Tobsha Learner was born and raised in England and has lived in both Australia and the USA. She is a playwright, novelist and also writes thrillers under the nom de plume TS Learner.

Please visit her website at www.tobshaeroticfiction.com or follow her on twitter @Tobsha_Learner.

Also by Tobsha Learner:

Quiver

Tremble

YEARN

TALES OF LUST AND LONGING

TOBSHA LEARNER

piatkus

PIATKUS

First published in Australia in 2011 by HarperCollins *Publishers* Australia Pty Limited
First published in Great Britain in 2012 by Piatkus

A CIP catalogue record for this book
is available from the British Library.

ISBN 978-0-7499-5906-7

Printed in Great Britain by Clays Ltd, St Ives plc

Papers used by Piatkus are from well-managed forests
and other responsible sources.

MIX
Paper from
responsible sources
FSC
www.fsc.org   FSC® C104740

Piatkus
An imprint of
Little, Brown Book Group
100 Victoria Embankment
London EC4Y 0DY

An Hachette UK Company
www.hachette.co.uk

www.piatkus.co.uk

For the Owl and the Pussycat
and all those other heroic lovers
who went to sea

CONTENTS

INK

It is an old story, an allegory of power if you like, of the tragedy that happens when two men overreach themselves, or the terror that fills a creator when he realises his creation has become more gifted than himself. It is one that even I, the most successful writer of my times, knows well, for we must all, eventually, give way to the young. And this story involves a very young writer, a passionate individual with the gifts of both beauty and rhetoric – blazing in his ambition. The now infamous D'Arcy Hammer. Perhaps you have heard of him?

D'Arcy Hammer put down his pen and slumped over his writing desk. It was a temporary submission, a nod to the gargantuan nature of the enterprise that the ambitious thirty-two year old had begun six years ago, when time seemed infinite and his future a mirage full of extraordinary possibilities. Now it was 1843, a hundred years after his subject – Joseph Banks – was born, and the biography D'Arcy had laboured over lay annotated in sections before him. By his feverish calculations he was only weeks away from delivering to his publisher, which meant they would have his opus to display in bookshop windows before Christmas.

'And God knows, I need the money,' D'Arcy spoke out loud, addressing the bust of the botanist he'd placed in one corner of the large study in the faint hope that by writing under the gaze of Sir Joseph he might gain his posthumous approval.

When D'Arcy Hammer had been a mere twenty-one-year-old student in his last year at Oxford, under the tutorship of his then mentor the eminent biographer Horace Tuttle, he had garnered an international literary reputation for a slim biographical volume charting the scandalous and sexually ambiguous life of the eighteenth-century Lord Hervey, himself, like D'Arcy, a one-time scholar of Westminster School.

The reviews had been generous and the dapper young biographer had become a regular attraction on the lecture circuit where he courted both infamy and an adoring (mainly female) public. But his success had come at a price. Horace Tuttle, a man he both intensely admired and sought to emulate, had grown to resent his protégé's easy acclaim and began an insidious campaign to undermine the young man's reputation. The two men fell out and overnight mentor became nemesis. However, the acrimony hadn't stopped D'Arcy from falling in love with Horace Tuttle's young niece, Clementine Jane Murray, the daughter of an influential aristocrat.

But over time the royalties and fame of his first book had evaporated. D'Arcy needed this new biography to be successful – hugely successful. He'd finally got engaged to the seemingly unobtainable Clementine and he knew it would fall upon him to keep her in the manner in which she had always lived. Then there was the unavoidable issue of his own father – Lord Hammer, a successful shipping entrepreneur and member of the House of

Lords. Unfortunately the aristocrat regarded his son's literary ambitions as a folly bordering on social suicide. An understandable attitude I, as a working author, can only condone, after all so few of us are commercially successful, and certainly, in my case, I was compelled by the dire circumstances of my family to make money from my art, whereas at least D'Arcy had had a choice.

Lord Hammer, an esteemed and august gentleman, had agreed to provide D'Arcy with a monthly stipend on the proviso that it should be regarded as a loan with a ceiling of five thousand pounds, a ceiling, at the telling of this story, that would be reached on the fourth of next month after which D'Arcy would be penniless.

The young biographer was near despair – he had thought he'd timed the writing of the biography to the very minute but he had run into debt months before. It was imperative he deliver the manuscript before his father's stipulated date in order to receive his publishing advance and stave off his creditors – of which there were now many. Despite all these irritating challenges he was confident of success. Defeatism and humility had never been part of D'Arcy Hammer's emotional repartee and as he glanced over at the neat piles of chapters – each containing episodes of vivid adventure and professional intrigue as well as graphic descriptions of Joseph Banks's libertine and rather salacious philosophies – D'Arcy had never felt surer of commercial potential. He even imagined it could be a subject for serialisation in a newspaper – a little like my own literary forays that were proving so successful.

He lit a cigar and walked to the window. The elegant townhouse belonged to his aunt – an unmarried gentlewoman who doted upon her nephew. Luckily for him she was only in London for the season; the rest of the year she joined Lord Hammer, her brother, on his country estate in Shrewsbury, leaving D'Arcy to run the house to his liking. The Georgian mansion was situated in Mayfair, just off St James's Square, and D'Arcy's rooms (a study, bedroom and small sitting room) were situated on the second storey. When his aunt was not in situ, the staff was reduced to one old butler and his wife, the housekeeper. The solitude and arrangement suited the young biographer perfectly. It enabled him to entertain in some style that was still affordable, and the infrequency with which the butler and his wife actually climbed the stairs to his rooms allowed him the peace and isolation required to write.

D'Arcy pulled open a window. The park in the centre of the square was luxuriant with foliage and flowers in full blossom. Lilac trees, their boughs heavy with white and purple blossom, were scattered between the flowering pink chestnut trees. Luckily the wind was blowing towards the Thames and the obnoxious ever-present odour of sewage did not undercut the scent of the lilac caught up in the breeze. It was early summer and already it promised to be an unseasonably hot month. D'Arcy exhaled a feathery plume of cigar smoke into the air where it hung suspended for a moment before drifting down towards the street. For once it felt wonderful to be both young and literary, and now that the completion of the manuscript was within sight – powerful. Sinking into the sweet reverie that comes with intellectual achievement, D'Arcy gazed down at the lilac trees, his mind drawn back to the last paragraph he'd written – a depiction of a particularly beautiful Polynesian beach Joseph Banks had described in his journals.

D'Arcy's initial attraction to the botanist was one of empathy, an imagined understanding between the biographer and his subject that, given half a chance, and the bottomless economic resources Joseph Banks had had at his disposal, plus the added advantage of being orphaned before he was twenty-two, D'Arcy himself might have lived such a life. The liberal nature of Banks's early years was a source of admiration for D'Arcy, particularly the open way he'd lived with his mistress despite society's disapproval. Such actions, D'Arcy had decided, depicted a man of both great courage and intense intellectual curiosity with little to no regard for how others thought of him – if only he himself had the courage to live in such a manner! These were the characteristics that had drawn D'Arcy to the gentleman explorer. And then there was Joseph Banks's account of his first visit to Polynesia, an account that portrayed the country as a utopia filled with uninhibited beautiful natives – both men and women. The diaries had fascinated D'Arcy and he had drawn liberally upon them for his biography, imagining his own portrait of the great man to be a source of simultaneous condemnation, secret envy and great curiosity to his own Victorian peers. The biography promised to be one of those irresistibly titillating books, condemned by the critics, bought openly by men and secretly by women. It *would* be a commercial success.

The ringing of church bells from nearby disturbed his meditations. D'Arcy pulled out his large gold fob watch – it was already two in the afternoon. He was then interrupted by a knock on the door. It was John Henries, the butler, a tall stooped man in his late sixties with the lingering dignity of a once-handsome man. He stood politely just outside the study, accustomed as he was to the biographer's explosive nature when writing.

'Sir, there is a young man outside, an employee of your publishers, I believe. He informs me that you are to visit them immediately, on an urgent matter,' he announced in a quavering baritone.

'Did the young man describe the nature of the matter?'

'No sir, he only reported it to be most urgent.'

D'Arcy's imagination spun wildly as he contemplated the myriad of requests, demands and dismissals that might be the reason behind such a summoning. But, as I explained before, our young biographer was both a narcissist and an optimist, and finally he concluded it was merely one of those fortuitous moments of synchronicity – he had almost completed his book and with whom else but his publisher to share the good news?

'Excellent. I have to see them anyhow. I shall be down momentarily.'

The offices of Bingham and Crosby Esquire might have been considered the rooms of an affluent and successful publishing house twenty years earlier – which indeed they were – but now they had the appearance of a fading courtesan ravaged by age and bad judgement in her choice of patron. True, the waiting parlour had both a well-stuffed French sofa covered in red velvet with two matching chairs in the Georgian style, but the velvet was worn to a thin sheen and the gold trimming frayed. And, for the first time, D'Arcy noticed that the secretary, whom he remembered as a young eager student of literature given to monologues expounding the literary virtues of whomever his employers had just published, was no longer young, no longer eager and indeed now exuded a positively sullen air. In fact,

D'Arcy realised as he waited, perched uncomfortably on one of the threadbare chairs, it must have been years since he'd last visited the publishers.

'Mr Crosby will now see you, Mr Hammer,' the secretary announced in a lugubrious tone before opening the door. Mr Crosby, a bewhiskered gentleman imbued with an elegance that had always reminded D'Arcy of a Renaissance statesman, sat behind his desk. An air of grim determination hovered about his person. His assistant, the younger Clarence Dingle, leapt up to shake D'Arcy's hand while Crosby stayed noticeably seated.

'Wonderful to see you, truly, and we are so excited …' Dingle's words spilled out like a cascade of flat piano notes – his enthusiasm seemed utterly perfunctory and mechanical, D'Arcy observed. The biographer, now a little nervous, flicked his jacket tails clear and sat down in a lone chair standing in the centre of the room.

'Dingle, cease your inane mumblings! You're not fooling anyone, least of all Hammer here, who's a very sharp young puppy!' the elder publisher barked from his leather-backed throne. Startled, the assistant sat down abruptly.

Mr Crosby leant forward, his halitosis drifting towards D'Arcy like a bad omen. The young biographer steeled himself. 'The truth is, Mr Hammer, we have called you here to discuss the import of a very grave rumour …'

'A very grave rumour indeed,' Dingle echoed for emphasis.

D'Arcy's face tightened in anticipation. This was not the reception he had expected. What had gone wrong? He had informed them that the manuscript would be in by the end of the month, and Crosby had replied, conveying the company's enthusiasm, by telegram. 'A grave rumour?' he queried, a break in his voice betraying his agitation. Crosby's hand crept across the marble-topped desk, his fingers curling around a paperweight that appeared to be a skull carved out of quartz crystal.

'It has been suggested that an associate of yours, the eminent Horace Tuttle, is also working on the definitive biography of the botanist Joseph Banks.'

Shocked, D'Arcy inhaled sharply. The animosity between Tuttle and himself was well known, but Tuttle was older by a good fifteen years and excelled in literary reputation by three more critically acclaimed biographies. If there were to be a rival biography by Tuttle, he would have the upper hand. The idea was unthinkable.

'That simply isn't possible. Tuttle has been wrestling with Lord Nelson for the past two years.'

'In that case Lord Nelson must have won,' Crosby replied cryptically, then reached into a large snuffbox and, after laying out two large rust-coloured pinches of tobacco upon the crook of his thumb, snorted them both up vigorously, staining his nostrils a dark red. He looked like a melancholic dragon, D'Arcy couldn't help noting. It was a distracting sight. Crosby coughed then continued: 'No, I'm afraid I have it on good authority that Tuttle has lodged the notion with Doubleday and Sons, and has promised a manuscript by next Easter. Heard it from the dog's mouth myself, in the gentlemen's cloakroom at The Garrick. Naturally this is of great concern to both myself and Bingham ...'

For a moment D'Arcy thought he'd misheard. As far as he knew, Bingham, Crosby's business partner, had been dead for at least five years. The elderly publisher's expression suddenly changed as he shifted his gaze beyond D'Arcy's shoulder. Unable to contain his curiosity D'Arcy swung around. A portrait of the esteemed but deceased Mr Bingham – in life, a man far more affable than Crosby – hung on the wall directly behind him. D'Arcy had the distinct impression that the shining jovial face in the portrait had suddenly winked at him. Dingle coughed politely and Crosby was immediately drawn back into the moment. '... and calls for a review of your own proposal and publishing timetable,' Crosby concluded gruffly. D'Arcy sank back into his chair, his fiscal strategies sunk. How could he afford to marry Clementine now? And how on earth would he be able to both pay off his creditors and avoid being pushed into his father's shipping business if his next book was a publishing disaster? But more than anything, how had Tuttle arrived at the idea of the very same biography as his own? D'Arcy's own venture was a well-kept secret between himself and the publisher. And even if Tuttle had heard of the project, it could only have been spite or perversity that inspired his rival to undertake the very same subject so late in the development of D'Arcy's own manuscript. But there was something else that filled him with a nauseating disquiet. Had his fiancée, who was an intelligent but frivolous young woman far younger than him, accidentally blurted out the topic of his labours to her uncle? Or even worse, had she unwittingly shown his rival some of his pages? The young author's imagination swirled up into paranoia – if this was true, it was even more of a horrible betrayal. Either way he had to save his biography and his own reputation.

'This is just ugly coincidence,' D'Arcy exclaimed more passionately than he'd intended. 'Besides, my manuscript is merely days away from completion. We will beat him to the shelves, I promise you!'

In the silence that followed, Crosby, in lieu of an answer, solemnly packed a pipe while D'Arcy fidgeted anxiously, convinced he was facing a verdict that would either make or condemn the rest of his literary career. Finally the tension was broken by Dingle striking a match dramatically. The assistant leant solemnly forward to light the pipe for his employer. Then, like Vesuvius, after exhaling a large plume of white smoke Crosby rumbled, 'Bingham and Crosby are not only men of the letter but also of our word. We will still publish, and we will publish ahead of Tuttle and Doubleday. However, you must guarantee that your biography will contain some new and hopefully salacious insights into Banks's early, morally dubious forays that will create enough hysteria amongst the scandalmongers and newspaper gentlemen to sell the godforsaken book!' He swung around to the portrait of his deceased partner: 'Forgive me, Bingham, but if we are to survive and become a "modern" publishing house, then we must surrender to the bestial demands of the Gods of Commerce,' he said before wiping his brow with a large purple silk handkerchief as if he had himself been sullied by such a declaration.

D'Arcy stared at him aghast. 'But every such event and proclivity is already embedded in the manuscript, sir!'

'Then find something else!' Crosby thumped the desk for emphasis, one precariously balanced manuscript falling with a bang to the floor. No one dared to pick it up. Softening, the publisher turned back to D'Arcy. 'My dear young man, research is the portal, but imagination the messenger,' he concluded with an air of pompous sagacity – an impenetrable remark that left the young biographer even more perplexed.

Crosby rose with a dramatic scraping of his chair against the floor then balanced his portly front against the edge of the desk. He had, D'Arcy noticed, become considerably plumper since last time D'Arcy had seen him. The publisher was again staring reverently at his deceased partner's portrait as if he were engaged in some kind of preternatural communication. 'And Mr Bingham tells me to tell you he expects the delivery of the completed and … *enhanced* … manuscript by the end of this month. Thank you, young Hammer, that will be all.'

The young biographer walked straight to his fiancée's townhouse. As he marched down Great Marlborough Street an intense fury began to build from the soles of his fashionable buttoned boots to the crown of his high top hat. Had Clementine betrayed him? Could she have been so foolish as to reveal to her uncle the subject of his secret dedication? He had to discover the truth. All the previous trust, the confessed intimacies of his ambition whispered to the young girl, seemed cheapened. As he examined the nature of their courtship – her passive yet delightfully innocent amazement at his passionate enthusiasm for the eighteenth-century botanist and his exotic adventures – D'Arcy could not envisage that Clementine would be capable of such disloyalty. As I have said, D'Arcy was young and still in the naive throes of the kind of egotism we all fall victim to at the beginning of our careers, and to D'Arcy's great disservice, Clementine had convinced him of his own genius. Any man would have fallen in love.

At twenty, Clementine was twelve years younger than him and utterly without guile, or at least he had thought so up until then. D'Arcy had been smitten the first time he'd laid eyes upon her – at her uncle's table seven years earlier when she was a mere thirteen years old and he a cynical twenty-five year old – the year in which he later fell out with Horace Tuttle. At the time he was in the middle of a protracted love affair with a married woman (who shall remain nameless on these pages at least, but suffice to say that the woman specialised in the seduction of gullible writers and I am shamed to confess that I was one amongst many). An erotically charged relationship involving complicated liaisons in obscure and extremely dangerous places (she was rather good), the love affair had exhausted D'Arcy both emotionally and existentially. Three tortured years later he encountered Clementine at her coming-out ball. Then sixteen, she seemed to embody all the virtues his older lover did not: virginal, uncomplicated and delightfully candid. At the time D'Arcy had despaired of the possibility of marriage, having come to the conclusion that he was now too jaded to experience the emotion of love. However, he broke off his affair with the married woman and took to pursuing the young girl, a pursuit further fired by her uncle's objections. A year later they were engaged.

Clementine's innocence had swept through his life like a scented breeze over a barren landscape, a metaphor he clung to as strongly as his cologne-infused handkerchief, now pressed to his face as he turned into the dense and pungent chaos that was Soho. The daily sewage-laden miasma of the Thames was now blowing in from the south, and in the unusually hot summer the stench in this densely populated borough was particularly disgusting.

Despite living in the comparative luxury of spacious, green and quiet Mayfair, D'Arcy was constantly drawn to the vibrancy of Soho, the bustling narrow streets with their tailors, leather-curing factories, coffee houses and inns as well as the once-grand mansions of Golden Square, now reduced to cheap housing in which whole families often lived in one room. But there was a warmth and rhythm to the place that the promenades of Mayfair lacked – a borough controlled and austere in its wealth. This seething mass of striving humanity was exotic to D'Arcy. And as a member of the titled classes, he could afford to indulge in its corrupt pleasures and, most importantly, get out when he wanted.

Indeed there was one particular prostitute he was fond of visiting who lived on Golden Square – a practical Irish wench who had scraped together the flimsy trappings of respectability. It was to here that D'Arcy, after a spiritually uplifting but frustrating evening with his fiancée, would often return, if only to enact upon the lady's rented body fantasies he knew he would never be able to execute upon Clementine's slender, lily-white frame. And it was at this very harlot's window that D'Arcy now found himself staring, his feet having guided him there by pure instinct. 'No, I shall resist,' he told himself, knowing that taking out his anger or frustration upon the prostitute would be counterproductive and, knowing her rates and his purse, economically disastrous.

'I really will confront Clementine. As suspicious as I am, I'm sure there is a completely innocent explanation – pure coincidence, for example.' It was an argument that failed to convince even himself.

Nevertheless he glanced wistfully back up at the window – the ironically named Prudence O'Malley was a comely girl with an earthy sensuality matched by an earthy laugh. She was also very good at the amusing but erotic scenarios D'Arcy found entertaining. In short, despite the heat of the afternoon, it would have been a very pleasant distraction from the young biographer's current troubles. The memory of their last encounter, during which D'Arcy had donned a leather saddle at her command so that she could ride him and whip him, made him harden. He waited until his tumescence had lessened into some semblance of decency then walked on – ah, the glorious dictatorship of a young body, I remember it well!

'What exactly are you trying to say, my love?'

Clementine, wearing a rose-coloured day dress, was perched very becomingly on the edge of a chaise longue, fingering the beaded fringes of her shawl; her escort, an ever-present maiden aunt, sat at a discreet distance in a window seat, theoretically absorbed in her embroidery. It was not an atmosphere conducive to either whispered confessions or confrontation. D'Arcy cleared his throat nervously. 'I find that I now face potential professional catastrophe, one that could prevent me from being able to support you in the manner to which you are accustomed once we are married.'

'Oh goodness,' Clementine yawned prettily, displaying rows of pearly white little teeth, 'it does sound tiresome. What kind of catastrophe? I thought you had finally finished with the great heroic literary tome you had embarked upon?'

For a moment it occurred to D'Arcy that if his fiancée hadn't been so imbued with both beauty and youth, he might care for her personality a little less, but like a cloud passing over the sun this observation was quickly lost and forgotten.'I have told you the subject of my biography, have I not?' he inquired dryly.

'You have, the extraordinary adventures and life of one

Joseph Hanks, I believe,' she replied, now fanning herself. 'The heat today is quite remarkable, remarkable and tiresome. But my love, you'd think if Mr Hanks was so extraordinary he would have had at least two surnames and a title.'

Really, D'Arcy thought to himself, if her lips weren't quite as red, her skin quite as pale and if those blonde tendrils that framed that cat-like face not quite so perfect, he might have taken her for being petulant and perhaps even a little stupid. On the other hand, he was comforted by the observation that if she couldn't even remember the name correctly, she was surely unlikely to have passed on the subject of his biography to her uncle.

'His name was Banks, Sir Joseph Banks, and he was, by the time of his death, one of the most significant English figures in science of his times, my dear. But I'm sure such details will only give your pretty head an ache, insignificant as he is in your delightfully girlish world, Clementine.' Indeed, it was the seeming purity of the trivia of this world that had attracted D'Arcy to Clementine in the first place. Although lately, to his faint amazement, he'd been finding her lack of intellectual curiosity an irritant. 'However, you wouldn't by any possible chance have told your uncle Horace about my biography? Mentioned Joseph Banks and my name in the same sentence, for example?' he asked, studying his fiancée's face closely. Clementine's expression appeared unchanged, although if our young biographer had been a little less infatuated and a little more astute, he might have noticed her fingers tightening around the handle of her lace fan.

'Now, why would I do that? I hardly see my uncle, and certainly not alone,' she protested, now waving her fan furiously at one flushed cheek.

'But you mentioned he escorted you to Ascot only last week!'

'He did? I had quite forgotten.'

'Just as you might have forgotten mentioning to him that I was writing the definitive biography of Sir Joseph Banks!' D'Arcy, unable to contain his frustration any longer, exploded. Behind him he heard the sound of Clementine's aged escort dropping her embroidery: it hit the parquet floor with a clatter.

Clementine's large blue eyes seemed to magnify as they filled with tears. 'I am sure I have not!' she protested. It was the first time in their two years of official engagement that either of them had raised their voices to each other and already D'Arcy was filled with remorse.

He edged forward and took her trembling hands in his own. 'You have to understand, Clementine, that not everyone is as innocent and without guile as yourself. Your uncle and I have a history that I have tried to explain before. We are in commercial competition. I am Brutus to his Caesar.'

'You mean to kill him?' Clementine's eyes widened even further and one tear, welling over the edge of her thick eyelashes, splashed down her cheek.

The sight gave D'Arcy a secret erotic thrill. Appalled to discover he found such power so exciting, he cursed his tight breeches as he crossed his legs. 'I mean that if your uncle has discovered I am writing about Joseph Banks, he might take it upon himself to match me with a biography of the gentleman himself.'

'He would not. Uncle Horace is a perfect sweetheart, and he knows I am engaged to you.'

'But, Clementine, he has! This was the professional setback I have been trying to explain to you. My publisher has received rumour that your uncle is also writing a biography of Banks! It is a calamity!'

'So there will be two books about the same man; how can this be so terrible?'

'Because your uncle is far more established than myself, his biography will have precedence over mine, with both the newspapers and with the reader. Six years, Clementine, six years of my life – and it is ruined! Are you absolutely sure you didn't, by accident, mention something to your uncle?'

Furious, the young woman rose, one hand worrying the emerald engagement ring he had given her. For a moment D'Arcy grew terrified that she might be about to pull it off to throw at his feet. In perfect synchronicity, her aged aunt also rose. The two women stood poised like figures from a Greek tragedy in the centre of the large Regency drawing room, until Clementine held out her hand imperiously to D'Arcy. He kissed it formally.

'At this moment I have nothing more to say to you,' she announced then, with a small nod, dismissed him.

D'Arcy strode down Regent Street, the tails of his morning coat flying behind him. Normally its wide promenade and sweeping elegance never failed to elevate his spirits, functioning, as it were, as a lodestone of wealth for the struggling writer. But today was different. Today he felt as if the mannequins and the displayed luxurious fabrics and dresses, the objets d'art, the tailored suits, the gold fob watches glinting through the shop-front windows, all represented a club whose membership had just been cruelly and unjustly snatched away from him, snatched away by one man and one man alone. Horace Tuttle.

The name resonated over and over, drumming its way through the heels of D'Arcy's polished boots as he walked the pavement, underscored by the rhythm of the clattering hooves of horses pulling carriages as they jostled their way down the thoroughfare, eating its way up through his fear, into his very soul. To be thwarted on the brink of such success – all kinds of tragic scenarios unfolded in D'Arcy's imagination: Tuttle triumphantly waving laudatory reviews in his face, the vision of a bookshop window displaying Tuttle's biography while his own book lingered neglected on some obscure back shelf. It was all too horrible to contemplate and yet, the harder D'Arcy tried to dismiss it, the more obsessed he became.

By the time he had descended back into the theatrical vulgarities of Piccadilly Circus, he felt as if he'd already lived out the appalling mortification of such a possibility. Tortured, he collapsed at the edge of the Eros statue and stared grimly out at the parade of humanity that streamed past – even the poorest beggar and rag picker seemed enviable. They, at least, did not have a rival prominent author about to publish a biography on the very same topic they'd given six good years of their miserable lives writing. It was a writer's worst nightmare, to have his subject stolen from under him – an insidious crime even harder to prove.

There only seemed two courses of action. He had to have access to Tuttle's biography and he had to discover an element of Sir Joseph Banks's life that was totally unique, scandalous and guaranteed to propel D'Arcy's biography above Tuttle's. As the reader no doubt knows, indecision is far more crucifying than decisiveness and so, cheered by his own resolve, D'Arcy leapt to his feet and decided that a brief sojourn at his club, the

Athenaeum, for a consoling drink before returning to the desk newly inspired would be in order.

The reading room at the Athenaeum boasted a high ceiling, unobtrusive waiters who served a good sherry to your very chair, a number of private alcoves in which it was possible to both hold court and hide out, and a selection of cigars a pasha would have been proud to serve. It was our protagonist's favourite place to daydream, a place where he had germinated many an idea for a novelette, essay or speech, and it was where he had now retreated, bathed in that warm glow of male exclusivity that every gentleman knew was guaranteed to restore world order and self-worth.

And thus, lounging in a leather chair, D'Arcy, hidden from his peers and elders by an overgrown aspidistra, ran through all the facts of Joseph Banks's early life, from his preparation for the memorable expedition on the *Endeavour* to his broken engagement to Harriet Blosset. All the salacious material was already in the book; to introduce anything else without hard proof would not only be a lie, it would also be doing the great man a huge disservice. And having lived with Banks for over six years, D'Arcy truly felt that he could not compromise either his reputation or the explorer's unless there was undeniable evidence. He had reached an impasse. This circuitous inner argument seemed to build and build when suddenly a voice booming out from another booth on the far side of the reading room jolted him violently back to the present.

'... I was just telling Thackeray the other day, never trust a pedant or an editor unless they are one and the same person! Eh, what?' The bellicose voice, laced with the kind of elitism D'Arcy loathed yet desperately wanted to be a part of, was instantly recognisable. D'Arcy froze in his seat, but the voice, oblivious of the young biographer and the disapproval of several other tutting members, continued bellowing through the rarefied atmosphere. '... Another wonderful occurrence, old friends, the drought is broken, Lady Fecundity is mistress again and I am writing! Yes, a veritable deluge of prose. A biography – one that will, like the last one no doubt, soar on the wings of literary excellence and land firmly on the footnote of posterity ...'

D'Arcy could contain himself no longer and, after swinging around, peeked through the leaves of the aspidistra. His nemesis, clad in a red smoking jacket and matching necktie, sat in a far booth, surrounded by a group of three friends. Horace Tuttle, bolstered by shameless enthusiasm for his own talent, waved his large hands about as if inscribing upon the air in invisible hieroglyphics declarations of great profundity. He was, indeed, a most tiresomely pretentious individual. Meanwhile the three friends – one minor publisher, one unimportant poet and a rather more important critic – leant forward enraptured.

'A biography!' the critic exclaimed. 'Do tell, Horry, *The Times* would be happy to print a teaser.'

'Let me guess,' the poet interjected eagerly. 'Robert Browning? He's terribly fashionable now, all the clever people love him.'

'Far too modern, no, this is someone who was a true Romantic scientist, a man who has defined our times ...'

'James Watt?' the publisher suggested hopefully.

'Vulgar commerce, no, no, my subject is ... Joseph Banks,'

Horace Tuttle concluded, pronouncing the name as if by doing so he himself was summoning the man back into existence.

D'Arcy could stand it no longer. Leaping to his feet he marched over. 'Tuttle ...' He stood before the seated group, his voice trailing away, his nerves having failed him at the last moment.

Horace Tuttle, an imposing, handsome man in his early forties, his hair as black as his niece's was blonde, drew himself up to his full height (which was over six foot and certainly taller than our hero) and extended his hand. D'Arcy's own arms remained conspicuously glued to his sides. The slight was noted and hung upon the rarefied air like a great fat question mark suspended precariously above them.

'Hammer, it is a pleasure to see you again, particularly as we are nearly family.'

D'Arcy still did not shake the proffered hand, which stayed frozen in mid-air. Before him he could see intrigue bleeding into the puzzled expressions of Tuttle's entourage. He had to say something, and swiftly.

'I'm afraid both our friendship and professional relationship is now at an end. I believe you to have deliberately and maliciously embarked upon the same biography I, myself, have dedicated the past six years of my life to, an endeavour you no doubt heard of from my fiancée, your niece. In fact, sir, if I were a lesser man I might even suspect you of stealing or accessing my manuscript in some form ...'

Horace Tuttle's hand curled into a fist as his smile transformed into a snarl. Startled, his face flushing with the vicarious excitement of the spectator, the minor publisher sprung to his feet and lay his hand rather limply upon Tuttle's wrist, as if to restrain him from any rash action. It was a symbolic gesture D'Arcy, if he had been less incensed (and a little more mature), might have heeded but, swept away by the conviction of his grievance, D'Arcy's diatribe knew no bounds.

'Indeed, of all the plethora and riches this country has to offer in terms of geniuses, poets and prophets to immortalise, is it not extraordinary that you, sir, should alight upon the very one I have chosen?'

'Are you, Hammer, accusing me of the heinous sin of plagiarism?' Tuttle's voice echoed around the reading room. Several newspapers and one slim volume of poetry were dropped as eminent members of the Athenaeum Club rose to their feet. There had not been such an accusation heard within those four walls since Thackeray had argued with myself and, trust me, that argument was not forgotten.

An icy silence descended upon the large chamber as D'Arcy became acutely aware of the unfurling drama he had initiated; a drama he realised, with a great swoop of his heart, he was now utterly powerless to stop. 'I am, sir, indeed I am. I charge you with having deliberately stolen the theme of my own biography, a manuscript well gone in its development, and I do suspect you of having read those very pages ...' But by now his voice was drowned out by the cries of outrage as literary men, now incensed in turn, sprung into action. The uproar in the reading room was unacceptably loud, and I should know, dear reader, for I was there.

Suddenly the two men found themselves surrounded by an audience. Tuttle's face darkened. He started towards D'Arcy, who was forced to jump aside, but the older biographer was firmly held back by the critic and the poet now flanking him. 'This is intolerable!' Tuttle announced, then, grabbing his gloves from the table, swung them in D'Arcy's direction in an attempt to hit his cheek. To his deep shame D'Arcy dodged the insult.

'Enough!' I shouted, my melodious voice instantly recognisable to all. Immediately the crowding men parted to reveal the source of the command. I stood at the far end of the chamber. Now, how to describe myself? I would like to say tall, charismatic, the embodiment of charm, but, perhaps for the sake of modesty, an elegant portly man in his forties will suffice. I was, at the time, arguably the most well-known author in the country so naturally I held some authority in the circumstances. Moving swiftly through the chamber I approached the two biographers who remained head to head, like a pair of fighting stags about to charge.

'Horace.' I nodded to Tuttle, who nodded back but did not remove his gaze from D'Arcy nor drop the hand that held the white gloves at the ready. Then, with the careful but exquisite focus of a consummate observer, I walked around them as if examining an interesting tableau or statue.

'Hammer, is it not? I did enjoy your first book.'

'Thank you, sir,' D'Arcy stammered, awed despite his anger, but he still dared not move for fear those white gloves might again come flying in his direction.

'The accusation is plagiarism, is it not?' I deliberately kept my voice mild, indeed, perhaps too mild – my very tone made the accusation sound absurd.

'It is, and a flagitious one at that,' Tuttle thundered while D'Arcy wisely remained silent.

'A duel would resolve nothing and would quite possibly result in a great literary loss for England,' I announced, passing my verdict. The men surrounding the two biographers murmured in agreement. D'Arcy, still transfixed by Tuttle's dangling glove, appeared vaguely aware that I'd been both diplomatic and strategic enough not to clarify the death of which biographer might be considered a great literary loss. Then to D'Arcy's visible relief, Tuttle dropped his glove. The younger biographer turned back to me.

'What do you suggest then, sir?'

'I suggest that such a duel is really Posterity herself and it is the one duel we writers all engage in whether consciously or unconsciously, willingly or unwillingly. Let both biographies be published. The reading public and history will decide which is the better book,' I concluded a little grandly. After which the whole of the reading room burst into spontaneous applause and D'Arcy was left with the vague but uncomfortable sensation of having lost. However, I couldn't help noticing that it was he and not Tuttle who retrieved the dropped white glove – the property of his nemesis. Intrigued by the possibility of a further twist of plot I said nothing.

That night D'Arcy dreamt he was attacked by copies of Tuttle's manuscript raining down upon him like a fatal hail only to be rescued by myself, the epitome of the successful Victorian novelist, smiling banally down upon him; apparently I opened an umbrella to protect him. It was not a good dream and he awoke with a frightful headache.

On arising, D'Arcy forfeited breakfast and went straight to the library of the Royal Institute, determined to discover in Joseph

Banks's archives some missed piece of research that might elevate his own biography. After greeting the librarian he retrieved the well-thumbed collection of journals, sketchbooks, essays and general reportage Sir Joseph Banks himself had bequeathed to the library. Fighting a strong sense of hopelessness he laid out the collection in order of events and scanned it mournfully. After six years of study the collection was so well known to him that if he closed his eyes and placed his finger down blindly upon a page he would have been able to recite the paragraph from memory. In fact the travel diary of the young Joseph Banks, written during his trip on the *Endeavour* to Polynesia, was so vivid to D'Arcy that sometimes he became confused between his own memories and that of the naturalist himself.

Resigned to a fruitless search he flicked through a hundred or so more pages then, as the study clock chimed three, closed the journal. There was nothing he'd missed, no new scandalous titbit of behaviour, anthropological observation, love affair or even a base sexual liaison between those well-worn pages. It was futile. His biography would have to stand as it was written thus far. He was condemned. No doubt Horace Tuttle's biography, whether superior or not, would eclipse his own by mere dint of Mr Tuttle's reputation. It was an unfair world, he reflected, and now one in which he was convinced he was about to lose reputation, hearth and possibly his engagement. He might even be reduced to working for his father. Deeply depressed, the young biographer stared out of the window. As if in response the sky was darkening with a summer storm. He would have to run home to avoid the downpour.

He arrived half an hour later at his aunt's house, half drenched from the deluge (which he hadn't managed to avoid).

He shook himself dry in the entrance hall, only to be informed by the housekeeper that there was a gentleman waiting for him. 'A financial gentleman judging by his frock coat and miserable demeanour, sir,' she added in a lowered voice.

Convinced his life was about to engender further misery as well as a possible new creditor, D'Arcy contemplated climbing out a side window and escaping to Calais, but as he turned back his father's lawyer confronted him in the entrance hall. The lawyer – an austere, humourless individual whose face wore an expression of perpetual disappointment, as if life had cheated him of some great prominence despite his professional success – snorted in disapproval.

'Master Hammer. Going somewhere?' D'Arcy winced; he hated the way all of his father's employees still addressed him as 'master'.

'I had just remembered I had forgotten something …'

'It can wait; we are due for a little talk.' With a notable lack of decorum, the lawyer pulled him into the drawing room. They stood in uncomfortable silence until the lawyer, realising no hospitality would be offered voluntarily, took it upon himself to help himself to a small glass of port from a bottle sitting on a side table.'As you are aware, your father has, for some time now, expressed considerable unhappiness at your choice of profession, eager as he was to have his only son join him in partnership at the shipping company.'

'Come to the point, Stanley, I am damp and there is supper waiting,' D'Arcy interrupted rudely, eager to avoid one of the longiloquent monologues the lawyer was prone to.

'The "point", Master Hammer, is simply that your stipend will cease altogether by the fourth of next month after which your father expects you to be able to support both yourself and your future wife through the profits of your profession. He also expects your stipend to be paid back in total by the time you are thirty-five. There is a biography due to be published, is there not?'

'There is, but ...'

'There are no buts, Master Hammer, not this time. Your father's decision is final,' the lawyer concluded, and then, after reading the young man's expression, placed a clammy hand on his arm. He was not a cruel man and, having known the writer since he was a child, was rather fonder of D'Arcy than the writer was of him. 'I am sorry, Master Hammer.'

Overwhelmed by this latest turn of events, D'Arcy sat down abruptly. Then, in a feeble attempt to conceal his reaction, covered his brow with his hand. It felt as if the whole world was conspiring to cause his downfall. How could he possibly afford to marry Clementine now, never mind keep her as a wife, without his father's financial support? And how could he possibly rely on his biography being a success now that his rival planned to publish the same biography? And as for the stipend to be repaid within three years – the only way he could imagine that to be possible would be to sell his very soul, an option that would not, in any case, bring him any great fortune as he suspected he might have sold it already, thanks to his extra-curricular activities with Prudence O'Malley. Life looked very bleak indeed. 'I do not blame my father, Stanley, he has been generous to have supported me thus far.' D'Arcy's voice was small, broken, as he now wallowed in self-pity.

'Indeed,' the lawyer added, then subtly placed a banknote on a side table. 'This should see you through until then, D'Arcy.'

And then, to avoid further humiliation for our now penniless author, he left, closing the door silently behind him.

Later that afternoon D'Arcy, still dazed by the reversal of fortune that had left him unable to recognise the confident writer of some twenty-four hours earlier, sat at his desk staring blankly out of the window in a manner young writers are so often apt to do. Outside the storm had cleared and late afternoon sunshine now streamed across the town square, transforming the tall, leaf-covered chestnut tree branches into luminous green giants, comforting in their optimistic beauty.

'I am defeated,' he said out loud, glancing across at his manuscript, untouched since the previous morning. 'I cannot even muster the enthusiasm to finish. I have been pipped at the post even before publication.' He finished his address to the bust of Joseph Banks; it sounded depressingly like an apology. His gloomy reverie was interrupted by a knock at the door, which he had intended to ignore, except that it occurred twice and then thrice. 'Come in!' he yelled, a little more bad-tempered than he intended. A chimneysweep bearing brushes entered. He tipped his cap politely.

'Sorry, Gov, the housekeeper told me you wouldn't be in. Should I leave, sir? Seeing you're working and all …'

'No, please continue with your task. The chimney does need cleaning …' Despite his anxiety D'Arcy welcomed the distraction. The sweep, a handsome lad of about twenty, appeared to be somewhat of a dandy within the confines of his uniform. His cap was set at a rakish angle, there was a yellow carnation in the buttonhole of his worn overalls and his moustache was groomed. There was an intelligence in his gaze and he seemed blessed with that particular optimism found in the working classes, D'Arcy noted, envying the simplicity of both the man's life and profession. After all, in that moment, cleaning chimneys appeared an honest day's work from D'Arcy's jaded perspective. Whistling, the sweep began to unpack his brushes. 'You a writer then, sir?' he asked after glancing at the pile of papers.

'A biographer. I write about other people's lives.'

'Sounds like a pretty living.'

'It is precarious like all others.'

'You're not wrong there, sir. Course it must help arriving at a life worth telling – wouldn't be much in me own, that's for sure. I'd be quite boring to read. Although what I've seen of others – now that would be worth telling.' The sweep laughed, a salacious chuckle that made D'Arcy a little uncomfortable, as if he too had unwittingly partaken in the workman's voyeurism.

'I only write about great men, men that have inspired and made a contribution to our great nation,' D'Arcy replied haughtily, then immediately regretted the sound of his own pompous voice. 'Like Joseph Banks,' he continued, 'the subject of my current work – although I am somewhat stultified having arrived at an impasse.' To his surprise the sweep immediately stopped unpacking his brushes and stood amazed.

'Joseph Banks – Sir Joseph Banks?' he asked, astonished.

'The very same. You have heard of him?'

'Heard of him? I sweep the chimneys over at the Royal Institute. I 'ave swept the very same chimney his honourable personage no doubt once toasted his honourable feet at, in what was once, I was told, his study. One could say I have stirred the embers of greatness.'

'One could say,' D'Arcy echoed, amused, 'but it is not such a coincidence. Mayfair is a small world, and you are a local business.'

'Indeed, sir. Perhaps you are right, but then I am a superstitious man,' the sweep replied enigmatically before covering the hearth and its surrounds with a sheet and returning to his brushes. He began assembling a particularly long one. As he screwed one wooden pole into another, he kept glancing over at the manuscript while D'Arcy, having again sunk into despair, reached for his snuffbox and sniffed a pinch as a consolation. 'Funny you should be writing about Sir Banks, sir, because I came, innocently mind you, upon a document I believe belonged to the man, when I was cleaning the very same 'forementioned chimney.'

It was an extraordinary admission. Startled, D'Arcy spilled his snuff all over his left hand. In a futile attempt to appear calm and indifferent he carefully swept the expensive powder onto a glass-topped side table. 'You did?' He kept his tone level; he didn't want the sweep to suspect that he might be in possession of something financially valuable.

'I did, sir, concealed halfway up, wrapped carefully in an oiled canvas bag so it wouldn't soil, a section of a diary, signed I believe by the knighted gentleman himself. Obviously it were something he didn't want his public getting hold of, I believe, else why would he go to so much trouble hiding it?' the sweep nonchalantly replied while vigorously inserting the long brush into D'Arcy's own chimney. As he pushed the brush energetically up and down inside the chimney, dislodging a small cloud of soot down onto the sheets, D'Arcy watched him, transfixed. Could this be his Gabriel in disguise? His angel of deliverance?

'Do you still have the section?' A note of tremulous expectation entered the writer's voice despite his feigned indifference.

The sweep pulled his brush out dramatically, a cascade of soot blackening the hearth and grid. 'I do indeed, sir, but I have it at my humble lodgings, in Soho.' Now the sweep turned and looked at him frankly, his gaze travelling from the writer's feet to his face. It was a gaze D'Arcy couldn't quite fathom the meaning of, but found it disturbing nevertheless. The sweep smiled saucily. 'Would you care to see it, sir?' D'Arcy's heart was now pounding so hard he was concerned its movement might have been visible through the cloth of his waistcoat. He slipped one hand into his trouser pocket to conceal his trembling fingers.

'I would indeed. Is this evening convenient?'

'You are eager, sir ...' the Sweep, still smiling, seemed almost provocative.

Suddenly D'Arcy realised he *was* being provocative. The young biographer blushed furiously. Ignorant as he was of the behaviour of men who desire their own gender, he realised he had not been aware of any such signal until now. And yet he still needed to lay his hands on that secret section.

'The diary, it does really exist? For that would be my only motivation for visiting you, you understand,' D'Arcy added, abandoning all etiquette to make sure there would be no further misunderstanding.

'Oh yes, sir, I can assure you of that.' And if the sweep was disappointed he concealed it prettily. Instead he turned back to D'Arcy's fireplace. 'Your chimney was really filthy, sir. It must feel a lot better 'aving all that dirt pushed out of your pipes.

I suppose that's why some call me "the good time man". After I've come they can breathe a whole lot easier,' he concluded cheerfully and seemingly without nuance. He began to pack his brushes away.

D'Arcy turned back to his desk, his heart still thumping. 'I will get my hands on this secret diary. I will,' he reassured himself, but sensing that both tact and strategy were required, he busied himself with some trivial footnotes as he waited for the sweep to broach the subject again. It felt like the workman was taking an eternity to gather his equipment. Finally the sweep turned to leave. Before he walked out whistling he placed a business card on D'Arcy's desk.

'Number ten, Golden Square. Ask for Harry. I'll expect you at eight on the dot and I'll have the desired object unpacked and waiting.' And then, to D'Arcy's disconsolation, he winked.

Stepping over the rivulet of raw sewage that wound its way between the cobbled pavement and the front steps of the Georgian house with the number ten welded into its rickety iron gate, D'Arcy wondered whether he might have been a little rash – it might have been wiser to have asked the sweep to visit him again at his aunt's mansion. But somehow it had felt safer and less conspicuous for him to visit the sweep. After all, he could not afford to be seen by any of his Mayfair or literary acquaintances and he wanted to be entirely confident the existence of the diary would not be leaked to Tuttle.

And so it was, dressed suitably casually in a sack coat (which he now found to be unseasonably warm), checked trousers and soft-crowned brown hat, D'Arcy came once more to find himself unintentionally in the vicinity of Prudence O'Malley, his moral weakness and object of great sensual distraction. Although her dwelling was situated on the other side of the square, the young biographer could even now feel the pull of her upon him. Forcing himself back to the task at hand, he approached a small female child of about six years or so, playing marbles on the step.

'Excuse me, young miss, I am after a Mr Harry – the chimneysweep?'

The red-headed waif stared up at him, then thoughtfully picked her nose. ''Ow much is it worth to you?'

Reluctantly D'Arcy handed her a penny. She bit it then, with practised expertise, slipped it into a pocket hidden in her dirty petticoat. 'He's on the top floor, is Harry. No doubt he'd be expecting a gentleman like you,' she added with a lewd sort of sophistication that D'Arcy found momentarily repulsive.

Ignoring the waif's comment, he stepped over her and entered the Georgian townhouse. Once a grand residence, it had, like all of its neighbouring fellows, fallen into neglect and decay. The entrance hall was dark and dingy – a terrible stench rose up from the cellar below and somewhere beyond the darkened arch at the back of the house D'Arcy could hear the sound of a baby wailing.

Holding a handkerchief to his face, determined not to catch some dreadful disease through inhaling the foul and polluted miasma, D'Arcy began climbing the stairs and the air became less foul as he ascended each landing. The sweep's residence was at the fourth landing, in what might have served originally as the servants' quarters. And Harry, out of uniform and dressed surprisingly in an elegant but obviously second-hand morning coat, was already waiting for him at the top.

'Prompt, sir, that is indeed the mark of good breeding, is it not?' There was a new shyness about the man, as if by removing the uniform he had removed some of the obvious social differences between them.

'Indeed, it is, Harry.' D'Arcy, winded by his climb, leant for a moment against the railings.

'Please excuse my humble dwelling – isn't a lot of money in soot,' the sweep explained as, holding up a smouldering oil lamp, he led the young biographer through a narrow corridor with a repressively low wooden ceiling towards a set of double doors. The smell of boiling cabbage became progressively stronger as they approached. 'Not until I own me own set of brushes and then I can employ some lads below me. See, I have ambition, sir, and in my position ambition is both a blessing and a curse,' he concluded as they reached the door. Behind him D'Arcy had silently begun calculating how much money he could afford to pay the sweep for the diary since it was now apparent that obtaining the diary would require commerce.

Harry knocked three times and a tiny woman, her white hair hidden under a grimy bonnet, opened the door. She looked eighty but was probably not much more than fifty.

'Mother, this is the eminent biographer we was expecting,' Harry announced. After a demure curtsey, she silently let them pass. The large room contained two beds and a table placed in a low window alcove that looked as if it served both as kitchen and dining table. A copper cooking pot hung over the hearth and there was a small washstand in one corner. Despite being meagre it was spotlessly clean, much to D'Arcy's relief.

'I live here with my four sisters, but they are all out working.

In the theatre. They are handsome girls and they do handsomely, don't they, Mother?' In response the old woman suddenly smiled – an expression that instantly transformed her face. To D'Arcy's surprise, he could see where the son might have inherited some of his beauty. 'Now to the diary, sir. Sit yourself down over there, Mother will bring you a mug of tea and I shall fetch it.' D'Arcy, his head lowered to avoid bumping it on the ceiling, made his way over to the table. Through the grubby diamond-shaped windowpanes he could just see the skyline of London, with a large, sickly yellow full moon rising up over the high roofs of Mayfair. It looked ominous and, again, D'Arcy wondered about the turn of circumstances that now found him in such a situation. The old woman poured tea out of a saucepan that had been sitting over the fire-grate, then placed before him with a delicate grace a chipped china cup of the dark brew. On the other side of the room Harry reached under one of the beds and pulled out an old tea chest. At the rustle of paper, D'Arcy turned. Triumphantly the sweep held a small canvas bag aloft. 'I knew I had it in here somewhere. I've not read it meself, out of respect for the great dead gentleman, but you, sir, are his official biographer so I'm sure he wouldn't mind …' Unable to contain himself D'Arcy snatched it from the sweep's hands and stepped into the only pool of light in the room, cast from a single oil lamp hanging from the ceiling. He pulled open the bag with his trembling fingers. The canvas smelt and felt old, at least sixty or seventy years of age. Carefully D'Arcy slipped out the collection of pages it contained. It was a slim notebook of ten pages or so, held together by string. On the thick oiled cover were written the words: *The pages of my journal kept only for myself to avoid condemnation from God, my fellow*

37

scientists and perhaps, even my future wife ... D'Arcy recognised the handwriting immediately.

The window was pushed as wide as it could go. Although it was past one in the morning, the temperature had not dropped and an oppressively humid heat rose from the pavements, seemingly mingling with the moon shadow that fell in broad blue-white bands, transforming the mundane into the mysterious. D'Arcy sat at his desk, the rest of the house hushed and sleeping. Before him lay the clandestine document. He held his hand an inch above the thick yellowed paper, fingers spread over the journal as if he were, through some feat of inverted gravity, absorbing the very soul of the great man up through the pages. It was an extraordinary intimacy, this communion, and the young biographer felt both the weight of responsibility and tremendous exhilaration. He was deeply conscious that the last person to have looked upon the manuscript was Banks and now he held it in his hands. It was undeniable; their lives were irretrievably woven together.

D'Arcy glanced back down, his mind reeling between disbelief, complete fascination and, if he were frank with himself, a deluge of sexual fantasy that had made it hard to continue reading with the cold eye of the scientist; the bulge in his trousers an uncomfortable confirmation of this distraction. In front of him were several paragraphs he'd marked in pencil – these contained the description of the climax of the ritual Banks had reported in the journal, a secret religious ritual of the native Polynesians that, if executed, imbued the main participant with great powers. But this ritual differed from other ceremonies witnessed by Banks and documented in his published journals. This one involved sex magic and of such detailed intensity that the ritual was not only extraordinary but transgressive. Certainly perverse enough to outrage those esteemed guardians of high culture, the Church of England, but also the members of the Royal Institute. D'Arcy couldn't have been more excited. The diary contained material guaranteed to compel all manner of reader to buy the biography. It was a writer's gold mine, a treasure of controversy that would make him famous. For the hundredth time in the last two hours, D'Arcy began to read the marked paragraphs:

It came about that Otheothea, my native 'wife', had a quarrel with one of her friends over some breadfruit and coconut crops she was convinced the friend had been stealing. And she needed evidence to prove her case before accusing the friend and seeking local justice. She explained to me that there was a secret ritual that if executed gave the truth-seeker the power, for a limited time, to see through the eyes of anyone they named. 'Truth magic' would be the nearest translation in our English tongue. She then asked me if I'd partake in the ritual, as it required two men, one of whom needed to be a Tupia (local priest), and two women, one of them a priestess. Eager to learn as much as I could about her culture and innocently thinking it would be a simple matter of the sacrifice of a few chickens and some chanting, I agreed. Never in the history of mankind has a man been so wrong …

After insisting that I should bathe and groom my hair, Otheothea led me to a clearing in a small forest beyond which it was possible to hear the pounding of the ocean

against the rocks. It was (judging by the position of the
stars and the lights in the sky) about two hours before
dawn, the time of which was significant to Otheothea
as she kept indicating my fob watch. She herself had
dressed in little more than a grass skirt with a garland of
flowers about her neck and woven into her hair that she
had loosened and wore down her back. Waiting in the
clearing was a young girl (perhaps as young as sixteen), a
girl Otheothea had noticed me watching – for the creature
was as lovely and comely as the young Aphrodite herself.
Instead of being consumed by jealousy (as would be the
custom of the women of my country), Otheothea had
smiled and asked if I desired the girl. At the time, fearing I
might insult Otheothea, I had denied it. But now I could
see that she'd read my emotions more faithfully than I
had assumed. The other person waiting in the clearing
was a native man, a Tupia, another magnificent specimen
of humanity, standing over six foot tall. His oiled and
muscular body gleamed in the light of the fire illuminating
the grassy plateau. Both wore ceremonial dress – grass
skirts, beads, and necklaces of scarlet feathers. There was a
formal, almost religious atmosphere, as if both were there
as participants in a solemn rite.

On the ground was laid a blanket the pattern of
which I recognised from the cloak of a man I had been
introduced to as a priest: a distinctive design of strips and
crosses. Upon our approach the young man lit a low
burner of incense and began chanting, rocking backwards
and forwards. The girl knelt slowly on the edge of the

blanket, her knees placed carefully on two points of the pattern.

Otheothea turned to me: 'She is for you. She is part of the magic. The four of us will make a window of pleasure, and together our joy will join to wake the Earth Lizard and he will give me the eyes of my enemy for half a day.'

At the time I thought I had misinterpreted her intention, a meaning lost in translation. But when she placed my hands on the oiled breasts of the young girl, and she herself had straddled the lap of the priest, the nature of this magic ritual was apparent.

An ember suddenly crackled in the hearth, startling the young biographer, absorbed as he was by the detailed description of the ritual. It was almost as if Banks had written the account as a set of instructions left, if not for himself, for posterity. Even if he had hidden the journal it was evident to D'Arcy that some part of Banks must have assumed its discovery sooner or later, otherwise why had he not destroyed the pages, or even not written them at all? It was a moral argument the biographer allowed himself to be pursued by.

D'Arcy stared into the fire. It was as if the four figures themselves danced amid the flames, bronze skin gleaming as buttock pounded into buttock, breast against breast, Banks's pale figure embraced by both man and woman – all abandoned to an instinctive animal force greater than the conventions of both D'Arcy's era and that of the late eighteenth century. This transcended the rationality of modern man. Gripped by inspiration, D'Arcy could hardly breathe. It was a powerful and seductive vision. He returned to his reading. The next two pages provided a detailed account of the ritual itself, involving an elaborate orgy the movement of which appeared to be so highly choreographed that the four participants would reach orgasm simultaneously, the intent being (as far as D'Arcy could ascertain) that the energy of this sexual climax would then channel directly into the truth-seeker, who had hung about his or her body objects belonging to the person she/he wished to see through the eyes of. In the ritual described by Banks it was locks of hair, and some beads that belonged to the woman his native 'wife' had accused.

Afterwards Banks wrote of his scepticism, but also of his intense pleasure in witnessing such a ritual. Then came the last paragraph, the content of which fascinated the young biographer almost as much as the sexual acts so beautifully and lyrically portrayed.

I had dismissed the whole event as an excuse for the usual indulgence of the senses these people (as innocent as children) so delighted in, and had just decided to regard my involvement as a delightful memoir I might return to when age and infirmity had made such pleasures unobtainable when Otheothea who, up until that moment, had been lying quietly beside me, seemed to go into an apoplexy. Her eyes rolled up into her head and she began to shake wildly. I could not bring her to her senses. This went on for just under an hour until, as swiftly as it had begun, the paroxysms ceased. Sitting up and smiling peacefully the native girl appeared to have returned to her normal self. 'I have been with her, Joseph, I have seen through her eyes and she is guilty.'

After these words she insisted I accompany her to the hut of her enemy, gathering witnesses along the way. Upon arrival, despite violent protests from the accused, Otheothea went straight to a wooden chest in the corner and opened it. Hidden inside were the stolen fruits and crops. The location of the chest was not obvious, and neither were the crops hidden within. And I could not find a rational explanation except to acknowledge that the sex magic had worked and Otheothea had seen through her enemy's eyes in order to locate the stolen crops.

Naturally the notion that such a ritual might indeed be empowering is deeply disturbing to me. I cannot afford such methods of promotion to become available to either my contemporaries or descendants. This kind of alchemy is not fit for either Christian or Englishman … and yet, it is mesmerising.

By the time D'Arcy had finished reading dawn was already creeping in under the curtains and the fire in the hearth was reduced to smouldering embers. He closed the journal. Already he felt like an entirely different man to the one who had sat down to study the journal eight hours before. He had been transformed. He felt as if his notion of perception, the borders of reality, even his understanding of what religious worship might be, had been blown apart. The discovery of the journal was more than just an extraordinary piece of luck that would doubtless propel his biography into a league of its own. It had also stirred D'Arcy to new heights of aspiration: to control the gaze of your enemy, to actually leave your body and enter another? These adventures promised to be as much a thaumaturgy of the senses as the orgy itself. And what if the ritual actually worked? He sat there staring across the familiar planes and shapes of his study and yet he was in Polynesia, lying naked and satiated in a jungle clearing by the smouldering remains of a log fire, his spirit having flown from his body and then returned, restored, renewed, the doors of perception yawning open. If only he had that power – to be able to see through the eyes of anyone he liked for an hour, to experience what they were seeing. What would he do with such a gift?

Just then his eye fell upon Tuttle's white glove that he had placed at the base of Sir Joseph Banks's marble bust as a kind of trophy or offering. Inspired by the sight, a small trickle of an idea started glinting in his consciousness, an idea of revenge, of empowerment, an idea that might reverse forever the calamitous set of circumstances he now found himself in. If D'Arcy had such a gift, even for an hour, he would be able to find out at exactly what stage Tuttle was in his book. He would be able to read the actual pages, gauge whether Tuttle's biography would be a real threat to his own. He would triumph no matter what.

Physically exhausted but with his mind racing with excitement, D'Arcy threw himself down on the daybed in a corner of the study. Strategies danced like dervishes about him. His plan would have to be extremely well executed. To conduct a ritual like that in London would not only be potentially ruinous (if it were ever discovered), it would also no doubt be illegal. And yet the advantage gained would be tenfold. Not only would he be able to thwart Tuttle's publication (a concept that was as delicious to him as any fought duel) he would also have undergone the same experience as Joseph Banks himself, and the idea of being thus fused forever to his great idol was almost as irresistible.

He lay there imagining all the consequences – himself basking in the fame of scandalous celebrity, the book sales, the sheer pleasure of trumping Tuttle in the reviews, the covert pleasure of being in his skin for an hour, perusing his notes … His mind was made up, he had no choice. It was as if the very discovery of the journal – the way it had organically arrived in his hands, the arbitrariness of Harry the sweep's appearance, the coincidence of D'Arcy having stayed in that afternoon when the chimneys were being cleaned – was destined; he was compelled to commit body and soul to the journal. He had to perform the magic.

But now, having persuaded himself, he was confronted with the bleak reality of planning the event. Who, if anyone, could he trust to take part in such a potentially dangerous ritual? Just then he was reminded of Prudence, his paramour at Golden Square. For the right price she would play a part. She had already proven herself a mistress of all kinds of salacious games – the kind of role-play found betwixt man and woman, games that turned nature on its head and always excited. She would be the perfect mistress of ceremonies for such an event. And it would be easy for her to recruit a young girl of her profession. But who could play the other man's role? He had to be handsome, open-minded in his lovemaking and desirous of other men as well as women. Just then an early blackbird began whistling outside D'Arcy's window. The birdsong immediately brought to mind the cheerful whistling of Harry the young chimneysweep.

*

'You want me to do what?' Prudence, known as Mademoiselle Inferno amongst certain members of parliament, looked indignant; indignant as is possible clad in a corset, stockings, riding crop and short fur cape. D'Arcy had disturbed her at work, insisting that he needed to speak to her directly despite the fact that she was with one of her more particular gentleman friends (as her maid put it). The prostitute, although well fond of D'Arcy, who was one of her younger and certainly more handsome clients, was not happy at the interruption.

'It is a magic rite, an ancient religious ritual, Prudence. We will be the first in England to have executed it,' D'Arcy clarified enthusiastically, swept away by his own rhetoric.

'I wouldn't be too sure of that, Mr D'Arcy. I've had some very peculiar libertines in my time. I just never thought you were inclined that way.'

'Prudence, this isn't just some simple orgy, this is genuine magic-making – communion with the raw power of sex itself.'

'Please, keep your voice down, Mr D'Arcy. I am a Catholic, I'll have you know. I don't hold stock with dancing with the devil nor doing anything else with him. I have my reputation to think of.' Prudence, who liked to think of herself as a cut above other working girls, pursed her lips.

'Trust me, Prudence. This isn't devil worship or witchcraft. This ritual is from the South Sea Islands, from a land the French once described as La Nouvelle Cythere, an island where a woman with your skills would be considered a queen and welcomed in the highest realms of power.'

Intrigued, the working girl looked up. 'Nice island that would be – where did you say it was?'

'Does it matter? Prudence, I am making you an offer of a lifetime. Who knows what might happen if it works? I'm also offering you twenty crowns.'

For the first time in their conversation Prudence looked interested, her pretty face sharpening as she made some quick mental calculations. 'Twenty-five … and ten for my … "assistant" …'

D'Arcy inhaled sharply. Twenty crowns was double her usual fee and thirty-five was exorbitant. He simply didn't have the money. Calculating wildly he realised he had no choice, he would have to visit at least two of his more sympathetic unmarried relatives to borrow the money and live off cockles and cheap beer for the rest of the month. But he was committed: he was determined to execute the ritual at any cost. 'Done. There's just one other point: there is another man involved.'

'Oh saucy, Mr D'Arcy, but I suppose two men and two girls could have a lot of fun. And it's lucky for you that I do like the occasional tryst with a pretty young girl. Still, servicing three is a lot more work. Is he a reasonable chap?'

'I think you'll like him. He's young, handsome and clean enough.'

'And you'll be the master of ceremonies so to speak?'

'I will be directing the movements of the ritual,' D'Arcy replied cautiously, settling on the word 'movements' because of the musical connotation, and thinking of the ritual as a benign symphony somehow gave the whole notion a dignified legitimacy. Reaching into his pocket he pulled out his last ten crowns. 'See this as a desposit.' He held out the crowns. Finally Prudence's fingers closed around the money. 'The rest we get on the night?'

'Gentleman's word.'

'Well,' the prostitute said, sliding the money into the large purse she always kept hanging off her belt, 'at the very least it will be an education. And I'm always looking for original ways to educate meself. I think this new girl Amelia has talent. She's very pretty and has an enthusiasm for the theatrics. Just tell me the time and place and what we should be wearing and I promise prompt and professional service, as always, Mr D'Arcy,' she concluded with a tiny flick of her very pink tongue.

The young sweep glanced about the private garden square then slid closer to D'Arcy on the park bench. 'You mean to say that we will all spoon together for the sake of ... 'ow would you call it ... magic?' His voice was a tense mixture of incredulity and excitement.

D'Arcy stared out at the small pond upon which a drake was strutting his prowess to a disinterested mate. If only his life was as uncomplicated as that of the lusty drake. Swallowing his own nervousness, he mustered up the last of his resolve. 'It is more in the pursuit of a native science, young Harry, and I will be following the words of the diary to the last letter.'

'And these are definitely the words of the great man himself?'

'Absolutely, I have verified both the handwriting and Banks's very turn of phrase. It is indisputably his reportage. You have made a great find, and I shall see to it that you are mentioned in my book.'

'An honour, sir, but I was hoping for a more fiscal kind of reward ...'

'Indeed, and I will, naturally, pay you well for partaking in our little secret ritual.'

'How well?'

D'Arcy knew he would not be able to borrow more than the sum of sixty crowns and already his expenses were mounting up. Disheartened, he ran through a mental inventory of all his assets, attempting to calculate which he could more or less happily part with. Finally he arrived at an old set of pewter drinking mugs he had inherited from his grandfather. At least one hundred years old, it was safe to assume they might be of value to the pawnbroker. 'I was thinking of the sum of fifteen crowns?' he ventured, assuming the young man's services might be worth less than the professional Prudence as, he reasoned, another man might actually be willing to pay as opposed to being paid to be included in such a venture.

'I'm in. Harry is always one to mix pleasure with commerce,' the chimneysweep retorted swiftly, winking and licking his lips as he broke into a broad smile. 'As long as I'm back at the chimneys by nine the next morning.'

'Nine? Oh, I can get you back to London well before nine – after all, the whole ritual climaxes at the crack of dawn. Then we all go our separate ways ...'

'I'm rather looking forward to it. Very titillating, Mr Hammer, even if I say so meself, making love and making history! Something to tell the grandchildren, I dare say.'

'Something you cannot ever tell of, sir. Unless you wish to condemn both of us to both notoriety and prison,' D'Arcy snapped back firmly.

'I was joking, Mr Hammer. I am as discreet as a monk in a nunnery. As far as I'm concerned, as soon as it's over it never 'appened.'

D'Arcy studied the young sweep, who returned his gaze, steady and unflinching. The young biographer then held out his hand and the two men shook on the agreement. From a distance it all looked very innocuous.

Later that day, D'Arcy visited two wealthy cousins and an uncle. He borrowed the total of sixty crowns then hocked his pewter mugs and received another forty crowns. After further study of Banks's description of the ritual he went in search of a number of other essentials: a piglet (required as an animal sacrifice to Atanua, the Polynesian goddess of fertility and of the dawn; a sweet vegetable called a yam, which was also required as a ritual offering; a ground cloth, upon which the orgy was to take place, that had to be marked up with magical symbols and totems exactly as described in Banks's notes; and, finally, a wooden bowl to be held up at the point of climax by the two male participants.

The piglet he rescued from a slaughterhouse in Smithfields market. The small cowering beast appeared so grateful D'Arcy couldn't help but feel a little guilty for the innocent adoration of the animal that had no idea that D'Arcy had merely substituted one nasty fate for another. The yam was harder to locate. After a lengthy search he remembered a shipping colleague of his father's who imported vegetables and fruit from the colony of the West Indies. He visited the offices of the company at the London docks and, after paying a visit to the bemused gentleman, left an hour later with a box of the strange, twisted, yellow vegetable. As for the ground cloth, he left this task to his tailors with a drawing of exactly how it should look. Discreet as ever, the Savile Row tailors asked no questions. The wooden bowl he bought from an importer of exotic goods off a small arcade in Bond Street. It was, to his immense satisfaction, actually from Tahiti. Finally the last but most essential ingredient of the ritual – an object belonging to one's nemesis, the person one wished to inhabit for an hour – was already in his possession: Tuttle's white glove.

And so, after an exhausting two days of hansom cabs and brisk walking, D'Arcy discovered himself one street away from his publisher and found he could not resist a spontaneous visit. Pushing past Dingle, the secretary, D'Arcy made his way straight into Mr Crosby's office and caught the corpulent gentleman in the middle of a prolonged post–afternoon tea repose. He was accompanied by a snore that rattled around the room like a trapped djinn. Crumbs of Stilton cheese were still caught in the whiskers of his handlebar moustache, blowing, as they were, like snowflakes, abreast every exhalation.

D'Arcy stood over the desk (with a dirty lunch plate ignobly placed over some poor fop's manuscript) and coughed loudly. The publisher woke with a small shout, his flailing arms scattering pages in his surprise, his eyes finally focusing upon the young biographer. 'Mr Hammer, you shocked me! I was deep in thought,' he announced as he hurriedly plucked the soiled napkin from his shirtfront and placed the plate behind the desk. 'You are audacious, sir, to interrupt a man from such a reverie.'

'Forgive me, sir, but it was the excitement of the hunt.'

'The hunt?'

'The hunt,' D'Arcy repeated.

'I understand,' the publisher replied gravely, when it was patent he did not. 'The spontaneous vigour of young writers, not least their imagination, is, after a time, somewhat tiresome,' he concluded philosophically, addressing the last observation to the portrait of the deceased Mr Bingham. D'Arcy, fearing another of Crosby's soliloquies to the dead, interrupted: 'You don't understand: I have found it!'

'It?'

'The element that will propel my biography into a stratosphere Mr Tuttle can never possibly imagine, never mind actually achieve! A secret account of a magic ritual conducted by the young Joseph Banks on the island of Tahiti – the contents of which are so scandalous, so un-Christian in the most titillating way that it will assure huge sales of the book. Sir, you and I will both be rich!'

The publisher studied the young man standing before him, taking into account his heightened colour, the feverish glaze of his eyes, the exhaustion that played across the taut cheekbones. He was fond of the young biographer, having nurtured him through his first manuscript, believed in him when others had not, nursed him through the bouts of insecurity and, on occasion, paranoia; why, he'd even been known to advance him money – but, most importantly of all, he had been at Harrow with D'Arcy Hammer's father, Lord Hammer, and in England that, as we know, counted for an awful lot.

'My dear young man, are you eating properly?' he inquired, brushing the last of the Stilton from his face.

'Did you not hear me? I tell you I have discovered the Holy Grail of biographies, the unpublishable heart of the great man. Why, the journal itself was hidden up a chimney in the Royal Institute – Joseph Banks's old study.'

'And you are absolutely positive it is genuine?'

'I am positive it is written in the hand of Joseph Banks and much of the reportage correlates with his earlier journal. Also, from an anthropological perspective, the description of the ritual, the artefacts used, names of gods invoked, these are all correct. There is one last piece of research I intend to carry out tomorrow night which will prove one hundred per cent that the journal is authentic. Once that is completed I will insert an account of the ritual and a description of the discovery of the secret journal into the manuscript within the week.'

'That alone will ensure an article in *The Times*.' The publisher, now infected with D'Arcy's enthusiasm, had already begun to embark upon a marketing strategy.

'As well as a lecture series, perhaps starting in the very room which houses the chimney the journal was found in,' D'Arcy added eagerly.

'Brilliant, my young man! I shall have it typeset the very day you deliver the manuscript! Now, about this last piece of research, are we confident you can ensure the authenticity of the material?'

D'Arcy smiled. He couldn't help but imagine Crosby's expression if he knew the exact nature of D'Arcy's 'research'. 'Oh yes, that and a whole lot more,' he concluded a little more mysteriously than he had intended.

D'Arcy had chosen a small wood in Essex – a two-hour coach ride during which Prudence, Harry and young Amelia had, with the help of a few bottles of stout, become noisily acquainted. Secured to the roof of the swaying coach was a small crate containing the squealing piglet, the ground cloth (meticulously stitched, pressed and folded, with a silk label reading 'Harringtons and Harringtons of Saville Row' fixed neatly into one corner), a quantity of black candles, the wooden bowl, rubbing oil, a portable clock, some water and, of course, one large yam. He had the precious white glove tucked firmly into the pocket of his frock coat. As far as D'Arcy could tell, he'd not missed any of the elements needed – now all that was required was precise timing, the actual orgy and the rising of the sun, the one element he was confident of.

By the time they had arrived at the entrance to the woodland, the others were quite tipsy with Harry the sweep entertaining the two women with bawdy jokes that had them roaring with laughter. D'Arcy wasn't quite so amused. The seriousness of the venture had finally impressed itself upon his sensibility. He had to execute the ritual precisely and he feared that any deviation, any action that was not in the actual account of the ritual, might destroy the sorcery.

As the coach entered the wood, D'Arcy was pleased to see that the clearing he'd chosen was as secluded as he remembered – a small plateau set slightly above a circle of oak and birch trees. It was a full moon and the canopy of branches and leaves threw a lattice of shadow and light upon the grassy carpet beneath. He glanced over at his companions, young, eager, uneducated and now drunk. They had no idea of the spiritual importance of the undertaking, and he worried they lacked the sophistication to understand. This disturbed him, taking, as he did, the anthropologist's view of another's culture: he felt it essential that they approach the experience with the same reverence they might approach a religious ceremony. 'But for them it is a mere orgy, a ribald indecent good time,' he observed silently to himself. 'After all, you've hired two whores and a chimneysweep – it's a far cry from an eighteenth-century Polynesian princess, a high priest and priestess. Would the ritual still work?' These doubts and a multitude of others had plagued him the whole two hours of travel, and yet, now that they had arrived, he was condemned to carry out his plan.

The coach pulled up with a jolt, sending Amelia flying into the biographer's lap, cleavage spilling over. She was a slender, heavy-breasted redhead with pale skin that looked to be almost transparent. Prudence had told him she was very popular with a couple of the brothel's painter clients. This gave the young biographer some hope that Amelia herself might be used to sexual trysts of a more artistic sensitivity. Laughing, and with her face still in his lap, she smiled then pursed her lips suggestively. D'Arcy's member hardened despite his determination to maintain a dignified detachment throughout, and to his chagrin, he blushed. 'Steady on, Amelia, we ain't even started yet!' Harry cracked, and again the coach rocked with laughter. Just then the coachman, a sober, cadaverous-faced man D'Arcy had bribed heavily to maintain both his silence and discretion, opened the door and the three younger people disembarked in a flurry of petticoats and heavy perfume. Without a word the coachman clambered atop the vehicle and handed down the small trunk and crate containing the now snuffling piglet, which finally seemed to have had a premonition of its fate.

The three stood now a little dazed on the damp grass, waiting for some direction from D'Arcy.

'I have some robes for us, if you would all like to change into them while I arrange the ground cloth upon which we are to execute the ritual.' He tried to sound authoritarian and sombre. Prudence glanced dubiously over at the piglet.

'What about the pig? You ain't said nothing 'bout the pig.'

'That's right, sir,' Amelia chimed in. 'I don't do animals.' She looked anxiously over at Harry, whose bemused gaze slid back to D'Arcy.

'Fear not, the pig is to be sacrificed to the goddess,' D'Arcy retorted brusquely.

'Sacrificed?' Prudence squealed in unison with the pig, which seemed to have understood. With a grin, Harry ran his finger across his throat to illustrate, a gesture that sent the girls into a cascade of shrill shrieks, more of delight than fear, D'Arcy noted.

Walking over to the small glade open to the sky, he threw down the ground cloth then used a small compass to arrange it so that the symbols faced in the correct directions beneath the stars. He pulled out the large clock he had brought and consulted it. It was three-thirty am; according to the Royal Astronomical Society dawn was to be at four-fifty that morning – they had just over an hour.

'Time to get acquainted,' he announced to the other three. The four of them knelt, one on each corner of the ground cloth, their foreheads daubed with pig's blood. The unfortunate animal lay over the symbol D'Arcy had calculated to represent the dawn goddess. It hadn't been easy killing it – in the end Harry had to slit its throat – but it had died swiftly enough with one last lingering glance of reproach at D'Arcy. The yam – also a food sacrifice to the dawn goddess – lay next to the slaughtered pig and the travelling clock (brought solely for D'Arcy to time the event exactly) was well within sight; a strangely contemporary artefact in a tableau that had already started to draw all of them into a more immemorial ambience.

It was undeniable; D'Arcy felt the mysticism of the ritual rush through his blood like an opiate. An air of eerie reverence had fallen over the others; even Prudence, the most earthy and cynical of creatures, now dressed in the thin white silk robe he had given each of them to wear, seemed spellbound, almost hypnotised as D'Arcy lifted his hands to the sky, one hand clad in Tuttle's white glove. 'Oh Atanua, great goddess of dawn and of all things fertile, we have given the spirit of this animal to you and we will give more – our very life-spirit in union. I seek the body-sight of my enemy – in your name, great Atanua, I seek to see through the windows of his soul. I beg, Atanua, in the name of all the valleys, rivers and oceans you have given birth to, grant me this wish ...'

Nearby, in a small grove of trees, D'Arcy could hear the coachman give a polite cough followed by the sound of his footsteps as he walked further away. Relieved, D'Arcy dropped his hands. To his surprise there was no embarrassment, no shame to his actions. It was as if now, here, psychologically prepared and dressed in the robe, he was the priest, the Tupia, described in Banks's journal; it was as if he had undergone this very ritual before, so powerful was its influence on him.

D'Arcy pulled off the white glove and placed it ceremoniously in the centre of the ground cloth, then looked across at Harry, the young sweep – his erection evident under his thin robe.

D'Arcy nodded. 'And now we will begin.' He moved over to Prudence and lifted her robe. The thick curls of her pubic hair sat neatly between her thighs, the small pert breasts with the large nipples stood high on her chest. Roughly he thrust his hand between her legs. To his surprise she was already damp, her labia sticky against his wrist. Her long blonde hair, now loose, hung down to her waist, and cascaded down to the ground as he lowered her onto her back. She gazed up at him with a look that was half-submission, half-wonder, and he could tell that the ritualised atmosphere of the orgy had transported even Prudence, a practised professional.

Cupping her two small breasts in his large hands he sucked each of her nipples in turn, nipping them gently between his teeth, then ran his tongue down the centre of her small body to the apex of her sex, pert and ready for him. As if on cue Amelia slid behind Prudence and, lifting Prudence's knees, parted the older woman's legs as if offering her to D'Arcy. Prudence groaned in excitement. D'Arcy parted her with his fingers and began to suck and lick the small hard bud of her sex, his fingers slipping into both entrances. It was as if Prudence's spreadeagled figure was the centre of the formation, the beginning of the dance they had to perform, the first position of a movement that had to culminate in a certain configuration – one that had been sketched in Banks's secret journal. It was an image that D'Arcy felt, hung suspended over his burning lips, his pulsating member, the roar of sheer pleasure pounding through him.

Looking up he saw that Amelia had moved her hands and mouth to Prudence's breasts and that Harry had pulled his robe off. His muscular body, oiled, glistened in the moonlight. He was erect, with a member that jutted out, disproportionately large, from his slender torso. The young sweep reached across and ripped the thin silk of Amelia's robe. Her full buttocks and heavy breasts immediately came into view, a sight that excited D'Arcy even further. Amelia, seemingly paying no attention whatsoever, continued to suck each of Prudence's nipples in turn, her fingers pinching and squeezing. The sweep, as if angry, pushed Amelia's back down so that she was forced to kneel on all fours. He then parted her buttocks, pushing them as far apart as he could. For a moment D'Arcy watched as the sweep paused, almost as if he were examining the young girl's nether parts, then his face disappeared as he buried his mouth and tongue between her buttocks. Moments later Amelia began emitting short screams of excitement, her pleasure exciting Prudence, D'Arcy noticed, as her sex began to clench around his tongue and fingers.

D'Arcy paused for a moment. He had to time all their climaxes to the exact same moment. This he had explained patiently to the other three during the coach trip, emphasising, despite their evident amusement at the difficulty of such a feat, that it was absolutely vital the timing was perfect.

Above him Harry shifted and, after lifting his face up, inserted himself into Amelia. For a moment the young girl gasped, no doubt surprised by his size, D'Arcy couldn't help observing a little ruefully. Then her pained expression changed into one of pleasure. Grabbing at her heavy breasts the sweep began thrusting into her: slowly at first, then faster and faster. He caught D'Arcy's gaze – again the young biographer was worried that they might climax too early. Catching the meaning of D'Arcy's expression, the sweep smiled back at him – confident and cocky – as if to say he was still in control, but there was something else in that smile, a magnetism that kept the two men locked in that gaze as they both made love to others as if they were making love to each other.

D'Arcy tilted his face so that he could see the clock – they had another twenty minutes before dawn, before the moment of climax. Following his gaze, Harry pulled out of Amelia.

Moments later D'Arcy, still kneeling with his face and lips on Prudence's sex, suddenly felt his own robe being pulled up, large hands parted his own buttocks, and with a startled moan (muffled by the thick bush of the prostitute's sex) the touch of a hot tongue penetrated him while large rough fingers encircled his swollen yard. D'Arcy had never felt anything quite like it, and it took all his concentration not to come. Two thick fingers probed him, easing him open. D'Arcy felt pinned, yielding in a way he'd never yielded in his life, yet it did not repulse him but excited him, and the thick blunt tip of the sweep's cock pushed into him. D'Arcy almost screamed in a pain that was so close to pleasure that the two became interchangeable as the sweep increased his tempo. In reaction his own fingers thrust in and out of the now soaking orifices of Prudence, faster and faster – two fingers, three fingers; deeper and deeper as her muscles contracted and rippled under his touch.

Above him he could hear the groans of all of them resounding in the glade. Somewhere an owl hooted, almost in response. He was too close to coming. He pulled himself away from Harry and stopped, sitting up. Harry leaned across and nuzzled the back of his neck, the alien roughness of a man's skin arousing him further. Standing up, D'Arcy moved around to Amelia, who now slid her face down to Prudence's wet sex. It was an arousing sight, the young girl's fingers spreading open the older woman, her tongue and lips eagerly playing the clitoris. Watching, D'Arcy took hold of Amelia's large buttocks and manoeuvred them so that she now crouched over Prudence's face. The prostitute needed no encouragement: her hands slipped around and parted the buttocks as if offering the young girl up to D'Arcy, while beneath she eagerly began sucking on the young girl's clitoris. Harry, watching him, lifted Prudence's legs so that they slipped over his thighs, his engorged member waiting to enter the prostitute from underneath while Amelia still pleasured her from above.

D'Arcy looked over at the sweep; they were nearly in position for the final act, the final movement – a formation he had planned with the sweep beforehand and the final position described in the ritual. He nodded at the sweep and then in unison both men entered Amelia, D'Arcy from behind and Harry from above, at the same time Harry buried his mouth into Prudence's sex as she stood over him. D'Arcy glanced over at the clock; there were five minutes to go. The dawn, a thin red streak across the horizon, was beginning to break.

D'Arcy began to thrust eagerly into Amelia, her tight youth grasping him like a silk glove, while Harry mimicked his every thrust. It was as if the four of them had dissolved into one organism. As white-hot pleasure soared through his blood, the groans and screams melded together so that D'Arcy could not tell his pleasure from Harry's nor Amelia's nor Prudence's. Now the red lip of the sun was breaking over the trees. Reaching down, D'Arcy picked up the wooden bowl of water and held it out to Harry. Together they lifted it over the writhing women to catch the first rays of sun in its waters and all four of them simultaneously reached a shuddering, howling orgasm. Moments later D'Arcy lost consciousness and suddenly found himself staring through the eyes of Horace Tuttle.

The next morning D'Arcy awoke and found he was safely tucked into his bed and wearing his usual summer nightgown. He lay there contemplating the sunlight dancing upon the ornate plaster ceiling – spectres of light that appeared to be fornicating and writhing with the same sensual pleasure still echoing through his body. The ritual had worked. It had worked! The startling intelligence of this realisation jolted him into a sitting position – but at what cost! The horror of what he had witnessed through Horace Tuttle flooded back. It was impossible to either ignore or dismiss and D'Arcy knew that any last trace of morality or belief in Man's better nature had left him forever. The whole experience had aged him, knocking the last remnants of naivety and idealism out of him. From now on it was dog eat dog – that was the true character of Mankind (biographers were no exception) and he had better get used to it.

Strengthened by his resolve, he swung his legs out of the bed and immediately went over to the framed photograph he had on the dresser. It was of Clementine, his fiancée, an elegant portrait of her carefully posed in flounced summer dress, lace-trimmed bonnet and parasol under a painted bower of flowers. She'd given it to him in the early days of their courtship, when she was forced to depart for Europe for a trip with her mother, Horace Tuttle's sister, to Florence, a trip meant to deter the young heiress from marrying. Such feigned innocence, he thought, looking down at the picture, such a deceptively angelic face.

Now D'Arcy was even more determined to both destroy and supersede Horace Tuttle – any lingering residue of respect for the older writer had evaporated. A sudden violence swept through him. Picking up the photograph he threw it against the bedroom wall. It shattered, showering the floor beneath in glass fragments and splintered wood. Leaving the debris there, D'Arcy hurried down to his writing room.

The mad scratching of the quill against the paper was the only sound in the study. The room had started to darken and with it came that timeless tranquillity that sometimes falls upon even the noisiest of cities. Henries, the butler, stood with the dinner tray at the open door. The absorbed young biographer, still in his dressing gown, did not look up from his desk. D'Arcy had been writing for hours with a fury Henries hadn't witnessed before. It was as if another, older man possessed the young writer – a new anger had hollowed out his cheeks, and his limbs seemed infused with a frenetic energy that someone else might have recognised as rage. The butler wondered whether he shouldn't inform Lord Hammer of his son's condition but, at a loss as to how to actually define the condition, he decided it might be wiser to wait and see what kind of creature emerged at the end. Sighing and filled with a dismay he couldn't quite fathom, the elderly servant quietly placed the dinner tray on a side table, switched on the gas lamps, which each burst into a warm glow, then picked up the luncheon tray: the food on it was untouched.

Four hours later, D'Arcy put down his pen. Closing his eyes he breathed in deeply then exhaled. The whistle of his breath rustled the pages, scattering them wildly across his desk, shuffling them like the cards of an ominous Tarot deck. D'Arcy opened his eyes and tentatively picked up the chapter he'd just spent twelve hours composing – Joseph Banks's experience of the ritual, transcribed and meticulously interlineated with footnotes. As he scanned down the lines a great surge of excitement began to thump against the walls of his chest. His mouth went dry. 'Genius,' he said out loud.

'"Scandalous, preposterous and utterly gripping. D'Arcy Hammer Esquire has written a biography of Sir Joseph Banks that has revealed the great scientist to be either an amoral libertine with a penchant for voodoo, or Hammer himself to be a great writer of fiction!" Mr Ernest Weatherby, *The Times* ... "This book should be banned and burnt on a Sunday!" Mrs Samantha Jenkins, the *Daily Telegraph*.' Mr Crosby, his naturally florid countenance even redder with excitement, lowered the newspapers he had been holding aloft.

'My dear young man, you have surpassed yourself! The orders are overwhelming. Why, only this morning a request arrived – delivered in a plain brown envelope, mind you – for another five hundred copies. Banned!' He chuckled, then, with remarkable agility for a corpulent man, he spun around on his heels, causing D'Arcy, standing in the centre of the office, to stumble back.

'Dingle!' the publisher bellowed in the direction of the reception room, then swung back to face the young biographer. 'Probably asleep at his desk, exhausted by the tragic paradoxes of this world. He's a misanthrope, Hammer. Never make the mistake of employing a misanthrope – no room for them in the creative realm, no room at all!' At that very moment the aforementioned misanthrope appeared at the door.

'You called, sir?'

'Sherry, Dingle, sherry!'

'But, sir, it isn't yet Christmas, nor indeed Easter,' Dingle observed solemnly, unaffected by the evident joviality in the room.

'We are celebrating young Hammer's extraordinary literary success, you miserable spittle of a man! He is to be banned!' the publisher declared with great relish, his own spittle spraying the now feted biographer in the face.

'Congratulations, sir,' Dingle told D'Arcy with the enthusiasm of an undertaker just denied a corpse. He scuttled over to a small Chinese cabinet in a corner and retrieved what appeared to be a dusty bottle of ancient sherry and several grimy glasses.

D'Arcy collapsed into a small armchair. It had been an exhausting month. The biography had been published a little over a week earlier and was already the scandal of London, Scotland and the Continent, the coverage of which was only matched by the reportage of an unusually severe outbreak of cholera just streets away from D'Arcy's own dwellings, ironically in Golden Square in Soho, the very square in which dwelled both Harry the chimneysweep and Prudence. Swept away by the demands of his literary success, D'Arcy hadn't even had time to read about the outbreak, never mind actually visiting his two new 'friends'. Life had become a whirlwind of press appointments, interviews, several public lectures, invitations to numerous salons both literary and social, and a worrying demand to appear before a committee of the Royal Institute to explain his source material. There was even a rumour that Her Majesty herself had made a request for a covert delivery of the book. D'Arcy Hammer had become the enfant terrible of the literary world overnight, and London couldn't have enough of him.

'Banned? But surely that would be the ruin of me, Crosby!'

'The ruin? It will be your making. Everyone lusts after the clandestine, my dear young author. Isn't that right, Mr Bingham?' Crosby asked the framed portrait of his esteemed but deceased partner. 'After all, where would the Bible be without Mary Magdalene, *Justine* without the notoriety of the Marquis de Sade. Elisha without Jebel?' he added obliquely. 'Besides,' he said, turning back to D'Arcy, 'they wouldn't dare to *actually* ban you.' With a clatter, Dingle plonked down a tray with four glasses and the bottle of sherry onto a small table before the desk, then poured out four drinks. He placed one solemnly under the portrait of Mr Bingham, then handed a glass each to D'Arcy and Crosby. The publisher raised his glass.

'Gentlemen, I propose a toast – to both Hermes and Dionysus. Long may they rain down good fortune upon this dear young author!' The three men had just clinked then lifted their glasses to drink when a loud and persistent ring of the front doorbell interrupted them. It was a messenger from Horace Tuttle's publisher and main rival of Bingham and Crosby, the notorious and ruthless Bill Scrunch. The messenger, a young man with sleek, oiled, black hair reaching down below his ears and a well-cut suit, dusty at the trouser cuffs from running, silently held out a plain white envelope.

'A challenge, sir?' Crosby, whose hatred of Scrunch rivalled D'Arcy's hatred of Tuttle, spat, then silently ordered Dingle to take the envelope from the messenger as if he did not wish to demean himself by touching it.

'It might be, then again it might not, but Mr Scrunch told me to tell you you've got till this evening to respond,' the messenger informed him. Then, after a flick of his coat tails and a short mocking bow, he departed.

Once the door had slammed behind him, Mr Crosby tore open the envelope and scanned the contents. He looked grimly across at D'Arcy.

'It is from Horace Tuttle. He claims your biography contains fictionalised material and he queries your sources. He has challenged you to a public debate, to be held in the Great Hall of the Royal Exhibition Building this Wednesday afternoon.'

'But that is only two days away! I refuse to lower myself to his pettiness!'

The publisher carefully placed the letter upright and open on the mantelpiece above the small grate. He considered D'Arcy thoughtfully until his uncharacteristic silence rattled the young writer. 'D'Arcy, the material is authentic, is it not?' Crosby finally asked.

Startled by this new vein of scepticism, D'Arcy leapt to his feet. 'I swear, Crosby, I would never have endangered both your reputation and mine!' Appalled, he stepped towards the door. The publisher patted his arm reassuringly then led him back into the room. 'In which case we will pick up the glove with relish. You must take up his challenge; you must attend the debate and defeat him with great wit! It will be a triumph of publicity. Why, Dingle, draw up the leaflet immediately! We shall emphasise youthful innovation over old prejudice ... Of course, naturally you will be required to produce the secret journal and verify your sources.'

'Naturally,' the young biographer replied, and if there was any doubt behind his veneer of brazen confidence he did not let it show.

The next morning, D'Arcy was woken by Henries clutching the morning papers – the headlines all screamed *Cholera!*. The newspapers warned local residents to stay clear of Golden Square and the infected borough of Soho. 'Sir, I strongly suggest that you adjourn to your father's estate or at least stay indoors for the duration of this pestilence. I am convinced this would be your father's wish, young D'Arcy,' the butler counselled.

'I cannot. I am to attend a public debate tomorrow, Henries, and my reputation will be in ruins if I should miss it,' D'Arcy replied. In fact despite the cholera outbreak, he was determined to visit Golden Square himself in order to see Harry, the chimneysweep, to ask him if he would consider giving a verbal confirmation of his discovery of the secret journal at the very same debate. Fortunately for Henries, D'Arcy kept this decision to himself, and it was only after both the old butler and his wife had retired to their own quarters that the biographer ventured out onto the streets of the West End.

D'Arcy stood at the kerb of Regent Street, now the great divide between the diseased and the unaffected, and looked down Beak Street. Behind him stretched the affluent disease-free borough of Mayfair, where fashionably clad shoppers and pedestrians still thronged the pavement, whereas before him there was a distinct lack of humanity. He lifted a handkerchief that he had drenched in a herbal concoction he'd purchased that was meant to ward off the toxic miasma blamed for spreading the noxious disease. After a silent prayer to Thoth, Zeus and any other deity he thought would be sympathetic, he hesitantly crossed Regent Street.

D'Arcy plunged into the narrow and dingy Beak Street. Normally a hive of colourful commerce and frenetic activity, this evening it was strangely desolate. Most of the businesses and shops were boarded up as many, fearing contamination, had fled to other parts of London or relatives in the countryside. The only business still open appeared to be the Lion's brewery on Broad Street. An old woman scuttled past, her gaze held steadily downwards, as if to look at him would be to invite the contagion. It was a disturbing and eerie sensation. Increasingly anxious, he made his way down to Golden Square.

A good half of the tall houses had their blinds pulled down, while many had black cloth displayed in their windows, an indication that there had been a death or deaths in that particular building. Fearing the worst, D'Arcy walked down to number ten – Harry the sweep's lodgings.

He stood outside staring up, not daring to enter. Black cloth hung in the windows of the first two floors, but he couldn't see the top window of Harry's family's lodgings. The small girl he'd encountered before on those very same steps months earlier, when he was a very different man, was still sitting there, seemingly impervious to the grim atmosphere, engrossed in a game of marbles. She looked up at him. 'Who are you after?'

'Harry the sweep.'

She held out her hand, the nails broken and filthy. Pushing down a wave of nausea that swept through him, D'Arcy, careful not to touch her, dropped a penny into her palm.

'Harry the sweep, top floor?' she asked in a voice flat with lack of emotion.

D'Arcy nodded, his handkerchief pressed against his nose and mouth, he dared not breathe in.

'Gone. Sunday morning, carried off by the cholera. His mum and a sister followed. I got her hoop,' she finished with a certain pragmatic triumph.

Shocked, D'Arcy stumbled then ran back to the safety of Mayfair.

Once returned to the sanctuary of his own study, D'Arcy stood nonplussed for a moment – it was hard to believe such youth and beauty could be wiped out so indiscriminately. Harry's presence now lingered before him, imprinted on both his memory and body. He could still taste his sweat, could still cast his mind back to that night the young sweep possessed him with such audacity. They had been linked by sex and magic, but also by discovery. But most disastrously of all, now that his only witness was dead, what chance did D'Arcy have to prove the legitimacy of his research, other than by his own word? His dilemma was interrupted by a tentative knock at the door. It was Henries informing him that he had an unexpected visitor – a Mr Horace Tuttle – who insisted that he see him immediately.

'This is an unexpected pleasure.'

The two men stood in the grand reception room of the mansion, facing each other warily. D'Arcy, fearing he would lose control of his own temper, kept his clenched hands thrust into his trouser pockets, while he noticed that Tuttle had not bothered to remove his coat.

'You are a master of disingenuousness, young Hammer, a trait I will not pretend to admire,' Tuttle, abandoning any semblance of etiquette, observed. It was a reply that sent a surge of fury through the young biographer, who immediately went to open the door, indicating that his rival should leave.

'Oh, I don't think you shall be so eager to see me leave, once you have heard me out,' Tuttle protested, not moving an inch.

'You have three minutes to interest me, but I suggest you save your argument for our great debate tomorrow, sir.' D'Arcy stayed by the open door, gripping the handle. Smiling, Tuttle threw down his cane and strolled into the centre of the room.

'Three minutes, eh?' To D'Arcy's intense annoyance, Tuttle produced a small gold case and lit up a cigar. 'Well, I promise it will be a devastating three minutes.' He exhaled a plume of cigar smoke with an air of smug triumph. 'D'Arcy, it was I who hired Harry Jones, the chimneysweep. A wonderful thespian for a working man, do you not agree, and so easy on the eye ...' Tuttle watched D'Arcy with the callousness of the hunter studying his prey as it dies in the trap. Shocked, the young biographer let the door handle slip from his grasp and the door swung shut with a bang.

'What do you mean, sir?' Ashen-faced, he turned to face his nemesis.

'I mean, Hammer, that the so-called secret journal of Sir Joseph Banks, the ritual to Atanua, was all fabricated by myself and planted as bait. Biography, young man, is a war – a war that you have proven yourself to be unfit to engage in. And if you don't expose yourself as having fictionalised Banks's memoir, I shall do it myself. You are ruined.'

'But it cannot be a fake!'

'I tell you, after studying Banks's handwriting, and his phraseology, I wrote it myself.'

'But the ritual works!'

'Don't be ridiculous. Anyhow, how could you possibly know that?'

'Because, Tuttle, I executed it myself, with the assistance of three other people – poor Harry and two ladies of the night, one of whom is a regular amour of mine ...'

Behind him the door clicked open, but D'Arcy was too impassioned to notice that a third party had entered the room. Instead he stepped closer to Horace Tuttle.

'I duplicated every movement of the orgy. I caught the sun in the cup and summoned up the goddess. I tell you the ritual works!'

'D'Arcy, how could you!' Clementine's voice rang clearly through the room. D'Arcy swung about and faced his estranged fiancée for the first time in months. He felt nothing but revulsion. 'How could you betray me like that?' the young woman continued, her voice thick with outrage. 'Why, you are nothing but a disgusting libertine.'

'You have no right to take the moral high ground with me, Clementine, and if you both care to sit down for a moment I shall explain why.'

Both Horace and his niece reluctantly sat, and, for the first time, D'Arcy noticed the familial resemblance between them.

'Mr Tuttle, you are lying, sir. I suggest you did not fabricate the ritual.'

'You're right, I copied it out of an old Grimoires, an old magic book I found in my collection. I merely changed the nature of the artefacts, but what of it? It was all nonsense anyway,' Tuttle barked back, flushing with indignation.

'I thought that must have been the case, because you see, my dear man, when I was possessed, when I was empowered with the magic ability promised from that ritual, whose eyes do you suppose I could see through?' An expression of horror slowly began to creep across Tuttle's face as he started to comprehend. Savouring the moment, D'Arcy continued. 'Your own, sir, and what I saw both appalled and disgusted me.' Now he noticed that Clementine had paled and the hand that held her parasol was visibly trembling. Determined to sink the dagger in, he did not falter for a moment.

'Uncle and niece making vile unnatural love. And so my original instinct was confirmed, that you, Clementine, had betrayed me and smuggled my manuscript to your lover –'

'You have no proof!' she screamed, abandoning all semblance of decorum.

'That night you both spoke of your first encounter only two years ago. I can tell you the place, day, even the name of the hotel at the time –'

'Enough!' Clementine shrieked, now holding her hands over her ears.

'What do you want?' Tuttle's voice was now little more than a broken whisper.

'A deal, Tuttle – a devil's pact, if you like. You withdraw your accusation and publicly endorse my biography tomorrow and in return I shall never expose either yourself or Clementine.

That way my literary success is assured, and you will never see the inside of Newgate. Do I have a deal?'

'You have a deal.'

And that, my dear reader, is the end of my little moral fable. Tuttle, of course, never recovered and as for Mr D'Arcy Hammer, well, that chapter isn't quite closed. Of course, you'd never read a tale of such moral depravity in one of my books.

FLIGHT

It was one of those long-haul flights, the overnight LA–London route, when the plane chases the sun north across the globe in a streak of perpetual dawn. Cocooned in the pastel-coloured luxury of the first-class cabin sat one entrepreneur, a minor Saudi prince and his wife, two American executives being flown by their company for a day with investors in London, a Chinese businesswoman and one film star: male, Australian and instantly recognisable.

Jerome Thomas, famous for his raven locks and piercing blue-grey eyes as well as huge donations to the starving orphans of Ecuador (all tax deductible, but that doesn't make it any less commendable), was London based and on first-name terms with British Airways special services. Dressed in black jeans (Versace), a white shirt (Tom Ford) and purple loafers (Paul Smith) in true Antipodean style, he affected a friendly casualness that belied an obsessive appreciation of anything luxurious, exclusive and elitist.

At thirty-nine, the film star was at that point when he could either fade into obscurity along with his looks or move out from the romantic hero roles that he'd built his early career on into more three-dimensional dramatic roles. Luckily for Jerome, his latest film, *Loser*, had been an international success and had landed him an Oscar. A psychological drama that had required serious acting and physical transformation, it was about a middle-aged American businessman who finds himself suddenly divorced, unemployed and without custody of his children. Then one day, homeless and sleeping under a bridge, the hero discovers a wild beehive and eventually finds spiritual meaning, new love and redemption by becoming an urban beekeeper. Much to both Jerome's and his agent's amazement, the film had become a runaway hit and the film star had safely made the transition from romantic hero to serious actor.

Jerome Thomas was still eerily beautiful to look at, a fact that he had struggled with all his life, a situation made even more poignant by the fact that the actor was also unusually intelligent with a capacity for empathy that he sometimes found paralysing. Celebrity for him had been a curiously painful process, a little like a slow-growing disease he'd only become aware of around the release of his fourth film. He had begun his career as an intense young actor, in the business not for fame but to lose the real and very awkward self-consciousness that can haunt the very beautiful. Jerome had been desperate to be taken seriously. At NIDA, the prestigious Australian drama school where he'd trained, Jerome was set on a stage career in London, preferably as a Shakespearean actor. Then, a couple of American producers had run auditions for a romantic comedy starring Meryl Streep, about a young male escort who falls in love with his much older female businesswoman client. Jerome hadn't even intended to go to the audition, but ended up accompanying his roommate who was almost speechless with nerves and needed serious moral support. As fate would have it, Toby Gladwell, the young Australian director attached to the movie, cast him on the spot, the film went on to make millions but Jerome Thomas was typecast. To his deep but secret vexation he'd wanted to be taken seriously, and, somehow in the passionate pursuit of that objective, had ended up hugely successful in unserious but very commercial projects. It was a paradox that Jerome had now escaped.

And so it was with a sense of sublime achievement rarely experienced by the extremely ambitious, Jerome had settled down in his favourite seat in first class – 1K – in the very nose of the jet with his customary two portholes. Here he could, without stretching his neck, gaze down on the carpet of lights that was Los Angeles as the plane swung to the left then backed momentarily towards the city before heading northeast towards Canada and beyond.

He'd been in LA for a week meeting with 'his people' and several directors to decide on the next film project, the script of which was now tucked securely in the magazine pocket in front of him. He'd also caught up with a lover there, a young make-up artist he'd seduced on the set of his last movie, a twenty-two year old from Kansas whose endearing lack of irony laced with naive optimism had reminded him of himself when he'd first landed in LA fifteen years ago. But on this latest visit Jerome had found himself increasingly vexed by her awe of him, and, yet again, he'd ended up feeling as if the dialogue she thought she was having with him was nothing but transference on her behalf, a discourse with some idealised version of him she'd created from various roles he had played. Jerome's true self was lost in celluloid, in that mirror of who his lover thought he was. It was a frighteningly familiar experience that always seemed to hijack his relationships, one that inevitably left him feeling disingenuous, guilty and inadequate, as if he himself was somehow responsible for his lovers' projections.

It was when he began to notice that his young girlfriend had started to spout lines he'd used in movies without even realising it, that he'd finished the affair, appalled. Since then an aphorism one of his drama tutors had always used – 'Wear the truth like a skin' – had begun to run through his head like a pop tune he couldn't get rid of. This sense of shifting identities was beginning to drive him crazy. Suddenly deeply aware that he'd actually started to lose his Australian accent, even to dress in the manner of some of his more famous roles, he'd become terrified he was losing his own 'truth'.

In reaction he'd secretly started to address himself by his childhood pet name, Rom, and had taken to scribbling notes to himself as a desperate way of staying emotionally anchored. He'd made sure that no one else knew the pet name. This was an identity that belonged to him, not to any lover, not his agent and certainly not his adoring fans. It was his personal totem, the anchor that held him together psychologically, but still he was finding it hard to be himself with an intimate.

Jerome longed to argue, to fight, to have a disagreement with someone who didn't know or care about who he was or how she imagined he would behave. He longed to be with someone who'd never seen a Jerome Thomas film, someone who didn't know him. Maybe then he would be able to get a measure of his true power – power as a basic human being and not some nebulous idol that millions of people had projected their fantasies upon.

This secret longing of his had blossomed into an obsession. Jerome desperately needed to know whether he could still attract someone with who he really was behind the façade of fame. Early that day, driving back from his agent at William Morris's office at Mid-Wilshire towards LAX, he made a pledge to himself. Before he was forty he would seduce someone who didn't know who he was at all. It was a pledge he took seriously, especially as his birthday was the next day.

The actor's gaze encircled the cabin. The entrepreneur, a jovial looking man in his mid-fifties, had ostentatiously ignored Jerome, even when he'd almost bumped into him hanging up his leather jacket in the wardrobe tucked behind the pilot's cabin. Such a reaction usually meant the other person had recognised the film star immediately and was shamming indifference – again, a scenario Jerome encountered over and over again, and one that at times had made him feel strangely isolated.

He glanced back over his shoulder at the Saudi prince and his wife, sitting in the centre aisle, side by side. Now that the plane was safely in the sky, they had finished reciting the Koran. The prince was studying a portfolio and his wife was engrossed in flicking through the deluxe in-flight shopping magazine. Jerome, applying the character research skills he'd learnt both at college and over the years, furtively examined the minutiae of the man – the way his shirt was immaculately laundered and ironed, the fastidiousness with which he kept pulling his cuffs over his wrists, indicating he was both controlling and nervous, characteristics, Jerome concluded, that were further underpinned by the bitten nails, chewed down to the skin, and a patch of eczema on the side of the prince's face. Despite his vast wealth and influence, the prince obviously had hidden anxieties.

Jerome turned his attention to the prince's wife. At least twenty years younger than her husband she was possibly a third wife, and one with young children, children who were probably waiting for her in London, Jerome guessed, gleaning a faint air of excitement and expectancy around her. This was a woman who was returning to something pleasurable. A beautiful Middle-Eastern woman in her early thirties, she smiled shyly across at Jerome from under her headscarf. Jerome smiled politely back at her then pulled out his film script from the front pocket, rather disappointed that she too had recognised him. That left just one woman in the cabin, a woman he'd already noticed in the first-class lounge. He opened the script and pretended to be reading it as he peered over at her.

She was sitting directly opposite him across the aisle and was the only passenger in full view. A small slim woman in her mid-forties whose beauty lay in both her fragility and the obvious skill she applied to her appearance. She was strikingly dressed in an elegant black Gucci suit – a short skirt and jacket. Her black hair was scraped back into an ornate bun, she wore a Patek Philippe watch, large diamond earrings that appeared to be real and a ruffled mauve silk shirt under her jacket, that promised (a fact Jerome had become acutely aware of) rather full breasts on a narrow torso. Jerome, who was well travelled in Asia, guessed she was Chinese rather than Japanese and after studying her he decided she must be a member of the newly ascendant class of Chinese billionaires.

But what fascinated him most about this woman was that so far she appeared to have no idea whatsoever of his celebrity. He'd already checked out his theory in the first-class lounge by walking past her several times while talking loudly to his agent on his mobile, and she hadn't reacted at all. At one point he'd deliberately looked over to her, waiting for that dazed gaze that came over people as they realised who he was, but nothing, absolutely nothing had registered in her sphinx-like face. It was this blankness that thrilled him to the bone.

'How are you today, Mr Thomas?' The hostess, offering the menu and wine list, startled him. Jerome stared up at her blandly smiling face, furious that she had used his name, and loudly enough for all the other first-class passengers to clearly hear who they were travelling with.

'Good, thank you.' He forced himself to smile through clenched teeth and took the menu. He glanced across the aisle and saw that the Chinese businesswoman hadn't even bothered to look up. It was as if he were a total nonentity, invisible. How was that possible?

He sat back, momentarily stunned. He couldn't even remember the last time he hadn't been recognised – it must have been at least fifteen years ago. The sensation was disorientating, a little like looking in the mirror and not quite recognising your own face. Was this what his audience, the constant excitement his presence engendered in people, had become to him – a mirror? It was both a profoundly liberating and deeply intriguing thought. And intrigue in Jerome's rarefied and choreographed world did more than excite him – it aroused him.

It then occurred to him that perhaps he should have a conversation with his agent about the Chinese distributors of his movies – was this woman's ignorance of who he was cultural disinterest? But he knew from the number of interviews he'd given Chinese magazines, as well as the number of adverts he'd made, that he was extremely famous in at least Shanghai and most likely Beijing. In which case where had this woman been for the past fifteen years? Did she not watch movies at all? Was she such an obsessive businesswoman she simply didn't have the time? Or perhaps she was the mistress of a top Chinese gangster – the

Chinese equivalent of the Japanese yakuza – being flown to join him on some dubious sojourn in London? Jerome surreptitiously ran his eyes down her legs looking for the telltale tattoos that were the insignia of such mafia. There were none.

He leant back against the soft leather headrest and allowed his imagination to weave storylines starring the mysterious woman. Could she be one of those female warrior types, descended from a great aristocratic pre-revolution lineage and imbued with great martial arts prowess? Suddenly he saw her floating down the aisle in a diaphanous tunic, her slim arms and legs outstretched in a kung-fu pose, hands ready to lash out. Would seducing her be fucking or fighting? He'd always liked rough sex, and a woman like that could flip him on his back in seconds. Or maybe she was more of a spiritual type, a kind of Buddhist high priestess able to meditate for hours … he saw her perched on a remote rocky mountain crag in Tibet, cross-legged in saffron robes, eyes closed, her long black hair flying back from her serene face. Perhaps she would be able to teach him to levitate or at least overcome the fear he still secretly felt walking the red carpet on Oscars nights. Somebody so spiritual probably also knew everything about tantric sex – they would be able to have sex for hours, slow, delicious, gyrating intercourse, the kind of lovemaking that really made you transcend your own humanity and enabled you to soar through space and time. But the idea that she had made her own money rather than married it excited him the most. A rich, beautiful woman, powerful in her own right who had no idea who he was – it couldn't have been sexier. Jerome sighed and nestled closer to the expensive leather headrest. Maybe he had been spending too much time in LA.

He stared across at her legs; a thin diamond anklet encircled a fine ankle, the bones as narrow and delicate as a bird's. Jerome imagined holding that ankle, imagined his fingers would be able to wrap entirely around it. She would be tiny against his six-foot frame, a doll he could manipulate. He thought about how erotic it would feel holding that ankle high against his waist as if she were straddling him, impaled upon him. And she would be small: a hot tight fist around his cock. Suddenly the weight of the script now resting across his lap felt heavy.

'Another glass of champagne, Mr Thomas?'

Startled again by the hostess's voice, Jerome sat up, hiding his erection with the script. Ever the consummate actor, he didn't even blush, instead he held up his glass to avoid the embarrassment of having the hostess bend down to fill it.

'Why not?' he replied, adopting the smile he'd crafted for his role in *Loser*. And now the smile, empty as it was, worked, and something in the hostess began to glow – some might have called it sexual hope – like the faint light of a ship caught in fog.

'I loved your last film,' she murmured, but loudly enough for the Chinese woman to have heard.

'Me too, wasn't that a fabulous role?' Again, Jerome let his gaze slide across the aisle. The mysterious businesswoman was engrossed in the in-flight magazine. It was as if she hadn't heard at all. She was utterly impervious. A shiver of pure ecstasy ran down his spine then tightened around the head of his penis. Oh God, did he want her now.

Oblivious to his flurry of desire the hostess bent over him to place a small bowl of cashew nuts on his side tray. A wave of the perfume Poison, sickly and cloying, drifted down with her movement: and for a second Jerome had a flash of the tiny apartment the hostess would return to between flights – the large flat screen that dominated the living room, the cat that would be waiting instead of the ex-husband, the cat litter tray beside the fridge in the tiny kitchen alcove. Suddenly Jerome felt very claustrophobic.

'And you did win the Oscar.' The hostess's voice dropped half an octave, an affectation he imagined she thought seductive.

'Oh, I blame that on the director and the screen writer – us actors, we're just glorified puppets, really,' he joked, hoping she would leave him alone but meanwhile adopting the false modesty that had endeared him to many a TV host and journalist – a rehearsed response. The hostess smiled indulgently then moved on to the next passenger, leaving him alone with the Chinese woman once more.

Jerome glanced across – still no reaction or even an acknowledgement. How delicious. Well, she could wait. He would seduce her but he would take his time, test his skills by doing it as slowly as he liked – after all, the flight was a good ten hours long and they'd only been in the air for an hour. Besides, wanting her was almost as erotic as having her, Jerome concluded, such was the mentality of a man who always got what he desired. Smiling to himself he opened the script he had to read for his meeting in London.

The lines of the first page seemed to writhe around seductively as Jerome tried to rein in his concentration. The script was an English period drama, set in the mid-nineteenth century, about a great rivalry between two famous Victorian biographers that had ended in a huge sexual scandal that had ruined both of them. Jerome was to play the part of the younger biographer, D'Arcy Hammer.

Restless, Jerome flicked through the pages scanning only his character's lines. He arrived at an extended monologue: a scene between D'Arcy Hammer and Clementine, his young fiancée, a role that had been offered to the latest English ingénue to be catapulted to Hollywood. Hoping to absorb himself in the psychology of Mr D'Arcy Hammer and temporarily forget the alluring woman sitting so close to him, Jerome began reading:

D'ARCY LEANS FORWARD AND POKES
THE FIRE, HIS FACE NOW FLUSHED WITH
EXCITEMENT AND SOMETHING ELSE – THE
MANIACAL GAZE OF THE OBSESSIVE …

D'ARCY

You have to understand, Clementine, what it must have
been like for Banks, suddenly finding himself in this
tropical paradise, this alien world where very few white
men had walked before, and to feel this great passion,
this irresistible attraction to a woman whose customs,
appearance and language were as strange to him as Eskimos
might be to us. And yet love or perhaps primal lust …

C/S OF CLEMENTINE BLUSHING AND YET SHE
CANNOT TAKE HER EYES OFF THE YOUNG
WRITER.

D'ARCY (CONT'D)

… I believe, transcends the constraints of civilised
society. It is pure, it lies in the heart of all of us, dormant.
Unbelievably dangerous, and yet …

HE LOOKS INTO THE BURNING HEARTH.

D'ARCY (CONT'D)
… the young Joseph Banks had the courage to thrust his hand into the fire …

C/S OF D'ARCY: HAS HE GOT THE COURAGE TO THRUST HIS HAND INTO THE FIRE? WILL HE INCLUDE THE SECRET JOURNAL IN HIS BIOGRAPHY AND RISK RIDICULE? HE GLANCES ACROSS AT CLEMENTINE – THEIR EYES LOCK.

CLEMENTINE
I believe in the real you, D'Arcy. I don't care what my uncle says, or what your adoring public believes. I know the truth of the man I love, whatever the future holds.

AND D'ARCY HAS MADE HIS DECISION.

Jerome stopped reading and gazed out of the window at the azure twilight that had become that moment's time zone, the dull roar of the plane's engines behind him. The role had caught his imagination. Here was a man who'd found someone who loved and desired his private persona, the vulnerable, fallible human side. D'Arcy had found someone who hadn't cared about his fame or money. Who cared if it had ended badly? This character could have been him, a hundred and fifty years ago, another brave explorer of human nature who yearnt for true intimacy, just like himself!

Now he could see D'Arcy crouched before that Victorian fireplace, he could feel his own chest encased within the tight velvet waistcoat, the starched stiff wing collars, the heightened pleasure of the proximity of the young woman D'Arcy wants but cannot have until marriage, the young biographer's ability to live through his subject's adventures – Jerome felt it all now.

As if in response one of the actor's eyebrows started to twitch as his face adopted the expression he imagined would suit a character like D'Arcy – a combination of haughtiness and vulnerability. He could make this work. He had run the same gamut of emotions as the troubled young biographer! He could play D'Arcy. All the acting possibilities began to run through his mind. Searching for role models for the character, gestures he could use that he'd observed in friends, other actors, the few young aristocrats he knew personally, he began to put together an emotional palette he could draw upon.

Just then a movement down the aisle distracted him. He looked up. The steward was now standing over the Chinese businesswoman, asking whether she was ready to order dinner. Her shining jet-black hair was illuminated by the pool of overhead light, the shadows transforming her pale face into a prism of sharp planes in perfect symmetry that was broken only by the length of her eyes and the large full mouth. And there appeared to be a gleaming wry intelligence in those black eyes.

Was he falling in love or in lust? He wondered then decided it didn't matter; the most important thing of all was that he was still unknown to her. He was every man and no one, plain Joe Blow with all the advantages and disadvantages that came with that. But there was something else that made the prospect of seducing her even more erotic, and that was the anonymity of air travel. In this nether-time they could be anyone. They were citizens of the sky, bound together by a restless need to keep moving. Surely that in itself indicated a need to reinvent oneself over and over with each new country, each new destination, so there was a double anonymity – the fact that he was unknown to her and the fact that both of them were literally in no-man's land. Jerome, fancying himself as somewhat of a philosopher, played with the notion. He'd always liked sex in the air, but up until now he'd only made love on private planes. The public domain was a whole other ball game, one that was far riskier and far more exciting – it violated all conventions.

With her he could choose to be his younger self; the idealistic and intense young actor with all the choices in the world or the questioning, more secretly vulnerable self he was now or anyone else for that matter, but one thing he would not be was Jerome Thomas the film star. And fuck, that was sexy. Now he was erect again, rock hard, his cock pressing up against the blanket over his lap.

Pretending to read his script Jerome surreptitiously studied the woman's every movement: it was the careful observation of the hunter. Again, she seemed to be oblivious of his interest. There was no subtle angling of the body towards him, no unconscious preening – the hand to the hair, tongue running across lips, fingers stroking skin – to indicate that she was even aware of the gaze of an attractive man, never mind a world-famous film star.

The steward described the menu. The businesswoman looked up at him. It appeared she didn't speak or understand English. The steward then repeated the menu in fluent Mandarin.

The woman broke into a smile and the severity of her beauty softened. It was then that Jerome was absolutely convinced he must act. Like the fearless D'Arcy Hammer he too would thrust his hand into the fire – or in this case, hopefully, between those smooth slim legs. Determined, Jerome lifted his pen from his breast pocket and wrote in the margin of the script: *Rom, you will have her by the end of the flight*. It was a promise to his secret self, his hidden persona. It was a commitment.

He pulled out the TV screen set into the side of the booth. The touch screen came on and he pressed the YOUR JOURNEY icon. Immediately a graphic of the plane flying across a curved map of the northern hemisphere came up. They were now somewhere over the icy plains of Alaska, as far as he could tell, and there were about eight hours to go before arrival. Eight hours to find a way of getting her attention, charming her without language or the advantage of his fame, and then seducing her without causing a disturbance or a newsworthy scandal. It was a deliciously erotic and extremely dangerous prospect, one worthy of both Jerome Thomas and D'Arcy Hammer – the question was, how? Across the aisle, the woman donned her headphones and, with eyes closed, appeared to be listening to music, her long delicate fingers tapping the arm of her seat. The in-flight magazine now rested on her lap, open. It was then that Jerome first noticed she was wearing a wedding ring. Good, he thought. In his experience married women were easier to seduce and less likely to have any emotional expectations afterwards.

Reaching into his trouser pocket he pulled out a second-hand wedding ring he'd bought years ago as a ploy to wriggle out of any unwanted advance; instead he'd discovered that presenting as a married man usually engendered one of two reactions. One was to make him even more desirable, which depressed him as despite never having been married himself he still liked to think the institution was sacrosanct. Or it would put women (and sometimes men) at their ease, as if the experience of marriage gave him both more gravitas and made him more trustworthy.

Just then he noticed that the in-flight magazine lying on the businesswoman's lap had flipped one page and was open at the movie section. The page was dominated by a large photograph from his latest film featuring himself in character dressed as a beekeeper – the lead character in the movie *Loser*. Startled, he almost got out of his seat; instead he forced himself to remain calm and, surprised at the intensity of his own reaction, tried to steady his racing heartbeat. He hadn't been this nervous since receiving his Oscar. It was an epiphany, a sudden understanding of how much the seduction meant and how the opportunity that now presented itself was once in a lifetime. Jerome had to stop her from seeing the promotional image in the magazine. He had to stay unknown to her. Had she already recognised him? Was his last chance of looking into the mirror and remaining anonymous lost? Fearing he was too late, he glanced across the aisle; her eyes were closed, she hadn't seen the photo yet. It was a matter of seconds – he had to move fast. Disentangling himself from his seatbelt, he got up and stood in the aisle. Pretending to reach for something in the overhead locker he swung and deliberately let the sweater that was draped over his shoulders fall across the lap of the Chinese woman. It slipped onto the magazine, covering the photograph completely.

The businesswoman opened her eyes. An expression of

outrage at having her personal space so rudely violated flashed across her face. She sat up, adjusted her skirt and broke into a torrent of angry Mandarin. Ignoring her fury, Jerome, adopting his most charming smile, apologised in English then bent over her to collect his sweater, keenly aware that by doing so she would certainly be close enough to catch both the scent of his pheromones (the allure of which he strongly believed in, especially as he'd been voted Sexiest Man of 2002) and his very expensive Parisian aftershave. As he collected his sweater he also managed to knock the magazine onto the floor. Again, smiling and fixing his most seductive look upon her, he handed the closed magazine back to her. The unspoken protocol of first-class passengers keeping themselves to themselves was broken. The woman gazed up at him. It was impossible to completely read her reaction in those black eyes, but Jerome was undeterred; if anything her apparent perplexity excited him further as did the sight of her slim thighs visible under the taut silk of her skirt. Still smiling, he pressed his hands together in front of his face and bowed as if he were a Tibetan priest. The gesture broke the tension as, laughing, she bowed back. Flushed with the success of the first strike Jerome returned triumphantly to his seat. 'The seed is sown, Rom,' he said silently to himself; now it was merely a question of time.

Moments later both the hostess and steward fussed around the two passengers, setting their tables with the customary white linen tablecloth and real cutlery, followed by their meals. The lights had now dimmed and each passenger booth was like a small island of illumination, the gentle drone of the engines like the great internal workings of a huge bird in which they were cocooned.

Jerome loved flying. He loved the neutrality of the environment

– it was timeless, nationless and best of all out of reach of the frenetic world stretched out beneath them. He finished his Dover sole and a glass of bone-dry sauvignon. Now he was intensely conscious of every movement his neighbour made, as if there were an invisible web linking his arm to hers, his hands to the small white fans of her own. He didn't have to look at her. It was as if he could feel the shift in the air around them with every gesture she made. It was a waiting game, a question of knowing when to reel in that taut thread of erotic possibility, he concluded, stretching his long legs against the footrest that, when raised, converted the seat into a full-length bed – useful in a private jet but not so useful in the polite and chaste atmosphere of a first-class cabin on BA, he noted.

Suddenly his reverie was rudely interrupted by a grape that came flying through the air from the direction of her seat. He caught it deftly with his left hand then looked across the aisle. The woman sat leaning forward, another grape impaled on a fork. To Jerome's delight she smiled slightly, a seductive half-smile, teasing. In response Jerome lifted the thrown grape to his mouth then rolled it between his lips, running it across his full lower lip while his tongue circled the purple flesh of the grape suggestively. Mimicking him she lifted the impaled grape to her own mouth, sucking on it as if it were him, his cóck. Jerome watched intently, her cupid bow lips dominating the narrow face, her dusky ivory skin heightened by the ink of her hair. She paused now, holding the grape between her lips. The action pushed out the flesh, and the grape glistened provocatively, ready. Mirroring her, his own lips came down upon the grape he held, both grapes spitting a tiny trickle of juice at exactly the same moment they both bit down: the climax, the pact, the moment of silent acquiescence.

Under his blanket his erection was close to bursting. Jerome picked up the fresh fig that was nestled between the camembert and gruyère on his cheese plate. He looked down the aisle; some of the other passengers were now tucked up in their individual booths, stretched out and sleeping, the lights above them turned off. He could even hear the faint rumble of the entrepreneur's snore in the booth ahead of him. Others were still finishing off their meals. Turning the fig slowly around and around he waited until the last of the diners had finished and were lying out in their individual booths either resting or sleeping. Most of the overhead seat lights were out and the crew were now discreetly out of sight, sitting in their rest area at the back of the cabin. Leaning down Jerome carefully rolled the fig across the carpeted aisle towards the Chinese woman. Tumbling as it followed the slight tilt of the plane, it arrived at her seat. She reached down and, after extending a slender leg into the aisle, rolled the fig over her thigh then beneath her skirt and into the recesses of her crotch. Jerome caught his breath, his own hand creeping under his blanket as he reached for himself, releasing his cock with a subtle lift of the hip and a quick soundless unzipping; in seconds it was in his hand, hard and hot.

Across the aisle the woman switched off her overhead lamp. Jerome peered through the dimmed light watching fascinated as she shifted her weight in her seat, her hand slipping down beneath her skirt and between her legs. He switched his own light off as his fingers wrapped themselves around the smooth skin of his penis, a heat bar pushed up against his stomach. Closing his eyes he executed a couple of quick tight strokes, the hot familiar pump of masturbation, the image of her lips flashing across his mind's eyes as he imagined her taking him …

The rustle of someone getting out of their seat startled him out of his fantasy. He glanced over. She was leaving, making her way down the aisle towards the toilet. He zipped up his fly and waited for several minutes to pass so he could avoid drawing attention to himself, then, after checking that the crew were still out of sight and that all his fellow passengers were asleep, he followed, his loose shirt concealing the bulging erection that would otherwise have been visible through his jeans.

He paused at the toilet door. The dividing curtain between first-class and business was pulled across while the first-class hostess and steward were huddled on the opposite side of the plane's aisle, engaged in a whispered conversation. They hadn't noticed him. Taking advantage of their distraction Jerome tapped quietly at the door. A second later he heard the bolt being slid across. He let himself in.

Dressed in expensive lingerie – purple lace he recognised as La Perla – she was pressed up against the washstand, her back against the basin. He squeezed in beside her, thankful for the extra space given to first-class amenities. There were only centimetres between the tips of her breasts and his chest. She was tiny next to his tall angular frame. He reached behind her head and pulled loose her hair. In a jasmine-scented cloud, it slipped down over her shoulders like black molten glass. She stared up at him, daring him to take her. He needed no permission.

Without a word he lifted her up and set her down on the closed toilet seat. He knelt on the floor as she too knelt on the toilet seat, thrusting her narrow hips towards him. He slowly peeled off the low-cut lace underpants. Her skin, the colour of pale honey, was as soft as kid gloves, and the feathering of black pubic hairs so fine it was like a dusting over her sex. He stretched his hands from the centre of her flat stomach to her hips, his fingers covering her entirely. Above him he could hear her moan as her body trembled beneath his fingers. He parted her with his thumbs; her sex was neat, symmetrical, her lips glistening and swollen with desire. Bending further down he nuzzled in, his tongue finding the small erect clit. She smiled down at him – beautiful, enigmatic.

As he inserted his fingers into her moist crack he found the fig, pushed up inside her, now protruding between her inner lips. He slipped a finger underneath and, nudging the fig out, began to eat it, pausing between each tiny bite to circle her clit with his tongue, stopping to suck gently before resuming, fig juice intermingling with her own juices, her thighs trembling wildly under each hand. Above him the groans continued, a little stifled. He glanced up over his shoulder into the mirror. She had clamped her own hand over her mouth to stop herself from crying out, her face flushed pink, his shoulder-length hair falling across her thighs, with only his brow and bridge of his nose visible. He liked this reflection, he liked the way his face was hidden, that he was unrecognisable. He had become every man and no man. He was finally a man who lived in his own skin, who was desired for himself alone and not his fame, who lived for his own expectations and not others'.

His cock was now painfully hard, bursting against his leg as he finished the last of the fig. She was slippery wet, tiny contractions fastening themselves around his finger. He judged she was close to coming but not quite there.

She was small: the promised tightness of her was almost enough to make him come there and then, even without entering her. Instead he lifted himself and stood upright, so that his crotch now faced her. She slipped her legs down so that she was sitting on the toilet seat and reached for his fly, unzipping him eagerly. He turned back to the mirror; his head and shoulders had moved out of the mirror's reach. Again he was without identity, invisible – all that was reflected was a man being serviced by a woman. For a man who was confronted with his own image as much as Jerome was, it was a profoundly liberating sight.

He tilted his body so that his penis came further into view. He liked his cock. He was lucky that it was as beautiful as the rest of him, well shaped and in proportion, complemented by testicles that seemed a good weight and size. Looking at his reflection in the mirror he ran his hands down the length of it. Then, still watching himself, he pushed his fingers through her long hair and pulled her down to him, rubbing his tip backwards and forwards across her lips, teasing. Grabbing at him she took him eagerly into her mouth, gagging slightly on his size.

Burning circles of tight pleasure spiralled around him and shot up through his groin and torso. Weakening at the knees, he put out an arm to steady himself, trying not to come. She was good, really good. More importantly, she seemed to be enjoying herself as much as he was. Cupping his balls she took him deeper and deeper, opening her throat like a professional. Was she a professional? The thought suddenly shot through Jerome's mind – the uncomfortable possibility that he might have been set up by some mercenary tabloid newspaper. It was almost enough to make him lose his erection. But as he glanced back down at her elegant face dipping to and fro, the diamond bracelets banging against her wrist, he was reassured: she was too well groomed, too well dressed, and there was that elusive quality about her, that independent self-assurance of the extremely successful woman that no hooker, no matter who she was, could emulate.

Comforted, his consciousness rushed back into his body, back into the tip of his cock throbbing in the hot cavity of her mouth. He had to stop. He was too close. Pulling away, he pushed his jeans to his knees and roughly pulled her onto his cock, her legs winding themselves around his waist, as he straddled the toilet seat for balance. She slipped over him like a silk glove; the snug fit made both of them gasp. It was ecstasy, it was the wettest tightest place he'd ever penetrated, and he was reluctant to attempt any further thrusts for fear of coming. She moaned loudly as he slowly began to move his hips, the pleasure spreading like a slow burn from the pinnacle of their locked sex organs. With each new entry she grew wetter and fuller and he felt as if all of his body had become his cock, every millimetre of pleasure, of skin on skin, resonating throughout his whole body, both of them now groaning, wet, faster and faster until the sex was driving him completely as he began pounding furiously into her. He slipped his hand into her long hair and yanked it back, while the other hand lifted one of her breasts to his mouth and he bit down on her nipple sharply. He thrust faster and faster, the roar of the plane engines now filling Jerome's head like his own approaching climax, like the roar of semen, of his own essence, identity, the inner nameless soul gathering up into one searing bolt of pleasure and he came, shuddering over and over, her thin arms clutching at him, her slender fingers trying desperately to muffle his groans. A second later she reached for the hand towel and covered her mouth to stifle her own cries as she came, her whole body shaking uncontrollably. In dim post-coital awareness Jerome found himself clutching onto her until she stopped quivering, suddenly somewhere between lover and fighter. In the silence that followed they half-sat, half-stood there, Jerome precariously perched on the closed toilet seat with the woman still wrapped around him. Reaching across he pulled up the window blind. Outside it was dawn – just below lay a perfect carpet of thin fluffy white cloud stretching endlessly around the plane. The sun hadn't quite risen yet and there was a band of glorious pink-red light above the cloud that bled into the azure of the blue sky above. It looked utterly elemental. A great wave of happiness rushed through the film star. He'd done it; he'd finally seduced someone who had no idea who he was, who'd desired him simply for being an attractive man. Staring out, a feeling of total wellbeing swept over him and for a moment he was part of that cloud, part of a greater truth, and it felt like immortality.

Ms Wei Chung walked swiftly down the tunnel leading into the arrivals lounge feeling particularly refreshed. British passport control had been easy to navigate and she was feeling invigorated after her long but interesting flight. And uncharacteristically for the normally sober businesswoman, she couldn't stop smiling. Xu Feng, her young PA, an ambitious Harvard graduate who was happy to work around the clock for one of China's most successful entrepreneurs, was waiting on the other side of the barrier beside the limo driver who was holding up a cardboard sign with her name written clumsily in Chinese characters. Xu looked grim. Wei strolled up and handed her hand baggage to him, thinking her news would be sure to restore his usual cheerfully wry expression. 'You'll never guess who I just screwed!' she told Xu in Mandarin.

BARROW BOY

'What school did you say?' Lord Harwood, Eddy's prospective father-in-law, looked up from his beef Wellington and studied the twenty-six-year-old metals trader with the air of an anthropologist who has just discovered that the tribe he'd dedicated his life research to turned out to be speaking bastardised French and not some exotic unknown tongue.

'Oh, Daddy, no one asks that question nowadays.' Cynthia, Eddy's fiancée of five months, laughed nervously, a high-pitched tinkle that Eddy had once associated with class but now found irritating. Eddy's narrow, handsome face sharpened as he glanced around the dining table. This was the moment both Cynthia and he had been dreading, the moment of truth when all his carefully laid plans could collapse as fatally as a house made of cards. Luckily they'd spent the week before devising a plausible back-story. Cynthia, despite her ingrained snobbery, was a pragmatist and she appeared to love Eddy regardless of his working-class roots, a fact that had never ceased to amaze him, but instead of endearing her further to him, as it should have done, it only made him feel more indebted to her, and Eddy, as a self-made man, hated feeling indebted to anyone.

Nevertheless, together they had concocted a plausible secondary and university education for the trader, and Cynthia had reassured him that a little white lie here and there wouldn't cause any harm, especially once her parents realised that Eddy's annual income was at least twice that of Lord Harwood's, who'd been living off the dwindling family estate since the 1950s. But the truth was, Eddy, or Edward as he was known around the table in question, was, to his deep chagrin, finding dinner at the Mayfair residence of the great family both intimidating and, in some inexplicable way, humiliating, for Eddy was the son of a fish stall owner at Berwick Street market. Good English working-class stock, his family had been running that particular fish stall for over a hundred and fifty years, a lineage one might, in other circumstances, have been proud of.

Yes indeed, Eddy was barrow-boy blood through and through, and the school he had attended was a minor comprehensive somewhere west of the Edgware Road, a place he could barely visualise as he'd spent a good deal of his schoolboy years playing truant or hanging out with his errant but entrepreneurial uncle, who was the one to introduce him to the intrepid seductions of the stock market.

At twenty-six, Eddy was the most successful metals trader in his bank, a small boutique enterprise that was extremely selective in its choice of clients and, with a turnover of more than two billion per annum, it could afford to be. It was the late summer of 2008 and London was still the glistening financial capital of the world, awash with both ridiculous wealth and pockets of bleak poverty. Like a great fat diamond with some facets shiny and some clouded by grime, one's experience of the metropolis really came down to which facet one was staring through and Eddy had made sure he was staring through the shiny one.

'I ask that question, I'm somebody.' Lord Harwood's voice rumbled down the length of the Georgian rosewood dining table and settled against Eddy's Wedgwood white china plate (also over a hundred years old) like a malevolent cannonball. Staring down at his pool of gravy Eddy was reminded of the pale green chipped china his own father, now divorced, ate off in his small council flat. He knew his socialist father would be appalled to see him now, all trussed up in black tie, speaking in a private school accent he'd recently finessed through watching an old DVD of *Brideshead Revisited*.

'Fuck it,' the ambitious trader thought to himself, 'now the lying begins. Still, what has to be done, has to done.'

Eddy prided himself on a certain mercenary ruthlessness that separated him from his forty-five-year-old dad, who was a bit of a hippie and who, to Eddy's annoyance, continued to romanticise New Labour, the benefits of the national health system and state education.

'Uppingham, sir, class of '98,' Eddy barked back, as rehearsed with Cynthia only hours before. The Cheltenham Ladies' College graduate and model had settled on Uppingham because, she'd concluded, Daddy was a Harrow boy and she was convinced that Eddy pulling rank would only incite her father to a bout of macho one-upmanship – the contemporary equivalent of duelling – a battle she dared not expose her inherently aggressive fiancé to as he would have to lose, and Eddy hated losing. Besides, although Uppingham was not one of the top three schools, Prince Charles had gone there and Cynthia knew this would shut her father up. Cynthia's mother, Lady Harwood, rotund in Chanel, looked up, her mouth puckering in disbelief.

'Class of '98,' Eddy repeated, flashing his killer smile at the aging matriarch, who, he decided, couldn't ever have been beautiful, unlike her twenty-one-year-old daughter, who was so preternaturally stunning she stopped traffic. Eddy froze his smile but kept his gaze steady, then very deliberately winked – his sexy I'll-have-you-in-black-lingerie-against-the-Louis-the-XIV-side-table wink. To his secret delight the matriarch dropped both her gaze and spoon. Bull's-eye. The old charm worked, especially given that what Eddy's parents had lacked in status and money they had made up for in good looks.

Back in 1981, Eddy's dad, then long-haired and dashing, had played in a punk rock band named the Aging Lotharios, a moniker that had led to the band playing one gig at the Playboy Club, booked under the misapprehension that the Aging Lotharios were a Rat Pack covers band. Although disastrous for the band it proved to be a fateful night for Eddy's father, for he had met Trish, a Playboy bunny from Conventry – a liaison resulting in Eddy's conception on the fire stairs between the eleventh and twelfth floors.

Uppingham indeed, Eddy mused, now tempted to share the wonder of his origins with Lord and Lady Harwood, if just to see the old man lose his teeth in his beef Wellington. But the young trader was committed to Cynthia – or at least he thought he was. Increasingly he'd begun to wonder whether they had enough in common for marriage and, more disturbingly, whether he could really trust her with his true self. He hadn't been entirely honest with Cynthia, fobbing her off with some story about how he went to a minor grammar school and his dad was a civil servant who'd dropped dead at forty from a heart attack – a blatant fiction. And now that the reality of getting married was looming Eddy had begun to feel more and more disconnected. Not just from Cynthia, but from himself. It was as if all the lying, the fake background he'd so meticulously built up, had suddenly become translucent. Worse than that, lately he'd actually had to stop himself from self-sabotaging. He glanced over at his fiancée. Pristinely beautiful, she represented more than a trophy wife. She was his golden gateway, his way of getting ahead, which, even in the glory years of early twenty-first-century London, meant some reinvention and the absolute necessity of becoming a member of a club. Carlton House, Cinnamon Club, the Athenaeum, the Army and Navy – whatever, Eddy didn't really care, he just desperately needed to belong and he was acutely aware that Cynthia was his only passport in. He would marry her, he would, he would!

As if intuiting his sudden reservations the heiress smiled back, a little quizzical, encouragement gleaming in her eyes. Determined to dismiss his own secret doubts and to further impress his potential in-laws, he launched into a diatribe.

'After Uppingham, there was PP and E at Oxford naturally, then the MBA at Harvard. I always thought a general education was important, even in business, eh, what?' Eddy elaborated, running the H's through his nostrils like a horse while thinking he sounded like an absolute tosser.

'Quite.' Lord Harwood coughed as Cynthia kicked Eddy under the table; perhaps he had overdone it.

'Which college at Oxford?' Lord Harwood's voice dripped with cynicism. A sudden chink opened in Eddy's normally impenetrable confidence. As he looked around wildly his eyes alighted on a Gainsborough portrait of Cynthia's ancestors: a dour-looking duke and his two sons.

'Trinity,' Eddy blurted out, convinced he'd heard the college mentioned in a radio quiz once. Cynthia kicked him under the table again.

'Edward's joking, he means Christchurch,' Cynthia told her father, just as Eddy remembered Trinity was in Cambridge.

'In that case you'll know my old friend Professor Huntington-Blithe. He teaches philosophy, politics and economics at Oxford. I shall ask him about you – probably come up with some dark history, eh?' the aristocrat retorted, then hooted with laughter.

'We'll invite him to the wedding. It will be St James and then the usual reception at Claridges?' Lady Harwood cut in, her blue eyes beady against the beak of her patrician nose.

'What do you think, Mummy?' Sarcasm was the nearest Cynthia ever got to wit, Eddy noted grimly. Now that the engagement was official and her parents seemed appeased, his fiancée appeared to be literally bouncing in her seat, reminding him of an overexcited Jack Russell terrier. It was a strangely terrifying sight.

'And I've already made the appointment at Hardy Amies. They have this wonderful new designer – you should see the dress I've picked out, it is covered in pearls! Real pearls, Mummy!'

'I expect *Horse and Hound* will want to write an article.'

'And *Vogue*! Oh, Mummy, it's going to be so wonderfully lavish …'

'And perhaps we can recoup by selling the rights to *Hello!* magazine,' Eddy chipped in helpfully. A deathly silence fell on the room.

'That's a little hoi polloi for the family, my dear fellow. The Harwoods haven't had to *sell* anything for over two hundred years,' Lord Harcourt pronounced, the aristocrat's obvious disdain for the word *sell* reverberating like a bad odour, making the hackles on the back of Eddy's merchant neck bristle.

And now you're marrying off your daughter to a barrow boy, Eddy felt like shouting up to the original Georgian ceiling. But he didn't. Instead he sat there meekly in a welling pool of self-hatred as the two women turned back to their wedding planning with renewed ferocity, expenses curling around them like a thickening fog, most of which Eddy would no doubt be expected to cover. He suddenly felt like vomiting.

He escaped two hours later, having managed to circumvent any further interrogation from Lord Harwood by engaging him in a vigorous conversation about the pros and cons of blue-chip against the perils of day trading. Outside it was dark and the usual residents of Mayfair had begun to appear like vampires emerging from their coffins: Russian oligarchs and their seventeen-year-old girlfriends; heirs to the Saudi empire; aging entrepreneurs cruising in their Lamborghinis and the like. In those days the extravagant money earnt and spent was comparable to the 1890s rather than the 1980s and London itself had begun to creak under a Dickensian disparity of wealth. It was possible to spend over ten million pounds in a small stretch of New Bond Street and only have a small shopping bag to show for it, and advisors to the wealthy were like courtiers at the Sun King's court – the more they charged the more desirable they appeared. Eddy was proud to count himself amongst this privileged set.

A light rain began to fall. Eddy, welcoming the cool pinpricks against his skin, loosened his tie and lifted his face to the wet night. The soothing drops helped wash away the heat of the heavy dinner and port. He knew he should go back to his apartment and read some background notes he had on a new client he was meeting the next day – a powerful Chinese businesswoman, one of the wealthiest in Shanghai, who'd flown in from LA that morning – but the evening had jolted him out of his usual equilibrium, the tight control he held over himself that he worked so hard to conceal.

The young trader lived in a converted penthouse flat in a red brick Edwardian apartment building on Marlborough High Street, an area that had just superseded Notting Hill in terms of hipness and was the latest abode of both ambitious young fashion models and aspiring actors. He'd received the two-bedroom apartment with media room, surround sound and roof terrace in lieu of a fee from one of his clients who'd gone through a particularly acrimonious divorce.

Eddy, sitting in the jacuzzi on the roof terrace with the steam curling up into the chilly London air, would often stare out over Piccadilly and the smudge of green that was St James's Park, and say to himself, 'You've made it, mate, you've bloody made it and you're not even thirty,' before sinking back into the piping hot water as if to marinate in the juices of his own financial success. But tonight his usual glow of self-satisfaction felt more than a little sullied. Had he sold out? Would he be happy with Cynthia? He sensed that under all the confidence she had from being monied and professionally successful as a model, she loved him. But why? For his own wealth? For the 'edge' he had compared to the usual private school boys and trust-fund crowd she normally hung out with? Was he just rough trade for her? And how would she react if she really were to meet his father? How would he ever bridge the gap of status between them? Cynthia never seemed to doubt or fear the future. It was as if she just expected things to work out, for success to simply shower upon her effortlessly. It had been one of the characteristics he'd originally admired so much – her lack of struggle. But now he felt alienated by it. This and a thousand other doubts whirled around his mind as he made his way through the milling crowds on Piccadilly.

It was that magical hour between dinner and before clubbing in which all manner of unpredictable encounters might ensue. Normally Eddy, a player to the max, revelled in this decadent twilight but tonight all he wanted was to escape the sense of being soiled, by both his own disingenuousness – the betrayal of class and family – and by the naked prejudice and avarice displayed by his potential in-laws, not to mention his fiancée. Eddy wanted to lose himself until he could feel normal again.

Looking up, he found that he had entered the narrow lanes of Soho; instinct had led him back to the streets of his childhood and his father's flat – or was it guilt? He checked his Rolex watch. It was too late to arrive at his father's door; the stall owner would most probably have fallen asleep on the couch by now, after a four-thirty morning start at the market. Eddy could envisage the sleeping bulk of him, a craggy silhouette against the back wall, snoring softly in front of *Match of the Day* or some such football reportage as the television blinked into the perpetually darkened lounge room. It would be cruel to wake him so late and besides, Eddy hadn't seen him in over twelve months. Not wanting to dwell on the reasons why, the trader sauntered on further into the warren of sex shops, upmarket delicatessens, boutiques and gay pubs. The streets were alive with tourists, day-trippers and the homosexual regulars as they window-shopped, ate at café tables set out on the narrow pavements and hovered around the sex clubs.

But it was hard for Eddy to forget who he was and what he'd compromised as he pushed his way through the pedestrians. His stomach ached from the heavy English food he'd felt compelled to finish at dinner, and his head spun from the cognac and cigar he'd shared with Lord Harwood. He longed for a pint at his local pub but that was at least three city blocks away. As he walked past the comic book shops and the rubber fetish boutiques, memories from his childhood bubbled up, dancing like jeering skeletons against his conscience. What kind of self-made man was he if he had to lie about who he really was? How would he explain his not-actually-dead father to Cynthia? And what was going to happen if Lord Harwood actually did ask Professor Huntington-Blithe about him? How was he going to orchestrate the wedding to avoid a collision between his world and Cynthia's world? What kind of public humiliations and other unimaginably awkward moments awaited him? The education and history, that profound sense of entitlement that came from such an upbringing – you couldn't fake that forever. Sooner or later his past would catch up with him and he would be bound to be exposed.

No matter from which angle he examined the dilemma, Eddy couldn't see a way to resolve it without revealing his true background, and that, in Cynthia's family circles, would be both social suicide and the end of the engagement. Perhaps he should break it off now. He stopped walking, imagining the scenario, Cynthia's disbelief and shock, the hurt. It was intolerable. The trouble was he really did care for her. If only there had been some glamorous wisp of childhood achievement he could hold on to – a scholarship, an unexpected friendship with Princess Diana when she visited Berwick Street market perhaps? Anything! But all he had were the long bouts of truancy and his early mercantile sensibility, none of which stood to win accolades from Lord Harwood no matter how much money he had in the bank.

He stepped off the kerb and was almost run over by a speeding Jaguar. Suddenly his frustrations erupted. He ran after the limo swearing and waving his fist in the air, just managing to thump the boot before it swung into a narrow lane. Gasping for breath he doubled over, watched by a couple of amazed tourists. Now ashamed, he tried to saunter off casually but his whole body was infused with anger. There was only one cure he knew of when he felt like this, one way of jolting him back into his own skin – a visit to a brothel. Sex did this to him, anonymous violent sex lacking emotion or expectation, just the clean morality of trade. And so, cheered by the idea, the metals dealer made his way to his favourite knocking shop on Old Compton Street.

Illuminated by a single tiffany lamp, the receptionist, a defiantly resplendent transvestite on the wrong side of forty with a face like a veil of sorrow, looked up as the bell above the door rang. 'Oh, evenin' Mr Jenkins, 'fraid your usual ain't in, got sick with the flu. But we got a new girl working who is very much to your taste. Does it all, bells and whistles, cocks and thistles,' she concluded in a flat monotone that excluded the possibility of irony. Suddenly animated she tidied a lock of fuzzy red hair that had somehow escaped her tortured coiffure. 'You interested then?'

'You know me ...' Eddy shrugged.

'I do indeed,' she replied without guile, 'just give me a minute.' She picked up the telephone and turned her back to him. 'I have a gentleman downstairs, partial to brunettes,' she said into the phone. '... Will do, dear,' she finished the conversation then swung back to Eddy. 'Room twenty-one, she's available now, same price.'

Eddy handed over his credit card and began making his way to the staircase at the back of the narrow reception room. At the foot of the stairs he turned.

'Has she got a name, then?'

The receptionist glanced down at her narrow black tome. 'Goes by the working name of Jezebel. Nice gal, no nonsense,' the receptionist added. 'Real polite.'

The girl was sitting with her back to him on the clean single bed with the canopy of cheap Indian silk slung above it. Her long black hair reached halfway down her narrow back, which was encased in a black rubber corset, her hips curving out beneath it. She had that pale English skin he was partial to, and looked to be full bodied. Eddy was old-fashioned in that way. He liked his women curvy, breasts and arse, something to bury yourself in. Secretly, he had never found Cynthia's fashionably bony physique sexy, as beautiful as she was. He stepped towards the girl; already he was hard with anticipation and his throat was dry. He was looking forward to the thumping violence of sex, to shaking off the restraint he'd maintained all that evening, through the humiliating dinner, through all the probing and questions, through the hee-haw of his own fake accent.

She swung around and he immediately lost his erection. They stared at each other. He froze, knowing she hadn't recognised him yet, while he would have known her anywhere, even in a black wig, rubber corset and g-string, after all those years. And, my God, was she still beautiful, he noted ruefully.

'Eddy? Eddy Jenkins?' The voice was the same, maybe an octave lower but then it had been a good ten years since he'd seen her and she would have only been sixteen then.

'Janey. Janey Lewis,' he said, his accent reverting to its natural cockney. 'A bit of a come-down, ain't it?' He gestured vaguely around the room and then regretted it as, to his surprise, a deep blush swept across her porcelain skin.

'You're not bloody wrong. Times are a little tight but you've got to make good wiv wot God gave yer, right?' She pulled the wig off and her naturally blonde hair cascaded down her back. 'They said you liked brunettes ...'

'I lied.' He grinned back, catching her awkwardness.

She pulled a black chiffon wrap over her shoulders. 'But you look good. You good?'

'Good? I'm wicked.' He tried smiling again but now found he was too nervous. And besides, he didn't know whether to stay standing or sit; there was only space to sit beside her on the bed and that would be a commitment. He stayed standing.

'Got a fag?' she asked, nervous herself.

Eddy reached into his pocket and pulled out a pack that he only kept for emergencies. This was an emergency, he decided, in fact the whole evening was shaping up to be one of those nights where the unexpected transforms itself into the epic whether one wants it to or not, and an old survivor like himself had no choice but to enjoy the ride. Fate. It was a bloody joker but he still didn't know whether to sit down beside her.

To his relief Janey took the cigarette then patted the bed. He sank down beside her, painfully aware of the scent of her skin, the depth of her cleavage, the warmth emanating from her thigh brushing up against his own and was instantly reminded of the back of the school playground; the smell of hot tarmac and wood, fake tanning lotion and cheap cigarette smoke, the muggy London days when they huddled together for an illicit fag between classes. Memories rushed in – Janey aged fourteen dancing to his stereo, laughing, her school shirt clinging to her breasts; Janey applying lipstick to help them get into an X-rated movie at the Marble Arch Odeon; Janey waiting for him at the school gate after he was held in detention.

It had been unrequited love from the ages of twelve to sixteen, one of those crushingly tormented obsessions that, as a teenager, had kept him wrestling the night for far longer than he'd ever admitted to anyone. In fact, he concluded silently, not having Janey had made him the man he was today. He knew that now, but then who was that man, that ingratiating idiot, who'd just had dinner with Lord fucking Harwood? It certainly wasn't Eddy the ambitious teenager who'd once boasted to Janey that he would never ever be ashamed of his background, no matter how successful he became.

He glanced over; she'd never known how much he'd wanted her all those years ago. Why not? Why hadn't he ever told her? he wondered, marvelling at the turn of fate that now placed him as the rich client and she – the indisputable and ruling queen of all his teenage wet dreams – the whore.

'I don't know who to be more embarrassed for: you the sucker for paying for it or me the scrubber putting out.'

'I don't 'ave to pay for it, you know.' He couldn't help sounding defensive. She smiled and placed her hand on his knee.

'Oh I know that, Eddy, 'andsome bastard like you. I should be paying you.'

At which they both burst into laughter and, for the first time in months, Eddy relaxed into his own skin.

'Eh, do you remember that time we played truant to go and see that reggae band play?' she asked him.

'And you almost started a race riot by flirting wiv the lead singer?'

'Yeah, well, Sean was a right jealous bastard.'

Sean had been Janey's official boyfriend, a big oaf of a seventeen year old, but what he lacked in intelligence he made up for in blinding loyalty. Irish and inclined to violence, he was extremely possessive, although in truth Janey did what she wanted with whom she wanted, with the long-suffering Sean in tow. 'Perhaps that was why I never declared myself,' Eddy thought as he furtively scanned Janey's chiselled profile, the long thick eyelashes batting her cheeks, the round green eyes and disproportionally full mouth that, set against her heart-shaped face, looked as if it had been stolen from another, larger-faced woman. He knew it had been fear of rejection that had stopped him declaring his infatuation, for to be rejected by Janey would have meant being rejected by all that he aspired to at sixteen, and, at the time, he could not afford the humiliation or the disillusionment. 'So maybe my reticence has paid off,' he rationalised silently. 'After all, I might have married Janey and be slumming it in a council flat with three kids by now.'

Nevertheless, now that he was here, in a position to be able to pay for her affections, it was not the same. If he paid he would never know if she really wanted him or just his money. And as he looked at her – those green eyes that were always a curious mixture of intelligence and tentativeness, the unspoken life of poverty they'd shared, those narrow pale shoulders crying out to be defended – he was filled with an overwhelming yearning to have her and, more than that, to be wanted by her; that night-wrestling, sweat-drenched obsessive love had never entirely disappeared, it had just lain dormant all these years, like some bloody great hidden iceberg waiting to smash into his life. Now frightened of betraying his emotions, he tried to sound casual.

'Wot do I call you, Janey or Jezebel?'

'Given the circumstances it might be easier if it was Jezebel.' She half-smiled a little sadly, then stubbed her cigarette out in the big glass ashtray which sat, along with a vibrator, a packet of condoms, KY jelly and peppermints, on the bedside table.

'So wot would you like, big boy?'

Her long fingers reached for his fly and for a moment he was tempted. Just then the shadow of a forgotten night, buried because it was too painful, came flooding back, the night that had ended up crushing his adolescent hopes. Now all the colours, gestures and emotions of his younger self lodged themselves firmly in the forefront of his mind. As if to bat away a moth he waved his hand, but the memory would not be denied. He even remembered the date – 15 June 1998. Perhaps there was a way of exorcising it. He pushed Janey's fingers away.

'There is something …'

They stumbled out into the street, Janey now wearing a demure day dress over her lingerie, Eddy in his suit. He'd paid a hefty sum to retain the prostitute's services overnight, and the receptionist hadn't even arched her famous eyebrows as the two stepped out.

The first thing Eddy did was to lead Janey to the Comic Empire on Firth Street. It had been there for years and had been on the walk home from school. It was at the Comic Empire that Eddy had first got up the courage to speak to the twelve-year-old Janey. He'd seen her over at the *Jackie* magazine section, her school skirt hitched up ridiculously high, tottering on platform shoes. To Eddy the boy she was the embodiment of all his sexual fantasies as she pulled a length of chewing gum from between her lipsticked mouth to carefully arrange it over George Michael's features, as seen on the cover of one of the magazines. He remembered her first words to him like it was yesterday: 'Oi, wot you looking at?' delivered with what seemed like exactly the right degree of poise and panache. Later Janey had introduced him to the four other teenagers who made up the disparate gang she hung around with. Even now he remembered his intense disappointment when Sean, who towered over him, pushed forward to introduce himself as her boyfriend.

At the door Eddy looked up at the old neon sign, now blinking erratically. It hadn't changed, and as they stepped into the shop he had the same rush of adrenalin he'd always experienced as a youth. The same old poster hung above the door as it had years earlier; the shop even had the same old paper smell, and it still displayed the same shelves piled up with editions of comic books, some dating as far back as the 1950s.

'*Fantastic Four* issue twenty-six,' Eddy whispered to Janey as the shopkeeper – who looked like a younger clone of the man who used to serve them – glanced up from a thick book.

'Done, and I'll have the issue in which Wasp Woman betrays the Hulk wiv the 'uman Torch, that's a fair dare,' she whispered back, grinning like a ten year old. It was a game the gang used to play – the shoplifter's challenge.

'Can I help you?' the shopkeeper asked, leaning forward.

'That's all right, we'll know what we want when we see it,' Eddy replied, and the two of them burst into laughter that made the shopkeeper conclude they were probably drunk day-trippers in to cruise the sex shops. Resigning himself to a no sale, he returned to his book.

Eddy watched Janey slip to the rear of the shop with professional ease. His mind flashed back to the first time he'd watched her shoplifting, nervous as hell, as he played guard for her, making sure the shopkeeper's back was turned – the way she loosened her school blazer to slip the comic in, the teasing manner with which she let her fingers drift over the comics all carefully wrapped in cellophane, the tightness of her short school skirt over her arse ... The fear of being caught fused with her furtiveness in a way he found impossibly erotic and the whole scenario had featured in several of his adolescent wet dreams. He was finding it erotic now, recognising the echo of the teenage thief in Janey's careful circling of her prize. Five minutes later he realised he had to hurry with his own shoplifting.

Afterwards they stood, hearts still thumping, grinning crazily at each other outside, Eddy with his issue hidden down his trousers, and Janey with her comic lodged between her armpit and the lining of her coat.

'As promised, issue forty-five – Wasp Woman does the 'uman Torch and the Hulk gets scorched.' He produced the issue with a triumphant flourish.

'And 'ere is the *Fantastic Four* issue twenty-six, still in its cellophane. We're even. Wot next, Batman?'

Under the street lamp he could now see the harshness of her life showing a little in her face, around the eyes, giving her beauty a knowing wisdom Cynthia didn't and would probably never have, Eddy concluded, as he battled the impulse to kiss Janey. Not yet, not yet – the timing had to be perfect if there was to be an exorcism.

Eddy glanced down the street. It was past one in the morning and the revellers were now out in force. The damp night air was laced with a tinge of Blitz madness – the existential sensibility that life is very short when one is burning so brightly and at such speed.

What had they done next on that momentous date? The night he planned to lose his virginity. For despite the precociousness of the other members of the gang, Eddy was still a virgin at sixteen. It wasn't for lack of choice, but he'd decided years before that Janey was to be his first and once Eddy decided something, rational or otherwise, his tenacity drove him to achieve it. It was a character trait that was to serve him well later as a businessman. For a good couple of years the teenaged Eddy had joked and joined in with all the sexual innuendo of the other boys, pretending he knew everything and more. In truth all he knew he'd gleaned from his father's well-stocked shelf of erotica and *Playboy* magazines – one of which featured his mother as centrefold of December 1981. Then, on the eve of his sixteenth birthday, he made a pledge – he had to have Janey or face the very real possibility of dying of sexual frustration. The young Eddy began to make plans.

He started rehearsing his first line, his first pass, over and over again, practising on an old dress-making mannequin his mother had abandoned when she left his father. He even rehearsed the awkward transition from friend to lover, or at least how he imagined it would be. He'd seen it all in his mind's eye, played the night out so often it was now almost part of his memory before he'd even experienced it. He was so certain nothing would go wrong. How could it? He was in love – that all-consuming shimmering kind of love that made you invincible, like Superman or his favourite Chelsea player Ruud Gullit. All he needed now was a strategy to get rid of Janey's constant entourage of boyfriend and best friend for one whole night.

He'd begun by saving the money he'd got working Saturdays at his father's fish stall to buy Sean a ticket to a Premiership match at Wembley. After that he'd tricked Janey into thinking her best friend was going to come along on the date too, then at the last minute bought the best friend a ticket to see her favourite band. He had the whole night orchestrated, climaxing in his seduction of her alone – away from Sean, the confines of his father's grimy lounge room and the ever-present television, away from all that kept them both ground down, unnoticed on the streets of London. They were going to soar, he imagined, on a carpet of both divine love and fantastically explicit dirty sex, having learnt from his libertine father that there was no paradox between the two, unless you were a practising Christian, in which case you were no fun at all. And then Janey was going to fall in love with him and they would run away and live on the top floor of the Savoy Hotel like the Arab millionaires whose cars he had sometimes washed. The sixteen-year-old Eddy was convinced of it, and he was ready, his heart and cock bursting for her.

Then came the pivotal moment, the moment he'd been waiting four whole years for, the moment when he finally had her alone, sitting by him on the damp grass in a place no one would disturb them, her bare leg actually touching his in a forest fire of excitement, his cock so hard in his jeans he was frightened of coming with just one touch. For a minute the air between them was suspended in glass, crystallised by expectation, and he knew if he was to kiss her it had to be then, at that moment – the silent tick of history turning over. But he hesitated – a sickly fear of rejection pinning his hands and arms to his sides, his heart suddenly pounding so forcefully he wondered if a plane hadn't flown overhead. By the time he turned to Janey the opportunity had evaporated like so many other things in his life – his mother, a decent school uniform, a decent school, his father's youth – and he'd stayed sitting there by her side, paralysed by his own failure, hating himself for his cowardice. Oblivious, Janey had chatted on, sharing confessions she might have shared with a girlfriend or confidante, but certainly not with a potential lover. Eddy couldn't look her in the eye for fear she would see his tears and his anger, so instead he'd stared at his knees then at the scrubby London summer grass, his hopes now as small as an ant.

They'd spent the rest of the night walking the streets – dodging cops, sneaking around bouncers, stealing the cream from milk bottles on doorsteps and nicking the morning papers. By the time London was grey with dawn, Eddy knew he'd lost her forever.

'You still wiv me, Eddy?' Janey's adult voice jolted him out of his reverie.

'Funny how time shapes us.'

'Time? Eddy, we're still young.' She checked her watch. 'And there's at least five hours to go, big boy.' She began walking him down towards Piccadilly. 'Green Park, wasn't it, Eddy?' she chuckled.

'So you remember that night?'

'I might, then again I might not,' she teased, leaving Eddy wondering. The gate was locked at the Piccadilly end of Green Park. After checking there were no police around, they climbed over the railings. Inside the grass glistened under the moonlight and the trees were magnanimous in their shelter. They walked barefoot, carrying their shoes, Eddy's naked toes luxuriating in the soft grass. The trader hadn't felt so calm and complete in years, so authentically himself. Nothing seemed to matter then, only the crisp damp smell of the leaves, the distant sound of traffic, the sudden warble of a blackbird.

Just then his mobile beeped. He knew it had to be a text from Cynthia; without breaking their pace he slipped his hand into his pocket and, feeling for the phone, switched it off, while Janey tactfully said nothing. Eddy scanned the line of mansions that backed the paved edge of Green Park. The old homes of the courtiers of the Royal Palace, the formal back gardens of these huge mansions lay like tantalising oases behind brick walls and wrought-iron fences, still contained within the perimeters of the park. These were the residences of the most prestigious families in Britain – the Rothschilds, the Spencers, the Duke of Westminster, to name a few. It was in one of the back gardens of these grand residences that the adolescent Eddy had planned to seduce Janey. It would have been the melding of two fantasies – one of having her, and the other of one day owning one of these palaces. He led her to the back fence of the large Georgian mansion, remembering the garden like it was yesterday.

Carefully avoiding the robotic swing of a surveillance camera as it scanned the lawn, Eddy helped Janey climb over the brick wall. Crouching, they ran across the grass towards a clump of trees. In front of them the high arched windows were shuttered up and the mansion stared back at them like a blind man. It was like stepping into a secret Eden as the sounds of London and passing traffic dropped away. Eddy was even convinced he could hear the soft croaking of frogs and crickets. A languid Venus frolicked with a marble Adonis in a fountain, and there was a line of perfectly landscaped gardenia and camellia bushes, the scent of which floated across the garden to mingle with Janey's perfume. 'Aren't you frightened we'll get nabbed?' Janey murmured, her eyes wide in the streetlight that fell over the wall and onto the lawn.

'Don't care if we do. Wiv a bit of luck we'll make the *Daily Mail*.'

'Wasn't it over here, Eddy?' She pulled him down beside her under a weeping willow.

'You remembered?' he whispered, feeling as if he was being drawn back into the sixteen-year-old Eddy. The possibility that she too had imbued that night with her own nostalgia filled him with a secret thrill.

'Hard to forget. I was waiting for you to make your move but all you did was rabbit on. All them plans about how you were gonna make your millions, get your dad his own fish shop …'

'Yeah, well, that never 'appened – the fish shop, I mean.'

'Yeah, well, if you remember, I was gonna become a TV actress, fancied myself on *Eastenders* … and look at me now – single mum and working girl.'

'You 'ave a child?'

'Daughter. Sean and I only lasted a couple of years. Old bastard's in the nick now. GBH and a couple of burglaries.'

'He always 'ad a short temper.'

'Didn't he just.'

And they both laughed. Janey wriggled a little closer to him and a shiver of anticipation fluttered in his chest.

'So what did 'appen to you after that night? We never did see you after that.'

He looked back over the lawn towards the darkened mansion and its imperial architecture, which seemed to scream 'you do not belong here', and the memory of the profound disappointment he'd felt that morning after walking her home to her mum's council flat came back to him.

'I ran off, see. Went to work for me uncle, who put me straight in the way of trading. He had a client who was looking for an office man and the rest is history.'

'So you did make your millions?'

'I did.'

'And you're 'appy?'

He didn't answer; he was thinking about Cynthia, about how she'd never known what it was like to fight to win something,

what it was to survive, how real loss and real poverty – things
that had shaped him – remained total abstractions to her. Would
she ever really know him if she didn't share these experiences,
and how could she love him if she didn't really know him? And
yet he'd chosen her. Why? Was it just the opportunity of social
mobility? Or did he really love her?

Wanting to escape his ambivalence he reached across ten
years, his arms as long as time itself and, after burying his fingers in
Janey's long soft hair, brought her mouth to his own. His tongue
searched out hers in a great shuddering collision of familiarity,
sharp desire and lust, a passionate embrace that hardened him
instantly. He was kissing her for his adolescent self, for the Eddy
he'd lost and for the man he was now. He was going to take her
and he was going to take her now and by doing so, the symmetry
of the world would be righted, all his confusion would be swept
away and he would be whole.

Instead Eddy froze.

'Wot's wrong?' Janey's face was dappled in the moonlight
falling between the branches.

'I dunno, memories I guess.' He looked into her face, but her
eyes were veiled and it was impossible to read her. His glance fell
down to her mouth, the full-blown gorged slash reddened by the
smudged lipstick – the haunting of his teenage years came back to
him. Oh what he had done to her in those dreams. As if reading
his mind she sat up and, reaching across, kissed him again. This
was the confirmation he was looking for, that she wanted him as
much as he wanted her. She looked at him, her cheeks flushed,
her lips like bruised fruit, her wide green eyes ironic. Losing
control he reached out and unbuttoned the front of her dress. His

hands slipped down into that soft flesh and lifted her heavy breasts out, the hard nipples erect. Full and ever so slightly pendulous, he fell in love with their asymmetry. Dropping his head down he sucked on each nipple in turn, hard in his trousers, his hand touching her face as if to find an echo, a memory, his fingers in her mouth. Moaning she reached down and pulled him free then pushed his cock between her breasts. Encouraged, he straddled her and rubbed his swollen cock between them, faster and faster, until he felt as if he might come. Holding the base to stop himself, he climbed off her and threw up her skirt, finding the velvet-soft skin above the tops of her stockings. He buried his face between her legs. She smelt wonderful, the perfume of her sex tangy salt undercut with rose musk. Parting her labia he found her clit, a hard erect button. He played it with his tongue, gently at first then, as he felt her thrashing above him, her moaning muffled by her skirt, he took her whole clit into his mouth and sucked it. His hands cupping her arse, his fingers slipped into both her vagina and anus. Now he was her master and she, the butterfly, was pinned out, spread for both their pleasure. He could feel that she was close to coming, her knees trembling against either side of his neck, and suddenly there it was, the clenching around his fingers, the shuddering wetness. Above him somewhere in the translucency of her dress and the dappled light between the branches were her groans. Fearing someone might hear her, he reached up with one hand and clamped it over her mouth, and she gently bit him in her ecstasy.

She pressed him back onto the grass, the crushed scent of it drifting up, the heavy weight of his erection now resting on his stomach. He still couldn't believe it was her as her face dipped down towards his penis, erect and thick. He could see both the young Janey in all her eager beauty and the adult Janey in the planes of her face, her laughing eyes, the wry mouth that closed over his cock as she sucked him hard, her tongue circling the tip in maddeningly sensual circles. He half sat up, pushing her long hair away from her face, unable to help his fascination as he watched her take him. Now kneeling, she slipped her hands under each of his buttocks and played his anus as if she were taking him, as if she were the man. He caught his breath; there was genuine abandonment and delight in both her face and movements, as if she were as erotically aroused as he was by the fellatio.

His mind flashed to Cynthia's face when they made love, an act which always seemed to entail Eddy serving Cynthia's needs over his own – the heiress's sense of entitlement extending to the bedroom. With Cynthia, Eddy always had to resort to imagining he was with someone else to bring himself off – it was hard not to resent her passivity, the way she lay back as if it was an honour for him to even be in the same bed as her. Janey was entirely different; her enthusiasm was almost as erotic as the extraordinary things she was doing to him with her mouth and her fingers. She was now taking him faster and faster, deeper and deeper, and he could feel his orgasm building. He sat up and pulled her away from him. He looked at her flushed face, a blush mottling her pale skin, her eyes bright, her mouth swollen as if bee-stung. 'That was for Eddy at sixteen,' she said, grinning, 'but Eddy at twenty-six is beautiful too,' at which they both started laughing until, unable to wait any longer, he pulled her onto his lap and plunged into her; the pleasure making both of them gasp. Slowly she moved up and down, clenching him as she swivelled her hips in a slow sliding dance. Deeper and deeper he lost himself in her, over and over, all his anger, humiliation, disempowerment of that evening vanishing with each new thrust. Then he moved faster and faster, the race, the galloping hunt, the cock and cuntiness of it all searing through him in a sudden epiphany. This is where he really belonged, in her arms, her legs wrapped around his hips. And in the blinding moment that he came he knew that for the first time in years he was completely and profoundly authentic.

Later they walked hand in hand like love-drunk teenagers, her shoes dangling in his left hand, his jacket draped over her shoulders. The dawn light was breaking over Mayfair. Outside the Savoy some of the night hotel workers were changing shift with their day counterparts. A garbage truck was crawling down the road. Already the day smelt of summer, and Eddy was charged with the kind of excitement he hadn't felt since he was a child. 'Oi, mate!' he yelled after the dustbin men. Three minutes later they were hitching a ride down to Piccadilly Circus, hanging off the sides of the large truck, laughing at the bleary-eyed who were just emerging from the nightclubs. At Piccadilly Circus they both climbed up onto the plinth and had their photo taken by a German tourist as they embraced Eros, Janey showing the top of her thigh as she wrapped a leg over the bronze boy god as the sun, now rising up between the buildings, caught the glass and the reflective steel in a sudden shower of light. Staring across, Eddy thought to himself all was possible now, he was going to win, score that perfect goal over and over. He was never going to compromise who he was or where he'd come from for anyone ever again. Laughing, he swung Janey down from the statue.

'I am greater than Eros,' he thought, 'greater, bigger, more fucking successful. I am a god!' he felt like shouting, staring down Piccadilly with the wealth of London flanking the broad promenade, Janey's lips now on his neck as she kissed him. 'I am invincible' – the notion resounded through his very cells, his psyche, as they climbed down to the pavement and he took in Janey's tumbling and dishevelled hair, small tufts of grass still tangled amongst the blonde strands. 'You 'ave made me invincible,' he whispered. But the roar of a passing delivery van masked his words and Janey, not hearing, smiled back blankly.

It was now five am and Eddy knew his father would already be setting up his stall. They walked down to Berwick Street market. Larry Jenkins, dressed in an old pullover that Eddy recognised from years earlier, stood with his back to them, unpacking fish from freezer boxes onto his stand. A small radio propped up on a nearby milk crate gave the track running order for the races later that day, while down the lane all the other stalls were setting up, the owners bantering and teasing each other while unloading boxes, fruit, flowers and cheese: it was a rapport so familiar that they didn't even bother to turn their heads towards the object of their ridicule. The humorous exchanges flew above their heads like errant darts as Eddy and Janey wove their way along the street, dodging handcarts and barrels, towards the fish stall.

'Dad!' Eddy cried out. Larry Jenkins swung around. Smoking and hard work had aged him a great deal since the last time Eddy had seen him, and for the first time he became aware of his father's frailty. He felt a pang of guilt as he hadn't visited him in over a year, yet he walked past Berwick Street market every day on his way to work.

'Eddy!' Larry Jenkins spun around to the other stall owners. 'See, Shirley, me boy 'as come to visit me!'

Shirley, a plump, dyed redhead who owned the flower stall next to his father's, waddled over, her gaudy make-up unchanged since the 1980s.

'Eddy? My handsome lover Eddy?' she crackled. Pushing past Janey she pulled him into a hug, her powdery perfume sending him back decades. ''Asn't he grown – he looks proper smart. Oh, Larry, you must be proud.'

'Course I am, Shirley, course I am – when I get to see the cocky bastard. Come 'ere, lad.' And he pulled Eddy into a pungent embrace of fish and tobacco emanating from his fishmonger's apron. Eddy pulled back, overwhelmed.

'We'd thought you might 'ave set up so we could 'ave breakfast wiv you – you know, the usual?'

'My pleasure, lad.' Larry winked at Janey. 'You know Eddy, a right elitist bugger he's become, but occasionally he likes to slum it wiv his old dad, like the good old days ...'

'I remember, Mr Jenkins,' she replied, smiling.

Taken aback he studied her. ''Old on, I know you ...'

'It's Janey Lewis, Dad – you know, my old school friend ...'

'Janey! Why so it is! Tell you wot, girl, you broke my lad's 'eart, you did.'

'I did?'

'Dad!' Eddy tried to shut him up, but Larry Jenkins would not be deterred.

'Gave it all up after that. Could 'ave gone to university, that boy. First in the family, could 'ave done something for society.

132

Instead off he went and become a capitalist, a bloody paid-up member of the Tory party.'

Aghast, Janey turned to Eddy. 'Is that true, Eddy, you ran away because of me?' He could not meet her eye, instead turning back to his father.

'C'mon, off your soap box, we're only 'ere for a fry-up, not a bloody lecture.' Eddy punched his father's shoulder good-naturedly and the three of them walked down to the last of the traditional greasy spoon cafés in Soho, a place where Larry Jenkins had been having his sausage and eggs every morning for over twenty years. Over baked beans and toast with a kipper staring up at her from a side plate, Janey leaned over.

'You haven't answered me, Eddy. Did you run away after that night when nothing happened between us?'

His father coughed with embarrassment then buried himself in a copy of the *Morning Star* while a blushing Eddy folded his paper napkin over and over.

'Did me no harm. Look where I am now, eh? If I wanted I could buy out Dad here and the rest of Berwick Street market for that matter.' Eddy couldn't keep the defensiveness out of his voice.

Janey and his father stared at him, neither smiling.

'And wot would that achieve, lad, eh?' his father finally answered softly, then turned back to Janey. 'See, no hope for the boy. It's all pomp and circumstance with him, all golden balls and hot air. Money don't matter that much, Eddy, not in the grand scheme of things.'

In lieu of an answer Eddy turned on his Blackberry, which had now been switched off for ten hours. To his horror, he noticed that there were a hundred and twenty messages for him. Two were from Cynthia, no doubt wondering where he was. The other hundred and eighteen were from the Asian offices of his investment bank, and that was far more worrying. He looked at his watch – six-thirty am; Asia had been open for five hours, his meeting with the Chinese businesswoman was at ten. Cynthia could wait. He turned to Janey.

'Quickly, give me your mobile number.'

'07325 678710.'

He tapped it into his phone as she spoke then, after standing and giving her a quick kiss on the forehead, moved towards the door.

'See he doesn't steal any of me toast,' he joked, indicating his father. He stepped out of the café into the morning light now sharpening with the sun, flicked his phone open and pressed the direct number to his counterpart in the Singapore office, who answered immediately.

'Where the fuck have you been, Ed?' Jeff, a brash Jewish New Yorker, was not renowned for his hysteria – Eddy's first thought was that there'd been another 9/11.

'What are you talking about? It's just gone six-thirty here.'

'I don't give a shit, Edward, two major banks went down today, there are rumours from Sydney to Shanghai, everyone's expecting the Dow to crash through the fucking floor. I've never seen it this bad. They're saying it's going to be worse than '29 – more like 1890! They're talking the end of the financial world here – get to your fucking desk! I have clients here who are threatening to kill me first and then themselves. Edward, do you hear me? Edward?'

But Eddy was already running for a cab.

*

The trading floor was mayhem, a flurry of panicked shouting and running suits. Some of the traders had worked all night, some were already slumped over leather armchairs catching a nap between markets. At the central hub there was a huddled bunch of anxious-looking young traders with eyes glued to the canopy of monitors that blinked down at them as they screamed into their phones. All the flashing figures on the screens were in red – the plummeting share prices from Tokyo to Shanghai through to Sydney – haemorrhaging funds as if the money god himself had slashed his wrists and now stood waiting atop the New York stock exchange like King Kong, blood cascading down onto the pavement below.

Eddy bolted to his desk, splashing his hand with scalding hot coffee from the Starbucks container he clutched – he barely noticed. Once at the desk he booted up his monitors and began selling and selling and selling … The world was in freefall, it was like clutching at snow. Eddy watched blue-chip stocks melting in value before his eyes as the switchboard was jammed with panicking clients trying to get through to their traders.

Just before ten in the morning the Chinese businesswoman's assistant phoned to tell him she was cancelling but not to sell any of her employer's portfolio – in fact she ordered him to buy up gold, silver and iron ore. Shouting over the raised voices of his colleagues, Eddy asked if she was serious about not selling the stocks that were plummeting. At the other end the phone was handed to the businesswoman herself.

'I tell you …' she said – he could barely understand her heavy accent – 'you are to buy now. Ignore panic. The calm

135

captain does not sink the ship. My assistant will text you the stocks.' Her melodious voice seemed to narrow the chaotic room around him down to a desert island on which he was standing holding the phone.

'You are sure?' he ventured.

'I am sure. I never do anything without great calculation – at least not business,' she replied somewhat enigmatically.

A minute later his phone beeped to announce the texted instructions. In the ten minutes he spent purchasing the shares they devalued by fifteen per cent, but a grain of curiosity had been planted, one he put at the back of his mind in order to deal with the ensuing chaos. It was bedlam. At one point he had the head of the biggest iron ore exporter in the world on hold while he calmed down the majority stockholder of the same company on the other line. But strangely, despite his lack of sleep, Eddy had never felt such clarity and emotional integration; it was as if the barrow boy, starving in his ambition, desperate for reinvention could now openly triumph with his street sense and chameleon abilities. He was himself, he noted as his fingers flicked wildly over the computer keys. His body, although exhausted and now starving, still glowed with post-coital warmth. He'd come home.

Just before the market closed Eddy glanced again at the list of commodities the Chinese woman had bought into. Using his own cash he had purchased a considerable number of shares which were now trading at half the price he'd bought them at three hours earlier. He then left the office whistling, much to the astonishment of his fellow traders, many of whom were contemplating their own demise in the fall-out that was bound to follow.

*

Eddy caught a cab to Cynthia's Chelsea Mews cottage and arrived unannounced. Cynthia was curled up on the couch, drying her toenails while watching a reality TV fashion show. She leapt up as Eddy entered the room.

'Where have you been? I tried ringing last night. What happened, sweetie? I was really worried.'

'I walked around all night. I had to sort out some things in my head, and then the stock market this morning ...'

Eddy collapsed onto the small chaise longue that he had previously associated with good taste but, for the first time, now recognised as chintzy. It was also extremely impractical and uncomfortable, characteristics he'd tolerated before, assuming one had to suffer for style. Now he found himself craving the old battered leather couch that was the one piece of furniture his father prized.

'I know, I've been following it all day. Even Daddy's worried. You were a big hit with him last night, by the way. I thought you might have overdone it with the Oxford story, but we pulled it off, Edward! Isn't that amazing?' She sat down beside him, nuzzling up. Eddy pulled away despite himself.

'Are you okay, sweetie? I mean, everything is okay with us, isn't it?'

There was a slight pause. Eddy felt as if the room had started to recede from him, as if he was drunk or suffering from vertigo.

'Cynthia ...'

Cynthia studied his face and now, suddenly too nervous to hear his answer, spoke over him.

'Daddy said you had real grit. He's even offered to put you up for the Carlton Club. Of course I'll have to recruit a few of the Pony Club to substantiate your story. What was the name of the school you went to again? The real school?'

He sensed the question could possibly be a trap – Cynthia might tolerate a grammar school background but certainly not a secondary modern. Eddy fingered the signet ring they'd bought for him at Christopher Graffs (he'd paid) when they'd bought her engagement ring. He pulled away. 'Sorry, I don't feel very well.'

He rushed to the bathroom and locked himself in. Inside he reached into his jacket for his Blackberry and dialled Janey's number. The line rang and rang. Eventually an automated voice came on to tell him the number had been disconnected. How was that possible? She had only given him the number that morning. Dread began to jangle his shot nerves as his emotions narrowed down to one desire only – to see Janey.

Outside Cynthia had started to rattle the doorhandle.

'Eddy, are you okay? Eddy?' The concern in her voice made him feel instantly guilty. Panicked, he climbed out of the bathroom window and bolted down the back lane towards a cab.

He directed the cab to the brothel, telling the driver he'd give him an extra ten quid if he got there in under ten minutes. They were there in seven. After instructing him to wait outside, Eddy ran into the building. The receptionist, cool as ever, looked up from her desk.

'Janey, is she here?' His heart was now in his throat, throbbing uncomfortably.

'Who?'

'Janey – I mean Jezebel?'

The receptionist, registering his desperation, put out her large man-hand, long red fingernails catching the light, and touched his.

'I'm sorry, baby, but she resigned this afternoon, no forwarding address or number.'

'Nothing?'

'I would help you, a regular, if I could. But you know these girls, especially the temps. Fly-by-nights, gone by the morning. I don't even have a real name for you, never mind a surname.'

Eddy didn't even wait for her to finish her sentence. He rushed back out into the street and instructed the cab driver to take him to an address he'd suddenly remembered from all those years ago, an address he'd once carved into a box he'd made in woodcraft in a hopeless act of voodoo.

He stood in the street staring up at the block of brand new luxury apartments, the For Sale signs attached to the gleaming glass windows. Gone were the old red brick council flats in which Janey had once lived with her mother, the narrow Victorian entrance with its single arch over the doorway. He would never find her now. Overhead the sun slipped behind a dark cloud and it began to rain.

The key clicked in the door and Cynthia looked up from her magazine. Eddy stepped into the flat, his hair and jacket drenched from the downpour. She dared not get up, frightened that her gratitude at his return would drive him away again. Now she sensed that nothing was certain between them and yet she still wanted him, perhaps even more.

'Are you okay?' Not being able to help herself, she stood and took him into her arms.

'I think so,' he murmured. 'Edgware Secondary Modern,' he suddenly said into her shoulder.

She pulled away and studied him. 'Darling, why on earth wouldn't you tell me before? I don't care, honestly. I love you.'

To his own horror Eddy began to cry.

FUR

It was one of those impossibly hot days, one of those apocalyptic climate change can-fry-an-egg-on-a-car-bonnet days that had become so prevalent in Sydney lately. May, a twenty-two-year-old university student, was on her way back to the small two-bedroom apartment she rented with her boyfriend Mitch in a Victorian terrace house in the suburb of Glebe. A pale thin redhead, she had forgotten her sunhat and was hopping from one patch of shade to another as she navigated her way back to the flat. Earlier that day she had worked for four hours in the small vintage clothing store owned by her sister. The income from this part-time job helped with her studies and rent, and normally the anthropology student enjoyed the eccentric, laidback atmosphere of the store, which was a stark contrast to the intensity of her own research work, but today was different. It felt to May like the whole world had suddenly tilted upside down and the intrinsic order of things – government, business and personal relations – had twisted up into something unrecognisable, something undefinably frightening. For a start the global markets had crashed badly overnight – it was in all of the newspapers and on CNN; the images of panicked stock exchanges with ashen-faced men gesticulating at TV monitors upon which numbers ran like terrified insects had upset May. She knew such financial panic was bound to filter down to universities and research grants and she was about to graduate. But more importantly, May's own life had also contorted violently that morning, like a reflection in a curved funfair mirror.

May, a late riser, had woken to the sight of Mitch, her boyfriend and flatmate, naked except for an old fur rug draped across his shoulders, staring at a red pentacle he appeared to have scrawled on the bedroom wall. This was remarkable for several reasons – one was that Mitch was a conservative young man who liked to keep his clothes on in bed, or at least his underpants, an irritating habit May had battled the whole two years of their relationship to her frustration. And secondly, despite the fur rug and the fact that it was at least thirty-five degrees, Mitch was still shivering.

May, stunned by this vision, had barely collected her wits when Mitch announced in an absurdly deep and serious voice that he was no longer Mitch Jackson, twenty-one, formerly of Pymble in the northern suburbs of Sydney, but Erasmus Jehovah, a warlock of the Mikulee tribe, and that she should address him as such. If it had been anybody else May might have dismissed this as an imaginative prank, but the two years with Mitch had taught her that the economics student, although top of his year and considered brilliant, was not the most imaginative of individuals, nor was he the most emotional.

In fact there had been moments when May wondered whether he wasn't borderline Asperger's but what Mitch lacked in emotional intelligence he'd made up for in physical beauty, monogamy and financial generosity, which made him a huge improvement on May's previous boyfriends. So naturally the sight of such a controlled individual so blatantly out of control was both deeply disturbing and, if May was honest with herself, incredibly amusing in a dark sort of way.

May stared at him, searching her mind for any tips on handling warlocks that she might have gleaned from her anthropological studies, but despite a number of lengthy footnotes on witch doctors and the practice of exorcism, not one useful fact emerged, which wasn't entirely surprising given her thesis was on the eighteenth-century tribes of Polynesia and not on the warlock myths of Scotland.

Regardless, and wary of the way Mitch alias Erasmus was now holding up a tennis racket as if it were some ancient wand, May decided the best policy might be to humour him and, assuming he was in the grip of a nervous breakdown and hadn't in fact been transformed into a warlock, bundle him off to the student counsellor as soon as possible.

That was eight hours ago and Mitch still hadn't rung her on her mobile to confirm he'd made the appointment.

'Bugger it,' May swore to herself as she hurried down the street, mentally running through the last few months, searching for the trigger that might have tipped him into such a delusion. It was only at her front door that she remembered the DVD series of *Buffy the Vampire Slayer* that she'd given Mitch for his twentieth birthday. Could that have been an influence? Then there was that night back in June when she'd come home from the library and found Mitch glued to the TV screen. The episode had been about Buffy's best friend Willow and her boyfriend Ōz, a werewolf who has to leave her to understand his inner beast.

Mitch had been fascinated. Had this storyline released some appalling psychosis?

As May turned the key in the door she dismissed the possibility. It was obviously the result of stress, a meltdown of nerves just before his finals, and given the apocalyptic nature of the sudden economic crisis it wasn't very surprising that Mitch might harbour some hidden dread of failure that had now forced his subconscious to flip him into another identity altogether. In fact it seemed both poignant and pertinent to May that Mitch, a rationalist inclined towards a resigned fatalism, had chosen such a magical persona as a warlock. Perhaps he had unconsciously concluded that such a persona might equip him with the necessary sorcery to succeed in the financial world? May hoped that a session of counselling might have restored Mitch to his predictable but lovable self, but as she pushed the front door open, her optimism evaporated. Inside the lights were off and from the kitchen came the sound of banging.

The economics student was standing at the workbench illuminated by a dozen lit candles perched precariously on the corners of the kitchen counters. Looking like some demented mediaeval murderer, he was in the middle of pulverising a large piece of bloody meat with a hammer. At least he was wearing clothes, May noticed with some relief, although his usual suit had been replaced by a raggedy old kilt and a bloodstained T-shirt.

'What the fuck?' she exclaimed, abandoning any possibility of handling his psychosis with sensitivity.

'Supper,' he growled at her, at which May, depressed by the sudden realisation that she might have lost Mitch forever, sank into a chair.

''Tis roo,' Mitch muttered darkly. He dangled the raw piece of kangaroo over his mouth and snapped at it, gobbling the dripping sinew greedily. May dry-retched, and then reminded herself that it was probably dangerous to display any signs of revulsion towards his behaviour.

'Delicious,' Mitch concluded, blood now streaking his chin. May manoeuvred herself closer to the door in case a fast escape might prove necessary.

'So how was the counsellor?' She managed to sound calm.

'The high priestess spake truths that totally aligned with my mindset. Amorous as she was of my paradigm, she hath summoned Mitch and thrown him from a great height and the economics scholar is no longer. Long live Erasmus.'

Which May understood to mean that the student counsellor had empathised with Mitch's need to segue into this new and possibly more liberated persona, a notion May thought both ridiculous and dangerous, but given that she herself had visited the student counsellor (an aging hippie with a penchant for the esoteric) once or twice, it was plausible.

'You mean, great Erasmus,' (fuck, she hated the sound of her own grovelling voice) 'Mitch, the economics student, is no longer of this world?'

'World, street, lecture hall and alas, fair maiden, of the matrimonial bed.'

This last item took May by surprise – she'd never considered Mitch a de facto, never mind a husband, despite having lived with him for the past two years. He was more a kind of pleasant passing phase, one she now reflected might have been somewhat of a misjudgement. But what exactly did he mean? That she was to sleep with Erasmus from now on and, if so, how would this affect their lovemaking?

She glanced over at the aspiring warlock. She'd been quite content with their lovemaking before; if a little predictable it was at least regular and enthusiastic. Mitch had been a good lover and if it was difficult to read his emotional responses it wasn't for lack of interest on his part. Now Mitch alias Erasmus suddenly grinned wolfishly at her, a fibre of raw meat still clinging to one tooth. Nope, there was nothing remotely sexy about this current manifestation of Mitch's personality. The meat fibre slipped off, dangling for a moment on his unshaven chin before falling to the kitchen floor. May made her mind up. Sharing a bed with Erasmus was not going to work; but could she rescue Mitch? He was, after all, her boyfriend.

'So there's no way I can summon the human individual Mitch back into this portal that standeth before me?' May asked, wincing at her own pseudo-Shakespeare speak sprinkled with a little postmodern techno-talk that appeared to be warlock dialect to Mitch.

'Not a hope in hell,' Mitch alias Erasmus answered cheerfully, then smashed the hammer into the benchtop as if he were finishing off the human Mitch himself. May tried not to jump at the noise. Saddened and more than a little scared she eyed the bloodied hammer cautiously then backed a little closer to the door to contemplate her options, knowing that some strategy would have to be applied to remove the warlock from both kitchen and house. One woman's warlock is another woman's schizophrenic, she observed then determined that self-preservation was probably the only course of action.

'Oh great Erasmus, I, a mere female human, am not worthy of being a repository for your great and mighty organ ...' she began, remembering that Mitch had always been slightly sensitive about the size of his penis. 'You have greater and more powerful horizons to conquer, therefore I release you from the confines of this cottage ...' she concluded, trying to remember whether warlocks belonged to the village scenario as opposed to the castle scenario. At which Erasmus alias Mitch dropped suddenly to his knees and began to rub his head against her knee like a dog.

'You are right, prophetess. I am destined for greater things and distant lands. I will leave by the next full moon.' A statement that had May desperately scanning the calendar hanging over the fridge. To her great relief, the full moon appeared to be two days hence.

'But you'll have to pack first,' she quickly replied, then patted the warlock on the head.

The next afternoon, after May had made several clandestine phone calls to Mitch's mother, Erasmus stood in the front courtyard surrounded by cardboard boxes packed with his possessions. The economics student was still wearing the kilt and hadn't shaved or washed. He was standing stock-still, his arms outstretched and his face turned up towards the sun as if he were in a state of worship. May stood at some distance, praying that Mitch's mother – a feisty criminal lawyer who'd brought Mitch up single-handedly – would, for once, be on time. May tried not to stare at the aspirant sorcerer and she also tried to resist the temptation to throw her arms around him and say, 'Stop, Mitch, it's May here, it's okay to be normal now.' Just then he made a noise that sounded suspiciously like a bark or a howl, and May reached for her mobile hidden in her skirt pocket, her fingers curling around it for comfort, trying to reassure herself that at least the police were only a phone call away.

She felt like crying. It was like Mitch had died, she might never see him again and she hadn't been able to say a proper goodbye. Meanwhile Mitch alias Erasmus started running from one end of the short street to the other, backwards and forwards past their gate. Christ, he looked completely demented, May thought to herself. Neither of them had slept all night. Instead he'd spent the night prowling naked around the tiny concreted backyard, occasionally stopping to genuflect towards the moon. It required all of May's charm and diplomatic skills, as well as the reassurance that he would be gone by the next night, to dissuade the neighbours from calling the police. Curiously, Mitch alias Erasmus did not seem emotionally affected by their approaching separation. If anything he appeared cheerful, relieved even, which made May suspect that perhaps Mitch had unconsciously wanted to leave her anyhow. Exhausted and near tears she leant against the front gate, determined not to get upset in case this triggered some unexpected reaction in her ex-lover.

Mitch's mother was due any minute and there was still no sign of Mitch re-emerging from under the hairy mantle of Erasmus. If anything, the warlock persona appeared to have gained in strength, the five o'clock shadow on his chin had become a stubbly beard, his thick black un-brushed hair looked as if it was about to divide itself into dreadlocks, and he'd taken to muttering incantations, which had terrified the Vietnamese postman earlier that morning.

As May watched him, a great sadness anchored her to the pavement. Would he ever recover or would he end up like her older brother, medicated and only half functional? She couldn't bear thinking about it. She glanced back at their apartment where another, more pressing issue awaited her attention – the rent, which was due in four days. May knew she didn't have enough money in the bank to cover it, and she couldn't afford to be late with the payment. Accommodation was really scarce for students; she couldn't afford to lose the flat and yet she couldn't afford to keep it on alone.

Just then Mitch's mother's car swung into the quiet suburban street. Mitch alias Erasmus, recognising the car, ran back to the gate and suddenly reached down behind some bushes. He pulled out a large cardboard box from which came loud scratching noises. Smiling at her, he thrust the mysterious box into May's hands.

'His name is Shadow, he is a familiar, he will protect you. This is my last gift to you, oh faithful female of the human species.' May was too frightened to ask what was inside, just in case it was something odd like a rat or a possum.

She watched the Lexus drive off. Already she could see Mitch's mother arguing with her son inside the car. Surprisingly, now that he was gone she felt nothing but relief. Had she really loved Mitch, she wondered, or had he just been a financial convenience? As if to answer, a loud scratching suddenly sounded from the cardboard box. May rested it against the garden wall and opened the lid. Inside a black cat peered out with uncannily intelligent eyes – there even appeared to be a glint of amusement in them. 'Shadow,' she said to the creature. The cat did not reply.

Sitting at her desk later that evening, May booted up her computer and posted a 'Flatmate wanted' ad on the university website. Shadow, who was endowed with great feline beauty, sat curled by her feet. To her relief he seemed to be remarkably self-contained, which was just as well as May was neither a cat person nor even a dog person. Pets worried her: they merely embodied more responsibility and expense, and cat food was one cost she knew she couldn't afford.

She picked the animal up, placing him on her lap. He was large for a cat, almost the size of a dog, with huge thin-skinned ears rising up from a noble, narrow skull. His only flaw was that part of his left ear was missing, as if it had been bitten off in a fight. Apart from that he was perfect. His eyes were large and green and unfathomable. His whiskers, feathery and long, seemed to quiver in the slightest breeze and his fur, although dense and short, had a texture and touch that reminded May of very expensive silk. It was a dense black with hints of what almost looked like purple under the light. And the animal didn't seem to purr so much as growl – a low, almost mechanical sound, like an engine running. She stared down thoughtfully, caressing him under the chin and behind the ears, his eyes half-closed in ecstasy. Shadow butted his head against her breasts as if to say, 'More, more …'

The animal seemed a strange legacy for Mitch to leave. They'd never talked about having a cat, and, like her, he'd always seemed indifferent to pets. Now that he'd left the reality of his departure had begun to dawn on May – a growing melancholy infused with a sense of both guilt and futility. Should she have fought harder? Should she have been more active in finding him help?

Casting a cold anthropological eye over the situation she wondered at her own callousness and reluctance to get involved. The childhood trauma of her brother's own breakdown flooded back. She had been nine at the time and her brother – older by some years – had suddenly started to hoard silver milk-bottle tops obsessively, convinced that laid out in the right order they would send psychic messages to aliens. Eventually May's parents had him committed to a psychiatric unit. He returned a few weeks later, sluggish and dim-witted on the drugs they had prescribed. He'd never really recovered and May had withdrawn from him, having little to do with him as a teenager, but she now remembered the faint revulsion and her unutterable fear that she might later develop whatever her brother had. Was this why she'd been so ruthlessly pragmatic with Mitch? Had his mental illness awoken a hidden terror of her own?

Unable to concentrate on her studies, May glanced over into the sparse bedroom. Mitch's cupboard door had swung open, forlorn and abandoned. The bed was stripped and the side table that had housed Mitch's collection of knick-knacks – a framed photograph of Donald Trump, a school rugby prize (a small battered silver cup), a Rabbitohs footy scarf, a salt shaker he had stolen from a restaurant as a memento of their first date together and, most telling, his first issue of *Warlock*, with Marvel comics character Adam Warlock on the cover circa 1975 – were all gone, swept away in his disappearance. She glanced back to the bed, the prospect of sleeping alone was daunting.

Resigned, May settled down on the couch to watch TV, determined to exorcise the emptiness that had now begun to slip into the shadowy corners. The cat followed her and after leaping up beside her in territorial fashion, curled up against her as she reached for the remote. Comforted, May turned the television on. Immediately images of another teenage witch series filled the screen. With the sound muted May watched in fascinated horror as a young man in a suit turned into a warlock in a flash of white smoke. He looked nothing like Mitch, she noted, but the idea that such a prosaic storyline could have triggered Mitch's breakdown was depressing in itself.

She switched channels and wasted an hour watching a documentary on the seasonal migration of stingrays from Mexico to Florida – thousands of them – cow-nose rays flying through the sea, their elegant yellow fin wings arcing slowly through the ocean depths in a timeless aquatic flight, a soothing distraction for May's overwrought emotions. Watching them made her want to be one of them. She imagined there would be great security in being one of many swimming along, seamlessly integrated into both their environment and their species, the cool ocean rippling across one's fins. No madness there. No unexplained warlocks or material greed rocking the world.

Around eleven pm she decided she would have to confront her fears and sleep in the empty bed. As if guessing her reluctance Shadow stretched his back then leapt down. The cat padded silently on his long, elegant legs towards the bedroom as if he already knew the way and had taken that path a thousand times before. Bemused, May followed him. By the time she arrived at the door he was already on the bed, laid out in an elegant arc across the side Mitch used to sleep on.

She switched on the bedside lamp and began undressing with her back to the cat. Suddenly she stopped. Unease swept across her body like a shiver as she was filled with a strong sense of being watched. She swung around. The animal was sitting upright staring directly at her, his eyes filled with an extraordinary human intelligence. It was uncanny.

'Stop looking at me, you fur-covered pervert.' May spoke out loud in an attempt to lighten the atmosphere. But the animal took no notice whatsoever. Instead his gaze panned slowly down her half-naked torso with the kind of appraisal May would normally have associated with a man. It was both disturbing and highly intrusive. May pulled an old dressing gown off the hook on the back of the bedroom door and covered herself, then retreated to the bathroom, making sure the door was closed behind her. She stared into the bathroom cabinet mirror.

'This isn't rational,' she told her reflection, the stress of the past two days now beginning to show in her eyes and thin-lipped mouth. 'It's only a cat, May, a harmless feline, incapable of anything remotely like human emotion. You're being paranoid, and even if your nut of an ex-boyfriend who thinks he's a friggin' warlock gave you the beast, it doesn't mean the creature itself is bewitched,' she finished, failing to convince herself. Was she losing her sanity the way her brother did? Was Mitch's condition contagious in some strange way? After all, she was also under similar stress, her own finals looming in a month or so, with no prospect of employment. Was it possible his breakdown could trigger one of her own?

'Stop it,' she told her reflection firmly. 'Stop it, stop it, stop it!'

Determined to bring some normality back into her routine, she brushed her teeth, washed her armpits and face, and thoughtfully massaged some body lotion into her skin. Her future suddenly loomed up as blank as her face looked cleaned of the heavy eye make-up. Then, hoping to shock herself out of unease, she splashed herself with some cold water then turned back to the bedroom.

Shadow was now lying stretched out on Mitch's empty side of the mattress. Somehow to shoo the cat off felt like surrendering to her fears, so, after locking the bedroom door, May slipped in between the sheets and, with her back to the cat, switched off her bedside lamp, plunging the room into a velvety darkness.

She closed her eyes, lulled by the sound of distant traffic roaring down Parramatta Road and the chirping of a lone cicada that hadn't realised it was nightfall, and was just dropping off when suddenly she felt the caress of fingertips running across her bare shoulder. She froze. The touch was so light, so delicate, that she wondered whether she hadn't imagined it. But then, just as she'd started to relax once more, it happened again, this time more firmly, more definite – the warm trace of human fingers running across her shoulder and then sneaking down and around to the hollow between her hip and waist. She lay there paralysed by shock as another hand slipped around the other side of her torso to cup one full breast and play one nipple. May opened her mouth to scream then, remembering the neighbour upstairs and his tendency to complain to the police at the slightest provocation, stopped herself. She had to be imagining the caress, she must be. After all, she had locked the bedroom door, the window was barred and she was sleeping on a mattress on the floor. There was no room under the bed for anyone to have hidden and no possible way for a man to have entered the flat.

Mustering all her courage, she switched on the bedside lamp and looked down at her body. No hand, no fingers, just her naked torso – thin, pale and horribly vulnerable. She rolled over and glanced at Shadow. The cat's face was tucked onto its paws and it seemed to be softly purring in its sleep, indifferent to the external world and any crazy hallucinations of her own.

Had she started to fantasise due to the shock of Mitch's sudden departure? Was this some weird manifestation of loneliness? May rolled onto her back and stared up at the peeling ceiling. Somewhat disconcertingly, buried beneath the fear was a kernel of erotic pleasure, a kernel that had now started to unfurl somewhere between her belly button and groin whether she liked it or not. Should she masturbate? Would this relieve her stress? Somehow such an action felt wrong in front of the cat.

Sighing, May switched the light off again and began to doze. Five minutes later she was woken by an intense shooting of pleasure from one nipple down to her groin. As her brain flipped back into consciousness (or had it?) she became aware of a soft nibbling of one nipple while a strong and undeniably masculine hand slipped its way firmly between her thighs. Whoever was making love to her knew what he was doing.

'If this is a dream I intend to stay sleeping,' she told herself as soft full lips made their way up her body. Reaching down she cupped the sides of his head, running her fingers across his face to read his features in the dark. High cheekbones, a flat wide nose, full lips, hair tight whorls set against a long narrow skull – there was a sculptural symmetry that suggested beauty and an African heritage May realised with a jolt as her fingers traced the muscular shoulders, the smooth, almost hairless skin on his chest and lower down his stomach. I should be frightened or at least shocked, she thought to herself, but the silvery darkness of the bedroom felt as if it had transformed into some netherland between dream and conscious life, as if they were making love underwater, in a subterranean world of shimmering light which was itself a manifestation of pleasure.

May lifted his face up to hers, her hands holding his high cheekbones, then, after retrieving one from her bedside cabinet, lit a small scented candle. The flame flickered across his dark features. He looked young, around twenty – a couple of years younger than her. His features were slightly aquiline, as if he might herald from as far north as the Sudan, but his skin was so black it almost looked blue in the shimmering light. His eyes were long and almond-shaped, and so bottomless that when May gazed into them she had the sensation of tumbling into outer space. They wore an expression of languid sensuality, of drawn-out unhurried sex. A wry smile danced across his lips, and somehow May knew that if she ended the silence between them, this tacit unspoken erotic contract would be broken. She would either wake up or he would flee or vanish.

Without removing his gaze from her face his fingers worked their way up her thighs in ever decreasing strokes as he circled her sex, the rough skin of his fingertips making her skin flame up in erotic yearning, until everything he wasn't caressing began to burn with the anticipation of his touch.

Suddenly reaching down while arched over her, he lifted her legs over his shoulders, forcing her thighs wide apart. He paused for a moment then, without any inhibition, licked the side of her face, nuzzling her neck as he made his way down to her sex, licking her skin furiously all the way. May fell back on the pillow, surrendering to the intense pleasure. She was already dripping wet, her hands clawing the sheets, wanting him to take her between those full soft lips, wanting him to fill her, pierce her, be in her completely. But he was in no rush.

Her skin was moist with his saliva as he bit her inner thighs, gently getting closer and closer, his fingers spreading her to the light, to the warm glow of the flickering flame of the candle now dancing over the plaster ceiling. His tongue pulsed with the same flame, building and building to a climax. Within seconds the cries of her orgasm resonated throughout the empty room, bouncing back off the walls. They sounded to May almost like another woman's cries, one she hadn't known was inside her until now. Illusion or no illusion, sex with Mitch had never been this good.

Before she had a chance to catch her breath he flipped her over so that she was crouching on all fours, arse up. He leant down and bit the back of her neck, then plunged into her. His thick cock filled her, pounding into her wildly without any decorum or want except for his own pleasure. His groaning desire reinflamed hers and as he rode her, plunging in and out, in and out, over and over, faster and faster, something even deeper, another buried inhibition, fell away inside May and she lost herself in total abandonment as thrusting and buckling they became one beast, until both of them came in one long great shout before collapsing together on the mattress. Afterwards she was lying there drifting off when she was startled by a small purr from the other side of the bed, she glanced across. The man was lying on his back, eyes closed, a smile upon his face. Sighing she turned and fell into a deep sleep.

The next morning May woke up with a pounding headache – it almost felt like a hangover. The sun had bashed its way through the blinds, heating the room in yellow bars of light. Half asleep, she opened one eye and reached across for the reassuring presence of Mitch's back. Instead she touched fur and heard a tentative miaow. The events of the last two days swept through her and then she remembered the lovemaking during the night. Surely it must have been a dream, some kind of psychological reaction to her abandonment – perhaps even an unconscious desire to get a new lover as soon as possible? May, a pragmatic young woman, was not given to erotic dreams. In fact she'd learnt to regard the pursuit of Eros with suspicion, the result of several early love affairs that, based on sexual desire, had, nevertheless, ended up breaking her heart. Even taking Mitch as a lover had been a reaction to those earlier affairs – she had thought him a profoundly sensible choice. What an irony, she thought to herself, and now I am reduced to bizarre sexual hallucinations.

She glanced back over to what had been Mitch's side of the bed. Shadow the cat was curled up, both eyes closed, the end of his tail twitching. If she didn't know better she would have been convinced the animal was just pretending to sleep. Tentatively she reached down and touched between her legs. She was sticky. When she lifted her hand to her face, it felt and smelt like semen – had it been more than a dream?

May glanced over at the alarm clock – it was past eleven, she'd slept in and was running late for her first lecture. She remembered there was nothing in the house that resembled cat food, and Shadow must be starving. She leapt out of bed and ran for her dressing gown.

The fridge was empty except for one carton of milk and an opened tin of tuna. She pulled out the tuna and swung the fridge door shut. The calendar above the fridge had rent day circled in red felt pen. May couldn't help noticing it was now only three days away and she was short at least two hundred dollars, and that was before paying for food. She wondered whether she would be able to sell some clothes or possibly some furniture on eBay to raise some cash. For a moment she thought about an old record player her dad had given her, then remembered she'd already sold it six months earlier to a vinyl freak to make one term's fees. All May could think of selling was a leather jacket that she might be able to get fifty bucks for if she was lucky.

Depressed, May reached for a plate and emptied half of the tuna onto it. Shadow was already circling her bare legs, rubbing his fur backwards and forwards against her bare skin, his back arched in anticipation. Last night's dream seemed a lifetime ago – today May just felt tired, abandoned and overwhelmed by a multitude of financial commitments, none of which she could meet. She thought about borrowing the rent money from her sister, but May knew she was also in financial trouble and the last time she'd borrowed money she hadn't been able to pay it back. No. She would try not to worry too much about the looming rent day, while trying to conjure up some other radical methods of making some cash. She put the plate on the floor and Shadow began eating hungrily.

She watched him – he was a very good-looking cat. Perhaps he might be worth something, even on eBay? If not him, maybe his fur? As if sensing this sinister turn of mind the cat looked up from his eating, his eyes wide and pensive. There was something about his expression that was strangely familiar to May.

'It's okay,' she reassured the animal, 'I'm not going to sell you to a furrier just yet. But you'll have to do something to earn your keep and you're eating my lunch.' As if in reply the cat miaowed a protest then leapt up onto the counter and sat angrily swishing his tail. Shrugging, May grabbed her bag and left the apartment.

It was during her morning lecture – given by her favourite tutor, Joanna Wutherer, on the cultural fall-out and impact of Joseph Banks's visit to Polynesia – that May found her mind wandering back to the events of the night before. The lovemaking had been so real she was finding it hard to believe it was a fantasy, or perhaps it was one of those rare, stress-induced hallucinations that occur between sleep and wakefulness. As she gazed up at the whiteboard onto which were projected romanticised eighteenth-century images of native Polynesians, she found herself remembering the touch of her fantasy man's skin, the smooth ripples of his torso, her hand trailing down to the hairless nest of his cock and balls – the wondrous weight of him cupped in her palm.

'May!' The sound of the lecturer's voice jolted her back into the lecture hall. May opened her eyes to the sound of laughter.

'Would you like to tell us which part of Rousseau's concept of the noble savage made you groan and why? Preferably from a twenty-first-century post-colonial perspective?'

May glanced around, embarrassed; several students grinned back.

'Was I groaning?'

'You certainly were.'

May thought furiously then finally answered: 'Involuntary disgust at the British exploitation of the unfettered sensuality of the locals ...' She was counting on the approval of Joanna Wutherer, who she knew to be politically sensitive to such issues.

'And quite rightly so – within decades the local population of Polynesia was decimated by syphilis, a gift from both the French and English sailors, who had begun to regard the islands as a sexual paradise free from the mores of their own worlds,' Joanna concluded dramatically.

But what world had her phantom lover come from? May wondered before forcing her mind back to the more prosaic dilemma of eighteenth-century trading routes and their influence on the spread of Christianity.

May's distraction continued all day, through the rest of her lectures, on the bus she took down Parramatta Road to the vintage shop, which almost caused her to miss her stop, and then all through the three hours she worked as a shop assistant. It was an emotional state her sister mistook for shock at losing Mitch.

'You can talk about it, you know, mental health isn't a taboo subject anymore – and, hey, we know all about it, don't we?' June, older and five months pregnant, volunteered, again drawing May back into the present.

'What are you talking about?'

'Mitch of course, all that warlock thing. It must have been horrible. I guess it brought back stuff about Karl's breakdown. God, those were horrible years.'

'It was a little disturbing ...' May stared absent-mindedly at her sister, wondering whether vivid sexual fantasy might also be deemed a mental health problem.

'And of course you're grieving now, break-ups are really hard,' June continued in that patronising tone that always seemed to insinuate that she had a monopoly not only on experience but also the higher moral ground. Nope, there was no way May could ask her sister to lend her the rent money now. It was a question of sibling pride.

'He gave me a cat.'

June looked at her blankly.

'You know, as a parting gift. A big black thing. I think it's about the most beautiful animal I've ever seen.'

'But you don't even like cats,' June blurted out.

'I know,' May replied and to her amazement found herself blushing.

After her sister left May checked her email using the store's computer. There was still no response to her posting about a flatmate. She then checked her bank balance – at the very worst perhaps she could pay the rent using one of her three credit cards, two of which were already well over their limit. Her balance appeared on the screen in black relentless fact. As she stared at it incredulously, she realised she was far poorer than she had imagined. A fluttery panic began to creep up through her stomach and she felt sick. She'd always relied on Mitch to manage their finances, and now the vague memory came back to her of being surprised that he hadn't asked to see her bank balance mid-month like he always did. Had this been another sign of his impending breakdown? Her panic grew – how would she find the rent in three days?

She opened a window onto the university website to look at her ad. 'Female student seeks flatmate. Two bedroom flat with garden, large bedroom, non-smoker please. $1000 per month including gas and electricity ...' The ad was sandwiched innocently between a couple of others, one for a male flatmate to share with five other male students in a large house, the other for a lesbian flatmate to share with two lesbians. May noticed that both advertisements involved considerably less rent than she was asking – was that why she hadn't had any responses yet? But she couldn't afford to drop the amount, not if she wanted to keep the lease.

Sighing, she closed down the computer and stared out of the shopfront window. It was almost dark. Finally it had started to rain, breaking the heatwave. Great sheets of water cut the streetscape diagonally, splashing against leaves and steaming pavement. The traffic had slowed and people rushed from bus shelter to shop awnings trying to keep dry. None of them had her problems, May thought bitterly. The neon light switched on outside illuminating the shop till. It seemed to gleam seductively at her. May knew the takings wouldn't be added up until the end of the week, by which time she might have found the money – who knows? Surely June wouldn't mind if she borrowed a few hundred dollars, especially if May returned the money before she noticed.

Quickly she opened the till and slipped several fifty-dollar bills into her purse. Trying not to feel guilty about it May grabbed her bag, locked up the shop, then ran out into the heavy rain. Hatless and coatless she was drenched to the skin in a few minutes. Lifting her face to the drumming caress she spun around. It felt like a baptism, a new beginning, yet she couldn't fathom why she felt so excited about doing something as simple as going home – home to an empty flat. Then she remembered she was going home to the cat.

The bath water was deliciously hot, hot enough to redden the skin and exorcise any conscious thought or anxiety, which was exactly May's intention. She stood for a moment in the centre of the bathroom, naked, the full-length reflection in the mirror a white and pink ghost, the cool tiles under her feet. In the hallway outside she could hear the soft scratching of Shadow's claws against the door. She'd locked him out deliberately. This was to be her time, an indulgence of the spirit, and she needed to think.

Earlier she'd been grateful for the company of the cat. She'd cooked herself a meal and served him the rest of the tuna. She had planned to feed Shadow by the back door with his plate on the floor, but after she'd served him and had sat at the table with her own plate, the animal had refused to touch his food. Instead he gazed at her with a hurt and slightly indignant expression. It was a stand-off until, finally giving in to the cat's unspoken demands, May had put his plate on the kitchen table, in the place that was traditionally Mitch's seat. To her amazement the cat immediately leapt up and sat neatly on the chair, waiting until she had begun eating before delicately munching the food off his own plate.

'Jesus,' she'd said out loud, 'you really do think you're a man, don't you?' to which he miaowed – just once – as if in agreement.

'Okay, but just this once – don't get any long-term ambitions. Remember you're on a lower rung of the evolutionary ladder.' But the cat chose to ignore the comment.

As she watched him it was uncanny how his presence felt so human. Every time she turned her back to him she could feel him observing her – but not in the instinctive way of an animal but rather in an intensely curious, intellectually alert manner. It was beginning to unnerve her, which was the reason why she had decided to lock him out during her bath. But here he was, scratching furiously at the bathroom door, demanding to be let in. Determined to ignore him she stepped into the water, perfumed by a mixture of baby oil and rosewater. A fragrant cloud lifted up as she broke the surface. Grateful for the luxury, May slipped down into the hot water, stretching her body out full length. A purplish mark on the inside of one of her thighs caught her eye.

She lifted the leg out of the water to take a closer look. It was a bruise, a distinctive kind of marking that reminded her of something else. A love bite. She ran her fingers across the surface – a faint pricking of pain ensued. That's what it was, not a bruise but a love bite. But how in hell had it managed to appear on the inside of her thigh? Unless … unless the lovemaking the night before had been real. The thought drifted up with the curling steam forming a remarkably phallic shape before dispersing. May closed her eyes for a minute, determined to dismiss all lewd thoughts.

Shadow's scratching at the door stopped and was replaced by a sudden yowl of discontent, startling her. Steeling herself, she sank back down into the embrace of the warm water; the bruise livid against her pale skin. It just wasn't possible. Or had her imagination transformed fantasy into such realism that her actual body had created external manifestations of those dreamt sensations? If phantom pregnancies were possible, perhaps phantom lovemaking and phantom love bites were also? It was not a comforting thought.

Shadow's yowling became louder and more desperate by the minute. In the apartment above, May could hear the slam of her neighbour's front door, followed by the soft plodding of his footfall. A taxi driver who worked morning shifts, he'd often complained when Mitch and May played music after midnight. The last thing he would be tolerant of was a loud cat. Swearing softly, May got out of the bath and, dripping water across the bathroom floor, let the animal in.

'Now for Christ's sake shut up or else I'll have to drown you,' she warned. The cat, as if in reply, leapt up and perched daintily on the toilet lid that was firmly shut. 'And don't look,' May added for good measure, still convinced the animal was preternaturally intelligent.

She stepped back into the water, sank down low and closed her eyes, determined to regain the delicious meditative state she'd been in before, a dancing colourful mind-state that involved no thought whatsoever. As she was just getting close a faint splash outside her consciousness danced across her mind's eye in the form of a white dot. She decided to ignore it, but it was followed by a louder splash then the brush of a foot against her inner thigh. She sat up with a jolt, displacing water that sloshed over the sides of the bath.

Standing naked looking down at her, his feet firmly planted either side of her legs, was the man who'd appeared the night before. Foreshortened, the most visible thing about him was his penis. Fully erect, it stood out from his torso and hung above her like some exotic fruit, full and dusky, blooming out defiantly.

Above that the muscularity of his body rippled upwards, prominent mauve nipples erect on each arc of his pectorals. His large veined hands hung down by his sides, the slight awkwardness of them in repose only adding to the beauty of the juxtaposition of his rippling torso.

Without thinking May reached up and, kneeling, took his cock into her mouth. The taste, scent and size of him was as real as the water dripping down her breasts and back. Above her she could hear the man groan (or was it purr?) as she increased her pace, curling her tongue around the large tip, taking him deeper and deeper into her throat until she sensed he could take no more. She lifted her face away and pulled him down to his knees. She stared into his eyes in wonder, touching his lips with her fingers as he took them into his mouth, sucking. Then her fingers wandered up to the sides of his head, her left hand curling around one of his ears. As she traced the lobe she noticed that the bottom half of the left lobe was missing, as if it had been torn off in an accident. The image seemed vaguely reminiscent of someone or something else, but before May could remember exactly why, she was distracted by him pulling her into a long, deep kiss. His tongue searching her mouth caused a flood of erotic desire to wash through her, forcing her to steady herself with one hand against the edge of the bathtub.

'Who are you?' she murmured, then instantly regretted the question, fearing he would vanish and she would find herself alone, waking out of her dream state. In lieu of an answer he bit her shoulder gently then lifted one of her pert breasts to suck greedily at her nipple. He then turned her so that she was on her hands and knees, water up to her elbows. He parted her buttocks and lubricated her anus with some soap with one hand while with the other he pulled gently at her clitoris. May watched their reflection in Mitch's old abandoned full-length mirror leaning against the wall. Her pale skin was a dramatic contrast to his shining blue-black body, his large hands pushed into the white flesh of her arse. It was hard to believe she was dreaming, and yet this was a scenario she'd often fantasised about during her lovemaking with Mitch – an affair that had always been a little predictable and lacking in imagination.

Now he was easing her wider and wider – she could feel the head of his penis nudging against her until he slipped in. At first the pain took her breath away but then as he moved slowly and carefully backwards and forwards she could feel herself loosening and embracing him as intense pleasure took the place of the pain. Reaching down she touched herself between her legs as he abandoned himself to his own pleasure, now thrusting wildly – they both came together. And in the silence that ensued there was the sound of bathwater dripping down onto the tiles.

May woke in her bed the next morning. She stretched and yawned, her body deliciously relaxed in a post-coital kind of way. Marvelling at how good she felt she glanced across the bedroom floor. Shadow was sitting on an abandoned bath towel, licking his paws in a smug manner. It was then that May remembered the sexual encounter of the night before.

'Jesus,' she said to herself as she climbed out of bed and pulled on her jeans and T-shirt. 'If I keep fantasising like this I'll have to see a shrink myself by the end of the week.' The sequence of events of the night before ran through her mind. May couldn't remember ever having such vivid erotic dreams before – there was absolutely no way of discerning real life from fantasy. Again she was worried she might be going mad like her brother. How well did she even know herself? Most frightening of all, perhaps there was a whole frustrated fantasist trapped inside her, jailed by all her pragmatism.

Her thoughts were interrupted by the sound of the postman outside. Grabbing her iPod and mobile she raced out, grabbing the mail on the way. She opened the envelopes at the bus stop. One contained the gas bill which was due in a week, the other a notice from the electricity company threatening to cut off the electricity if the overdue bill wasn't paid in full – the cut-off date was the next day and the amount was four times their usual bill. How was that possible? Again, complete panic began to build from the pit of her stomach. Who had used that amount of electricity? It hadn't been her. She cast her mind back to that first day Mitch had appeared as Erasmus. He'd had the heater on – how long had he been standing there in front of the heater at full blast? Now she seemed to remember he'd been at home during the day that week studying while she'd been at university. Was it possible he'd had the heater on all that time? How long had this been going on? Weeks or months? Maybe he had been doing this for much longer than she thought. She glanced back at the bill – he must have had it on for over twelve hours. The amount was nearly four hundred dollars – all the money she'd 'borrowed' from her sister's till. If she paid it she'd have nothing left over for the rent due the day after. It was then that she remembered the rent was due the next day and that the landlord had finally refused to take any more late payments – if she didn't pay on time she would be evicted. It suddenly felt as if all these events were conspiring to force her to abandon her flat. No wonder her unconsciousness was taking refuge in erotic fantasy – the real world was just too unsympathetic and shocking to deal with, she concluded.

She caught the bus and got off at the post office to pay the electricity bill in cash. As she counted out the fifty-dollar bills – the same ones she'd taken from her sister's till – she wondered how on earth she would be able to find the money for both dinner and cat food, never mind the rent, when she suddenly noticed the rings that she'd inherited from her grandmother. She'd been wearing them for so long she'd forgotten she even had them. One was an Edwardian engagement ring with three small diamonds in a pearl setting – it had to be worth something. She decided to visit the pawnshop on the way to university.

The man behind the counter gave her a hundred and fifty dollars for the ring – fifty dollars short of what she needed to make the rent and about sixty dollars short after she'd bought dinner for herself later. Depressed, May pocketed the money and began to wind her way down to the university gates. She was interrupted by a chorus of wolf whistles from a group of road workers. Unused to such admiration she looked over her shoulder imagining they must be whistling at someone behind her. When she realised they were whistling at her she panicked thinking some part of her body must be exposed. She was entirely covered up yet the men were grinning appreciatively at her. Were they picking up something new about her? Had her fantasy left some invisible mark or scent about her person?

The day at university went a lot more slowly than usual. Although it was the day of all her favourite tutorials, May found herself increasingly excited as the hours ticked by. All she could think about was whether or not she would be visited that night. It was as if this incubus, this fantasy creature, had released some primal force within her, tapping into a raw sensuality she hadn't even known she'd had until then. And others had begun to notice as well. One of her friends – a very handsome womaniser with whom she'd only ever been platonic mates – suddenly started flirting with her, which appeared to surprise him as much as her. It was as if he'd only just noticed that she was female. She seemed to engender male attention everywhere she went: the bus driver had let her off her bus fare when she hadn't had the right change, and one of her male tutors had given her an extra week to complete an essay without her even having to argue the point. Although pleasant looking, May knew her male counterparts considered her interesting but never sexy. It had always been force of personality and a strong sense of self-deprecating humour that had attracted men to her. For the first time she felt like a femme fatale, a sexual magnet. It was a seductively empowering sensation: heads were actually turning in her direction.

Just then her mobile phone rang and she almost walked into a lamppost. Collecting herself she answered it. It was one of her girlfriends wanting to know whether she was going to their usual trivia night at the local pub. May had forgotten all about it.

'Come on, it'll take your mind off Mitch,' the girlfriend insisted.

'The warlock, you mean?' May corrected her.

The girlfriend broke into stifled giggles then pulled herself together.

'I'm sorry, it must be really terrible. I mean, living with the guy all that time then finding out you don't really know him at all.'

'It has been difficult …'

'Yeah, but you don't sound devastated and don't take this the wrong way but I saw you today on the other side of the Quadrangle and I've never seen you look so good. Like hot. May? Is there something you're not telling me? Like who's the new bloke?'

'Do I look that good?'

'Babe, I didn't recognise you. I swear your aura was lit up like a Christmas tree. Whoever he is he must be good.'

'The best …' May murmured dreamily into the phone before realising she'd actually spoken aloud.

'I knew it!' the girlfriend, whose main currency was gossip, squealed, causing May's ears to ring. She held the phone at a distance.

'Trin, there is no one, I promise.'

'Sure, and I'm guessing you're about to cancel tonight to be with this no one, right?'

'Afraid so.' Relieved that she'd been offered an excuse not to go, knowing she wouldn't have the money to buy her friends drinks, May resigned herself to an evening alone at home. Normally this would have depressed her and yet she actually found herself cheerfully swinging her arms as she walked towards the apartment in the evening sun. Impending financial crisis be damned, she concluded, it can all wait until tomorrow.

On the way home she dropped by the fishmongers to ask for free fish scraps. She was given two salmon tails – one of which had quite a lot of meat on it. She could feed both the cat and herself and somehow she felt Shadow had earnt it.

The cat was waiting on the garden wall outside. As May turned the corner and caught sight of him she was amazed (and slightly ashamed) at the depth of emotion that swept through her. She felt as if she were greeting a new lover. Again, it seemed both irrational and a little hysterical to her and May did not like feeling out of control. Had she begun to transfer the affection she would have given Mitch to a dumb animal? It was an uncomfortable supposition.

Determined to repress this new, ridiculously placed affection, she barely acknowledged the cat as she opened the garden gate. Rebuffed, the cat ignored her in turn and stared arrogantly out into space as she passed. It was only after May had slipped the front door key into the lock that he jumped down from the wall to follow her silently into the flat.

That night May laid two places at the table: one for her and one for Shadow. The salmon tails were then ceremoniously decorated with a few sprigs of rosemary (stolen from next door's bush) after being lightly marinated in lemon juice (the lemon having also been stolen from next door's lemon tree) then baked for ten minutes in the oven. Shadow watched the preparations with a reverence May had always associated with religion-worshipping humans and certainly not cats, but she liked the sensation of his approval.

She also found herself liking the way he sat watching from Mitch's old chair, his tail occasionally twitching in barely contained excitement. His feline gaze upon her was almost an erotic one, something May found hard to admit to herself. Humming happily she put on a CD and sat opposite the cat, who again didn't start eating until May had lifted her fork.

The salmon tails were delicious, although meagre, and though the potato and piece of broccoli were barely enough to stop

May from waking up hungry in the middle of the night, she felt triumphant. She was surviving without Mitch, without a man to oversee all the economic realities she'd avoided these past two years. And even though the nagging fear that she might not make the rent loomed, she felt surprisingly self-contained and contented.

May glanced over at Shadow, whose ears seemed to twitch to the music. She smiled at the comedic sight, amazed at how the animal appeared to keep perfect time, his frayed left ear butterfly-like as it fluttered in time with the right. His bitten left ear. His bitten left ear! May stared down at her plate. The image of a black human ear with a section missing out of the lobe suddenly seemed to float over her plate. How was it possible? Could it be coincidence, or some kind of projection of hers onto the innocent creature? And why had Mitch given her the cat? Did he know something about the animal that she didn't, that it had some extraordinary power?

Nina Simone's song 'I Put a Spell on You' floated out of the speakers and drifted across the kitchen like a dangerous perfume. Suddenly she felt that the presence across the table had changed. May froze, terrified, still staring down at her plate, too afraid to look up and across at the cat. In this position she heard the chair scrape the floor as it was pushed away from the table, she heard the heavy footsteps as he walked towards her. She felt his breath on the back of her bare neck, his large hands slip around, finding her breasts, finding her nipples, until finally she managed to whisper, 'Who are you?'

She was answered by a loud miaow. The sound made her look up to see the cat sitting just as it had been a minute before, on the chair at the end of the table opposite her, its yellow-green eyes wide in innocent surprise.

*

Later that night May made Shadow a nest of an old pillow and a blanket in one corner of the living room. While she packed them into an old straw basket she'd found, the cat wound itself around her legs miaowing plaintively.

'You can't sleep with me, you just can't. I need to know, Shadow, do you understand? I need to know before I go mad,' she told him, pausing to caress him behind the ears. She was interrupted by a cough outside. Gary, her neighbour, had paused outside the open window on his way to his own back door. He grinned sheepishly at May who, mortified, picked up the cat.

'Oh hi, Gary ...'

'Hi.' He stared warily at the cat. 'The landlord doesn't allow pets, May, you know that.'

'It's my sister's, I'm looking after him while she's on holiday. He'll be gone by tomorrow afternoon,' she lied, trying to smile at him. Gary hunched his shoulders defensively.

'Glad to hear it. Can't stand the animals meself. But you should know, they don't usually speak. At least not human,' he added, guffawing at his own joke before disappearing down the garden path and out of view. May collapsed, hugging her knees. In response Shadow rubbed himself affectionately against her legs.

'What does he know, eh, puss? Nothing, but then again maybe I really am going mad, like Mitch. Maybe he really was a warlock and now he's cursed me and you ...' In response the cat sat on its haunches and, lifting a paw, touched her face. May's resolve wavered for a moment. Would no cat mean no lover? Either way she had to find out.

May slipped between the sheets and listened out into the silence. There was nothing. Earlier Shadow had settled into his basket without a protest, his whole body infused with sad resignation. Indeed, there was such finality to his movements that May feared he might slip away into the night, and she didn't want to lose him. She realised, with some surprise, that she'd developed a dependence on the animal. She thought of him now, curled up on his pillow, his long tail wound around his face and whiskers, no doubt twitching slightly in his sleep. Would her man come with the cat firmly banished, or were the two inexplicably linked?

The silence in the bedroom thickened with the encroaching darkness. Her body, expecting a sudden caress, the surprising brush of fingertips as light as a breeze, tensed in anticipation, but there was nothing, not even a rustle in the shadows. May lay back and tried to unravel the complexity of her reaction. She was both relieved and disappointed, both sad and intrigued that she couldn't just summon her incubus through sheer will. He appeared to have a will of his own. Staring out across the bare floorboards she finally fell into a dreamless sleep.

What seemed like just minutes later she was woken by the sound of heavy knocking on the front door. Blinking in the sunlight that was now streaming in through the blinds, she sat up bleary-eyed from sleep. The clock showed ten am – she'd overslept again. The knocking on the front door persisted. Just then the telephone began to ring. Swearing, May reached for the receiver and picked it up. It was her sister June.

'May, you'll never guess what's happened, I've just done the books and someone's stolen four hundred dollars out of the till. I guess it's one of the temps – you can never trust them. I'm really upset. I've put a call through to the local cops ...' May froze, the receiver in her hand, paralysed by guilt, not knowing whether to tell her sister or not that she'd taken the money.

The knocking continued. May told her sister to hold then climbed out of bed and pulled on her dressing gown. As she ran to answer the door it occurred to her that it might be her landlord demanding the rent. She paused at the door, unwilling to let him in.

'Who is it?' she demanded through the door.

'Hello? I'm interested in the room.' It was a man's voice, a young man's, velvety and deep, laced with a foreign accent May couldn't identify.

'The room?'

'The one you advertised, on the university website?'

May's heart leapt. All her problems could be solved if only she could rent the room today. Hurriedly she unbolted the door.

He was dressed in an elegant pair of linen trousers and a loose cream shirt. Towering over her, standing with the sun behind him, the first thing May saw was his silhouette against the light. But she recognised him immediately.

'You,' she could barely whisper.

He stepped out of the light. He was even more handsome by day than by night. There was a sensitivity to his bone structure and eyes that she hadn't noticed until now.

'Sorry, do I know you?' He looked both surprised and bemused.

May blushed. 'No, you just look like someone I used to know,' she hurriedly said, then blushed some more, frozen on the spot in confusion.

He misunderstood her hesitation. 'I can put the deposit down immediately – if I like it. I really need to find something by the end of today.'

'That would be fantastic – if you like it, that is …'

'Oh, I think I might. Any chance of actually seeing it?' he asked hesitantly. He appeared to have no memory of her whatsoever – it was as if he'd never met her.

'Sorry, of course, come in …'

He stepped into the hallway after her. For a moment she paused, then turned. 'There's just one thing – you're not allergic to cats by any chance?'

He paused, doubt clouding his eyes. 'Actually I am. Is that going to be a problem?'

May turned and continued walking through the flat – Shadow was nowhere to be seen.

'Not now, it isn't,' she replied with a sudden smile.

TIGGER

Let me tell you about real intimacy, the kind of intimacy in which over the years your lover shares so many of her memories that osmosis occurs and you can no longer define which are hers and which are yours. That was the love we had, love that transcends the approval of society, the kind of love that is purely and undeniably instinctive. The kind you fight for – whether you want to or not. Joanna's story begins more than three decades ago, in the last days of the twentieth century, and I know it as well as I knew her.

At the beginning of this story Joanna, or Tigger as her friends called her, was of a certain age: the age at which a woman starts lying to both herself and others. It wasn't a question of vanity, pride or even professional necessity. It was a question of survival. Up until now Tigger had only ever experienced relationships that would run for two years or so and then either the man or Tigger would suddenly leave. In those days she was, as she told me with that wry crooked smile of hers, a serial monogamist with an attention deficit disorder. A bed-hopping heartbreaker who'd had her heart broken, she'd say, smiling a little sadly. It was hard to believe – it wasn't the woman I'd known – but I suspect that when Tigger was young she misused the power of her own allure and squandered it in reckless choices. I never made that mistake, but I digress.

At the start of my story Tigger's habitual restlessness had gone on for over two decades, although lately she'd begun to notice that it was more the men leaving her than her leaving the men. To make matters worse they all seemed to go on to successful long-term relationships straight after her, as if living with her was the catalyst for them to go running into marriage with another woman. She had convinced herself that the last one to leave had been the great love of her life, or at the very least the only man she'd ever truly loved up until that point in her life. She had certainly not fallen out of lust with him, or been driven away by boredom as had happened with so many before him. Nevertheless he had abruptly left her for a younger woman and, even more mortifying, a single mother.

Tigger still hadn't got over the shock. His sudden departure, and even more wrenching absence, had robbed her of not only her self-esteem but also the possibility of ever having children. Even if she fell in love tomorrow, she wasn't about to have children with someone she hadn't known for at least two years, by which time she would definitely be perimenopausal, and as she had no intention of ever becoming a single mother (having being brought up by one); adoption was not an option as she was too old. At the time it did appear a very barren horizon. And no matter how she shrugged off this fact to her friends – usually with a pinch of self-deprecating humour – this decline of fertility had affected Tigger's perception of her own sexual charisma.

It was, she told herself, gazing down at her long white naked body, as if the juice had suddenly gone from the fruit, or so she told me. Cupping her breasts in her hands she would weigh them carefully each morning trying to guess whether her voluptuousness was diminishing or increasing with age. It wasn't a rational obsession, but then, as she explained to me, nothing before or after menopause is ever rational. And despite this obsessive scrutiny of her body and loss of confidence, it wasn't as if she was less lusty. Quite the reverse in fact, Tigger observed, wondering if the sexual poise and emotional courage one gains with age was in inverse proportion to the dwindling amount of sex one actually gets as one gets older – especially as a woman. Sighing, she would pluck out another grey pubic hair and console herself with the fact that at least she looked younger than her real age.

Tigger was blessed genetically – neither of her siblings remotely looking their age either – and she had kept slim, although staying fit was taking up an increasingly greater portion of her time. She was an attractive woman in an interesting, strong-faced sort of way, and I would challenge anyone to argue otherwise. But what Tigger had that elevated her above other women was physical grace: however unconventionally pretty she was, when Tigger moved it was profoundly erotic. The woman didn't walk so much as flow, as if she were water shifting from one point in the room to another, or an assemblage of fluid molecules seamlessly gliding through space. She had always moved like this, and the best of it was that she was completely unaware of the effect it had on men. It was this that got her noticed at parties, at bars, at conventions, at the lecture podium, even in crowded airport lounges. Motionless she was almost invisible, but as soon as her weight shifted upwards and she tilted forward on a trajectory, it was as if a wonderful unfurling mass of silver mercury had been unleashed upon the world. Watching her reminded men of their potential: of the smell of the air after rain, of the times when their thighs burned and it was still wondrous to feel stubble on their chin, of the first time they had entered a woman. Let me tell you, Tigger walking awoke a sexual joy that made all men feel young again.

Even in her mid-forties Tigger still had this grace. And if she was feeling a little more invisible at the time of this story, it was purely because she thought she was. In truth, men still noticed her but Tigger had stopped noticing them. She had convinced herself no one would want her anymore. How wrong could she be?

In those days Tigger was a lecturer at Sydney University in the anthropology department. She was good, one of those rare teachers who didn't just inspire but who seemed to be able to envisage a whole gleaming future for a favourite student; she was an alchemist of hope. But in truth, she confessed to me once that she'd sacrificed her own dreams years before. She'd wanted to be one of those popular human science television presenters, someone who might be seen striding through an Amazon forest or along a Polynesian beach while talking enthusiastically to the camera about ancient tribes or colonial travesties. Eventually she'd channelled her ambition into academia instead, and by forty she was already a senior lecturer with tenure, her own terrace in Paddington and hordes of eager young anthropology students who respected (and occasionally lusted after) her. A gregarious individual, a giver, she was famous for her optimistic and sunny nature. And God, did I love her for that.

But back then she'd begun to feel as if this ability to exude friendliness and her desire to smile back had taken on an independent life of its own. Sometimes she told me she even felt as if she was possessed. Often, after teaching for eight hours straight, enthusing her students with the same stories, historical records and images she'd used year in and year out, staying on her feet, reassuring anxious students, counselling those who felt she was more approachable than others in the department, Tigger would collapse at the end of the day overwhelmed by a desire to be thoroughly nasty or at least honestly indifferent to somebody else's needs. The sensation would surge through her like a sudden influx of hormones, and nothing except a punching match with a pillow or a screaming match with the television would alleviate the feeling. In her darkest moments she wondered whether the last ex had sensed this repressed aspect of her personality: the disingenuousness of nice. Was this why he and all the other men had left her?

It was after a conference of international anthropologists that she'd both organised and fronted at the university, a conference that had deteriorated into a series of petty debates on nuances of reportage, leaving her both exhausted and disillusioned, that Tigger decided she needed a change, or at least an affair – failing that, a one-night stand. She'd told me she'd been determined to lose herself in any way possible, even if it meant behaving uncharacteristically. That very night Tigger booked a flight to Melbourne to visit her closest friend Elise, an installation artist.

In Melbourne's CBD in the late 1990s, there was a miniature facsimile of Paris, or at least what Melburnians liked to imagine was a facsimile of Paris. It had evolved in the centre of the city from an old nineteenth-century warren of narrow lanes that had somehow avoided urban development. And the whimsical old-world atmosphere had inspired a couple of young entrepreneurs to set up cafés along the grey stone streets, capitalising on the influx of young artists who had rented cheap office space for studios above the narrow labyrinth.

Gradually tables and chairs outside the cafés had hijacked the pavements altogether; filled with customers, they spilt out into the lanes like an overbooked wedding reception. Along with the cafés and a government push to encourage residential living within the city, a plethora of tiny bars had sprung up like errant nocturnal fungi illuminated only at night and accessible only to those in the know – in other words, the young, artistic and extremely hip. In actual fact the bars and cafés were more reminiscent of Barcelona or Bilbao than Paris, the confined imaginative spaces they occupied often so cramped that people became as familiar with each other as family. But then Melburnians, in their cultural elitism, preferred the Parisian association.

Since her divorce Elise, Tigger's artist friend, had become an honorary grande dame of this bar scene – her rarefied and highly aesthetic installations provided a counterbalance to the fast bold graffiti art and photomontage of many of the younger patrons. Elise also had a passion for younger men, a propensity resulting from the fact that the last time she had been single and hunting she had been much younger.

Elise had been married for seventeen years, from her twenties to her late thirties, and had emerged on the other side of the marriage with the same erotic gaze she had entered it with – her eye hadn't caught up with her biological age. Her utter indifference to any societal disapproval of this aspect of her character was admirable and a sign of a true maverick. Tigger envied Elise's cavalier attitude. Secretly Tigger had always felt confined by her own sexual conservatism, constrained by the inherited mores of her middle-class mother. No one but I ever knew that, but as I explained before, by the end of our relationship we were as close as identical twins.

There were things Tigger should have done when she was younger but didn't – unfulfilled erotic fantasies that had grown over the years to bloom suddenly, unexpectedly, in her dreams. Now she was frightened that if she didn't act on them they would haunt her for the rest of her life. It was, she later confessed to me, as if something was driving her to act, to shake up and even destroy the pattern of her life up to that point. Maybe it was a mid-life crisis. Maybe it was a reaction to her last relationship breakdown, but whatever it was I shall be eternally grateful.

And so Tigger set out that night with Elise leading the way, both of them dressed to seduce as they advanced upon the various bars Elise knew would be populated by eager young men also indifferent to social orthodoxy. They started the evening with an exhibition opening. It was summer and the evening was warm, one of those languid, stretched-out evenings in which the air is laced with possibility. I seem to remember a full moon that had risen early – a faint silver ghost twin to the setting sun. The actual opening was in a small passage off Flinders Lane, one blind alley hung with light boxes and chipboards painted with graffiti. Gazing up at the old stone walls punctuated by these windows of illumination, Tigger wondered whether this was art. She was infinitely more conservative about these matters than Elise. But it was pretty, she remembered thinking of one particular work, a light box displaying a photograph of the sun setting behind an endless sea of red earth – no doubt the Nullarbor Plain. The light box itself growing more and more luminous as the actual sun set behind the tall buildings. It was intriguing, this small, increasingly intense portal into the huge hollow landscape of the continent, hung as it was on a grey stone wall in a narrow lane that, by contrast, felt claustrophobic. Tigger wasn't sure where she would rather have been – Melbourne or the great interior desert. Either way the light box had begun to feel like a metaphor for hope, but then Tigger wasn't completely sure this wasn't the effect of the two margaritas she'd drunk.

A small café run by a couple of very handsome young Italian-Australians, fiercely proud of the authenticity of the Italian coffee and pastries they served, was hosting the opening. A multitude of young people clustered self-consciously, leaning against the walls smoking or sitting on the milk crates grouped around the canopy of the café, plastic beakers filled with cheap Australian champagne clasped awkwardly in their hands. Mainly art students, some looked as young as eighteen, and the eclecticism of their vintage clothes married with a neo gothic punk style reminded Tigger of her own youth – a direct mirror reflection of the clothes she wore as a student in the streets of Melbourne almost twenty-five years earlier. She told me it was a strange feeling, as if time had momentarily folded in on itself, and staring at these young people, the look of which had been so familiar to her when she'd been eighteen, made her forget her true age, made her eighteen again. But that was Tigger, acutely empathetic to the point of taking on the persona of those she observed. This was another reason I'd fallen in love with her, but again I digress …

It wasn't just art students at this open-air exhibition. There were a few older patrons of the cafés, as well as art buyers and the odd art gallery owner. This diverse crowd mingled and broke up into knots of vivaciously chatting people, hands flying passionately, cigarette smoke twisting up towards the strip of sky above, as interwoven as the conversations and flirtations. All the while Tigger, my Tigger, looked on with a certain ironic distance, perched on a milk crate, margarita in hand.

Melbourne is a small city – or large town, depending on who you ask and their particular world view. But there was one truth that was indisputable: most people knew each other, and a good number had slept with each other or were sleeping with each other or would eventually sleep with each other, which made for a certain relaxed intimacy. And in those days, no matter how Melbourne might assume it had evolved in cultural sophistication, architectural beauty or culinary superiority, it had remained a large town that hungered for the vitality and rejuvenation of fresh blood. Gleaning a certain veiled curiosity about her, Tigger realised she had been away long enough for people not to recognise her. She was, indeed, fresh blood and this gave her a certain cachet, and, as she later confessed to me, ladies of a certain age know that they need as much cachet as they can muster.

Elise sat beside her sporting a Comme des Garçons dress, white silk stockings with French slang elegantly stitched into the seams (by La Perla) below which a pair of state-of-the-art Nike runners squatted incongruously. Her gaze was set with flirtatious determination as she scanned the crowd.

'Portside, red shirt,' Elise suddenly murmured, with the discretion of a ventriloquist; Tigger wasn't entirely sure she'd spoken at all. Nevertheless Tigger cast her gaze to the left and immediately sighted a lean young man who appeared to be ostentatiously ignoring her (although whether he was or he wasn't I cannot remember). He looked like the kind of man she used to be attracted to in her early teens. More disconcertingly, he had exactly the same look she had affected during that era: shoulder-length hair, T-shirt, flared jeans and a sultry pout. He bore a strong resemblance to the young Mick Jagger, his physique glimmering with an unabashed feline sexuality. Now, to her amazement, she saw him looking back at her. She almost checked behind her, wondering whether she had mistaken the direction of his gaze. Elise nudged her sharply in the ribs, spilling a little of the margarita into her lap.

'Want an intro?'

'I dunno – is he legal?'

'Don't be fucking stupid, of course he's legal. I know him, he's a traveller, a Californian, been working here for a couple of years. He's got a wild reputation but, hey, you're not after marriage, right?'

Tigger glanced back at the young man, her heart and groin uncomfortably jumpy. If I remember, and I should, he was very good looking in that dark, troubled way, with high cheekbones, intelligent eyes and a kind of self-deprecating posture that she immediately responded to. Tigger recognised herself in it, or so she told me. Okay, perhaps at a younger, more self-conscious age, but nevertheless she empathised with that prickly awareness, that inability to completely own your own power – sexual or otherwise. She wanted him but why on earth would he want her? He was far too handsome; he could have had any of the young girls milling around the tables. Or at least that's what Tigger thought.

'Go on then,' Elise prompted.

Tigger glanced at the youth again. He met her eyes, smiled, then looked down at his feet. His jeans were torn, a slash of tanned and muscled thigh visible through the denim. She battled the urge to glance appraisingly at his crotch, uneasy with what she felt might be blatant gender reversal. But she knew the longer she waited to drum up the courage to speak to him the harder it was going to be.

'Jesus, Tigger, what's holding you back?' Elise, frustrated by her hesitation, pulled at Tigger's arm.

'I don't know. It all seems a bit predatory. Besides, how do you know he even likes me?'

Elise rolled her eyes. 'Okay, this is what you're going to do. I'm going to get a glass of champagne and take it over to him. After a beat you follow, walking towards us with that famous hip-fuck of yours, alright, and you hook him. Got it?'

Before Tigger had a chance to answer, Elise had grabbed an extra drink from a passing tray, sauntered over and sat next to the youth. Elise now waited with a plastic beaker of champagne in each hand, signalling wildly to Tigger with her eyebrows then nodding in the direction of the unsuspecting youth, indicating it was time to make her approach. Tigger nearly died with embarrassment.

Finally the terror that Elise might actually tell the youth that her friend fancied him drove Tigger into action. She stood and began walking over. As she moved she tried not to think about what she was doing but instead allowed the inherent grace she was so famous for to flow through her: from the way she placed each foot on the pavement to the ripple up the slender thigh to the hip, the faint shudder of gravity, of momentum, undulating upwards through the pelvis, diaphragm, ribcage and up through the throat to finish like a lingering sweetness at the back of her tongue. Within seconds she was aware that several men had turned to watch her, the heat of their eyes brushing against the thin cotton of her skirt.

Reluctantly, Tigger joined Elise at the young man's side. For a moment the three of them sat in uncomfortable silence.

'Seth, isn't it?' Elise handed the youth the beaker of champagne. 'I met you through Mark, right?' Mark had been Elise's younger lover at the time, an aspiring website designer with a penchant for custom-made skateboards.

Trying desperately to retain his cool, the youth nodded. And again, the three of them fell back into an uncomfortable silence while Tigger frantically searched her mind for witty opening lines.

'Seth … Tigger … Tigger … Seth,' Elise announced pointing to the two in turn. 'So, I'll leave you two to it,' Elise concluded before getting up and walking away, to Tigger's secret dismay.

She stayed glued to the milk crate, surprised at her sudden apprehension. This is what older blokes must feel when confronted with a far younger and better looking female, she thought – fear of rejection. Then she reminded herself how all her womanising male peers (and she knew a few) always seemed to have an infinite supply of confidence. They were never frightened of rejection, so why should she be? Besides, all she had to lose was her pride, and one of Tigger's great strengths was always to regard pride as an obstacle.

'Seth – so you're the seventh son, right?' She was careful to sound as nonchalant as possible.

Surprised, he looked up. His eyes were a disturbingly deep green, or so she told me later.

'Wow, you guessed.'

Back then his accent had the flatness of a Californian surfer with an undertone of irony. I remember he grinned; one of his front teeth was chipped, an imperfection he was deeply conscious of, but Tigger focused on it as a counterbalance to his otherwise perfect beauty.

'What are you, psychic?'

'No, just a good detective. Seth is a biblical name, associated with the number seven. And isn't there an American movie with "seven sons" in the title? One of them's a Seth.'

'Yeah, I think my parents were into that film. They're total film buffs – old hippies, really.'

And probably only a couple of years older than me she noted darkly, after which they both fell into the kind of silence that makes you want to tear your clothes off and dive in, regardless of the consequences. Tigger shifted to the edge of her milk crate and clutched the hem of her short dress, terrified her body language would give away the wave of lust swelling through her. Many years later she told me she was even frightened that she had started to radiate a scent, a dangerous musk that screamed, 'I want you at all costs.'

'So you're from California?' Her voice echoed in the sexual tension that hung between them. To her ears it sounded thin and pathetically transparent in its intentions; to his ears it was the key he'd been praying for.

'Totally. Encinitas – it's a small town just south of San Diego.'

'Sounds very exotic.'

'In a New Age meets *The Last Picture Show* kind of way.' He rolled his words out languidly, a very deliberate vocal mannerism he'd spent hours practising, convinced it was sexy. And you know what, it was. 'I guess that's why my parents chose the town – that and the surf. My dad was a total gypsy; he used to run organic vegetables down Big Sur from Northern California. My mom had a wholefood café right next to the old twenties movie house that's still there. They met at a full moon ceremony on the beach. It was lust at first sight. It still is,' he concluded, his eyes telegraphing the clear message that lust at first sight was a family trait.

Flushed, Tigger took another sip of her lukewarm champagne.

'It sounds like an idyllic place to grow up.' To her embarrassment her voice squeaked with nerves – not that he noticed: after all, he was as secretly nervous as she was.

'It's okay for the first twelve years – after that there's no edge. And I hate LA.'

'I guess that's why you're in Melbourne – lots of edge here,' she replied, deadpan.

The youth laughed. He liked the irony and there was a sophistication about this woman that he hadn't yet encountered in Australia – plus she had great breasts, and he was a breast man. Still is, actually.

'I kinda landed here and liked it. I got involved with a local artists' co-op – they needed a talent manager, someone who could promote and help show their work.'

'Really? You manage an art gallery?' This time she failed to keep the incredulity out of her voice. She thought he didn't look old enough to have that kind of responsibility or ambition. He picked up her patronising tone immediately.

'It's a collective. Some of my artists are just graduating and they're really good. It's important to get in early while I can sign them.'

And then it happened. They smiled at each other, one of those gloriously spontaneous smiles unrelated to their actual conversation, a kind of mutual unspoken acknowledgement of attraction, the kind that has you soaring through all kinds of impossibilities. Again, Tigger wondered whether she was imagining it. But he, in all the blind courage of his youth, he knew. An instinctive flash of intuition and in that moment he wanted her more than anything.

Unable to maintain the gaze without blushing, Tigger glanced down at his hands: long sculptured fingers, broad palms, and the tips of his fingers slightly blunted and thick. She wondered how they would feel touching her, in her, her mouth, her sex, between her thighs.

'And you?' He interrupted her erotic reverie. She breathed in, reassembling herself.

'I lecture at Sydney University, in the anthropology department. At the beginning I had these illusions of fronting documentaries about ancient tribes, educating the world about the wonders of the indigenous civilisations of the Pacific.' She didn't know why she was telling him all of this, it just spilt out of her like a confession. Perhaps it was his youth, some unconscious reminder of an enthusiasm for both life and the world that she had once had herself.

'What happened? You didn't want to pursue it?'

'Financial realities set in – that and the limitations of the Australian market back then. I guess I was before my time.'

'There is no "time", only now.' A philosophy you might think all youths subscribe to, but this one really meant it.

He stood, the full height of him unfolding. In those days he was at least six foot two, and for a moment the seated Tigger was presented with a view of his crotch as he stood directly in front of her. She tried to stop that automatic evaluation of his hidden penis all women succumb to sooner or later – hardwired as it was – feeling as though that would be too exploitative of her. But he felt her gaze and loved it. It felt like a caress, like long cool fingers around his cock.

'Are you going on to the Velvet Glove later?' He looked down at her, not moving, totally aware of his provocative stance.

The Velvet Glove was a bar that a lot of the young artists frequented and Tigger knew Elise planned to take her there.

'I think so.'

'I'll see you there then.' His eyes travelled across her shoulders, cleavage and skirt, a blatant sexual appreciation of her figure.

'Nice blouse by the way. Vintage, right? Some things just seem to get better with age.' He grinned then winked before walking away, his hips rolling ever so slightly at the top of his long slim legs. It was another mannerism he'd practised in front of the mirror – ah, the insecurity of youth! Tigger, trying not to stare after him, reached for another drink.

'He's yours, for sure.' Elise had magically reappeared beside her.

'Is he?' Tigger groaned faintly, wondering whether she had the emotional stamina for such a sexual adventure.

*

The Velvet Glove was at the top end of the city in a narrow nineteen-thirties building. It had a small bar and dance floor on ground level with a roof garden on top. Iconic images from the sixties and seventies were projected on the back wall of the dance floor and electronic punk boomed out. Elise led the way through the crowd – mainly young art students and a few businessmen packed into the bar. Perspiration seemed to be steaming up from the young skin of the patrons to drip down the walls, which seemed to be sweating too. Tigger clutched her bag as she was shoved up tightly against young hot bodies. It was uncomfortable for her – if her personal space was to be invaded she liked the purpose to be clearly delineated, and she found that the promiscuity of such ambiguously close proximity was distressing.

Yet she was impressed with the respect her friend engendered: Elise was greeted like an honorary leader or muse. The young male art students – pretentious in their finery – waved at her, some even abandoning small entourages of fellow intellectuals to push their way over to the artist. Here Elise was queen, shouting introductions over the pounding beat, pointing to Tigger as if she were a trophy. Barely able to hear anyone over the music, Tigger smiled back blankly while surreptitiously scanning the room for Seth. She told me later that was all she could think about. But he was nowhere to be seen.

Surprised by the jolt of disappointment that ran through her like some love-struck teenager, Tigger reluctantly followed Elise into a booth by the dance floor. Mike – Elise's lover –

squeezed in beside them. While the two gossiped about the
gallery opening and cattily critiqued other artists' work, Tigger
took in the various courtships unfurling around her: nearby the
awkwardness of a lone bespectacled young girl hovering beside
a table reminded her of when she was young, how the hierarchy
of what was perceived as 'cool' dictated one's whole outlook
− and one's prospects. Tigger had been lucky, she'd been
attractive and in her youth the priorities were different − they
hadn't cared about money or material stability. Back then it had
been about experience, cramming in as much as they could and
escaping what they perceived as the terrible ennui of living in
Melbourne.

The hovering girl − who looked as if she'd just come in
from the country − was peering self-consciously from under the
long greasy hair hanging over her face. Tigger couldn't help
but feel her anguish and isolation. As she watched the young
artist fiddling nervously with the beads around her neck, Tigger
noticed a sudden change come over the girl: she lit up as if an
attractive man had just entered her orbit. Following her gaze,
Tigger saw that Seth now stood framed in the entrance to the
bar, the neon light outside making a silhouette of his tall slim
figure. Holding her breath she wondered whether the young girl
might be a lover of his, but then he glanced across at Tigger.
Her heart leapt like a teenager's. He nodded and she nodded
back, desperate not to appear too eager. Seth then made his
way through the crowded dance floor over to the bar. Even
surrounded by people pushing to reach the bar he appeared
curiously remote, his height and beauty making him stand out.
It was almost as if he carried an aura of faint light around those

glowering dark features. But I can tell you, he was completely oblivious to the power he held over others, which in retrospect might have been a good thing.

'Not only is he too young, he's also too beautiful,' Tigger thought to herself, trying to repress that old huntress impulse – sexual desire – that had by now formed a rope through the centre of her body, from her groin to the edges of her mouth, tugging deliciously, reminding her of how alive one can be. This rope seemed to run like a silver thread from her mouth, looping and curling around the dancers, over the glass-topped coffee tables and up Seth's trouser leg to curl lovingly around the tip of his penis beneath the denim, and he must have felt it. Indeed, I'm convinced he felt it.

Meanwhile the bar was becoming louder and more rowdy by the minute and all manner of couples ground slowly against each other on the dance floor – boys with boys, girls with girls, and boys with girls. The DJ, sitting in a raised glass booth in one corner, spun records, many of which were covers of older songs Tigger recognised, like revamped versions of 'Ziggy Stardust' by David Bowie or 'London Calling' by The Clash. The whole effect just amplified Tigger's feeling that she was in some curious time dimension in which elements of her own youth overlapped and intercut with the young people around her. She was jolted out of her reverie by the sudden shouting of male voices. Tigger looked up to discover that a young girl wearing a man's suit and see-through crocheted top had climbed on one of the coffee tables and was slowly stripping with her girlfriend – an uber-femme young creature in pencil skirt and bustier – to the vocal approval of the audience watching.

'Do you want to dance?' Seth had somehow managed to appear before her. The stealthy approach was another thing he'd perfected through practice. Tigger glanced apprehensively at the dance floor: she would be the oldest person dancing by at least fifteen years. Elise and Mike looked up from their conversation, watching her reaction. Elise grinned at Mike then turned back to Tigger.

'Tigger, the man's asked a question.'

Tigger looked back at Seth, shifting shyly on his feet.

'Come on, it's not that bad out there,' he smiled, 'and I promise I'll bite.'

If I remember correctly it was she who followed him out onto the dance floor. Luckily it was so packed it was hard to do anything more than shift one's hips from side to side, and out there, with the beat pounding up through the wooden floor, Tigger remembered that she used to be a good dancer, her natural sensuality arching through her body as she spun, lacing her hands through the air as her hips shook rhythmically to the music. Seth followed her movements in a muted mirroring. In those days Seth had real elegance for a tall man, putting to rest Tigger's fear that they would look ridiculous together.

The other dancers cleared a space for the weaving couple. Just then a Motown track came on that Tigger knew really well. She immediately fell into dance steps from decades ago, grinding her buttocks against Seth and as she did so she felt the blind promise of an erection. Wriggling closer, the hard bar of him felt large and alive while her arse felt so much like paradise to him that for a moment he worried the rubbing of her firm cheeks would make him come in his tight jeans. Trying to distract himself Seth glanced up at a high window where the moon hung against a velvet sky. It seemed to dance with them, adding to the illusion that they were at some ancient Dionysian orgy – a fervent joyous celebration of both youth and sex, uninhibited and innocently exhibitionist. It was then that he thought to himself, 'I shall never forget this moment no matter how old I live to be, how the years pull me down.' And you know what? He didn't.

They danced for another few songs then suddenly Tigger's energy left her. As if sensing this, Seth stopped dancing and pulled her to the edge of the dance floor.

'I think I need to get back to Elise's, that's who I'm staying with,' she murmured, unsure about the etiquette of the next step of seduction. She knew she couldn't take Seth back to Elise's house, so she waited for some indication from him.

'Can you give me a lift back? I'm banned from Australian roads.' He grinned cheekily.

'How come?'

'I got pulled over for drink driving. The crazy thing was, I was on my pushbike at the time. They decided not to book me when they heard my accent, but warned me if I got pulled over again they would fine me. Now I can't even cycle back home,' he answered, feeling like a total idiot.

Christ, she thought, he hasn't even got a car, but the image of a police car pulling over a bicyclist weaving drunkenly across the road made her smile. Besides, what harm would there be in merely driving him home? She was already talking herself out of a seduction that might seem brutally revealing and unwise in the blazing light of the next day.

'I have a hire car parked outside.'

*

Tigger drove the hire car carefully, suspecting she might be over the limit herself. They drove through the streets of North Melbourne, an area she used to live in as a student, decades before. Memories loomed up as the car turned into streets she hadn't been in since then, but what had been small low-rent cottages lived in by poor immigrants and students was now gentrified, and many of the broader streets had lines of trees running down the centre. In her youth the area had been run-down and vibrant in a dangerous way and had made all her peers feel as if they were the first rebels to rise out of the greener suburbs encircling the CBD.

'It's here.'

They pulled up outside an elegant Victorian terrace. Tigger glanced across at the house surprised; she'd imagined he would live in humbler accommodation. Reading her reaction Seth told her the owners had just rented it to him and his two roommates while putting it on the market to sell.

He stayed sitting in the car, trapped in that awkward moment so many men find themselves in – whether to make the first move and risk rejection or be dictated to by the fear of rejection and just leave. Seth didn't want to leave. He wanted her.

'Would you like to come in for a cup of tea?' he asked in the sexiest voice he could muster. He stared out of the car window as nonchalantly as he could, as if by looking at her he might jinx her response. Tigger told me later the offer was so quaint and unexpected from a man who looked as if he would have been more comfortable wielding a microphone or a whip rather than a teapot, she had trouble not to burst out laughing.

'I do have to get some directions back to Elise's place …' she responded, careful to keep her own face turned away.

'… And I do have a map inside.'

They both swung around to face each other at the same time, suddenly becoming shy now that they were away from the anonymity of the bar with its noise and transient intimacy.

'Tea and directions then.' She started to unbuckle her seatbelt, praying that the lights weren't too bright inside his house and that he wouldn't get a shock seeing her full age.

Inside, the narrow entrance hall was awash with dirty clothes. Torn posters hung off the walls and a couple of bikes were pushed up against the new white paint. The lights were on, the front door ajar, and yet the house appeared empty.

Two bedrooms ran off the narrow Victorian corridor, both doors gaping open to reveal maelstroms of unmade beds, discarded jeans, underpants, abandoned weights, PlayStations, half-read magazines and other male messes she didn't care to examine too closely. It also smelt. It's hard to describe how badly it smelt – old runners and the musky scent of young men – but none of us cared. Tigger grimaced.

'What do you expect? I live with two twenty-four-year-old men,' Seth answered her grimace before leading her into the kitchen and lounge area adorned with a retro vinyl sofa and a small table covered with a miniature film set made entirely of Lego. A laptop was wired up to a tiny camera, also made of Lego but with a real lens. Seth sauntered across the room to switch on a CD player. Tigger found his movements so seductive that she had to put her hands behind her back to stop herself from reaching out for him. Again, she was secretly appalled at her own lechery, but Christ she wanted him. Did it show?

The melancholic tones of Leonard Cohen filled the room giving Tigger a bizarre sensation of déjà vu.

'Who listens to Leonard Cohen these days?'

'I do.' Again, Seth tried not to sound defensive. Tigger stopped herself from telling him that Leonard Cohen was one of her mother's favourite singers, figuring mothers, family or anything that enabled him to pin down her age might be unwise. Desperate to change the subject she walked over to the miniature Lego film set.

'You play with Lego?' She failed to keep amazement out of her voice.

Insulted, Seth now stood with a teapot in hand. 'It's not just any old Lego, it's a model of a Spielberg set. You can point the camera around the interiors and play the image back on the computer.'

To Tigger it seemed like an adult manifestation of a childlike interest; she could feel Seth watching her. Acutely aware of her own body language and his proximity, she sat down awkwardly, sinking into the old vinyl couch. She glanced back at the model, trying to work out which Spielberg film the set was from — suddenly she recognised the strange mould in the front room of the miniature bungalow.

'*Close Encounters of the Third Kind*, right? Richard Dreyfuss's house?'

'You got it!'

'It was that scene where he's obsessively trying to recreate the mountain the aliens are going to land on – I'll never forget it.'

'Yeah, it's my favourite scene, too.'

'I loved the way he used dream, creative expression and coincidence to drive those people to tell their experience of the UFOs ...'

'But that's how it is, isn't it? In real life. We glean intelligence from all different kinds of sources. Experience isn't linear, it's a collage.'

Christ, can I remember the kid's passion, his blind conviction, like it was yesterday. Now Seth watched Tigger, wary that he'd given too much of himself away. To his delight she smiled.

'Are you sure you're only interested in being a curator? You talk like an artist.'

He took a deep breath in, wondering if he could trust her, really trust her.

'I do draw, small sketches. But I've never shown anyone. I don't think they're good enough.'

'Show me.'

The sudden whistle of the kettle boiling interrupted them.

Seth put the teacups and teapot down on the coffee table in front of Tigger then walked over to an old chest of drawers in one corner. He reached into the bottom drawer and pulled out two small thick sketchpads.

Seth sat down beside her, noting the closeness of her body. The warmth of his leg running alongside her own, the elegance of her slender thighs. He placed the sketchpads on the coffee table, his hands hovering over them for a moment, almost reverently.

He dared not look at her; not wanting to betray his nervousness at such exposure, but then, I remember, he reasoned to himself: 'This is a woman who doesn't know me – her opinion will be entirely objective, what have I got to lose?'

'You sure you want to look at them?'

'Of course I do. And trust me, I'm known for my brutal honesty and I know good art when I see it.'

'These are from my travels. The first sketchpad is Europe, the second is Asia.'

He pushed the sketchpads towards her. She picked the first one up and opened it. The image was startling: a mass of thick black pencil lines and smudged charcoal, a bull charging a bullfighter. The energy of the collision between the two was palpable, dynamic and undeniably sensual. She flicked the page – the next was of a young girl emerging from the sea. Her thin pubescent body just about to break into adulthood seemed like a metaphor for her emergence from the ocean itself. Again, the drawing was frenetic, both sparse and dense – the rhythm of the image itself suggesting a maturity far beyond the years of the youth sitting in front of her.

'These are extraordinary,' she murmured, unable to keep the awe from her voice.

'You're having me on.'

'No really, Seth, this has to be your career, promise me.'

He gazed at her. No one had ever really believed him capable of anything extraordinary before, not his parents, not his teachers, not any of his other lovers – which frankly for his age had been rather a lot. A great energy suddenly roared through him as her belief crystallised something that up until then had been vague, nebulous. Together they pored over the open book, their heads almost touching. Seth flicked through the pages excitedly.

'This was Spain, this was Morocco, after that I went over to Algeria …'

His fingers both animalistic and elegant distracted her momentarily from the drawings. Tigger found herself wondering about the shape and size of his penis, as often she had noticed a correlation between the two.

Sensing her distraction he looked up suddenly and their faces almost bumped. Then just as suddenly he reached across and kissed her, pushing her back onto the couch as his tongue found her tongue. His lips, intelligent in their exploration, took her lips, softly biting, catching at her tongue, both of them now swallowing each other in an orchestration of promised lovemaking, of technique, of knowing how to fuck, how to make love, how to lose oneself in the pure sharp heat of good sex. His hands reached down into her blouse to cup her breasts, both of them forgetting themselves entirely in that instant rush of eclipsing lust. It was one of those moments that so easily could not have happened, a decisive act of courage, one that would change lives.

He led her up to his bedroom, a small room off the landing. Sheets were draped across the window and there was a mattress on the floor. Piles of books rested up against the walls which were painted black: a young man's bedroom – a very young man's bedroom.

In fact she told me, only a few months ago, that at this point she found herself suddenly wanting to run, as if sensing that perhaps this might be more momentous than she consciously realised. 'What am I doing here?' she'd thought to herself. 'Why now do I want to run and from what? Uncomplicated blinding pleasure? From possible heartbreak? From the sheer vulnerability of nakedness – emotional and physical?' These and a hundred other doubts flashed through her mind in a kaleidoscope of apprehension.

She stood in the middle of the room not knowing what to do next. There was nowhere to sit so she stayed standing, wondering how many other women had stood there feeling just as anxious – a shadow-line of past conquests trailing from her trembling hand. Seth, oblivious, lit some candles, slipped a CD into the player in the corner, then led her to the bed.

He began to pull her clothes off in clumsy haste, wanting her right then but, a little put off, she stopped him with a smile. And what a smile. I still remember it, a tantalising half-smile of experience, a smile that said 'I am going to lead'. Teasingly, she slowly lifted her dress up over her shoulders, now regretting the rather functional white cotton underpants she'd worn that night, but thankful for the push-up bra which displayed her full bosom to advantage.

Taking charge she pushed him back so that he knelt opposite her. His green eyes, captivated by her body, glinted in the candlelight. His cheekbones and mouth, she later told me, looked like a prism of sharp planes all promising sensual assault. Tigger could smell his sweet young sweat mixed with a salty tang, as if he might have been swimming or surfing earlier that day. It radiated off him and filled her nostrils with forgotten memories of youth, of fucking in sunlight in some beach house, blonde hair and sandy skin of aeons ago, and in that faded memory Tigger forgot who she was and where she was. Everything now narrowed down to one sharp point of pure desire, both of them so fiercely in the moment. To Seth's delight she suddenly wrenched his T-shirt over his head and flung it to the other side of the bed.

Of classical proportions his shoulders were broad, his chest and stomach a washboard of compact youthful muscle. There was a faint dusting of chest hair between his dark but pronounced, erect nipples. Tigger had forgotten how hairless and smooth-skinned younger men were. Tigger thought this man was beautiful, as beautiful as he would ever be. Awe rose in her throat like sorrow and she paused, rocking back on her heels.

Seth reached across and pulled the sheet from the window. Moonlight flooded the room and settled like white snow along the curves of his chest and thighs. They were both now kneeling face to face. He was watching her like an animal, knowing there was nothing in his gaze except the need to fuck. He lifted one hand and unbearably slowly ran a finger across her lips and down to one breast. Lifting it out over the bra cup he teased the nipple, a slow tracing circle followed by a sharp pinch that sent a taut spike of erotic excitement down to her groin.

'Don't move,' he commanded, watching the growing excitement in her face like a professional. He ran his fingers down her torso, tracing her moist clit through the thin cotton. Tigger closed her eyes. Her thighs were trembling. Her breasts ached as if they wanted to be bitten, to be taken into his mouth, the nipples hard for him. She opened her eyes again. Seth was smiling at her, his fingers pressed into the wet crack of her vagina through her panties. He was still wearing his jeans, the bulge of his erection straining against the cloth.

'Your turn.' His voice was almost a growl. He moved even closer, so that they were now only centimetres apart, and suddenly she understood the game he was playing; he was manipulating the erotic charge between them like an invisible balloon that swelled and grew tauter according to how aroused they were. It was the kind of heightened foreplay you could only have with strangers, when there was nothing at stake except the sex you were about to have – no emotional expectation, no history, no guilt or secrets. Tigger couldn't remember the last time she'd felt as excited, or liberated.

She leant forward. She could smell him now, a delicious perfume of sweat and musky cologne undercut with the smell of excitement, of the sex pheromone. His eyes were narrowed like a lion's, a sheen on his skin glistening in the light. She pulled his lower lip into her mouth and pressed her teeth down gently. He groaned. She then raked her nails across his shoulders, over his nipples and down the centre of his midriff, hard enough to let him know who was in control. His skin was impossibly soft, impossibly youthful, but she wanted his cock. Her fingers found the buttons of his fly, for a moment her clumsy fumbling made the invisible balloon of erotic tension between them deflate. Finally she released him, the weight of his cock falling against her palm. His cock was long and of decent girth, like his capable fingers. She couldn't believe her luck.

He arched his back, pushing his groin proudly towards her like a gift, but in those days he was arrogant like that. She hauled his jeans down over his hips and, falling back, he wriggled out of them, now naked and gloriously erect, his cock appearing thick against his slim hips, his mouth and hands now greedy in their abandonment. After burying her face in the sweetness of his testicles she took him into her mouth. The length of him almost made her gag. After circling the bulbous sticky tip with her tongue she took him deep into her throat, feeling his excitement rise like sap.

'Stop, I don't want to come like this.' He pushed her head away and sat up. 'Come here.'

She moved towards him as he pulled her underpants off and, reaching behind her, undid her bra, her breasts falling heavy against his chest. He then pulled himself beneath her so that his face was under her sex.

'No, stop,' she groaned, but he didn't stop.

Tigger pressed her hot face against the wall, faintly appalled at his obvious sexual prowess and experience. This was no virgin. She could feel her own excitement building and building down in the kernel of her body. She couldn't remember the last time a man had served her like this. Certainly sex with the ex in the last months of their relationship had deteriorated into her serving him, a warning sign Tigger should perhaps have heeded. But here, now, Seth was an entirely different proposition.

Close to coming herself she pulled her hips away from his mouth. Lowering herself down she was relieved to find him as hard as before if not harder. The tip of his cock now rested just inside her lips. This was a moment Tigger always relished in lovemaking, a tantalising lingering tease, the moment before bearing down and being filled by a delicious tightness. Tigger had always regarded this as the litmus test of sexual compatibility – whether the man filled you or not. For her it was a harbinger of what was to come: she was convinced that a sensible woman should take heed if they did not, for inevitably this misfit would sooner or later become an issue in the relationship.

Slowly, she pushed down onto his cock. The sense of being filled was overwhelming, a visceral reminder of what it was to be female, to be the receiver. She rode him faster and faster, clasping herself tightly around him. Then suddenly he pushed her up and after slipping both his hands under each of her buttocks, lifted her up first onto his knees then, with her legs curled firmly around his back, into a standing position. Carrying her, still inside her, he walked over to the wall and pushed her hard against it as he slowly began thrusting, getting faster and faster. Their mouths pressed together, his tongue thrusting in and out in time with his cock. The power play was reversed; now he dominated, abandoning himself to his own pleasure. Paradoxically, this excited Tigger, who was so used to the self-consciousness of lovemaking with her ex, both of them too involved with the necessity of pleasing each other to the point of ridiculous sacrifice and some disingenuousness. But this was different. Immediate, primal, unabashedly self-serving, it was as if they were there to serve some invisible god – ancient, wild, instinctive. Seth slowed his pace then paused, allowing the ripples of sensual throbbing to vibrate through their bodies. They both came screaming.

She watched him sleeping, his fluttering eyelids a veil of surrender across his face. Suddenly he looked younger than his twenty-one years, and it was hard not to feel that she had exploited him. Apparently she took solace in deciding that his sexual prowess had indicated a decadent and far from innocent lifestyle – at least that's what she told me.

Tigger glanced at the window, the sheet now hanging down, the moon half in, cut by the diagonal edge. There was a promised timelessness in the faint scent of night jasmine, the distant roar of traffic. Her whole body was abuzz with the warm afterglow of orgasm, her deliciously aching muscles languid in their pain. She felt alive, capable of anything. She felt, for the first time in years, as if her whole future was stretched out before her and, more importantly, contained every possibility imaginable.

Over her shoulder she heard Seth groan and turn in his sleep. She looked around, surprised that the thin blue light of dawn had already begun to illuminate the student squalor of the room: the pile of dirty linen in the corner, a pair of worn-down runners still filled with the ghost of feet at the end of the bed. An ashtray overflowing with cigarette butts and screwed-up cigarette papers, the stained and worn carpet, the dust piled up in the corners. And all those one-night stands she'd had as a student came flooding back – the sexual conquests, some of which were the climax to an elaborate courtship, some not, but all of which she remembered. And all those early mornings she'd wasted lying there, watching some young man sleeping in a post-coital stupor, her own eyelids pinned back by hope, praying that he would want to stay for breakfast then perhaps even the whole day, and then after that who knows …?

Dawn had now crept along the bed covers and was minutes away from falling over Seth's sleeping face. Tigger suddenly caught sight of herself in the chipped mirror resting up against the wall. Her body looked flushed but voluptuous, her soft middle-aged belly a curve of an earlier aesthetic, her breasts now pendulous. She examined her face: the make-up from the night before was smudged down both cheeks and those crow's feet that now came from not sleeping and were impossible to conceal had appeared like the lines on fine parchment. The morning would not be kind, so as silently as she could manage, Tigger slipped out of bed and grabbed her handbag, underwear and dress, not daring to dress in the bedroom in case she woke Seth. Standing in the musky corridor just outside the door, she slipped on her clothes and tiptoed out of the house.

Outside the air was alive with a chorus of birds. Stepping back into her rental car was like stepping back in time, to 'before'. She started the engine up, jolting the radio into life, and as she drove through the sleeping city, accompanied only by garbage trucks crawling like giant beetles through the dawn streets and the occasional cab driver racing to get off his night shift, she realised she hadn't felt this free in years.

And this is where I come in. I remember I slept through until about one in the afternoon that day only to be woken by the afternoon sun streaming in. I remember reaching across the bed in that half-awake daze, hoping to find her, hoping she'd stayed. Even thirty years later I remember the intense sense of loss and, more than that, the overpowering sense that I had to follow her, to make her mine.

Seth looked up from the fireplace. A handsome man now in his early fifties, bereavement had nevertheless made its recent mark. May hadn't deliberately prompted such an intense confession but had stayed back after the wake of Joanna Wutherer, her old anthropology lecturer, sensing that Joanna's younger husband needed to talk, to exorcise some memory of the woman he loved. What she hadn't calculated on was the power and sensuality of the story of the couple's first night together. It was embarrassing, moving and confronting all at the same time. But then what did she expect from a painter famous for his erotic drawings?

May glanced across at one of Seth's drawings hanging above the artist's head. It was a recent one of Joanna – even dying Seth had captured the seventy-year-old's beauty and vivaciousness. He really was a great artist.

Somewhere in the house the female voice of a computer announced the time. It was nine pm and May knew she had to get a ten o'clock flight back to Sydney and her family, but there was something both poignant and faintly seductive about Seth's grief. He was the kind of man that you wanted to comfort, to hold even …

'Thirty years, May, thirty years of happiness. What do I do now?' He asked softly.

PUSSY AND MOUSE

Where I live has kind of closed down the last two years, a little like me. I've closed down. I now wear my life on the inside, like a second luminous skin no one else can see. Unless they know me another way. The only way. My name is Cassandra Whool. Kind of a fancy name for a twenty-two stone, thirty-eight-year-old woman who you wouldn't look at twice. I mean, hey, I wouldn't look at me twice. But I guess my parents didn't know that when they named me. Cassandra I believe was some crazy Greek mystic. There ain't nothing mystic or mysterious about me, except in my head. In my imagination.

I live in Southern California, in a new development north of San Diego. We were one of the first to move in five years ago. It consists of rows and rows of small white stucco houses, each with identical garages and a small yard at the back. It's gated and just off the 5 freeway. They call it the Greenways Community, which is surprising to me because I ain't seen much community except for the Fed Ex guy and the Mormons who sometimes knock on my door, and since the drought there's nothing much green except the golf course next door.

I moved in with my mom, but she passed three years ago leaving me with a $40,000 mortgage and a room full of them porcelain heritage dolls that she collected. I have no other family except one sister who lives in Encinitas – she married a hippie artist and now has seven children. We argued about God years ago and I ain't seen her since, except for Mom's funeral. None of her kids have amounted to anything, 'cept for the youngest, Seth, who's living in Australia. Seth. I used to babysit him before me and my sister quarrelled. Cute kid. Now it's like I'm alone since Mom died. I still ain't cleared out her bedroom and her clothes are still hanging in her cupboard. Sold the dolls, though. I hated them dolls. But Mom, she left a hole in this house like a runaway train. Sometimes when I'm sitting here of an evening I hear her calling out from her bedroom. It's the strangest thing.

Like I said before, around here things have kind of closed down. People are losing their homes, their houses repossessed before they even have time to put their own furniture into the place. It's getting ugly and I'm happy I have kept my job, thank the good Lord. I mean, it ain't a career, but it's a living, a place where I get money for just answering the phone but that's more than most folks have got these days.

The Tolgate Call Center, Head Office, La Mesa, Southern California is where I work. It's called the head office because I guess it once was the head office. Now it's about the last call centre left in the United States of America. The rest of them have moved to Mumbai or Delhi or one of them places that are economically blossoming, while here in God's own they're saying Capitalism is dying with a big groan and a small c. As if I care.

My workplace? It's a big old building in the back of a shopping mall that looks like every other shopping mall north of the Mexican border. In other words, a large anonymous concrete building, open plan, with about a hundred of us at our switchboards, headphones on, answering them calls from all over the country. Plastic palm trees inside, real ones outside. But the building has air con and the job health insurance and the boss is a relaxed kind of guy. The partitions around my desk are placed so that my computer is concealed from the other workers. I am the only one there to have a third partition. This is my privilege as the longest-serving employee. Twelve years I've been answering phones in that building, day shift only. I even have a plaque on my desk that reads: 'Cassandra Whool, C.C. La Mesa, employee of the decade', C.C. standing for call centre of course, but the dumb thing is that I am the only employee of the decade, considering the other workers that come through only last six months or maybe a year. There's too much echo coming off the white walls, bouncing back all their personal grief and misery for most folk. See, I have something they don't. I have Second Life.

Second Life is where I do my living: every lunchtime and from seven to eleven every night at home. Why, I even eat my dinner in front of the computer screen, but that being said, putting real-life food into my real-life body is secondary to booting up the computer. In truth booting up is more important. That machine is my window into happiness, into forgetting myself. Since I became a member of the Second Life community on 13 May 2006, my real life has faded away into periods of grey time, of waiting until I log on again. Second Life is my ecstasy and my salvation. It allows this great hefty body of mine to escape gravity, to soar. It gives me a portal through which there is hope, light, colour and best of all – sex. Yep, you heard me, sex: great, forbidden, pornographic dreamscapes in which I am queen and hallelujah to that.

Okay, I can hear you all preaching at me already. I mean for all I know you could be a born-again Christian or even a Charismatic. Lord knows there's enough of them around here, but the way I see it is that a woman is a woman. And even if she don't look like it, don't think there ain't a thread of desire in her. Call it sin, call it what you like, but that drum is gonna keep beating. And what could I do? I ain't had a man since 1990, and that was a drunken one-night stand. I'd given up even talking to the opposite sex with any romantic intention because I'm a realist – no man is going to take on a big heifer like me, not in this world anyway. I wanted to meet people, but not like this, not like me in real life – IRL.

It started innocently enough. I think my first visit to Second Life was to Holiday Paradise Island, kind of like a futuristic Club Med where everyone is beautiful, slim and young and some of them even had tails and wings, but everyone was kind of nice and friendly – and best of all, no judgement. My avatar was cute but she was no great shakes. So when I was approached for sex, I could not wait. I immediately went to Xcite and got me some genitals and nipples and upgraded my skin. And suddenly that thread of desire in me began to take shape and became my avatar now – Tasinis – everything I am not in real life. Let me put you in the picture: the real me – Cassandra Whool has short brown hair that is too thin to grow long, small brown eyes and pasty skin that is discoloured by large sunspots. My mouth is my best feature but at my size it's kind of buried by my cheeks. My dress size is 22, I can't remember the last time I saw my feet, my breasts hang down to my waist and I'm five foot one inch tall.

The 'skin' that I originally used to construct Tasinis cost me over 4000 Lindens and I got a Second Life artist to design her specially to my instructions. My avatar is six foot tall, with waist-length strawberry-blonde hair that flows down in those Barbie-doll waves. She has wide hips, a narrow waist, broad shoulders and DD cup breasts. I gave her super long legs with the latest Xcite interactive thighs, which cost me half a week's pay packet. I've also got Tasinis a special edition clit and long X3 nipples that can actually get erect. Finally I gave her this really sexy deep voice, kind of like Aretha Franklin meets Eartha Kitt – with a growl. Okay, some might find her kind of a gender-bender, but I like it. It's the kind of voice that makes men hard and the hairs stand up on the back of your neck. Constructing Tasinis was like playing God. It was like giving birth. It was the most creative thing I have ever done in my whole miserable goddamn life. I swear it.

I had five outfits designed for her but my favourite is an armour-like corset that cuts above her thighs exposing her crotch and ass, and thigh-high stiletto-heeled leather boots with silver spurs that can convert into small silver wings. There's a clip-on belt she wears on special occasions that has pockets for Xcite toys such as a silver dildo, a small silver-handled whip, steel handcuffs and an Xcite Violet Wand. The only non-human addition I gave her was a small pair of silver horns that poke up through her thick blonde hair. I'm telling you, she is mighty fine looking.

Tasinis is twenty-three – she hasn't had a birthday since I enabled her four years ago while in real life I'm thirty-eight going on fifty. And I can't remember the last time I stood in front of the mirror naked. In truth I can't remember the last time I was aware of feeling anything more than cold and warmth on my human skin. In Second Life Tasinis orgasms all the time, which is ironic because I don't reckon I've ever had an orgasm – not by myself, not with anyone else IRL, not once. I mean, it's not like I don't feel anything. I get excited when Tasinis comes, but my body – well, it's asleep, dormant like some huge hibernating animal that's never been woken up. Maybe I don't like myself enough to let go. You know even when I was young I found the feel of my own body revolting. I've never even masturbated. I tried once in the shower when I was about sixteen, but Mom walked into the bathroom and told me I was committing a sin. It was real traumatic. I started to eat big after that. It was like I was punishing her by not growing into one of those perfect petite china dolls she collected. Wow, I've never told anyone that, not ever. Now I'm making up for it big time through Tasinis, through my avatar. And, Mom, if you're up there in heaven I hope you can hear this, because my Tasinis is the most sinful kick-ass dirty-chick doll you're ever gonna see. And she has no trouble pleasuring herself or anyone else for that matter. I even gave her labia that light up when she's aroused to let the other avatars know. I made her the goddamn sexiest avatar in the whole wide Second Life, and it worked. She's a star, a cyber idol, while out here in the real world I am less and less visible. I mean hey, I could die of a heart attack in my bed one day and I don't reckon anyone would come looking, but if Tasinis left the net there would be a riot. I swear it. She is that famous.

I'll never forget the day I introduced her to the dark side of Second Life. I clicked on Gothic Dungeon Sex Island and flew Tasinis in. As soon as I saw her there floating like a huge love goddess in the perfect blue sky, I was her. A horde gathered to watch me as I hovered over the dark forest that stood in front of a gothic castle, breasts heaving and my long blonde hair undulating in the cyber-wind like tendrils. It was Kali meets Barbie and

226

the Ice Queen all in the same massive sex doll, and it felt like total power, total adoration. And for somebody who was used to people averting their eyes from them, this was enormous, it was the nearest thing to love I'd ever experienced.

I made Tasinis yell, 'I have arrived!' and the crowd roared. Tasinis didn't even make it to the huge wooden front door, I couldn't resist all those arms reaching out for her. I floated her down and let them pull her to the ground. In seconds Tasinis was involved in a group orgy that was a hundred times more exciting than anything I'd thought up in my imagination. It was kind of shocking yet thrilling. It was like civilisation stripped back to the bone, to raw instinct. But I wised up. Next time I visited the island I equipped Tasinis with a whip twirling wildly in one hand and a nightstick raised in the other. Immediately several avatars flung themselves down, begging Tasinis to flagellate them. I've never felt so powerful or so wanted. That pure feeling of control and dominance charged through me as I sat at my desk, my waistband cutting into my belly, the loose T-shirt hanging down to my knees to conceal my weight, the heat sticking the cotton to my back and armpits.

It had been a really bad morning – some of the workers were away sick and the boss had shouted at me – but I swear, when I logged on to Second Life that lunchtime, watching Tasinis standing victorious over the other grovelling avatars, the curling lash of her whip coming down again and again, was the most sexually exciting thing that had ever happened to me. It was like I was finally somebody. I was finally visible.

Just before I left for home that day my boss came in to tell me he had taken on a night worker who was to share my desk.

'A guy called Hector Lopez, a Latino, a nice guy. A loner like you, I think his wife's passed recently. Not that you'll ever get to meet him,' he joked.

Lately I've been spending more than six hours a day on Second Life, on Xcite and Gothic Dungeon Sex Island. Maybe I have an addiction, but hey, it's not like I'm doing drugs or crime. All I can think about is getting back inworld, to the chains, the whipping posts, the pain/pleasure on my victims' faces, the flashing pose balls, and the creak of the dungeon doors played over and over again. Tasinis has become top bitch, the ultimate dominatrix. Folk fly in from all parts of Second Life just to be whipped by her. There is even a fan club that meets every month to exchange stories. And last month a Second Life rock star named Lassorow composed a song about Tasinis and it's number five in the Second Life charts.

But the really weird thing is that I should feel good, I should be firing, but lately when I've gone in I haven't got the same kicks watching my avatar blindfold and humiliate some blond avatar, erect penis flashing. Something's missing. I feel it and Tasinis feels it.

The night worker who shares my desk, this Hector Lopez, he starts 7 pm then leaves 5 am. I start 9 am and leave 5 pm. We haven't met and we won't ever meet. I can't get a read on him, and why should I, given that he's nothing but a seat warmer. There's nothing on the desk that's personal. Nothing. Unless you count my collection of souvenir pencils with different sands in them I bought in Tijuana. But he hasn't messed with my things. To me he is like a shadow, someone who flitters across my space and is forgotten by the morning. Of course, no one at work, including

Hector, knows about Tasinis or what I'm like on Second Life. I only ever play on my laptop and I take it everywhere I go.

So there was this day and it would have been like any other day in that I got up, ate my usual oatmeal, maple syrup and blueberries, 'cept when I looked at the calendar on the fridge I realised it was my birthday. 'Shoot,' I said to myself, 'Cass, there's no one left to know that since Mom died three years ago,' and it promised to be another hollow, dry sort of day only maybe a little sadder.

So while I was stuck on the 5 in my clapped-out Civic Honda between Escondido and Carmel Valley I got to thinking about what might be waiting for me that afternoon on Second Life and how in my real life lately I'd started to dream from Tasinis's point of view like I was actually trapped in there, in her body, those long legs floating above the ground, my skin so smooth, so soft and tight, like I was agile, taut like I imagine an athlete might feel. And me/Tasinis, we were swinging that whip but there was no heart left, nothing but a faint curiosity, like maybe we'd tortured one too many, like all them chisel-jawed, big-dicked avatars with their cheesy come-on lines like 'Give it to me, big mama' had started to look the same, even the ones with the wings, the tails and the hermaphrodite options. Then my freeway exit came up and before I knew it I was at work again, parking in the parking lot along with a hundred other workers, with the morning sun already coming down like thin white knives burning the back of the brain, and then I was at my desk answering the phone, my mind on automatic, like some friggin' sleepwalker waiting to be woken up, a junkie hanging out for her fix, a baby screaming for her mother's milk, until five came around and I knew as soon as I logged on I would be alive again.

*

Gothic Dungeon Sex Island: 18.03 6/30/09

Tasinis is perched on a rafter of the Dungeon, long legs swinging, just observing the scene unfurling below. I'm in the zone, like there is no time here, and if there was, I reckon it would pass real slowly. There are three pose balls in the area, two blue and one red. In the sawdust-covered arena below, several avatars are tied by the wrists to whipping posts, two male avatars and one female. An avatar with dark skin, dragon wings and a ridiculously huge black cock stands in the centre, his arm holding a long whip which repeatedly descends with a jerking motion when the tail of his whip catches the buttocks of the three prisoners. Automated cries sound out from one of the men and the young girl; the second man seems to have the wrong sound pack attached as shrill female yelps of pleasure appear to be coming from his wagging genitals. Time to make myself known.

I leap down from the rafters, my long blonde hair streaming up behind me as I fly through the air. I land, strong interactive thighs parted for action.

'Welcome, Mistress Tasinis. I am your slave, your love pump puppy,' Hercules10, one of the male avatars tied to the whipping post, the one with the steel cock ring, says, his disconcertingly high-pitched voice emerging suddenly from my laptop speakers.

'Utter not a word, you filthy dog, I will make you howl,' I instruct Tasinis to growl back while prodding him with my Xcite Violet Wand. Over and over, harder and harder.

'Ouch! Ouch! Ohh, ohh!' he whimpers, showing his appreciation by flashing little lightning streaks that strobe up and down his erect member. I make Tasinis yawn. Her indifference drives him crazy. Suddenly in real life a gardener walks past my window with a noisy leaf blower. I get up and pull down the blind. The sound fades away but the spell is almost broken.

By the time I shuffle back to my desk there's a new visitor to the Dungeon, an avatar I haven't seen before. He's slim and tall like all the others, but there's something different about him I don't recognise at first. And then I get it – there are some deliberate flaws in his 'skin'. For example, his nose and mouth are both slightly crooked, and his hair, instead of the usual generic perfection of Second Life, is uneven, long and messy. In stark contrast to his physical features he appears to be dressed in an expensive suit, made by one of the top designers in Second Life. He looks like he's wandered into the wrong area. This is really confusing as Second Lifers all know it requires both money and motivation to access the Xcite adult locations: no one just stumbles in.

I'm curious; this contrived naivety is kind of sexy. I touch my mouse and move Tasinis closer. She/I look down at him from the height of her five-inch spiked boots. I say nothing.

The new avatar appears a little nervous and his arms flutter up and down like his operator doesn't quite know what to do with him. He looks around with an almost ironic expression then suddenly sits on a blue pose ball. Immediately the pose ball's animated sexual instructions begin as the avatar is thrown into one sexual position after another. The first has him on all fours; at the second command he leaps to his feet and starts gyrating his crotch, and finally he sticks his tongue out and starts waggling it suggestively. 'Hi, I am Starboy 8 and I would like to suck your cock ...' He appears to be talking to me. 'I mean clit. No, I mean ... DAMN IT!' The words flash in the instant messenger box as the newcomer struggles with the technicalities of cybering. I peer closer. It seems Starboy 8's creator hasn't bothered buying the software to give him a voice and the avatar is reduced to communicating the old-fashioned way, via voice messenger. I guess he is a greenhorn to the whole Second Life experience and has decided to go play with the big boys without learning how to catch first.

Just then Starboy 8 leaps up off the pose ball and appears to wobble slightly on his feet. I make Tasinis stride over to him. His face is at breast height so to make him feel more at ease I erect her nipples as if the sight of him has aroused her. This is a compliment in Xcite world but unfortunately one of them looks like it's poking him straight in the eye. Confused, Starboy 8 stumbles back on long gazelle-like legs.

'Hey, Starboy, you are way out of your league here. This is serious fetish town and besides …' Tasinis's husky voice booms through the place. I look him up and down, my gaze stopping at his Ken-doll-blank penis-less crotch. The avatar flicks her hair dismissively back over her shoulder. '… you seem to be missing some very basic accessories.'

'Yeah, fuck off, neuter! We have some Sodom and Gomorrah to get on with here!' One of the chained avatars is getting impatient. Starboy 8 gazes up at Tasinis.

'You're beautiful. There is no love here. I could rescue you.' I stare at the typed words emerging letter by letter. The guy hasn't even got an audio pack. This isn't a sex trade, it's some kind of romance whitewash. I can't believe the audacity, but also the ingenuousness, just where does this guy think he is?

'This is a sex dungeon, not Lovescape, and I'm a consenting adult. I don't need rescuing, buddy.'

'If you don't need rescuing, why are you always in here losing yourself?'

Dragonman marches towards the new boy who backs up against a nail-studded torture rack. Starboy 8's attitude has started to upset the natives. Tasinis drops her whip in surprise. Pushing past Dragonman, Starboy 8 picks it up and hands it back to her.

'Bye,' he types in softly before vanishing. Behind Tasinis the three chained avatars begin whimpering and wriggling their hips expectantly. For a moment I swear I hear Tasinis sigh before reaching down into her belt for her strap-on dildo.

That night I couldn't sleep. Maybe it was the heat; when you get to be as big as I was, you learn to dread the summer. Maybe it was just because it was my birthday and I was one year closer to forty, the year my daddy dropped dead because of his heart. And I was convinced I would be going the same way. I lay there hating myself, the silence of the whole housing complex folding around me as my sweat seeped into the sheets. I hadn't engaged emotionally in real time like that for a while and it wasn't pleasant. But something had shifted in my universe, a small thing, a thing I couldn't name but could sense growing.

The next morning was a Saturday but I was going into work anyhow as I always worked the weekends for the extra cash – cash I would usually spend by Wednesday shopping in Second Life. I had my reputation to maintain. I mean, damn it, who would have guessed that Cassandra Whool was a cyber celebrity? But I was, or at least Tasinis was. And she *was* part of me, wasn't she?

I got up, showered, pulled on the old track pants and sweater I always wear on the weekends then glanced in the mirror on the back of the bathroom door to check my hair was at least in a civilised condition. The mirror, full length, was taped up with cardboard so that I could see only my head and shoulders in the reflection. I'd taped on the cardboard years ago, just after Mom died. It made me feel better. It made me feel like my body below my neck did not belong to me but someone else, someone that was a lot heavier than Cassandra from the neck up.

That morning my hair was looking kind of greasy and thin. I ran a comb through it cussing. I've always thought grooming for a woman like me is a waste of time. Smoothing a tuft down I grabbed my morning donut and rushed out to the car. While I was trying to get down the driveway as fast as my weight allowed me, a pain shot through my chest like a tight belt crushing my ribs. I stopped and rested, my hand on the garage wall. For a minute it eased off and I climbed into the car. I kept thinking that if my time was up I wanted to go quickly like Pop and not slowly and painfully like Mom. She took months dying, and her insurance ran out. No one deserves to die like that, not even my mother.

In this part of the world your car becomes an extension of yourself, a metal cocoon to navigate the racing strips of time and noise that are the freeways. Everything else is an island attached to the end of these strips: the shopping mall, the call centre, the gated community and the nature reserve. I like driving because no one can see me. It's the only time in real life I feel empowered, like my body is my car, my real body invisible. The races were on at the Del Mar track that day and I was clever to miss the traffic, lines and lines of cars slowly moving bumper to bumper like a ribbon of silver snake sweltering in the sun.

I pulled up at the lights. I had Black Sabbath blaring out of the radio. In the lane next to me was a thin blonde in a Mercedes convertible, late thirties, with a chiselled look that smelt of money and good genes – two things I have always lacked in real life. I turned Classic Rock FM down. I couldn't help thinking how she had that glossed-over, air-brushed look of an avatar. All she was missing was the perfected skin, the impossibly enhanced breasts, lips and massive baby-doll fuck-me eyes. Was that how Tasinis would look in real life? Just then the thin blonde sensed me looking over and turned in my direction. Luckily the red light changed in that second and I sped away before she could really see me.

Back at the call centre the parking lot was empty apart from a few cars. Weekend workers like me. It always spooked me to see it like this, I guess because it made me realise how friggin' big that place was. Like a desert, a concrete flatland with the concrete block that was the call centre squatting barrenly against all that endless sky. Infinity. I would like to say it was timeless but it wasn't. It was definitely America, though, America at the end of a noose. 'Is it any wonder,' I said out loud as I pushed through the heat already coming off the tarmac, 'I git confused between this world and my second world? Is reality where you like to be or does it just fall over us like night?' My words scared a couple of crows picking at something dead on the sidewalk and up they flew, cawing against the blue. Me, I was just glad to get out of all that blasting white light into the cool air con.

As I walked towards my desk a man hurried past me in the corridor – short like me but skinny, and with those handsome Latino features that Mom used to call Valentinoesque, after that twenties film star. There was something sad and nondescript about him, and I have to confess in my hurry to stay invisible I hardly noticed him. It was only after I got to my workstation that I realised he might be the night worker, my mirror parallel Hector. Was he as invisible as me? Another shadow artist?

I put my headset on: 'Yes, ma'am, that is correct. The Abdominal Toner is twenty-nine dollars ninety-nine before shipping, which is an extra ten dollars ... within the United States ... Yes, ma'am ...'

While answering the call I scanned the weekly updated list of products and their instructions. Suddenly I noticed the bottom left hand corner of the page. Scribbled into the margin was a tiny pen drawing of a thigh-high winged boot.

The rest of the afternoon evaporated away like most of my working days do, in a haze of calls and coffee breaks. If you asked me, 'Do you remember that day, Cassandra?' I would have to say, not really, except for one image, the picture that grew in my head. That drawing of the thigh-high boot with the little wing fixed to its ankle, because I swear, it wasn't me that drew the goddamn thing.

Later at home I'm sitting in front of the computer eating my usual Saturday night dinner, which is one In-N-Out king-size cheeseburger, Animal Style, with double fries and onion rings, a king-size Coke, one slice of apple pie and vanilla ice-cream and a chocolate chip cookie for afterwards, all sitting in their cardboard tray – the burger oozing cheese, the apple pie oozing ice-cream, the cookie sweating chocolate – perched on one side of my desk next to my credit cards laid out ready to use. And I'm sitting there, mayo running down my chin, mouse in one hand, burger in the other, and I'm inworld, on Second Life.

And on screen I am Tasinis, dressing for the kill, for my night feed of worship.

Tonight I have decided to excel myself – I'm out to impress, I'm out to be queen, I'm out to be worshipped. Maybe it was that thin blonde and her smug air of entitlement, maybe it was because it was Saturday, but I am restless, I need a hit of major adoration. I have enhanced Tasinis's body – she now has a triple D 44-inch bust, two new silver nipple piercings and another through her labia. I've also narrowed her waist by three inches, which felt real good, felt like I was giving the finger to that blonde in the Mercedes. Then we visited the hairdresser's at Cybermop Salon, Voyager Road, Freedom Island. I instructed Claude, Tasinis's favourite hairdresser, to design her a sixties beehive with a twenty-first-century wildness. I've dressed her in a Gucci leather-panelled corset, La Perla stockings and suspenders (both purchased from Haute Couture Paris, Second Life store). I then squeezed her into a skin-tight silver pencil skirt and matching stilettos – with six-inch heels. She looks great, kind of like the ultimate wild-child Barbie doll, and she is totally my creation. Three clicks of the mouse later and she's poised outside the orgy pit of Pleasure Dome 3, Venus, awaiting my instructions. I finish the cheeseburger, stuff a handful of fries into my mouth and, trembling with anticipation, walk my baby in.

Pleasure Dome 3, Venus: 18.10 7/01/09
The area is a large silver dome with swings, ropes and racks hanging from the ceiling. The walls are hung with cascades of shimmering circular mirrors, melodious music plays and there is an indoor spa and swimming pool set into the floor at one end. Naked avatars, male, female and hermaphrodite, frolic in the

water, in the corners writhe pink knots of a slowly revolving orgy, others are just displaying their glistening bodies.

In the centre of the dome a young female avatar, totally naked except for a belly button stud and a ring through her clit, lies upside down tied and splayed on a rack that is slowly rotating. I peer closer, marvelling at the realism of the programming that has her hair cascading in the right direction as the wheel turns. Below her, on the ground, one male avatar is fucking another male avatar while another avatar takes him from behind – the third avatar's a female with her hermaphrodite function turned on so that a penis has sprouted above her vagina. All three have eyelids fluttering in simulated pleasure and mouths with thick plumped lips that open and shut in a mimicry of orgasm.

Some of them look like they have their audio packs on. I reach for my mouse and push the volume up on the computer. Immediately my bedroom fills with the sound of human moaning and groaning. Worried about my neighbour I get up to shut my window and return to the desk. By the time I look back at the screen the orgy has progressed.

A female avatar stops the rotating rack with the girl strapped on and goes down on her, while she herself is being propositioned by an avatar I recognise. His name's Horny-Corn and he's half human, half horse, with an extra penis sprouting from his forehead like the horn on a unicorn. A sex addict, I've never seen him anywhere inworld except for the adult realms, and although Tasinis has had sex with him, I've never warmed to his crude overtures. Now he trots up beside the female avatar that's now going down on the one strapped to the rack and, lowering his head, directs his forehead penis between her buttocks.

'What do you want?' she asks, her voice sounding like a robotic Minnie Mouse.

'I want to take you in the ass, hot bitch,' Horny-Corn replies, then neighs enthusiastically – not the most sexy sound.

'Okay, but go slow,' she replies, a command he ignores altogether as his avatar finally manages to enter the avatar whose buttocks immediately begin to vibrate and shake violently. X3 ass model nine I note to myself – 400 Lindens with guaranteed realistic action.

I touch the commands and Tasinis goes flying through the air and lands on Horny-Corn's back. Lifting her silver whip she begins flailing him lightly on the flanks as he pumps the female avatar with his cock-horn. I can't say it's particularly erotic but it's fun – the whole orgy room is beginning to look like some totally weird circus act.

Just then another avatar – a young blond male with an erection emblazoned with multiple piercings descends from the rafters, hanging upside down on a swing. He hovers over Tasinis then, freeing his arms and hands while still hanging from the swing, he begins to massage her breasts, while she continues riding Horny-Corn and whipping him. I activate Tasinis's interactive thighs and she starts bouncing vigorously up and down on the creature's back.

I peer closer at the screen. I'm telling you I'm in that room, in her skin. It's like I could smell the skin, the fur, the sweat and the sex. I/we are watching, and both Tasinis and myself are the MC, the conductor orchestrating the orgy. Now every time Tasinis brings down her whip, Horny-Corn penetrates the female avatar, the flat innocuous smiles on all of the avatars' faces gives the orgy a strange, childlike, joyous glee – naughty not dirty.

That's what I like about cyber-sex – it is fantasy, pure fantasy. Anonymous, safe and yet subversive.

Just then I notice Tasinis's name on the instant messenger board. I have been concentrating so hard I haven't noticed that Starboy 8 has entered the room and is standing by the entrance, leaning awkwardly against a rack of sex toys and handcuffs as if he has nothing better to do. He still lacks genitals, nipples and voice. It's like suddenly he is a lot more naked than the other avatars with all their fancy dangly parts and boobs. I can't help liking him for it. It's like he doesn't give a damn. A blue pose ball appears beside him as if prompting him to participate in the orgy. He pushes it away with an aggressive punch. Several of the avatars look up from their cyber-sex disapprovingly.

'Tasinis, aren't you bored with all this robotic pumping yet?' Starboy 8's words appear on the instant messenger board, as archaic as ancient hieroglyphs to us seasoned Second Lifers. Tasinis ignores him while I try and work out how I'm going to answer him.

'Get lost, buster, can't you see she's busy?' yells Swingerjoy, the blond avatar hanging upside down massaging Tasinis's breasts. His long blond hair waves in the cyber wind.

'Yeah, get in or get out!' Sexkittenblue shouts.

'I'm talking to Tasinis. Do you want a date?' Starboy 8 persists – the typed letters seem amateurish and juvenile compared to the electronic voices of all the other avatars.

'A date? What is this, nineteen eighty-five?' Horny-Corn mutters from under Tasinis.

A date? Why was this guy interested in Tasinis, an avatar obviously designed for everything but dating? What does he think? That she's relationship material? But I'm telling you, something about the guy not caring what the other Second Lifers think of him gets to me. That takes courage, that takes individuality. It's like he's happy being himself; he hasn't invested anything in proving himself to the other avatars, in looking attractive.

I make Tasinis climb down from Horny-Corn's furry back. 'Where?' I find myself making Tasinis whisper. My avatar seems to stare out from the screen at me, her huge blue eyes wide with surprise. Then again, I might be imagining it.

'Sam's Tropical Bar, Hideaway Island. In five?' Starboy 8 replies.

'See you there, big boy,' Tasinis finally growls back, now in her more familiar and reassuring mode of seductress.

'Big boy? He ain't even got a dick!' Horny-Corn shouts, but we are already gone.

Sam's Tropical Bar on Hideaway Island was the kind of place I imagined wealthy celebrities might go for secret liaisons in real life. It was an exclusive bar that was at least 40 Lindens per avatar to enter, on a fantasy island that resembled Dr No's luxury hideaway in the James Bond film. I spent ten minutes redesigning Tasinis in more demure clothing that was appropriate for the occasion – a Donna Karan dress I'd seen Scarlett Johansson wear to the Oscars a couple of years back. I have to say my girl looked great – although the triple D breasts and hips were a little of a giveaway. I put her in flats so she was at least kind of average height. I paid her entry fee and walked her into the bar.

Sam's Tropical Bar on Hideaway Island: 18.30 7/01/2009
There's a ripple amongst the people sitting around the bar: heads turn, eyes look up, stare then turn away. I feel that small ripple

of pleasure (the nearest thing I'd ever experienced to an orgasm) that Tasinis has been recognised.

Starboy 8 is sitting in a red leather booth at the back of the bar, in the shadows. He stands as Tasinis sits down. Then he orders champagne, good French vintage champagne. I like that. It shows real class. With his clothes on and his hair swept back, he looks a lot cuter, and it doesn't seem to matter that under the clothes he is minus a penis and other vital accessories. He smiles a kind of pensive smile that is remarkably human-like.

'So how long have you been on Second Life?' Tasinis asks sipping her champagne with cool detachment.

'Just over a week, I guess. I thought it would be different,' Starboy 8 says. Tasinis nearly drops her glass in surprise. Starboy 8 has a voice and it's nice: a smooth tenor, really friendly. There's even some emotion in it.

'Different how?'

'I guess I thought you wouldn't be judged like you are in real life. I thought people could be more honest standing behind an avatar.'

'But they are.'

'No, they're not. People are judged in here just like in reality. On their appearance. I mean, look at you.' Starboy 8 points to my avatar's body.

Just then a cute male avatar that looks like a pumped Johnny Depp approaches the booth and asks for Tasinis's autograph. She's just about to sign for him when Starboy 8 tells him to get lost. The really weird thing is I find myself excited by his possessiveness, but I couldn't tell you what Tasinis was feeling at that point. I think it was about then that me and my alter ego started peeling off from each other, like an ovum dividing in the womb, pink, unformed, blind in intent.

'What about me? Don't you find me attractive?' Tasinis cocks her head then flicks her hair over her shoulder (seductive gesture command 10).

'You look like a sex doll. There is nothing real about you.'

'No one in Second Life wants reality; we're all escaping reality. In reality I'm invisible.'

'So you make yourself super-visible in Second Life?'

'Something like that.' I make Tasinis sip her champagne in a demure fashion. It looks a little awkward, like a stripper trying to look coy. But it's a difficult moment. I want to tell Starboy 8 more but Tasinis is holding me back.

The conversation is not going the way I need, and yet I can't unhook myself. It's like Tasinis has started to want to prove herself to Starboy 8. She turns away from him, her long blonde hair falling down her face. I have to stop myself from hitting the command that would make two large glistening tears roll across those high cheekbones.

'Sorry, I've upset you,' Starboy 8 says.

Tasinis doesn't reply.

'Guess I should buy myself a penis. I mean, how long do you think I'll survive in Second Life dickless?' Starboy 8 continues.

In real life I laugh out loud then make Tasinis turn and smile back at him.

'If you stay a voyeur you'll be okay.'

Starboy 8 returns her smile. His hand lifts and slides across the marble tabletop, his fingers touching Tasinis's own.

'Do you have someone on the outside?'

I stiffened. I'd been so long in the adult areas that I couldn't remember the last time an avatar had asked Tasinis anything personal.

'No one. You?'

'I had someone but she died recently. Guess I'm in here escaping reality too.'

'I know what that's like. To lose someone and be alone.'

'Do you think we're running?' Starboy 8 asks softly, his hands creeping over Tasinis's fingers – they look absurd, they are so much smaller than hers, but I let him touch her.

'Sure, we're all running, aren't we?' she growls back, a little less confident than usual. 'Running from our shit real lives, real jobs and real bodies. But here I'm totally free, totally visible. I revel in being seen.'

'But who is living which life?'

I stare at the screen; I'd been inside Tasinis so long I'd never thought about it like that. To me I had been living. Suddenly I become aware of my body, my human body: my back aches from sitting down so long, there's a pounding in my temples and I feel a little nauseous from the burger. Outside it's night already and I know I should be sleeping. More than anything I want Tasinis to leave and fly back to the safety and anonymity of the adult areas. I'm scared, it's as simple as that. Inworld has started to blur with outworld.

I make Tasinis stand up and walk away without casting a backward glance. I can even hear the swish of her dress against her thighs.

'I want to see you again!' Starboy 8 shouts out on the messenger board, 'Tahiti! Tomorrow – eight o'clock!'

'I'm making no promises,' Tasinis mutters darkly, then walks through the bar door.

The next morning I woke up feeling a little different, like there was a thread of excitement weaving away inside of me. Like something had started to unravel. For a minute I lay there wondering if there hadn't been an earthquake in the middle of the night that I had only been unconsciously aware of, and some part of me was still on red alert.

I climbed out of bed and shuffled to the bathroom. After showering I pulled open a drawer that still held all my mother's make-up. I couldn't remember the last time I wore make-up – I'm guessing years. My hand hovered for a moment above all those shiny tubes and jars, all those magic tricks Mom used to keep her beautiful. Finally I selected a lipstick: coral pink. With the towel still wrapped around my body, I stood in front of the mirror. I took a big breath and carefully applied the lipstick, then loosened my damp hair and let it fall around my face. And you know what? I looked kind of okay.

For the first time in twelve years I found it difficult to concentrate at work. That day was hard, I'm telling you. Like I'm sitting there and I can feel the air con blowing across my skin, I can hear the chatter of the other operators rising and falling like waves over the partitions, distracting me. Making me angry for no reason. I was not myself. Like when I took my usual morning coffee break I picked up an apple and not a donut from the stand. I keep thinking about Starboy 8 and the date. How Tasinis made no promises, how if I/we did meet him it was bound to get personal, and personal was what I'd been escaping all these years. And I started to think about Mom and how I was always such a disappointment to her, how I was never thin enough, never beautiful enough, and how she made me feel that afternoon screaming at me in the bathroom, calling me a sinner, and how I'd never been able to touch myself since. And all of the memories, those old fears and bad images, lifted up inside of me like a tornado, only I was the tornado and the outside world was spinning around me and I thought I was going to throw up. So I stayed frozen to my desk taking deep breaths in, calming myself down before anyone noticed. Five minutes later I'd made up my mind.

Cass didn't do personal therefore neither did Tasinis. We were both terrified. I couldn't do it, I couldn't afford to let anyone in, in this life or the Second. I had good reason: a Pandora's box of nightmares.

That evening I sent my baby in full leather gear straight to Gothic Dungeon Sex Island. It was like I needed to get violent, to get lost in the frenzy. I needed to shake off my real-life skin and get as impersonal as possible. At least I thought I did.

Gothic Dungeon Sex Island: 20.00 7/02/2009

As Tasinis strides into the circular arena, sawdust swishing around her eight-inch spiked heels, a steel-cage visor tugged down over her eyes, hair pulled back severely into a waist-length ponytail, she cracks her whip.

'Okay, scum, time to feel the anger of my whip!' It isn't my best dominatrix command but it works anyhow: immediately three male avatars in neck cuffs and leather hand bindings begin grovelling at Tasinis's feet.

'Line up, dogs!' Tasinis orders.

The three crawl into position. Naked on all fours, cock, balls, feathers and tails all hanging down.

'Yes. Yes. Harder. Harder,' one of them, a muscular redhead with tattoos who for some inexplicable reason has a black penis, screams.

'Ohh!!!#@!! I'm coming. You bitch goddess of the lash,' the avatar at the end – a shaved humanoid head with a small dog's tail poking out from between his buttocks – moans, the tip of his modified cock flashing red. This is a sign that normally would have had her/me excited by now, but Tasinis feels nothing. I feel nothing. For the first time the room looks kind of tawdry. The ropes and metal harnessing hanging off the old stone walls appear fake, and I suddenly notice the way the simulation dissolves into obvious pixels at the edges. The jerky fashion in which the avatars wriggle their hips and legs making them look like wooden puppets, and the way their genitals bob up and down, orifices mechanically opening and closing, is kind of weird. The usual rush of excitement I feel when Tasinis's whip touches avatar skin is gone. Totally. I can't lose myself in Second Life. For the first time I can't lose Cassandra.

I look at the time displayed in the right-hand corner of my desktop: it's already ten past eight. Starboy 8 will be waiting in Tahiti. Suddenly I'm terrified I've left it all too late. In seconds I pull Tasinis out of the dungeon and send her straight to Tahiti, a fantasy island set in the 1800s.

Tahiti, Fantasy Island: 20.15 7/02/2009
I find Starboy 8 dressed as a shipwrecked French sailor sitting amongst a group of native Polynesians watching a ceremony.

I haven't had time to re-dress Tasinis and she looks ridiculous standing in full leather gear at the edge of a jungle clearing surrounded by native women and men wearing grass skirts. Starboy 8 doesn't seem to care, he looks across and immediately leaps up and leads her by the hand into the jungle. She/I walk through the trailing vines, the chattering monkeys, and the brightly coloured parrots that suddenly burst out of the foliage and fly across our path. Finally the two avatars arrive at a waterfall with a grassy outcrop hanging over the rushing water beneath. Starboy 8 and Tasinis sit on the grass.

'I thought you weren't coming,' Starboy 8 begins.

'I wasn't, then I changed my mind.'

'Let me guess – you were in Gothic Sex Dungeon?'

'How did you know?'

'Your outfit kind of gives you away.'

A large crocodile's head emerges from the pool and snaps harmlessly at Tasinis's leather-clad feet. It doesn't look right; somehow I'm not convinced Tahiti would have crocodiles living on it.

'Are you from California?' asks Starboy 8.

'Maybe.'

'Do you have many friends on the outside?'

'No. I don't need them, I live here most of the time.'

'In the dungeons and sex islands? Is that what makes you alive?'

'No. But it gives me power over others. It's an equation, isn't it? I guess the less power you have in real life the more you seek it in Second Life,' Tasinis replies. It was the most personal she'd ever been.

I can't believe what I'd just made Tasinis say. I'd never even thought about it that way before. Never. But somehow looking at Tasinis sitting there, her long legs folded under her a little awkwardly on that lush green grass, her metal visor now pushed over her head, her huge blue eyes sightless and blinking, makes a crack in me, in my avatar. Starboy 8 moves closer.

'Can I take your glove off?' he asks, and I swear it was the sexiest thing anyone had ever asked me on Second Life, something as innocent as that, after all the bondage, the orgies, the sex toys.

'Yes,' Tasinis whispers back before I'd even given her permission to speak. Starboy 8 takes her hand and peels off the glove. I feel a tingle in my special edition clit, or at least Tasinis felt it; me – I'm wriggling in my desk chair.

'I'm from California too,' Starboy 8 murmurs as he caresses Tasinis's long fingers. Involuntarily my heart leaps in my chest. A tight feeling, but exhilarating, the feeling that something's changing, something I have no control over, no choice.

'In Second Life we have no places, past or history. We're born new.'

'No one is born new. Listen, there's a sex addicts clinic on Health Avenue. Avatars meet, talk, admit their addiction.'

'Is that what you think, you think I'm a sex addict?'

'I think you need to empower yourself on the outside, in real life.'

It suddenly feels hot inside my bedroom. My bedroom in real life. A mosquito bites my arm and I kill it with a slap: a red streak of blood. My blood. I look back at the screen. Starboy 8 is poised,waiting, for a reply. I make Tasinis crack her whip and catch the leg of a passing parrot. Casually she dashes it against the trunk of a palm tree. In a flurry of scarlet and purple feathers it falls to the ground.

'Why do you care?' she says.

'Because I think you're like me. I may be missing a dick, nipples and other enhancements, but for all the sexy bits of your skin and the sex that you have, you're missing something far more important.'

Starboy 8 moves his face closer to Tasinis's. It's like I can almost smell him and I know he will be fresh and young, spice and hope. The tingle in Tasinis's groin becomes a flashing light as her labia lights up. Under my old T-shirt I become aware of my own sex, the tight warmth of it between my legs, and I become wet.

'There's something else. I want to get to know you – the real you. But I want you to want me for me, not my X3 dick or ass, not the special edition nipples or hermaphrodite option, but me. Imagine this was real life, imagine we were fallible.' And then he kisses her/me and in that instant I am there in Tasinis's skin. The touch of his lips, his tongue penetrating me tentatively, gently, and the sensation of it sending a jolt through my body, an explosion that bursts from my clitoris and ripples out up my belly and down both my legs, making me shake in my chair, a great white wave of contractions throws me back, my mouth opening as I moan involuntarily. My very first orgasm in real life. Shocked, I stay sitting as wave after wave of pure sweetness ripples through me; my body feels like it's made of white light. I feel beautiful.

I was woken by sunlight across my face. I rolled over to stare at the alarm clock. I'd overslept for the first time in twelve years.

Without getting out of bed I picked up the phone and rang work. I told my boss I'd be in late that afternoon. I didn't even bother to listen to his reply.

After hanging up the phone I stepped out of bed and stood in the middle of the room. The place looked different, brighter somehow: the colours of the walls, the way the sunlight was falling over my dressing table, picking out all the glinting silvers of my hairpins and Mom's old jewellery. Even the faded colours of my old robe looked brighter. I wrapped the dressing gown around my body, the brushed cotton incredibly soft against my skin. Everything was more vivid, each sensation heightened. It was like I'd woken up in a different world, one flooded with light and colour.

I ventured into the bathroom. The sunlight streaming in from the skylight filled it, transforming it into a prism of blues and greens. I showered, the hot water spraying thin needles of pleasure across my back. I climbed out, dried myself, then stood naked in front of the full-length mirror with the bottom half still covered by the sheet of cardboard. I worried my fingers around one corner, closed my eyes and tore it away, then counted to ten.

I opened my eyes and stared at my full reflection for the first time in three years. The white full curves of my body rippled down my sides, my breasts, large and pendulous, hung almost to my waist, my thighs were covered in stretch marks, and my belly almost obscured my pubis. But you know what? It was all me. I was finally looking at me.

I skipped breakfast and drove to the local shopping mall. At the huge Walmart store I bought a new red T-shirt and a long cotton skirt covered in small embroidered flowers. I hadn't worn a skirt in years. Back at home I put on the skirt and T-shirt. It was like the colours were floating off the fabric and colouring my mood. Butterflies of dancing light. I didn't want to question or doubt, I didn't want to frighten this new Cass away.

I retrieved four large cardboard boxes from the garage and carried them up to Mom's bedroom. It took me three hours to empty her cupboards and drawers and pack those boxes, but when I was finished I swear I felt a hundred pounds lighter.

That afternoon I drove to work with my car top open. The wind ruffled my hair and blew against my sunglasses. I had Classic Rock FM on and they were playing Steely Dan. I sang along at the top of my lungs. Driving beside the seafront through Del Mar, I thought I saw the water spout of a whale.

I got to the call centre around three in the afternoon. Walking through the parking lot I noticed how red the bougainvillea was that was planted against one wall of the building. I'd never even seen it there before. Once I was in the office, several of the other operators looked up from their desks. I could see the surprise in their eyes, like they saw I was different but couldn't work out how. I got to my desk and sat down. Perched in the centre of the desk, resting against an old pebble I once found as a child, was a postcard. A postcard with the words: 'Welcome to Tahiti, island of joy' printed under a view of a green island in a blue sea. I turned it around. It was addressed to Tasinis, Second Life and, in the message space, someone had scrawled the word 'Hello'.

I stared at it for a moment then carefully slipped it into my drawer. And I knew then that I wouldn't be logging on that night. I was going to wait to meet Hector the night worker, my shadow-self. I figured we might have a lot to say to each other.

WEATHER

It was one night after work before Alan came home that Phoebe first saw him. After an item about a two-headed kitten surviving in Basingstoke, an earthquake in Mid-west America and yet more trouble in the Middle East, the BBC news had cut to that inevitable mollifier of the English middle class – the weather report. Nestling into the old leather armchair, cup of hot tea held between her knees, Phoebe found herself staring into the large, slightly bewildered brown eyes of Rupert Thornton, the new weatherman.

'Hello, he's nice,' she thought to herself, allowing her eyes to wander over the tall, angular frame of the man. He looked to be somewhere in his mid-thirties, his thin wrists protruding from his shirt sleeves with a certain poignant vulnerability, the longish blond hair receding slightly from the domed forehead, the strong nose and cheekbones and large heavy-lidded eyes all united in a pleasing handsomeness – an old-world elegance. He looked, she thought, as if he'd just been dropped in from the nineteenth century and not 1987, a year she'd already decided was rather horrible, even if it was only July. Not wanting to dwell on her grievances, Phoebe glanced back up at the TV screen to concentrate.

Rupert Thornton stood in front of the map of the British Isles, arms raised as if he was about to conduct an orchestra: '… Tomorrow is looking a little more optimistic with a warm front sweeping in …' and here he lifted both hands and, in a curiously erotic gesture, circled the air as if he himself were pushing the warm front from Ireland towards Devon.

Phoebe sat up in her chair. The weatherman's hands were well shaped with thick fingers, she noted, and before she could help herself she began wondering about the size of his penis, which was testimony to the lack of sex in her marriage, she observed ruefully. For the tenth time that day the image of her husband Alan flashed into her mind, the mottled, rugged landscape his naked back presented every night as he turned to switch the bedside lamp off – his way of signalling that any possible intimacy was now off the menu. It had been like that for months, maybe even a year, Phoebe calculated, trying to remember the last time they had made love. Christmas 1986 came to mind, but even then she wasn't sure she'd had an orgasm. It was a depressing scenario especially, Phoebe reminded herself, as she was only twenty-six and considered attractive. Plenty of men would want her even if her husband didn't.

She glanced at the faint reflection of herself caught on the TV screen with Rupert the weatherman gesturing blindly behind her, almost as if he were trapped behind the glass. Phoebe was a curvaceous blonde of average height with a wild mane of hair and even features that were unremarkable except for her intense green eyes that she always dramatically highlighted with blue eye shadow and thick black mascara. She had the kind of prettiness that was pleasant but not in

the least exotic or sophisticated, and this had been a source
of disillusionment for Phoebe who, at the age of sixteen, had
changed her name by deed poll from the very plain Mandy
to Phoebe (after a character in a novel). She'd wanted to be
glamorous and dramatic but growing up with an alcoholic
mother on an estate on the edge of Acton hadn't really allowed
for such ambitions, and it was indicative of Phoebe's strength
of character that she had escaped home as soon as she could –
marrying Alan had been the greater part of that escape.

It wasn't as if she lacked self-esteem or sexual confidence,
Phoebe thought, wondering how and exactly when her husband
had fallen out of love with her. It certainly wasn't something
she'd done deliberately. If anything, she suspected that Alan, a
control freak, had lost interest once he realised he had won her
– or, more sinisterly, now had control of her. A sudden excited
utterance from the weatherman pulled her out of her reverie.

'… a glorious abundance of cumuli coming in from the
north-east will be followed by a darker patch of cumulonimbus,
rain clouds to us mortals …' Cumuli. Cumulonimbus. The words
seemed to drop from his mouth like an overripe plum, and again
his body arched in a gesture that seemed to ripple up from his
hips, travelling with a shudder down to his fingertips. Cumuli.
Phoebe found herself imagining that she was riding naked,
sprawled on a bank of fluffy white clouds as they drifted across
the English countryside. It was a sensually pleasing vision and
Mr Rupert Thornton was a sexy weatherman, Phoebe decided,
smug in the knowledge that, out of the three million viewers
watching the six o'clock news, there was no doubt she alone had
come to that conclusion.

Part of Phoebe's grand plan to reconstruct her persona was to think herself capable of exclusivity, of originality, of finding qualities in others that no one else had noticed. A less generous person might have called it imaginative projection on her usually fairly innocent subjects, obsession even, but Phoebe saw herself as a liberator, someone who could burrow into personalities and discover aspects unknown even to the individuals themselves. There had been some unfortunate incidents in the past – the milkman who was forced to place a restraining order on the then seventeen-year-old Phoebe, a school janitor she used to follow home – but all those were in the past, long before she'd married Alan, and besides, she still liked to think she'd seen qualities in these men that even they were not aware of. And so it was that she now relished thinking of the unwitting Rupert Thornton in a way that she imagined nobody else had ever thought of him – as a kind of sexual weather god.

The timer over the stove pinged, jolting her back to domestic reality. It was Alan's way of reminding her that he'd be home in an hour and she should start preparing supper. The sharp sound also brought into focus the more immediate consequences of Phoebe's imaginative embellishment of others. It was partly responsible for her marrying Alan in the first place, she reminded herself somewhat bitterly as the six o'clock news finally ended and the program cut from Rupert's slightly uncertain smile to the closing credits.

Phoebe had met her husband at the insurance company they both still worked for. Alan was an actuary and Phoebe was a clerk in the accounting department. Alan was involved in calculating risk – his speciality was acts of God: storms, floods, lightning strikes – and his clients ranged from farmers to owners of vulnerable historical buildings. In her role Phoebe was little more than a glorified secretary, filing, typing and taking dictation – a tedious job that led to much daydreaming.

She'd only been twenty-one when she noticed the way Alan kept wiping and adjusting the objects on his desk so that they were kept both clean and orderly. His precision was intriguing, quite the opposite of the violent chaos of the dysfunctional home she'd grown up in. Now, five years later, she recognised Alan's need for control as compulsive, perhaps even mildly pathological, but back then she'd thought this sense of control was both urbane and inspired. And she had loved the fact that he was so much older than her and owned his own house and a nice car, as she had worried she might end up impoverished and on benefits like her mother.

It had been an easy seduction. The way she'd originally got Alan to notice her was to incrementally mess up his desk, starting with small details. She moved his pencil sharpener, swapped his paperclips for the staple gun and left his phone off the hook, all of which seemed to throw the man into confusion then a rage (seeing him so suddenly animated turned her on). When her strategy climaxed with her 'accidentally' spilling a small pot of ink over his desk, she had his complete attention. Before he could explode into irrational rage she'd asked him out – which totally disarmed him. To both their surprise he'd said yes.

'It wasn't like he wasn't a passionate man,' she spoke out loud, startling the cat who dived under the kitchen table. It was just that sex had to be on his terms, and this meant a lot of ritual and preparation. The bed had to be folded down exactly right, they both had to have had a bath beforehand, he couldn't make love on a full stomach but not on an empty one either, and so on. It left absolutely no room for spontaneity and as the marriage had gone on Alan's prerequisites had become more and more inflexible until he appeared to lose interest altogether. Phoebe was reduced to furtively pleasuring herself whilst clinging to the cold edge of the bed, hoping the bed springs wouldn't squeak and wake him. It was, as her mother used to say with a great deal of relish, a miserable state of affairs.

From the other side of the house came the sound of the front door opening. Knowing that would be Alan returning from a late session at work, Phoebe hurriedly placed his plate of fish fingers and creamed broccoli on his placemat, adjusted the wine glass so it was exactly central to the placemat, pulled the chair out for him and switched the radio on to Classic FM. She then stood waiting beside her own chair. Alan, a short man a little squashed by life, entered the room, kissed his wife on the forehead then without a word sat at the table. Phoebe followed suit.

'Lovely broccoli,' he said after five minutes, a comment he made every Tuesday – their fish day.

'Thanks, sweetie,' Phoebe responded – it was her standard reply. Outside it began raining, droplets of water splashing against the windowpane in a sudden fecundity. Cumulonimbus, Phoebe remembered, and something inside her started to moisten.

That night Phoebe dreamt she was tied spreadeagled to the TV weatherboard, and her body had become the weather map Rupert Thornton was reading from: a relief map with mountains, gullies, lakes and river-ways all jutting out ripe and ready for him.

Every time the weatherman mentioned snow sweeping in from the northern peaks of Scotland, his long elegant hands would inadvertently brush against her nipples. Then when he said a warm front was moving up from France, his fingers would wander blindly across her wet lips and clit. She quivered with pleasure but it wasn't just the touching that was erotic, it was the fact that he had to ignore her and play to the camera. She was both his prop and at his mercy, and yet she knew she was invaluable to him. And Phoebe so wanted to be invaluable to someone.

She woke to discover that Alan had pulled the bedclothes off her in the night. Aroused by her dream, Phoebe crept her hands around the soft hairy circumference of his belly and found his nestling penis.

'We'll be late for work,' Alan mumbled, pushing her hands away. He sat up, his broad shoulders slumping forward. The vulnerability of his chest – the hair greying and the slight curve of his stomach – clenched at Phoebe's heart. The trouble was she still loved him. Fighting a sense of profound rejection, she sat up and they both swung their legs around to the opposite sides of the bed, naked back facing naked back. Staring out the window Phoebe noticed the rain had stopped, and suddenly she found herself wanting to cry.

The day passed intolerably slowly. All that Phoebe had to occupy herself with was a new box of insurance claims to file and several reports to type up. Several times she found herself wondering what the weatherman might be doing now – talking to the Meteorology Board, checking barometers and weather gauges himself?

The day was unseasonably warm even for the end of July, a sultry overcast day that threatened thunder but didn't quite deliver. The silk of her blouse stuck to her back and as she swivelled around in her desk chair she was aware of the way her underpants chaffed against her sex. Neglected, I am neglected, she thought, her gaze falling upon the young intern – a pimply lad of about nineteen. But despite her frustration, it was hard to muster any sexual enthusiasm for her young colleague, who was paralysed with shyness every time she spoke to him. No, it had to be the weatherman.

Her mind wandered back to the BBC weather report the night before, the way Rupert Thornton had his fingers outstretched when describing rain, like he was running them through hair, her hair. Again, she glanced hopefully at the window. If only the perfect blue sky would suddenly manifest a light shower or two – then she would see him do the same tender caress on the TV that evening. That would give her something to look forward to.

The ticking of the wall clock seemed to bore through her skull and it was only three in the afternoon. Bored and frustrated, Phoebe glanced back down at the report. The mundane sentences describing a small fire that had destroyed part of an old tower attached to St Leonard's Church, Heston, had a certain poetic rhythm to them. It was an old seventh-century church building that was historically listed, and the report mentioned that the botanist Joseph Banks was buried there. The damage included several statues, some of which were accidentally damaged by the overenthusiastic firemen engaged in putting out the fire.

One outstretched stone hand broken off at wrist
One grinning gargoyle lost nose
Nymph's arms upheld towards heaven now missing
Breasts of Virgin smashed

Phoebe read the clipped sentences out loud, her mouth shaping the consonants, mimicking Rupert Thornton's rounded vowels. Again she thought of the weatherman's sensual gestures. He had moved as if he lived in the air, as if he were deeply aware of his own physicality and fluidity, as if the small gestures mattered. This had made him beautiful and it made her want to touch him, to absorb through some strange process of osmosis that particular grace of his.

It was the total opposite of the way her husband Alan moved: a man who aggressively bustled his way through life, as if angry at the very fact of his own existence. If Alan was a building that got burnt down no one would really notice because he would be replaceable, but if Rupert Thornton were a building he would be a thing of both architectural grandeur and sensual beauty; the weatherman would be memorable – he would be listed, Phoebe thought wistfully as she doodled on her notepad. She noticed the doodle had become a large penis that was ejaculating not sperm but droplets of rain.

By the time she'd finished typing up the report she was in love.

Knowing Alan wouldn't be home until seven thirty, Phoebe raced back to the house. She got in at five minutes to six. Without even bothering to take her coat off she ran to the kitchen and switched on the television. This time she listed all the weatherman's physical gestures as he made them, in the order in which she found them the most erotic: rain, sleet and threatening clouds all constituted a dramatic flourish of the hand followed by a curious flutter of the fingers that reminded Phoebe of the way she touched herself; a particular technique she had despaired of Alan ever intuiting. After listing the eighteenth movement – a shrug of the shoulders made with both palms held upwards prompted by 'a gentle break in the cloud front' – Phoebe realised that the weatherman was far more animated by reports of severe or violent weather – as if he relished the drama. This was indicative of a mentality she could relate to: she too loathed monotone, monotony, the sameness of poverty, suburbia; she too craved drama. Now determined to somehow find a way of feeding this unconscious hunger she sensed in the weatherman, she moved closer to the TV screen.

Predictions like 'a storm front sweeping in from the north-west will gradually clear' involved the weatherman's whole body and a wry smile, body language that Phoebe fantasised into a post-coital embrace that finished with a touch of disbelief or cynicism – the wry smile was particularly sexy. It suggested intelligence and some self-parody, again a wonderful contrast to the deathly seriousness of her husband.

'Fog' was interesting – a short push with both hands, the word itself sounding a little like a grunt, suggesting to Phoebe that despite the weatherman's perfectly rounded private school vowels, he might be capable of a little rough play – maybe even some light S&M. 'A little break of sunshine …' came with a hip thrust, while 'hail' dipped down into a baritone and made Phoebe think of penetration and how the full weight of the tall weatherman would feel on top of her own body. That alone was almost enough to make her come.

By the time the weather report was over and she had the table laid, Phoebe had a list of twenty-five weather conditions linked to Rupert's particular illustrative body movements. She sat back in her chair, the list in hand – it was like code, erotic code, and her pants were wringing wet. Needless to say it was at that moment that Alan came home and Phoebe found that she had burnt the lamb chops.

That night Phoebe dreamt of a vast empty sky which seemed depressingly hollow. Then just at the point where she thought she might have to wake herself up to escape the despairing sensation that nothing would ever change – not the weather, not her marriage, not her job – a faint grey cloud appeared, swiftly followed by several others galloping behind like eager greyhounds. To her utter joy the sky was soon a dark grey with a crack of blue, and the phrase 'a bank of nimbostratus coming in from the south-east' shuddered through her sleeping consciousness like an orgasm. Phoebe woke and realised it was an actual orgasm.

This time staring across at her snoring husband in the blue morning light, Phoebe found herself feeling, well, just a little less desperate.

The rest of the day was depressingly sunny. At work all Phoebe's colleagues appeared to be imbued with that particular banal cheerfulness that sunshine induces in the English. The nineteen-year-old intern sharing her office even attempted a clumsy flirtation and complimented her on a skirt she'd actually been wearing all week. But Phoebe remained indifferent. She retreated to the small courtyard at the back of the building and, with cigarette in hand, stared mournfully up at the blue sky, praying for a thunder cloud, or at least a sudden shower.

Again, the same emotion she'd felt in her dream, the crushing sense that nothing was ever going to change in either her life or her marriage swept across her. She looked over at the window of Alan's office. She knew he was halfway across the country doing a site assessment just outside Newcastle – the roof of a betting shop had been struck by lightning during the Grand Prix and Alan had warned her he'd be home late.

She glanced back up at the sky – one faint white cloud drifted lazily across it, but it looked uneventful and static. If only something would happen that would contort the weatherman's body into another of his delicious little dances. Her longing was palpable, a dull sexual ache. What could Rupert offer her tonight with such boringly perfect weather?

That evening at the magical hour of twenty-five past six the weatherman stood for a moment as if waiting for the camera to focus on him. In that split second Phoebe wondered what Rupert was thinking. Could it, through some weird osmosis, be about her? Could he feel the heat of her gaze tunnelling down the tube, down into his eyes, into his consciousness? Could he distinguish her gaze from the millions of other viewers? The erotic tension she now felt, poised on the edge of the kitchen chair, staring intently at the screen, was surely mutual. How could such intense longing not be? Then, as if to answer both her prayers and her question, Phoebe suddenly noticed the tie Rupert was wearing: a new tie, a tie she hadn't seen in any of his previous appearances. She gasped, her hand instinctively reaching down towards her skirt – the tie and the skirt were made from exactly the same fabric. Thinking she must be imagining it, Phoebe moved nearer to the television screen, now kneeling on the floor beside it. She held the edge of her skirt up against the screen.

No, she wasn't imagining it; the tie and the skirt were the same pattern (a distinctive tartan) and the same colour. A thrill ran through her body. It was a message, it had to be – they were linked, destined for each other. The weatherman was sending her a signal, a signal that he knew about her, he had felt her watching, empathising. They were soul mates in a wind tunnel, two lost people reaching out for each other across a huge savannah of rain, hail, tornados and generally foul weather – but love would prevail.

'Hello, folks. Well, what a day, eh? What a glorious English summer's day, one to cherish, for there are some changes on the way. Let's turn to the northern part of the country, to the very top of Scotland …'

Rupert's baritone voice resonated right down to the tip of Phoebe's clitoris, and the way he swung around to the weather map was positively muscular. She pressed her breasts against the chilly glass of the television screen, imagining Rupert's chiselled profile buried between them. Just then he repeated 'glorious English summer's day', illustrating the phrase with a new gesture Phoebe hadn't seen before – a gentle bending of the knees followed by a sweep of the arms with upturned palms. She was enthralled. Instantly she envisioned her naked body wound around his, legs wrapped over both his hips, his cock buried deep within her, thrusting simultaneously as he articulated the word glorious. With her skirt pushed over her hips and her breasts hanging out of their bra, she reached for her notebook and wrote in her own lexicon of Rupert Thornton's weather phrases: 'Gesture number thirty-seven: the knee bend summer's day'.

Oblivious to her intense scrutiny, Rupert continued: 'We start the day with a stunning empty clear blue sky but as you can see from the map there is a small amount of cloud building up in Scotland which will be followed later in the day by a bank of nimbostratus coming in from the south-east ...'

A bank of nimbostratus coming in from the south-east! It was the very same phrase that had resonated in her dream the night before. Could she really have dreamt the weather before Rupert predicted it? But what was even more thrilling was that the actual order of the words had triggered a gesture from the weatherman that had Phoebe, within seconds, in a sexual frenzy. As she reached down into her panties a glorious sense of omnipotence flooded her. She spent the rest of the weather report pleasuring herself, timing her orgasm so that she came just as the sentence 'And that's all from me, folks, until tomorrow,' fell from Rupert Thornton's lips.

Afterwards, lying there in a fetal position on the kitchen floor, her hand still buried between her legs, the cat wanting to be fed purring and butting itself against her back, Phoebe thought about the way they had both chosen the same material, him for his tie, her for her skirt, the manner in which they appeared to be psychically linked, the coincidence of the way he seemed to like the same weather as herself, and she came to the overwhelming conclusion that she was morally obliged to take their relationship to the next level.

Alan didn't come home that night until late and when he crept into bed at about one am, Phoebe, who'd been woken by the click of the bedroom door, pretended to be asleep. But to her surprise, he reached for her, his long arms encircling her waist. Pulling her towards him he made love to her. It was their usual routine: first he played with her breasts in a slightly distracted manner that, unfortunately for Alan, had always reminded Phoebe of the way her gynaecologist handled them. Then he gave her a little manual stimulation, enough so that he knew she was ready for him. Finally, after a little pant of exertion, he mounted her. Puffing in her ear as he neared his climax, Phoebe realised she would have to resort to fantasy if she was to come at all. Her imagination conjured up the weatherman. Magically, Alan's panting breath became a howling wind sweeping across the weather map of her own body as his body lengthened, his face narrowed, his hair turned blond and thick, and she imagined that it was the weatherman's penis thickening within her. And then, to complete the fantasy, she imagined Rupert's voice whispering 'torrential rain' over and over. This was the final trigger, and Phoebe reached her second orgasm of the day. It was shaping up to be a better summer than she thought.

Over the next few weeks Phoebe lost weight, cut and dyed her hair and filled much of her wardrobe with sexier clothes – shorter skirts, tighter blouses, higher heels. Alan, whose sudden sexual interest had abated again, began to notice and, convinced she'd taken a lover, bribed the young intern his wife worked with to spy on her. But the nineteen year old hadn't noticed any specific change, except that Phoebe seemed to take an unusual interest in the weather forecast on page fifteen of *The Sun*, a fact the intern dutifully reported back to Alan, who then fatally dismissed it as an innocent hobby.

As for Phoebe, well, she thought she was in love, and thinking is the same as being for many of us – whether the love is mutual or not. Our heroine was on a mission. She was convinced she had met her psychic soul mate. Every day for the past month she had correctly dreamt what the weather would be like forty-eight hours later: She would dream it, Rupert would predict it that evening and the next day, without fail, the weather would appear. The weatherman's faithful reproductions of her dreamt predictions thrilled his young devotee to the point of orgasm – sometimes even more than one. He was, Phoebe concluded, the most wonderful of all her lovers, even if she'd never met him. He was capable of plummeting to imaginative depths and then soaring with her to the highest peaks of her most secret and perverse desires.

But as erotically fulfilling as their 'relationship' was, it did not come close to the sense of absolute power her predictive abilities gave her. It was as if Phoebe herself – a mediocre comprehensive school kid who had barely got three O levels – was now unwittingly controlling the weather for the whole of the British Isles, weather that affected transport, plane flights, race meetings, harvesting, the army, the Oxford and Cambridge boat race and the Queen's visit to Windsor Castle. The list was dazzlingly extensive and aroused Phoebe every time she thought about it. It was, well, like she was God.

Phoebe contemplated telling someone – like her older sister – about her extraordinary new-found powers, but she couldn't think of anyone who would take her seriously or, worse, not question her sanity. Certainly her sister had voiced her unfavourable opinion about Phoebe's propensity to imaginative flights of fancy. But Phoebe had to confess her supernatural abilities to someone to validate them, so instead she took to talking to Rupert's image on television every night in between bouts of intense masturbation during the weather report.

'Didn't I tell you it was going to get windy on Thursday? There'll be hail too, along the coast of Ireland, and don't forget the patches of fog in the north-east ... oh yes, oh yes, sweeping rain, and yes! The breaks of sunshine!' she shouted, coming with a shudder as Rupert, smiling brightly into the camera, encircled the air with both his palms as if caressing large breasts.

It was all going along nicely, Phoebe concluded: Rupert was always on time, never disappointed, never answered back, and he made her feel both beautiful and connected to important things – like choreographing the English weather in her dreams. It was the perfect affair and even her marriage was beginning to benefit. The distraction of her obsession had distanced her from Alan, and Alan, sensing this new separation, suddenly felt insecure. Still convinced she was having an affair, he'd taken to vetting the post and on more than one occasion had broken into the secret drawer she kept locked in the chest of drawers in the bedroom, convinced he would find a stash of love letters. To his great puzzlement, he'd found a pile of newspaper clippings, all of which appeared to be weather reports since mid-July, and a small plastic dome (the kind you'd give to a child) that held a miniature skyline of London that, if turned upside down and back again, got snowed upon. This disturbed Alan greatly, although he couldn't quite work out why. He started to wonder whether he shouldn't bring forward the planned date of conception he'd imposed on his young wife, thinking that perhaps having a baby might be the solution. But then, as Alan never got home before seven-thirty, he remained totally oblivious to the real cause of Phoebe's distraction. Alan's solution was to make love to her more often; a reminder note he pencilled in his diary carefully noted the days he knew she was fertile.

Phoebe took her husband's sudden efforts in her stride; it was nice but too late, she told herself, as she was now deeply in love with another, a man she regarded as the love of her life. A couple of times Phoebe had shouted out what sounded like 'Rain!' at the point of climax, but Alan, a pragmatic man at the best of times, decided it was better not to question her on this new habit. After all, he consoled himself, it wasn't as if it was the name of another man. So, over the next couple of months, life went on as normal in the small Victorian terrace house, but perhaps with a little more excitement, the only creature directly affected by Phoebe's obsession with the weatherman being the cat, who had begun to lose weight as her supper got later and smaller every night while her distracted owner pleasured herself.

It was all running along smoothly until one evening in mid-September. Just before cutting to the weather report, the newsreader, an annoyingly jocular brunette who looked and sounded as if she had kept a pet pony in her childhood, congratulated Rupert on the news of his engagement. Watching, Phoebe frozen in horror, her fingers already curled in her pubic hair. The camera cut to Rupert blushing and smiling awkwardly at the camera as he stood stiffly in front of the weather map.

'That's right, Cindy, I have popped the question and she said yes.'

'Have you set a special date, Rupert?'

'Er … we're in no rush …'

'Better make sure it's sunny that day.'

The camera cut back to Rupert, who immediately launched into a detailed account of tomorrow's weather, all of which Phoebe had dreamt of the night before – especially tailored to her needs. *Her* needs. An anguished tirade built up in her mind. How dare he betray her with another lover, never mind a fiancée? Didn't he realise what he was destroying? There was no way he had the same connection with this other woman, no way possible that she could share the very special psychic relationship (not to mention the sex) that Phoebe and Rupert had, she argued out loud. It was obvious that Phoebe had to stop him making a terrible mistake. She had to rescue him from marrying the wrong woman, and the more she thought about it the more frantic she became – she had a moral and spiritual duty to save him.

It took Phoebe almost an hour and five awkward phone calls before she discovered the correct R. Q. Thornton in the phone book. The very fact that the weatherman had a listed number angered her. It was outrageous. Didn't the British government realise how important Rupert was? Didn't they understand how vulnerable it made him? And what did the Q stand for? She talked out loud in frustration, imagining that this might have been how his fiancée tracked him down in the first place, through the telephone book. 'That's what happens to famous people, they get exploited, used. Rupert is in great danger,' she told herself as she wrote down his home address. 'Rupert needs protecting from this woman. She's just out to exploit both his fame and talent!' Her angry voice startled the now starving cat, who made a dash for the back door.

Sighing, Phoebe picked up the telephone and rang the BBC to find out which Met Office they sent their weathermen to, just in case she would have to book a long-distance train trip. She was relieved to discover that the weathermen always broadcast from their studios in Shepherd's Bush and only visited the Met Office in Exeter occasionally. She was convinced she needed to watch over Rupert both at work and at his house. Now she just needed a plan.

Later that night Phoebe refused to allow Alan to make love to her for the first time in their marriage. To his secret delight Alan found this new assertiveness made his wife more erotic than she'd ever been before, while on the other side of the bed Phoebe tossed and turned, terrified she was about to lose the first man in her life who really understood her. Rupert Q. Thornton. Finally she fell asleep counting clouds.

That night she dreamt of heavy fog lifting at midday, then a period of bright sunshine broken only by a late afternoon shower. It was like heaven.

The next day at work, acting on a hunch, Phoebe accessed a file of car owners and their numberplates through a car insurance plan run by the company she worked for. To her utter joy she found Rupert Q. Thornton's details filed under T: his numberplate, the model and colour of his car and his home address. Phoebe couldn't help noticing that Rupert, like her, drove a Volvo and it was also blue – not the same model as her own, but close enough; yet again, it was another indication that they were destined to be together. The last piece of the jigsaw was in place.

Later that day she lied to Alan about why she would be home late. When the six o'clock news was over and Rupert had again performed the exact gestures that signalled fog, sunshine and light rain, leaving Phoebe luxuriating in post-coital bliss, she was more convinced than ever that they were the most synchronised lovers in history, and the sooner she put him on the right emotional path the better. She put on her raincoat and drove over to Shepherd's Bush, determined to encounter the weatherman as he left the BBC studio.

Knowing his numberplate made it easy for Phoebe to locate Rupert's car in space number four in the underground car park at the BBC. Flanked by empty parking spaces, the blue Volvo, with an almost mournful air, seemed to be waiting for its owner to return. Phoebe parked opposite, careful to conceal her own Volvo behind a pillar. She turned the engine off, struggling to control the growing excitement that had begun to sweep through her in waves.

Ten minutes later the steel doors of the elevator opened and Rupert Q. Thornton stepped out. A jolt of recognition shot through Phoebe's body so intensely that she had to stop herself from shouting out. Instead she slipped down in the car seat, watching through the side mirror as the tall lanky weatherman strode across the concrete car park. He was much more handsome than he appeared on TV, she noted with delight, one of those rare individuals who looked much better in the flesh. His hair was longer and a blond forelock hung rakishly over one eye. He was wearing orange corduroy trousers and a brown leather jacket which, in contrast to the formal suit he always wore for the weather report, gave him a youthful air. He certainly didn't look like the dreamy, slightly academic man Phoebe had imagined – if anything, he looked far more dangerous, and far sexier. His expressive hands swung by his sides as he moved with an endearing idiosyncratic gait, and he appeared to be humming to himself.

Oblivious, he walked right past her car – literally within two feet. Phoebe ducked then peered up through the window, catching sight of a well-shaped pair of buttocks she felt she had clasped so many times in her imagination that the shape of his arse seemed to echo in the palms of her hands. Rupert Thornton reached his car, flicked the blond forelock back then got into his blue Volvo.

A minute later Phoebe followed him out of the car park. Outside it was dusk, and the sunny day was threatening to transform into a breezy rainy night – just as her dream had predicted the night before his evening weather report: she'd dreamt that that night and the next day would bring rain. She watched the heavy raindrops begin to fall with great satisfaction, feeling even more powerful with the weatherman within her sight, who she was now convinced she was psychologically manipulating, at the wheel of the car in front of her. If only Rupert knew how intuitive she was, that alone would be enough to make him abandon his fiancée for her. The thought rang around her mind obsessively, distracting her from the hypnotic rhythm of the windscreen wipers, the roar of the city traffic, the rattle of her car engine. It was as if the world contained only two people – herself and Rupert – and that an invisible ribbon now ran between the two cars in perfect equilibrium. He was pulling her as much as she was following him. All those hours she'd spent staring at him through the television screen, now all she needed to do was to punch her hand through the glass between them and he would be hers.

'I control you,' she whispered to the windscreen wipers, to the silvery drizzle, her car interior a confession box, the steering wheel a silent witness. 'We will be together, Rupert darling, I promise you.'

As the blue Volvo turned in front of her she too turned in perfect synchronisation – it was a dance, like lovemaking itself, Phoebe concluded.

She tailed him all the way to his small townhouse in Chiswick. Driving past him as he pulled into the driveway, she continued around the block so that he wouldn't get suspicious. By the time she re-entered the narrow suburban street and parked opposite, Rupert was just entering his front door.

The lounge room lit up as someone switched on the lights. Phoebe leant forward with interest. A leather couch and matching armchairs, a modern steel lamp, a print of a Rothko painting were all visible through the large windows which were uncovered. Just then Rupert, pulling his jacket off, walked past the windows. A tall brunette – skinny, Phoebe noted with some disgust, no meat on her bones, no sensuality whatsoever – entered from another door on the other side of the room. Rupert and the unknown woman (his fiancée presumably) met in the middle of the room in an embrace.

Shocked, Phoebe inhaled sharply. It was near impossible to dismiss the piercing sense of betrayal: betrayal that built to an overwhelming anger. How dare he even consider any kind of intimacy with anyone other than her? Didn't he know that they were soul mates? One of her hands suddenly slipped and she became aware of how hard she was gripping the steering wheel. Outside the rain abruptly got heavier, now hitting the car window with unleashed fury. Phoebe, trying to get a better view, pressed her face against the car window. Inside the house the couple finally separated and Phoebe found that she could breathe again.

Rupert started pacing the room while his fiancée sat in one of the armchairs. He appeared to be describing his day, or at least that's what Phoebe imagined. The weatherman walked to the window and looked blankly out, his back to his fiancée. Phoebe's heart jumped. Can he see me, she wondered, perhaps even sense my presence unconsciously? It was a delicious thought. Phoebe contemplated getting out of the car and running towards him to meet him, to rescue him from the mistake he was so obviously making. She was so convinced he would be thrilled to see her that her legs began to shake with the anticipation of movement. They belonged together, it was as evident as the sun travelling through the sky during the day or the moon at night. Surely somewhere in his soul, his mind, even in his heart, Rupert Thornton understood this?

By this time Phoebe had worked herself up into a frenzy. Only the thought of possible arrest or, worse still, Rupert misunderstanding her very genuine motives stopped her from stepping out of the car and racing across the rain-streaked lawn. Just then there was a huge peal of thunder and a streak of lightning hit the tree in the small front yard. With a loud crack a large branch bent then fell off in a shower of wet leaves onto Rupert's blue Volvo. This was another sign, it had to be – the weather god responding to her frustration, to the 'unnatural' order of things.

At the window Rupert's expression turned to horror. He raced out of the house then, as the rain soaked his trousers and plastered down his hair, attempted to pull the branch off the crushed roof of his car. His fiancée stood in the doorway, poised but obviously reluctant to step out into the pouring rain. Phoebe, fascinated, could now hear both of them clearly.

'I could do with a hand, darling!' Rupert sounded tense, infuriated even. The strong aggressive tone thrilled Phoebe; it was so much more assertive than his TV voice. Phoebe looked across at the fiancée, who appeared to be indifferent to her lover's distress. She glanced down at her shoes sceptically.

'I would help but these shoes are brand new and they're suede, they cost a fortune!' Well-bred, exclusive girls' school accent: immediately Phoebe pictured where she might have grown up – a Georgian mansion in Chelsea – spoilt, sheltered, impossible to please. Rupert glared over his shoulder towards her. Again Phoebe had the impression he was on the brink of losing his temper.

'This branch is a little heavy for one person.' His voice was icily polite. His fiancée tossed her long chestnut hair.

'Oh, sweetheart, I suspect my shoes might be worth more than your old Volvo,' she tried to joke, shrugging helplessly.

Rupert, now dripping wet, had his back turned to her as he pulled heavily on the large branch. Phoebe could see an expression of pure fury crossing his face. Elated that the couple obviously had problems, she started up the car and accelerated out of the small street. Now she knew she had a chance.

It was past ten by the time Phoebe got home. Alan was already in bed, his suit, shoes and tie neatly folded on the chair. Navigating the dim bedroom, Phoebe managed to pull her clothes off without waking him. She slipped in between the cold sheets, curling her feet up against his shins to warm up. Outside she could hear the rain dwindling down to slow steady dripping. She fell asleep with the image of Rupert's furious face suspended before her mind's eye.

That night she dreamt of a huge storm with hurricane force winds hitting most of the south of England: great winds bending trees almost in half as they swept through forests and fields, cars skidding across roads as the wind pushed them blindly into each other's path, huge waves lashing the seafronts, people trapped on their roofs because of flooding, people dying ... She woke in a state of rigid fear, her body drenched in cold sweat. She glanced over at the clock: six am, 14 October 1987. Alan was still sleeping, his snore a small wind that whistled around the corners of the bedroom.

Phoebe pulled the bedcovers back and stepped onto the carpet then made her way over to the window. Beyond the lace curtains the day was breaking across the small concrete patio. Beams of early sunlight illuminated a family of sparrows pecking hopefully around the foot of a potted rose bush. Phoebe sighed in relief: maybe this nightmare hadn't been predictive, maybe it was born out of guilt, guilt that she'd actually stepped into the life of the man she was obsessed with. Maybe this was a warning telling her to leave the weatherman alone.

Behind her she could hear Alan getting up and padding his way to the toilet; three minutes later it flushed. The sound of rushing water pulled her straight back to her nightmare – there had been the sound of rushing water in the background, and distant screaming. The image of a huge bank of dark blue cloud rolling across open sky, the shadow of which turned the water black below it, came back to her. It was a storm of biblical proportions, a storm that could change history. No, she hadn't summoned this weather – rather, the storm had called her to it.

Her reverie was broken by the sensation of a warm body pressing against her back and bottom; a warm body with an erection.

'Fancy a quickie before work?' Alan murmured into her ear as his hands slid around to her breasts and his hips executed a couple of comical thrusts which, unfortunately for Alan, made Phoebe think of an overenthusiastic dog.

'We've got about ten minutes,' he continued, a little more eager in his movements. For a moment Phoebe wondered whether Rupert's foreplay would be so ribald and clumsy. She couldn't imagine so; the weatherman seemed far more sensitive and romantic.

'Oh, what the hell ...' Resigned, she allowed herself to be led to the bed.

That morning Alan drove her to work. Inside the office building they parted to go to their separate floors. Once Phoebe had reached her desk she was hijacked by one of the senior clerks wanting her to take dictation for a lecture he had to give at a conference.

Sitting in front of a large window with the warm sunshine falling on her back, Phoebe found it harder and harder to concentrate as his voice droned on. Once or twice she found herself doodling on her notepad – great stormy clouds, showers of heavy pencilled dashes, hail. Was it possible there would be a huge storm the very next day? If anything the weather seemed unseasonably warm, even slightly humid, like an Indian summer.

Her predictive nightmare was beginning to feel like a huge ethical dilemma, but who could she warn and who would believe her?

Phoebe gazed through the glass partition at the rows of young women in the typing pool – all of them would be thrown into a maelstrom tomorrow, she couldn't helping thinking, remembering the image of trees flung like matchsticks into the air, electric wires vibrating like demented guitar strings between telegraph poles before snapping. People would die. People would drown. Thank God Rupert would warn them tonight, she thought, and again the warm rush of absolute power flooded through her. He would hear her dream, like he'd faithfully heard all the other dreams, regardless of any influence his fiancée had over him – true love would win out.

At lunch in a small Greek café around the corner from work, Phoebe fielded Alan's questions about where she'd been the night before.

'At my sister's,' she told him, gazing innocently into his eyes. 'You know how she's been having trouble with her husband.' Disbelief did not leave his face. Phoebe leant across and caressed his knee under the table. 'It was nice making love this morning,' she lied. 'Let's go to bed early tonight …' Phoebe tried smiling seductively.

'I won't be back before ten, I've got to finish some reports at work.' Alan, still suspicious, fumbled with his pita bread. Phoebe's hand moved up his thigh.

'Never mind, love, I'll still be waiting,' she purred. Alan, placated, dropped both the pita and his questioning.

*

Phoebe poured herself a small glass of sherry, fed the miaowing cat early then switched on the end of the six o'clock news just in time for the newsreader to make some wry comment about a very late Indian summer before the program cut to the weather report. Rupert, in his suit, stood smiling, holding the pointer up against the map of the British Isles.

'Well, apart from the slight blip of the sudden squall early last night, with the mercury promising to hover around 60 degrees Fahrenheit, the weather has returned to being unseasonably warm for this time of year. Tomorrow we're looking at fairly clear skies, with the promise of a shower early afternoon ...'

Phoebe let her glass fall to the floor where it shattered. Profoundly shocked, she didn't even bother to look down at the spreading sherry.

'The storm! Why don't you tell them about the storm?!' she yelled at the TV screen, causing the cat to bolt out of the room.

On the screen Rupert seemed to hesitate, almost as if he'd heard her. Then, after a slightly perplexed smile, he continued: 'This will be good news for gardeners or farmers who are hoping to slip in some last-minute gardening before the winter frosts ...'

Phoebe's heartbeat quickened to a nauseating fast pace and her mind raced. She couldn't let this go – images of the nightmare swam across the kitchen ceiling, each increasingly more apocalyptic. Panicked, she picked up the telephone and dialled through to the switchboard of the BBC. Near tears, she pleaded with the operator who, swept up by her obvious distress, put her through to the newsroom. Holding her breath, Phoebe watched the screen as Rupert appeared to receive a message through his hidden earpiece.

'We've just had a phone call from a concerned viewer, a Mrs P. Rodehurst from Acton.' Phoebe winced: at least they could have got her surname right. Rupert continued: 'She's phoned to tell us there have been reports that a major hurricane is about to hit southern England.'

Phoebe held her breath. 'Now, now is the last chance you have to redeem yourself, Rupert,' she said, speaking to the screen, convinced that he could hear her somehow, in a dim, remote, semi-conscious way. 'Now is your chance to be the first to give the warning – this could make your career!' She thumped the table, making the laid cutlery rattle.

To her horror Rupert smiled weakly, his voice taking on a patronising, soothing tone, as if he were speaking to a distressed four year old.

'Well, Mrs Rodehurst, let me reassure you – we don't have hurricanes in England. And certainly looking at the reports from the Met Office plus the patterns of both temperature and wind change of the past few days, there is really no need for alarm ...'

'You bloody idiot! How could you betray me!' Phoebe screamed, throwing the remote control across the room where it bounced against the wall. Unperturbed, Rupert continued, now pointing towards the right side of the map.

'There is actually a warm front coming in from France which should push the cloud build-up we experienced earlier today further across to the north-west ...'

Phoebe didn't bother waiting for the end of the program. Grabbing her car keys she bolted towards the front door.

Twenty minutes later she found herself waiting in a corridor outside a door marked 'STUDIO FOUR: News/Current Affairs and Weather'. A young girl carrying a clipboard came out of the door followed by the newsreader whose face was covered in heavy make-up. Phoebe recognised her immediately. The newsreader was talking intensely to a small bearded man who Phoebe immediately assumed must have been the director of the program. Wrapped in conversation they didn't even glance at Phoebe, who pretended to be interested in the rows of photographs that lined the walls: celebrities all posing with the newsreaders. A second later Rupert stepped out into the bright fluorescent light.

'Rupert!' she blurted out, deluded by a sense of intense intimacy. Surprised, the weatherman stopped in his stride. He glanced over at the pretty blonde woman who, despite her rather obvious sexual allure, had a strange feral grace that, against his better judgement, he found attractive.

'Do I know you?'

'Yes … well no … sort of. But that's not important, Rupert …' Again he found the way she pronounced his name – as if she'd known him for years – at once deeply disturbing and erotic. '… you are wrong! So wrong you don't know how you have endangered both your career and the British public,' she announced in such an authoritative tone that for one horrible moment Rupert thought she might possibly be government – or worse, MI5 – coming to pursue some awful transgression he had unwittingly made on air. Best to play dumb, he told himself, but damn it, she was rather attractive. He started towards the exit; to his irritation Phoebe followed, running to keep up.

'I'm not sure what you are referring to but I'm sure my researcher will be able to –' He was forced to respond but kept his pace up anyhow. Phoebe grabbed his arm.

'The storm, Rupert, it's going to be huge, well into hurricane proportions, and it's going to hit Britain later today and for most of tomorrow.'

'Mrs Rodehurst ...?' He stopped still, the memory of the whispered phone call during his report came back to him now with sickening clarity.

'Mrs Rosehurst. To you, Phoebe.' She reached down and squeezed one of Rupert's limp hands, immediately sending a wave of desire through him that added considerably to his confusion. Phoebe held on to his hand, now raising it up near one of her large breasts in a dramatic fashion. 'After all, with an understanding like ours ...' she continued breathily.

Rupert's logic reached out beyond the fog of sexual desire that had temporarily derailed him — along with the maddening perfume that enveloped the woman. He snapped into professional detachment.

'Look, I appreciate your interest in the program, and in particular the weather report, however you really have no need to panic. You have both my and the London Meteorological Board's word that Britain will not be under siege tonight or tomorrow — not from the weather, not from the French, not from the Soviets and certainly not from the Germans,' he joked, then saw with dismay that Phoebe hadn't smiled. In fact her expression had now intensified into one of deathly seriousness.

'Oh, Rupert, if you only knew how terrible the mistake is that you're making. I know you're wrong, and just think how this is going to impact on your reputation, Rupert — you will only be remembered as the one who always got it wrong, because

I can reassure you that this storm will be the storm of the century, I know it.'

'Does this prediction have any scientific basis? Or is it all just tea leaves and the way the autumn leaves are curling?' he snapped tersely, then remembered to snatch back his hand. Phoebe planted herself firmly in front of the tall weatherman, took his chin between her fingers (a gesture that thoroughly unnerved him) and made him look into her eyes.

'Do I seem familiar to you? Think hard, Rupert. Is there anything about me that you remember? My face, my eyes, the sound of my voice?' Again vertigo swept through Rupert as, for one ghastly minute, he recalled a particularly woeful period of promiscuity just after finishing university. The idea that Phoebe might be one of the young girls he seduced then abandoned rattled through him like sudden indigestion. Surely not …yet somehow she did seem familiar.

'Are you a friend of Penelope's?' he ventured, rather hoping she wasn't.

'You mean your fiancée?' Phoebe didn't bother to disguise the disgust in her voice. Rupert nodded cautiously. She certainly didn't sound like one of Penelope's upper-class girlfriends, many of whom were an annoying combination of stupid and arrogant.

'Absolutely not. Does she ever actually watch you, you know, on TV?'

'Weather's not her thing,' Rupert retorted. 'She has other attributes.' Although at that moment he was having trouble remembering what they were. He glanced down the corridor, the exit sign was beckoning – he couldn't afford to be seen with a mad fan, he had to get rid of her or at least get outside. He started walking, again she followed.

They turned a corner and walked into the car park lift. It was empty. As the doors slid closed, Phoebe suddenly realised she was alone and within intimate proximity of her idol.

'Then how can she really know you, or appreciate your genius?' she murmured as sexily as she could.

'That's not important to me,' Rupert replied, now acutely aware that he was lying. The fact that Penelope displayed no interest in his career was a source of great secret frustration to him.

'It is to me. You see that's how you know me. I've been watching you for months, and you might not know it consciously but we have a connection, a psychic connection.'

Rupert glanced at the light panel indicating each floor, suddenly aware of how long the lift was taking. Despite finding her physically attractive, the intensity of this strange young woman made him nervous. Phoebe moved closer, the scent of her closing over Rupert like a fog, a suffocating miasma. The weatherman shuffled discreetly backward until his back was against the wall of the elevator.

'I don't believe in such matters, I'm a scientist,' he protested.

Stretching up on her toes, Phoebe started to mimic the weatherman's gestures and vocal inflections.

'Tomorrow will start with a gloriously sparse blue sky. By midday there will just be a sprinkling of cumuli ...' Her arms and hands swept through the air in perfect mimicry, her fingers copying his particular flourishes – it was beautiful, it was genuflection, it was worship, and it was disturbingly exact. Watching her, Rupert was surprised to find himself both blushing and hardening. He thrust one hand into his pocket hoping she hadn't noticed his erection.

'Okay, so you're a fan, but what's this got to do with whether tomorrow will bring a hurricane or not?'

'I dreamt it last night.'

The lift shuddered to a halt and the steel door slid open. Rupert stepped forward but Phoebe blocked him.

'You have to believe me. I've dreamt the correct weather for the past few months. And every following night on the six o'clock news you've given the weather report exactly how it's been in my dreams, except for tonight's program. Tonight you got it wrong. Profoundly wrong. Please, Rupert, people are going to die and it's going to be on your watch. Are you going to be able to live with that?'

She's mad, stark raving mad, Rupert thought, his mind now racing wildly. She was one of those psychos who only happen to other people, other more famous people who work at the Beeb, he concluded, pushing past her, but it was flattering – his very own stalker. Not even that guy from *Blue Peter* had one.

'Please, I have a bus to catch.'

'Yes, I know, your car got damaged by a tree.'

He stopped, shocked. 'How did you know that?'

'I told you I care.'

She stepped aside then followed him, running to keep up with the long stride of the meteorologist.

'I can drive you,' she insisted, her hand clawing at his jacket as he tried to ignore her.

They reached the entrance to the car park. To Rupert's surprise rain had now begun to fall in angry squalls carried by sudden blasts of bitterly cold wind. The temperature had dropped at least five degrees since they'd left his office, Rupert calculated – now that hadn't been predicted by the Met Office. He glanced down at Phoebe – she might be mad but she was sexy. She smiled, a lingering sensual appraisal that felt like fingers on his body, experienced fingers that wanted to give him pleasure, unlike the reluctant and clumsy fumbling of his fiancée, who always seemed happy to receive pleasure but not to give it. Why did this strange young woman look so familiar? And what if she was right? It was an extraordinary claim, this psychic meteorological connection, but Rupert, despite his assertion of scientific rationalism, was not opposed to the extraordinary. After all, he'd often felt that his interest in meteorology was more of a spiritual calling than a scientific interest. Was he not a little like a prophet? Was it not a noble crusade to inform the British of the weather, a subject that shaped both the nation's lives and conversation?

A flicker of pride burst into flame somewhere below his belly button. It felt suspiciously sexual and he struggled to ignore it. But he liked the feeling, he liked to feel important, indispensable to the British public, and here was a woman offering him the opportunity to become heroic.

As if intuiting his thoughts, Phoebe leaned into him, the tips of her soft breasts pressing against his chest. He could not or did not want to move.

'You see, Rupert, you are a national treasure, the weather vane of the nation. Unlike Penelope, I really understand the quintessential power of both your talent and position. You must take action!' Her voice and eyes were mesmerising but even more seductive was the idea that if she were right, he would be the first to raise the alarm, an act bound to both immortalise him and place him onto the plinth of history.

'What have you got to lose by believing me? If I'm wrong, your original weather report will keep your reputation intact; if I'm right and you act, you will be famous.'

It was all too much for the weatherman, who'd only been promoted to the six o'clock news three months before, his previous posting being the Norfolk rural radio station.

'Okay, we'll drive to the Met Office in Exeter. If the readings bear out your story, I'll organise an emergency news bulletin.' As soon as the words were out of his mouth Rupert regretted them, but it was too late now. Phoebe flung her arms around him and pulled him into an embrace.

'You see, I knew we were destined to be together,' she murmured into his left ear.

It took over an hour to get out of London. The temperature had dropped another five degrees, and it had grown so blustery that Phoebe's small Volvo kept getting pushed across the motorway. Rupert stared out of the window, increasingly dismayed by the deteriorating weather. He already had an image of his producer berating him in the morning. He glanced at the clock set in the dashboard. It was already quarter to nine. He knew the Met Office was bound to be manned tonight (it always was in weather emergencies) but as the heavy rain rattled down onto the roof of the car he wondered how they could have got the predictions so wrong. Judging by the direction of the wind, the weather must have arrived from mainland Europe. Surely the Met had had warnings from Holland, France and Germany? For one horrible moment Rupert wondered whether there wasn't some sinister political motive for keeping England in the dark, a conspiracy to bring down the country.

They turned onto the M3, driving past an accident now hauled onto the emergency road. A truck had turned onto its side and several cars following it had crashed into it. The red and blue lights of the ambulances and police cars blinked like demented beacons in the thickening fog and increasingly Rupert had the uncomfortable sensation that the two of them were like pilgrims driving out into the great unknown.

There was also the undeniable erotic tension between him and Phoebe. It was inevitable that his long legs kept accidentally brushing against her hand as she worked the gear stick. Or was it accidental? Rupert had the impression that the strange but hypnotically attractive woman sitting next to him might be touching him deliberately. He sneaked a look across at her, her determined profile illuminated in splashes of blue and red light. She appeared to be enjoying the crisis, even relishing the way she accelerated through endless gushes of water. And yet Rupert, normally a conservative man, found her obvious enthusiasm for the appalling weather immensely exciting. He too had always found that storms released the animal in him (or perhaps the anima, as a good Jungian mate of his would have called it) – a kind of instinctive joy, a wild revelling in the knowledge that there was something bigger than man, something that could throw ordinary life into utter chaos. Had he found his soul mate after all? And if so, where did this leave Penelope?

Meanwhile, at the wheel for what seemed like the first time in her life, Phoebe felt as if she was in the right place at the right time and, for once, sitting next to the right man. She would prevail and he would see how perfectly they were suited, would have a sudden epiphany, and the secret recesses of his psyche would spring open and he'd realise how many times they had already made love in their imaginations. In the meantime she was determined to get the weatherman to the Met Office before midnight so at least Rupert could broadcast a warning for the next morning for areas yet to be hit by the storm. The most important thing, though, was that he believed her.

But it was difficult to drive without being distracted by his physical presence. It wasn't just the unerring sense of finally being with someone you'd imagined making love to every night for months, it was also the way the weatherman smelt that was driving her crazy. His scent was a delicious combination of a dry lemony aftershave, faint sweat and a whiff of old leather. She could almost taste him. And already she was convinced she knew how his mouth would feel, the soft shimmering texture of his skin, the long slim legs, his chest covered with feathery blond hair and, most distractingly of all, the feel of his cock inside her. Her fingers tightened around the knob of the gear stick, the bulbous hot plastic suddenly flesh in her palm. She swerved suddenly as a cat dashed across the road.

'Whoa! You don't want to get us killed en route, Phoebe.' Rupert rested his hand over her hand on the steering wheel, and immediately a bolt of electricity shot through her. He'd used her name, he'd used her name! All those nights she'd imagined that voice whispering her name at the height of passion, legs straddled over each arm of the lounge chair, and now he had spoken it. Her erotic reverie was broken by an awkward cough from Rupert.

'Look, I think I should phone the Met Office to let them know we're coming, and perhaps I should phone home, my fiancée will be waiting …'

'But we'll be there within two hours …' Phoebe sped up the car hopefully.

Rupert peered out of the side window. If anything the weather appeared to be worsening. Sheets of water were beating down and the trees on the bank opposite the freeway were now bending like palm trees in a hurricane. To Rupert's horror, he suddenly realised they were elms – he'd never seen English trees so stressed. Now for the first time that evening he was afraid they wouldn't reach the Met Office in time.

'Look, turn off the next country lane. I think we should at least try to find a phone booth. Please, Phoebe!'

Phoebe turned at a sign reading 'DOGSWOOD VILLAGE – 3 miles'. The road immediately narrowed into a bumpy country road then narrowed again into a lane. Visibility was bad. On either side of the car there seemed to be nothing but the looming shadow of forest, which now appeared to lurch from side to side like drunken demons. Frightened she might blow a tyre on the uneven surface, Phoebe slowed down. The car bumped and groaned over the road surface like a ship on a stormy ocean. Anxious, Rupert unwound his window slightly. The car was immediately filled with the sound of creaking and the loud roar of the wind. There was no sign of a phone booth or any other mark of civilisation. Suddenly Phoebe screeched to a halt, jolting Rupert forward violently in his seat.

'What was that?!' he yelled, thankful he was wearing a seatbelt. Phoebe leant forward, wiping the misty window with her hand. In front of them, only about a metre away, lay a large tree, the tangled abandoned mass of leaves and branches stretching from one side of the narrow lane to the other.

'Great,' Rupert muttered. Phoebe switched the car heater up and settled back in her seat.

'Look on the bright side – we could have been killed if we'd driven into it.' Surrendering, she smiled. 'It's wild out there, wild and unpredictable.'

As if in reply, there was a sudden loud crunch followed by a crashing just behind them. Both swung around – another tree had fallen, barely missing the back bumper by inches. This time it was a massive oak. It looked as if it might have been living for centuries.

'What is happening?' Rupert whispered, both terrified and awed by such carnage.

'This is,' Phoebe replied firmly, and turning around she took his mouth in a long deep kiss.

Rupert sank back against the seat as Phoebe, feeling blindly for the lever, pushed his seat back so that it was almost horizontal. Still kissing him she slipped her leg over his waist and mounted him, her hands searching under his shirt, down into his trousers. Tongues still intertwined Rupert moaned; he'd never wanted someone so immediately and without the usual courtship preamble, the crippling shyness he had on occasion experienced. The sheer sexuality of the situation felt almost spiritual to him. He didn't think; his mind was blank except for the overwhelming drive to be inside her, to have his cock completely engulfed and buried within her. He tore off her jacket and then violently hoisted up her jumper; her ample breasts were cradled by a simple black cotton bra. The fullness and firmness of them amazed him (Penelope was small breasted) and he paused in his surprise.

Smiling down at him Phoebe unclipped her bra, letting it slip down to the car floor. Her skin was milky-white, her nipples wine-red and large, and now pertly erect. She lifted his hands, fluttering her own fingers through his in imitation of the weather-telling gestures he used on TV.

'Cumulus or altostratus?' She laid his hands over her breasts, the nipples hard eager points in the centre of his palms. An overwhelming sense of coming home flooded through Rupert – finally, here was a woman who spoke his language.

'Two large banks of fluffy white cumulus laced with sunshine,' he replied, abandoning himself entirely to the moment, his voice throaty with lust.

He reached across and, cupping one breast with both hands, took the large erect nipple between his teeth and bit down, ever so gently. Phoebe felt herself moisten, a delicious tingle ran like electric lines forming a vibrating taut triangle between each nipple and the tip of her clitoris. She wanted him so much it was as if she could taste him in the back of her mouth. One of Rupert's hands found its way between her thighs, slipping in between the edge of her wet pants and her labia. He caught her hardened clit between two long fingers and began expertly pulling backwards and forwards.

'And what do we have here? A sudden wet trough …'

Between her gasps Phoebe managed to murmur back: '… leading to rain …'

'Of the relief variety,' Rupert added firmly, the image of warm moist air rising up from the sea over mountains to fall as rain now curled around his imagination in perfect synchronicity with Phoebe's obvious excitement that was engulfing his fingers.

He pushed her back against the dashboard and lifted her skirt, pulling the edge of her underpants to one side of her sex. Engorged with blood and dramatically visible through her blonde pubic hair, her sex looked like an exotic orchid with her clit a small dark red tongue. He pulled her legs and buttocks further up his torso so that arching, with her hands pressed palm upwards against the car roof, Phoebe's sex was close to his face. Outside a sudden violent gust of wind shook the car. Mirroring the wind's motion, Rupert blew across her sex, her labia quivering in response. Phoebe moaned, wanting him so much to take her into his mouth that the very anticipation of it was almost making her come.

Rupert blew again as the wind outside rattled the car once more.

'Take me,' Phoebe whispered then, reaching down, tore the two sides of her underpants so she was able to rid herself of them. Rupert firmly grasped both her buttocks. She tasted like the sea, he thought, like the moist earth, like the wild rain that hammered against the sides of the car like thrown gravel. Sucking gently at first, his two fingers playing her, he accelerated his tongue circling around her clit between the sucking, his other fingers slipping in and out.

Above him Phoebe thrashed with pleasure, alternately trying to balance against the car roof and trying not to come. Outside in the lane the weather intensified, and a small stream hidden in the forest to the right of the lane burst its narrow banks as water began to race along the forest floor like the tendrils of some mud-covered spider. Finally Phoebe could stand it no longer. She pulled her hips away from Rupert's mouth. She reached out and freed his cock from his trousers. The size of him sprung up rock hard. He had a kind of blunt tip, the kind she liked to fantasise about, and he was easily as large as she had allowed in her imaginary lovemaking with him. She held herself over him, catching his penis between her well-lubricated labia. They looked into each other's eyes and both, within that moment, imagined they saw all kinds of swirling cloud and weather trapped within each other's pupils, a meteorological drama that transcended the pettiness of their own existence; if it wasn't love it was certainly passion.

'And now the apex of the storm.' Phoebe's words hung within the confines of the car like a prophecy both now knew was impossible to escape. And with the word storm still sounding, she pushed down onto him. And oh, the size of him was magnificent; it filled her in a way she'd never been filled before, pushing out all memory of her husband or any lover before that.

She was born anew. The sexual pleasure mounting within her felt as if it were an extension of the accelerating storm around them, the crash of thunder, the loud creaking of the trees, all building to a crescendo. As for Rupert, the tightness of her held him like wet silk as she slid up and down, holding her lips apart so he could watch his cock push into her, playing her clit as his own groaning sounded around him. He had never felt more in his own skin, as if his consciousness now was his skin, as if all that mattered was the present tense and this excruciatingly pleasurable gallop towards orgasm. Phoebe arrived first, screaming suddenly as she contracted over and over and over again in the longest orgasm she'd ever experienced. Triggered by her contracting vagina, Rupert couldn't hold off any longer. He too began yelling as he came. Just at that moment lightning hit a tree nearby and a heavy branch fell with a crack as loud as a gunshot, missing the car by just a few feet – but neither Rupert nor Phoebe noticed.

Phoebe woke first, with a terrible crick in her neck. She was still straddled over Rupert, her head resting up against the side of the driver's seat, the grey of dawn illuminating the weatherman's sleeping face. Gazing down at him she wondered whether she should wake him. Outside it was still raining, and although there was a break in the clouds, there was also another bank of black sinister cloud creeping over the horizon, swallowing the blue before it like some huge evil dragon.

'Jesus, what time is it?' Rupert woke with a start. Phoebe disentangled herself from him and climbed back into the driver's seat. She glanced down at the car clock.

'Six-thirty.'

'Christ, I'm screwed.' Rupert reached across and switched the car radio on. The car was filled with a burst of static then, as he tuned the radio, a clear voice emerged.

'… the most severe storm seen this century has taken most of the country by surprise. The Met Office has even taken the unheard-of action of issuing an apology, claiming they had received no warning from Europe. The storm, which has been of hurricane proportions, has uprooted hundreds of thousands of mature trees, caused severe flooding in some parts and ground all flights from Luton airport and further up the country. There have also been several fatalities reported. A twenty-three-year-old woman, Penelope Morgan, drowned in a swollen river in Kent …'

Rupert's face turned ashen; Phoebe reached across for his hand.

'That's not your Penelope, is it?' But Rupert's face answered her question. Before she had a chance to switch the radio off, the voice had moved on to the next fatality.

'... While forty-year-old actuary, Alan Rosehurst, working in the insurance industry, was struck dead by lightning. The Prime Minister will make a statement later ...'

'Alan ...?' Phoebe whispered, and for a moment it was like the wind in the trees answered back.

FLOWER

Sara yawned, opened one eye, allowed the thin English sun to fall across her face then shut the eye again. She liked the one-sided dimension this skewed vision gave her. It seemed to simplify her complicated world and the endless financial responsibility that had coloured everything lately.

'2009, 2009,' she thought to herself, 'where have the last two years gone?' She lay in bed a little longer but the rose-coloured heat leaked in under her eyelids. 'I can only shut the day out for so long,' she thought, snuggling down further into the cool Egyptian cotton sheets. 'Besides,' (and at this point her eyes snapped open) 'life is vitality, vitality is good and I am vital,' she murmured with as much enthusiasm as she could muster. It was the mantra her life coach/trainer had instructed her to repeat every morning upon waking. It was meant to counteract her current malaise, a post-divorce depression that had lingered for months matched with downward-spiralling self-esteem.

'I'm here to triumph, make a new start and all that other New Age bullshit,' she concluded, failing to keep cynicism out of her voice.

Swinging her legs out of the bed she stepped down onto the Persian rug. The high-ceilinged Regency bedroom was large and beautiful in its proportions. She had deliberately kept it sparse, a restraint that had irritated Hugh, her ex-husband, whose own taste ran to the baroque and anything else that shouted wealth. In contrast, Sara's furniture was a mix of original Empire and a little Louis XIV, then peppered dramatically with a couple of startling sculptural contemporary furniture pieces. In front of the curved floor-to-ceiling window bay sat a white marble table, its sweeping organic curves rendering the stone near translucent. Although functional, it resembled both a desk and a large white flower, yet somehow the ornate Louis XIV gilded chair sitting beside it made perfect visual logic. That was Sara all over. Despite her inherited wealth and despite both parents having little to no taste of their own, she had managed to forge an aesthetic lexicon of her own − no mean feat in the social circles she moved in.

The floor was cool under her bare feet. She walked over to the large mahogany cupboard and opened the door, revealing the full-length mirror that was set on the inside. Pausing, Sara took a deep breath, let her dressing gown slip to the floor then looked up at her naked reflection. It was a ritual she'd adopted since her separation and divorce − a kind of brutal self-examination to track any visible signs of either emotional or physical disintegration. In fact she'd lost weight, initially from the shock and then deliberately with the help of her life coach. After all, looking fantastic was at least some balm to the soul after being left for a younger woman. But Sara's soul was not quietened. If anything, a spiritual restlessness had set in upon her return to London, a sense that her life was now futile and meaningless, and the murmured mantras had failed to exorcise the feeling. Now that she was no longer Hugh Lander's wife she wanted to do something, be something. But what? She lifted her gaze to her reflection.

Our heroine was of average height, average weight and average appearance, one of those women you might glance at casually at a party then look away again. Up until her marriage Sara had dedicated quite a lot of time and skill to achieving invisibility, a reaction to her very visible and very wealthy parents. Her mother had been a famous fashion model of the early 1960s and her father was a European aristocrat who graced the social pages of the era. Sara had spent most of the early part of her life as a source of disappointment to her mother, who'd wished for a daughter who reflected her own beauty, and a source of thwarted ambition to her Italian father (he'd wanted a son), and now that the gloss of youth had left Sara, she'd finally succeeded in achieving what she'd craved as an unloved child – to be ignored.

She glanced across at her breasts and liked what she saw. The chest exercises had lifted her heavy breasts a couple of inches, and despite the weight loss further down her body, they'd remained firm. Her waist that had started to thicken in the manner of most women over forty seemed to have diminished slightly and her thighs and hips were definitely lighter. Her gaze travelled across her sex, where she'd noticed a change too. It was as if her ex-husband's rejection had made it wither slightly in disappointment, and it had become just a little more furrowed, a little less plumped. Her sense of being a sexually vibrant being had certainly been demolished. Although there had been intellectual incompatibility in the marriage, the sex had always been great, at least from Sara's perspective, and Hugh's sudden absence from her bed had made her feel as if she were missing an annex of her own body. His lovemaking had defined her, had drawn her physical perimeters like an outline in an etching; without him she feared she was lost.

She looked down her torso and, parting her legs, looked for grey hairs. To her consternation she discovered a whole outcrop clinging together like some old man's whiskers. She pulled them out with violent relish, noting grimly that if the greying continued she'd have to consider a Brazilian with just a little landing strip or even shaving the whole lot off – a practice she considered to be both vulgar and brutally American.

She held the hairs up against the sunlight – some of them were pure white. It was deeply depressing; she was only forty-two and she still held hopes of having a child. The white hairs made her feel like old fruit, as if both her sexual and reproductive fecundity were wasting away. She looked down at her labia once more – she didn't remember her vagina looking that wrinkly when she was young, but back then it was still *verboten* to discuss the aesthetics of one's genitalia – unless, of course, you were a man. Back then young girls didn't look between their legs, Sara noted, remembering how she'd been shocked the night before by the subheading on the cover of a teen magazine a young girl was reading on the Eurostar: 'You and your labia – when the crease is pretty'. Was it good or was it bad to have such mysteries reduced to banality? In some ways it was good – at least young men now knew where the clitoris was, and if they didn't they could always look on the internet, she thought to herself, remembering some of her more awkward first teenage encounters. On the other hand, though, the current view of sexuality seemed so expedient to her, all so exposed and clinical

– the inherent romanticism that had always been her Achilles heel now battling her pragmatism.

Sighing, she slipped her dressing gown back over her shoulders and reached for the Chanel suit she planned to wear for her outing.

Sara hated going anywhere alone. It was a hangover from being the sole offspring of socialites who had little time for her. The memories of her mother were of an impossibly beautiful woman who floated in and out of the house and only seemed to pay attention to Sara when she was hosting dinner parties during which Sara was expected to perform to amuse the guests: either playing the piano or doing little dance routines. Sara had loathed it. She still had a blown-up photograph of her mother in a bikini, aged eighteen, hanging up in the master bathroom. Originally shot for French *Vogue*, her mother had put it up decades ago, and since her death, Sara, despite a strong dislike for the photograph, hadn't had the courage to take it down. And so it had stayed hanging, a constant reminder to Sara of her own inadequacies.

As a child during the late 1970s she spent long afternoons wandering around the museums of London with her nanny in stifling silence, the ennui of which even now made her feel panicked. This was probably why she'd ending up marrying her ex-husband in the first place – Hugh had been wildly gregarious and compulsively social. He was someone who didn't really exist unless he had an audience and then he would light up, blazing like the Christmas lights on Oxford Street and boy, was he good. Easy on the eye as well, Sara thought ruefully, gazing over at the wedding photograph that still sat in the middle of the white marble desk like a shrine.

Taken in 1992 outside the Mayfair church they were married in, both Sara and Hugh looked ridiculously young. Hugh was tall with an angular face, blue eyes and thick black Celtic hair with dramatic black eyebrows. He looked like a handsome young wizard, oozing sexual magnetism as he stared out at the viewer, daring them not to find him attractive. In the photograph the younger Sara, dressed in a cream silk suit, stared up adoringly at her husband. The pose was indicative of the marriage that followed, Sara reflected bleakly – she had worshipped him while he had continued to look for an audience.

Apart from her ex-husband's obvious indifference and her obvious adoration, the other striking aspect of the photograph was the imbalance of beauty between them. He had been, in every way, far more beautiful than her. She'd known it then and she knew it now. Even-featured, Sara was pleasant looking but not striking. She had not taken after her mother in any aspect except her strawberry-blonde hair. This was her most attractive feature but she had to have it back-brushed and styled every day to disguise its thinness. Hugh had told her that her best assets were her smile and laugh. He'd loved the way she laughed at all his jokes – in fact she'd laughed at most of his utterances, but this wasn't appreciation as much as a nervous reaction. In truth she'd been intimidated by his intellect and her laughter was her way of disguising the fact that often she simply couldn't follow his references or subtle nuances. No wonder he'd finally left her for an academic, she thought bitterly.

The imbalance of beauty: Sara said the words out loud. Beauty meant a lot to Sara, maybe too much, and like many who had suffered the curse and blessing of great inherited wealth, it meant far more to her than money, for as much as one tried to procure it, one could never really own it as beauty was inherently transient: ethereal in spirit, elusive in nature and fickle in choice. The only consolation was that one could invite it to dinner, sleep with it for a while or hang it on the wall until inevitably beauty moved on. But at least one got to live with it for an exhilaratingly brief time, Sara concluded, reflecting on her own marriage. It was the philosophy by which she had always lived, for Sara was an art collector, a serious buyer of seriously expensive art, and this was the one area she knew she excelled in. Her taste was impeccable, a delightfully eclectic mix of both contemporary and classical: Impressionists hung next to Damien Hirsts, Rodin beside Elisabeth Frink. And yet there was always a harmonious theme that linked them all.

Sometimes Sara wondered whether this was what her marriage had been – an art purchase. Perhaps she had collected Hugh for his aesthetic appeal and then perversely he had put her back on the shelf. But then there was the money. Hugh's departure had been swift but that hadn't stopped him hiring the best divorce lawyer in London and dragging her through the courts to usurp the pre-nuptial she had made him sign. The publicity around the case absolutely terrorised Sara. A desperately private person, she was a watcher not a performer and her family were old European money with a lineage that stretched back to thirteenth-century Venice. Monte Carlo was awash with gossip, many of her cousins still living in mainland Europe were scandalised, and the news had been all over the tabloids. Sara had been forced to retreat to Morocco for several months to be forgotten. Now it was October and she was back in her Georgian house in Mayfair, ready to step back into the raging torrent of gallery openings, charity balls, gala dinners and opera events that roared through the upper echelons of society as ruthlessly and indifferently as time. It was either that or social suicide, and our heroine wasn't ready to become reclusive just yet. And then there was the matter of her quest, her desire to do something useful with her life and the little talent she thought she actually had. Over the last couple of weeks an idea had occurred to her. Nebulous and shape-shifting, it was about as formed as a ghost, but she knew this much: she wanted to start an art collection, officially, then auction it off and donate the proceeds to a charity. The problem was, she hadn't been able to decide which charity. She had toyed with retired donkeys, abused greyhounds, Greenpeace, Shelter and the anti-whaling campaign, but none of them had really caught either her imagination or empathy. And as the proceeds could easily amount to more than six figures, she wanted something that she could commit to passionately. It was a dilemma.

Sara finished buttoning the grey linen jacket and, after throwing on a YSL blue faux-fur coat, headed down to Cork Street where she was meeting with one of her gallery owners.

'My God, you look amazing. Isn't it wonderful how divorce is always so good for the complexion!'

June Smithers, the gallery owner Sara regularly bought from, stood admiring Sara's outfit while rubbing her hand across the polished leather surface of Sara's new Louis Vuitton handbag that resembled a sculptured leather pillbox as her gaze panned down Sara's body. For a moment Sara was convinced she could see the price tag of each item of designer clothing reflected in the gallery owner's pupils. Code, Sara thought wryly, one's persona is an assemblage of codes and labels that translate into monetary figures by which one is judged.

'I don't know about divorce but I can tell you I never realised love could be so expensive!' Sara joked back in her soft, seductively lilting voice. Her accent was impossible to place, unless you had spent time as a child in the palaces of the Mediterranean surrounded by various nannies and great aunts who would switch fluently from Italian to French to occasionally dipping into formal German (a concession to the more distant relatives), and then you would have recognised Sara's accent immediately.

'So, I believe you have someone I should meet,' Sara continued while discreetly retrieving her handbag, the rubbing of which had taken on a near-masturbatory nature.

For several years before Sara was married, June Smithers had taken responsibility for the heiress's cultural and artistic education. She'd achieved this through engaging (at Sara's expense) a series of handsome male 'walkers', all of whom had been homosexual. They were usually either aspiring curators or art critics, and all were socially ambitious and elitist.

'And here he is now!' June, who was excitable by nature and an enthusiast by calculated choice, leapt forward as an impeccably dressed man of about thirty entered the gallery.

The young man, who was well over six foot tall, was immaculately dressed in a Paul Smith suit. Although he appeared to wear his body more than his clothes, moving in a sensual manner that suggested he was both proud and aware of the physique which was no doubt a result of hours in the gym. His face was broad and almost Slavic with long narrow eyes that were a piercing blue, high cheekbones and a strong mouth with a fuller lower lip. His thick blond hair was trimmed close to his skull. In short, he appeared so perfect as not to be human at all.

'This is Sven,' June declared as if she were announcing the arrival of a new marketing campaign, 'and today he is to take you to the Frieze show – which, this year is, I promise you, sublime!'

Sven held his manicured hand out to Sara.

'Norwegian father, Essex upbringing – so Stephen to you.' His voice was unpretentious and surprisingly estuary in its accent. It didn't fit with either his persona or his fashion sense. Nevertheless Sara found herself taking an instant liking to him.

'Sara Le Carin,' she said, shaking his hand. To her pleasant surprise his grip was strong, masculine. His large hand engulfing her own ignited a sense of femininity in Sara that was momentarily thrilling.

Smiling, he leant forward so that he was out of earshot of the gallery owner. A wave of Gaultier's Le Male swept over her; he smelt delicious enough to eat.

'Love the bag, but it doesn't go with the stockings,' he murmured.

'That's the point,' she whispered back, grinning, making them both instant co-conspirators, an evident intimacy that had June in a self-congratulatory slather. The gallery owner watched the two for another second then brusquely clapped her hands together.

'So, Sven is my latest discovery, an up-and-coming art curator, actually more of an art philosopher than critic, and one of the best young commentators on contemporary British work – as yet unknown. You couldn't be in better hands, Sara. So go! Go! Go and conquer!' June exclaimed dramatically while ushering them towards the door, half an eye on another client who had just entered.

As Sara was about to step back out onto Cork Street, June called across the gallery: 'Oh and, Sara, whatever he tells you to buy, you buy! He has the best eye in the nation!'

Outside, backlit by a sliver of sunshine that had escaped between the tall buildings, the critic's beauty was a little more intimidating than Sara had bargained for. Thank God for the accent, she told herself, grasping the one flaw that made him human.

Stephen slipped his arm through hers, presumptuous but friendly, and utterly non-sexual in a gay male/female friend sort of way.

'June exaggerates,' he informed Sara as they strolled down towards Piccadilly.

'She does?' Sara inquired, although she intended it to be more of an ironic statement than a query.

'Oh yes,' he reassured her, deadly serious. 'I have the second-best eye.'

Frieze was the largest annual art show London boasted. Set in tents and buildings in the centre of Regents Park, it was the last art show in a series of important art shows, but it was considered the most fashionable and serious one to be seen at and to buy from. Sara had missed the one the year before due to her deteriorating marriage and, as this was her first outing in public life since the divorce, she felt excruciatingly self-conscious as they entered the white-walled art sanctum.

Sara glanced at her companion. Was it obvious that Stephen was a walker – a professional social escort? She was hoping he might be mistaken for her latest boyfriend – at least at a distance – for in truth his sexuality was as apparent as his beauty. But it was still flattering to be seen walking beside such a paragon of male perfection; his handsomeness reflecting on her own good taste.

As if sensing her anxiety, Stephen paid for their admission then led her to the first stall he claimed was interesting. A photography exhibition, the first two walls of three were covered in blown-up images of young adolescent girls who, although in contemporary evening dress, were obvious references to the Pre-Raphaelite concept of beauty. The third wall was hung with close-ups of body parts, isolated and blown up in a montage of skin creases and crevices that looked very sexual in an ambiguous way, so one could not tell breast cleavage from a pressed armpit, a buttock crack from the top of thighs.

'A little obvious, but he's very collectible at the moment,' Stephen commented after reading the dismay that momentarily swept across Sara's face.

'It's just so ... visceral, which is not part of my emotional language at the moment,' she replied, tight-lipped, feeling very middle-aged surrounded by the bevy of exotic, gorgeous young men and women who always seemed to appear at such art shows. Drifting through the exhibition in groups of three and four, they were like lost muses just waiting to be discovered by some unsuspecting artist. Such blatant physical beauty reminded Sara of her ex-husband, and her mood shifted down a gear to a darker, more miserable place.

They moved on to the next stand, which displayed a triptych

of abstract canvases consisting of a block of colour with various fluorescent grids set over the top. As hard as she tried Sara just couldn't see the point of them. She felt as if they were trapped in a kind of stupefied, misplaced reverence as they stood for a good five minutes in front of one canvas. Her gaze slid sideways towards her companion and she wondered whether he disliked the art as much as she did. She coughed politely and fidgeted until finally Stephen, clutching the catalogue, flicked it open decisively.

'I do think any art that requires extensive catalogue notes to appreciate it is suspicious ...'

'Of course, but I have to confess I do need a little narrative, you know, something my imagination can get hold of. Perhaps I just haven't the intellect to understand something so abstract ...' Sara replied, wondering if the grid might have some religious symbolism – the Christian cross perhaps? But as much as she tried, the painting just looked like a glorified traffic sign to her, a reaction she dared not share with the critic. As if reading her mind, he interrupted her reverie.

'Don't beat yourself up. Art is about emotion, instinct, gut reaction – if it doesn't move you it doesn't move you, nothing to do with intellect. This is cold, constipated, emotionally indifferent.'

Hugely relieved, Sara turned to Stephen, grateful for the validation.

'I'm so glad you think so. My ex-husband used to accuse me of having a plebeian eye,' she confessed, then immediately wished she hadn't.

Sensing her sudden vulnerability, Stephen lightly touched her arm. Sara found it a comforting but strangely erotic gesture.

'Ouch. I'm assuming that's why he's an ex-husband?' he asked, but Sara fell silent. It was painful for her to talk about the divorce and she now regretted even mentioning Hugh.

'Are you buying with a purpose?' Stephen asked, changing the subject.

'Actually, I am. I'm thinking of starting a collection, you know, officially, to eventually auction for a charity. The trouble is, I can't seem to be able to decide which charity.'

'I find that once you start collecting, the shape or tone of the collection will dictate its eventual home. Maybe you should just start and wait to see what presents itself organically.'

'But you think it's a good idea?'

'I think it's a fantastic idea. The Le Carin Collection – it has a nice ring to it.'

It did have a nice ring to it, and the more Sara thought about it the more she liked the idea of the family name being immortalised in such a manner.

They strolled past a stand where the centrepiece was a Jeff Koons-like graphic sculpture of a couple making love. Cast in shining bronze it would have been tasteful except that there were bronze flowers sprouting from both the man's and woman's anuses, a motif underscored by a bronze rose clutched between the male figure's teeth. Wistfully Sara noticed that the female seemed to be enjoying herself with her eyes shut and her mouth open in an orgasmic cry. Unconsciously Sara found her own lips twitching in mimicry – she had been celibate for months. Without realising it Sara sighed out loud, a long wistful sigh that was suspiciously close to a moan, emerging far louder than she had intended.

A young couple gazing at the sculpture looked over, the girl grinning cheekily at Sara. Stephen swung around and Sara found herself blushing. With a gentle push to the waist he herded her away from the sculpture and on to the next stand.

'Sex does seem to have experienced a revival this year. I suspect it's a counterbalance to the economic doom and gloom. A kind of finger up to grim reality,' he murmured, his vaguely peppermint-scented breath drifting across her cheek.

'Maybe in the art world but certainly not in mine.'

'I know exactly how you feel,' he replied archly, a sad smile flittering momentarily across those perfect features.

Surprised, Sara faltered for a moment: 'But surely a man like you …'

'A man like me was left six months ago by the boyfriend. An older, far wealthier businessman who decided he wanted his freedom. I think it was some kind of hideous mid-life crisis from what I can glean from his behaviour since, but I did love him – still do, most unfortunately.' His fingers played with the collar of his Paul Smith shirt and for the first time Sara saw him as vulnerable.

'But someone like you would have all the choice in the world?'

'I'm fussy, monogamous and ridiculously loyal. And I do not do casual sex, absurd as that might sound coming from a gay man. All of which leads to great stretches of celibacy between relationships.'

The way he pronounced 'great stretches of celibacy' made Sara think of the two weeks she'd recently spent in a retreat on the edge of the Western Sahara in the hope that such sensory minimalism would awaken some dormant spirituality and exorcise the all-pervading sense of loss the divorce had induced. In fact all the retreat did was to fill her with boredom and an inexplicable thirst for B-grade horror films and popcorn, leaving Sara doubting whether she was capable of any spiritual profundity above and beyond a love of beauty.

They were now standing in front of a tapestry, a deliberately naive craft-like wall hanging with motifs of religious figures interspersed with the occasional rock god: an embroidered Iggy Pop floated over a sequinned Krishna, Mick Jagger genuflecting at the feet of Inca, a demon-headed God. Kali, the Hindu goddess of destruction, Sara noticed, seemed to be holding a scarlet-threaded vagina in her four upraised arms. Wondering whether her imagination had taken on a theme and she was projecting, Sara peered closer. Constructed out of meticulous, tiny stitches, there were indeed miniature female genitalia scattered amongst the imagery. The heiress tried hard not to stare. Stephen coughed politely.

'This artist is now practically a household name, very collectible, but you do wonder whether she would have been considered as avantgarde if she hadn't adopted the cross-dressing. Fantastic PR.'

'Spin does seem to be almost as important as the work itself nowadays,' Sara murmured. Still fascinated by the needlework, she was trying to work out whether the sequins sewn onto the tiny vaginas symbolised clitorises, or whether in fact they weren't vaginas at all but eyes. Either way the vagina-eyes appeared to be winking at her as if mocking her current state of celibacy, an effect Sara found very disconcerting. She couldn't help herself, in her enthusiasm she grabbed Stephen's arm and pulled him closer to the tapestry. In that instant she realised that she found the combination of his eau de cologne and faint but distinctive body odour disturbingly arousing. An undeniable sexual flush washed over her. She began fanning herself furiously with the catalogue, hoping he hadn't noticed her blushing face.

'Are those vaginas?' she asked in a stage whisper.

'Well, it's been a while, but I think I'd recognise one if I saw one,' Stephen joked before peering closer, his face just inches away from the hanging tapestry. Now Sara could see the young woman looking after the stall glancing over at them anxiously, obviously nervous about their proximity to the work. Finally Stephen spoke up.

'Yes, I think we can safely presume Kali is depicted here with a superlative number of orifices. I guess the artist is making a statement about the destructive side of sex.'

'I guess,' Sara replied faintly, thinking that the only destructive aspect to sex that she knew of was not getting enough.

'Are you okay? You look a little pale.'

Pale? Sara felt as if her body was on fire. She stepped back from him, anxious that her body might betray her desire in some mortifying fashion.

'Jet lag and possible culture shock. It's been months since I've been out in public and to anywhere so crowded.' She fanned herself with a glove.

'God, I'm sorry, I didn't realise this was to be the first big outing since the divorce. June said nothing. C'mon, let's break for a coffee or something stronger.'

He guided her through the crowd towards the hospitality area, a temporary coffee bar with tasteful white tables and chairs placed around a tree that soared up through the tented ceiling. Arm in arm they made their way past the small gatherings of socialities and art dealers grouped around a wine tasting. A tall, rather cadaverous man in his late fifties stood alone by the tree, empty wine glass in hand. He seemed marooned by his own loneliness, exuding a kind of sad isolation. He looked vaguely familiar. Sara tugged on Stephen's sleeve.

'Who's that?'

Stephen turned and glanced across. 'I think that's Rupert Thornton – you know, that weatherman who made such a fool of himself a while back.'

'That's right, he failed to predict the big storm of eighty-seven. God, he's aged.' Sara had been in her early twenties but she remembered vividly how shocked the nation had been about Rupert Thornton's failure to warn them of the catastrophic weather. But boy, did he look as if he'd paid penance now, she thought.

'I guess so. I can barely remember what he looked like.'

The weatherman smiled hopefully in Sara's direction. She smiled politely back then continued on her way, Stephen leading. Just then Sara noticed an acquaintance of hers staring at them, a glamorous sixty-year-old who had made millions through her last divorce. A notorious maniser, the femme fatale had frozen in mid-conversation, champagne glass in hand, while her eyes travelled up and down Stephen's body, lingering at the crotch. Sara was momentarily reminded of a documentary she'd watched on the Discovery Channel about praying mantises entitled *Deadly Females: Cannibalism and Sex*.

For a moment she felt deeply protective of Stephen – perhaps even maternal. It was fleeting, the emotion giving way to an immense rush of self-glory as the socialite gave Sara a subtle but definite thumbs-up then mouthed, 'Love the new boyfriend!', her cosmetically pumped-up mouth moving up and down like a fish. Behind Stephen's back Sara returned the thumbs-up then gestured to indicate the critic had a big penis. The socialite almost dropped her glass. Life was looking up, Sara decided. Without realising it, the heiress straightened her back and began to walk taller as Stephen, oblivious to the exchange, led her to a table.

They sat over two almond croissants and a single cappuccino. For fortitude Sara had ordered a glass of decent burgundy, even if it was only 11.30 am. The wine trickled through her, casting an optimistic glow on the morning's events. Out of the corner of her eye she could see the socialite flitting from one table to another, no doubt spreading the rumour that Sara Le Carin – normally a rather conservative mouse of a woman – had wasted no time in getting herself a gorgeous new lover since her divorce. Several people had already discreetly glanced over, evaluating Stephen's assets. No doubt the gesture about the large penis was the clincher, Sara decided, and found herself wondering whether Stephen did indeed have a large penis. She was so distracted she found herself ordering another glass of wine. Still unaware of the excitement his presence was causing, Stephen dipped his croissant into his cappuccino, biting into it with a bestial gluttony that Sara found heartening.

'That last piece ...' she ventured, hoping to engage him enough to prevent him from turning around and noticing the interest his presence had generated. 'I suppose I was brought up to regard certain parts of the human body as sacrosanct. I mean, surely to remain erotic something has to stay at least a little mysterious?'

'I guess it depends on how you define mystery. Mystery can be internal, an implied narrative within, and not contained in the physical visual depiction.'

'We are talking vaginas?' she asked sweetly.

At this point Stephen nearly choked on his dripping croissant. Sara banged him on the back politely. He regained his composure.

'Here they are used very much as a symbol, above and beyond the need to shock – birth-gates, death-gates, the beginning and the end. To the male heterosexual eye, anonymous tight wet pleasure; to the female heterosexual eye, bald-faced vulnerability ...'

Sara winced and crossed her legs. 'But why this year? The last couple of years it's been dead animal parts, a sort of butcher's carnival, but now it's ... pussies, or what my grandmother used to call the "la-la".'

'They do seem to be the leitmotif of the season, and it does seem to be de rigueur to own one. Perhaps you should consider buying one of your own?'

I have one of my own, she felt like replying, but stopped just in time, now a little tipsy.

'It might be a little confrontational for me at the moment, given the current state of my own love life.'

'Confrontational is good. It's cleansing. Out with the old, in with the new. Perhaps it could be the start of your new collection?'

'I'll drink to that.' And she lifted her wine glass to toast his coffee cup. To the curious onlookers, of which there were now quite a few, they looked like a loving couple toasting their good fortune.

That afternoon with Stephen's encouragement, Sara purchased a white china sculpture by a young Australian sculptress in the style of Louise Bourgeois which resembled a chintzy porcelain centrepiece of tulips and lilies, except when examined closely it was obvious the flowers were in fact vaginas, crinkly and delicately moulded. A couple of the blossoms were decorated with the odd drop of clear glass dew sitting precariously on the petals/labia.

Sara couldn't decide whether it was too kitsch to be art or too arty to be kitsch. Either way Stephen convinced her it didn't matter, the artist was going to be 'huge' and Sara could always resell at a profit if she found she couldn't live with it. In truth Sara was both fascinated and appalled by the piece; a gapingly feminine sculpture, it seemed to fuse two aspects of womanhood – the domestic and the intimate. She particularly liked the way each vagina/blossom was bespoke – not cast but individually moulded with painstaking precision.

The art dealer handling the sculptress promised to have it installed the next day – after they'd packed up the art show.

That night Sara had a terrible nightmare in which her own vagina grew so large it folded out and up over her head incarcerating her in her own labia. The sensation, which was not the slightest bit erotic, was like being smothered to death. Convinced she was about to die she woke herself up and found herself in the middle of a scream. Forgetting recent events she reached across expecting to find the comforting body of her husband. Instead she encountered nothing but cold sheet. Memory rushed in intermingling with the dream so that for a moment Sara wasn't sure what was real and what was fantasy. Pitch black, the bedroom felt stiflingly hot. It had been a muggy London summer night and the humidity had continued on relentlessly. The silence was broken by the faint wail of a police siren followed by the screech of brakes – a car was parking outside. Sara, fastened to the bed with fear, listened as she waited for her pounding heart to slow down. She glanced across at the bedside clock – it was only two am, still a civilised time on the west coast of America. Without dwelling on what she was about to do, she reached for the phone and dialled the one mobile number she'd never been able to erase from her memory.

'Hugh?' There was a beat, a silence on the other end in which she was convinced she could hear her ex-husband thinking. He then burst into full baritone.

'Sara, darling!' It was his actor's voice, the one he put on when he was being overheard.

'Are we friends?' Sara asked tentatively; she badly needed a truce.

'Of course we are,' he replied warmly, 'what's past is past.'

Suspicious, Sara pushed her ear closer to the receiver. In the background there was the excited crescendo of a party going on. It was interrupted by a young female voice asking Hugh who was on the phone. As if answering both her and Sara simultaneously, Hugh said, 'My favourite ex-wife.'

'Your only ex-wife,' Sara growled into the receiver.

'So far,' Hugh replied cheerfully. He sounded as if he'd been drinking or as if he was stoned.

'Are you alone?' she couldn't help asking although it was evident he was not. Immediately the background ambience began to grow fainter. She glanced up across the bedroom catching a faint glimmer of her reflection in the mirror, a ghostly outline. Somehow it made her feel pathetic, but she still did not put down the phone. There was a crackle on the line as Hugh returned.

'I am now. Are you alright, darling? It's rather late for you, isn't it?'

'I had a nightmare, Hugh, a very bad nightmare, involving labia and dying.'

'Sounds like a bad case of vagina mortis,' he chuckled.

She decided to ignore the comment. Sara had always hated Hugh's boarding school sense of humour.

'Hugh, just answer one question – am I pretty down there?'

'Down there?'

'You know – down there.' Sara bit her lip, Hugh's obtuseness suddenly reminding her of darker times – and then there was the constant frustration of him only speaking English, for Sara's natural inclination at this point would have been to break into French or Italian, which were somehow more suitable languages in which to discuss such matters.

'Oh! Down *there*.'

'Exactly.'

'Oh right, I see. Sara, does it really matter? I mean, it's not like us men look at a woman that way. I mean, smell, lick, taste and touch, but do we spend hours looking at the old Bermuda triangle? No. Besides, I seem to remember you looked fairly decent, normal, pretty if you like. Jesus, Sara, what is this, some kind of female hormonal crisis?'

'And we had a good sex life, didn't we, Hugh?'

'Christ, we've gone through all this before – sex was not our issue. Listen, Sara, I have a house full of guests, I have to get back.'

'It was this nightmare, my labia kept growing and growing and then I was lost in my own sex.'

There was a beat of silence in which Hugh's incredulity seemed to rush down the phone line.

'Should you be discussing this with your ex-husband?' He suddenly sounded wary, as if he was worried Sara was setting some kind of trap.

'Well, who the hell should I be discussing it with? My great aunt?'

'Sara, I think you need to see a shrink, I really do, but if you're really worried, go and see a cosmetic surgeon to get yourself tidied up – a lot of chicks do it over here. Not that I give a fuck, but apparently they all like to look like porn stars – you know, nice tight boxes with no dangly bits ...'

Sara's heart sank. Was it possible she did have a problem and Hugh was just being polite?

'So you do think I have a problem?'

'Sara, that is not what I said, I just said ...' Hugh was interrupted by the same young female voice asking when he was coming back to the party.

'Hold on a minute, Sara ...' Faintly Sara heard the words: '... I'm just having a conversation with my ex-wife, she's worried about her box! Yes, you heard right – friggin' box!' The two then broke into peals of laughter. Humiliated, Sara shrank into the bed feeling more alone than ever. She contemplated hanging up but before she had a chance Hugh's voice came back on the line.

'Sorry about that, Sara, but listen – on the sex front, sweetie, we're divorced now and you're not meant to be ringing me in the middle of the night.'

'I miss you, Hughie ...' Sara slipped into that baby voice that Hugh had once found irresistible but now found irritating. She waited for his reply, hating herself for still wanting him, for demeaning herself in this way, but it was like an addiction. She couldn't help herself. She did miss him and she still found it hard to accept the reality of his departure.

'Sara, don't start with the pleading again, please.'

'But, Hughie, we were so great together ...'

'No we weren't. Now please, we have no intimacy anymore and my psychologist told me it was bad for me to be in communication with you so move on, Sara. I'm getting remarried, remember?' He hung up.

In the silence of the bedroom Sara found herself holding the receiver up like a wand, the buzzing dial tone a tiny beacon in what felt like a gathering storm. Finally she replaced it in its cradle. Feeling pathetic and unbelievably lonely, she got up and wandered into the en suite bathroom. As she sat perched on the toilet she found herself staring at her mother's portrait hanging on the opposite wall. Slim in a bikini with long, perfect legs and a high, full bosom, stretched out on a rock beside a turbulent sea, the eighteen-year-old Future Mrs Le Carin seemed to stare down at her daughter with all the arrogance of impossible female perfection.

'Fuck you,' Sara told the photograph, then wiped herself and flushed. Back in the bedroom, she wrapped herself in a dressing gown, sat down at her desk and booted up the laptop. The screen flickered into life. Sara pulled her dressing gown closer around her shoulders then hit the internet key and typed 'VAGINA' into Google. She selected the first link on the long list that appeared and found herself on a site for a charity campaigning against female circumcision and mutilation of female genitalia. There were several photographs of the crotches of young girls who had had their clitorises cut off and, in some of the images, their labia. Their stories appeared beneath the images and they were all heartbreaking and poignantly provincial in tone. Sara noticed the cases ranged from Turkey to Ethiopia. Reading it, it was as if she could hear their voices, soft, matter-of-fact, none of them self-pitying. They hung in her head. It was all too confronting, and not what she was looking for.

She exited the site and typed in 'XXX'. Within seconds a list of porn sites appeared. Steeling herself Sara began to plough her way through the group orgies, young women with legs splayed, men opening the legs of young women, women opening their own legs, bending down, leaning up, on their sides, upside down, in swimming pools, in baths, on fur rugs, on beds, in hotel rooms, in fields, on the beach, perched on the back of horses, on the back of ponies, on the back of goats ... Sara stopped noticing the context as she surfed through images that were free to download. She even stopped looking at the rest of the women's bodies, her eyes obsessively fixated on just one body part. She was on a mission, a search for the perfect vagina. Big outer lips, small inner lips, big clit, thin outer lips, big inner lips, tiny clitoris, no lips at all, barely a clitoris ... The variety was endless, but after a while she began to notice a hierarchy – an elite of symmetrical, younger looking vaginas that were neat, with the inner lips barely visible and the outer lips plump but not protruding – as she gazed at the genitalia, assessing each one for beauty.

She bookmarked several then put them up on the screen in a line, trying to decide which was her favourite. She settled on one belonging to a blonde – a natural blonde, she assumed. The vagina was neat, pink, with no inner labia showing at all. Sara highlighted the image and hit on print. In the study next door the printer whirred into action. Sara got up and collected the printed image from the machine. Back in the bedroom under the lamplight it looked garish. After drawing a neat square around the vagina and the spread thighs of the porn star, she stapled to it the business card of a plastic surgeon that a girlfriend had recommended a couple of years ago. She glanced over at the alarm clock – it was nearly five am. She collapsed onto the bed then reached into the side drawer and, after taking a couple of sleeping pills, fell asleep cradling herself.

Sara spent the next morning at the gym with her trainer/life coach. As she ran on the treadmill the memory of her call to Hugh, along with the accompanying sense of mortification, gradually faded, almost as though she were literally sweating her need for him out of her body. But afterwards, in the changing rooms, she found herself painfully aware of the other women's bodies – all of them younger and fitter – as she changed back into her clothes. She caught a glimpse of herself in the mirror looking flushed and overweight. In that moment Sara was convinced she would never attract another man. It was a terrifying thought. To prevent herself slipping further into depression, she averted her eyes and left.

Back home, her housekeeper was waiting with a deliveryman. Rosa, a deeply religious Catholic Filipina with a shrine's worth of religious icons stashed in her bedroom, stood with her arms crossed, staring disapprovingly at the man, who seemed a little embarrassed.

'Is there a problem, Rosa?' Sara asked, her heart sinking. It was ridiculous to be intimidated by one's housekeeper, but she was.

'This man, he has brought some art he tells me you purchased, Mrs Le Carin.' She pulled Sara aside and continued in a stage whisper: 'It was filthy pornography! I told him, wrong address! Wrong address!' Rosa glared at the deliveryman while crossing herself as if he were some kind of infectious demon.

'Where is it now, Rosa?'

'In the dining room, on the table.'

Throwing her coat off Sara strolled into the dining room. The large white porcelain sculpture had been placed unceremoniously onto the table and sat shrouded in a large tea towel. It looked like some strange domestic offering. Sara whipped the tea towel off. Rosa gasped.

'Madam, this thing should stay covered, it is not proper!' Behind her the young deliveryman grinned at Sara, who was having trouble keeping a straight face.

'Why is that, Rosa?' Sara innocently asked.

'Because it is un-Christian!'

Sara walked slowly around the table. With the light catching on the petals, the piece had taken on a pleasing luminous quality.

'Un-Christian? I think not. After all, the Holy Mother might have been a virgin but I'm positive she had genitals,' Sara replied sweetly, and deliberately wide-eyed.

Muttering grimly in Spanish, Rosa crossed herself again then flounced out of the room. Sara didn't bother stopping her. She tipped the deliveryman five pounds then found herself alone with the piece. She stared at it, then had the uncomfortable feeling that it – or at least the sixteen or so vaginas perched at the end of each flower stem – was staring back at her. It was a disconcerting sensation.

'Madam?' Startled, Sara jumped. Behind her Rosa stood defiantly dressed in a coat with a Hermès headscarf (a hand-me-down from Sara) knotted sternly under her chin. 'I have to go to church now, Madam,' she stated in a tone that seemed to suggest the visit was non-negotiable.

'Is it Sunday?' Sara asked, knowing full well it wasn't.

'No, but I have rung ahead and Father Keelan is expecting me. I feel as if my soul needs …' her eyes slid towards the sculpture then back to Sara, '… purging.'

'Indeed, I have always thought of Father Keelan as a kind of celestial plumber.'

Without waiting for permission, Rosa was gone.

Sighing, Sara turned back to the artwork. She couldn't leave it on the dining table. As attractive as it was, she suspected some of her more conservative dinner guests would be put off eating. And yet conversely it might prompt some of her more liberal guests to indulge in pleasures other than culinary. Two years ago Sara would have found the image of an orgy initiated on and around her dining table both amusing and more than a little intriguing, but now the thought just reminded her again of her own celibacy.

Saddened she picked the piece up and carefully carried it out into the reception hall where she placed it on the Empire side table. She moved back to get a clearer view. There seemed to be a hundred china vaginas reflected in the large oval gilt mirror that hung above the side table – it was an interesting effect.

She stepped outside the front door then stepped back in. The sculpture was the first thing that caught her eye. It dominated the whole entrance hall. 'What kind of message would that give my guests?' she wondered. The first impression one had of the piece was fragile beauty but there was something a little odd about it that compelled one to look again. This time one always noticed the genitalia. She imagined the piece might be more appropriate for, say, the entrance hall of some lesbian power-monger like Annie Leibovitz, or failing that a female politician who was a defiant feminist, although when she stopped to think about it no one came to mind – not even Margaret Thatcher.

Now the piece seemed to be mocking her. Had she made a mistake in buying it? Encircling it with her arms, she carried it slowly into the adjacent sitting room where, after crouching down, she placed it on a low coffee table. Now she had a bird's eye view and from this angle the piece looked a little like white coral, thick branches dividing into smaller branches and so on – all tipped with the inevitable crumpled flower.

She collapsed on the couch and touched one of the 'buds' carefully, the smooth surface of the porcelain cool under her fingertip. Like a young girl's the bud/vagina was barely unfurling. Such innocence, such simplicity. The hallway clock striking four brought Sara back into the present, her gaze still fixed on the bud/vagina. It seemed to personify all the youth and beauty she now felt she'd lost. A sudden desire to smash the whole sculpture to bits swept through her. Not trusting herself she gripped the arms of the chair and allowed the sudden fury to dissipate before carrying the piece upstairs to her bedroom.

There, after pushing aside her wedding photograph, she placed it on the circular table that sat in the large window alcove opposite her bed. Again the sculpture seemed to dominate and Sara realised that the only time she would escape the sight of it was when she was lying on her back in her bed. Could she live with it? It reminded her of her own aesthetic failures, the inevitable comparison people always made between her and her mother, and how she was always doomed to disappoint. The sculpture was a ringing alarm clock, an alarm clock of birth, sex and death, chiming out the passing of the years. Again a growing panic rumbled up below her rib cage as her internal monologue grew wilder and more irrational. She glanced back at the sculpture. For a minute she thought she saw the lips of each vagina open, quivering in the golden summer light, whispering viciously: Sara, you are going to die an old maid! Childless, sexless and withered!

Sara picked up the business card for the cosmetic surgeon and began dialling the number. At the other end a well-spoken man answered the phone. Silence stretched like a spider's web from her end of the phone to his as Sara lost the courage to speak. Abruptly she put the receiver down.

I will not live with this oppression, I will not, she told herself as she searched for the large heavy shoehorn – an old-fashioned object with a heavy silver handle – that she kept in her cupboard. She was moving towards the sculpture ready to smash it when suddenly the doorbell rang. She froze for a moment, forgetting that Rosa was out at church. The doorbell persisted, an angry buzz that echoed up through the spacious house. Whoever it was wasn't going away. Slowly Sara lowered her arm. The buzzing felt as if it were now drilling behind the back of her eyes. Swearing (in French) she ran downstairs, across the hallway, ready to tell whatever salesman or religious busybody it was to bugger off, then somewhat breathlessly opened the front door.

Stephen stood in the doorway with a huge bunch of pink lilies and tuber roses tied tastefully with white ribbon. Without asking to be let in, he pushed the flowers into her arms and walked into the house.

'I brought these, to celebrate.'

Hiding her surprise at his arrival behind the huge bouquet, Sara followed him into the reception room.

'Celebrate?'

'Well, the sculpture's arrived, hasn't it?' he asked eagerly. 'I promised to help you install it.'

'Oh, that's right.' Sara was finding it hard to sound enthusiastic.

'Should I come back? Is this a bad time?'

'No, it's fine. I'm just finding it difficult to know exactly where to place the piece. The theme is somewhat dominating, you know, in a domestic setting. Not that there isn't a place for eros in the domestic, but something so ... implicit, so ... intimate ...' She placed the flowers on a sideboard and turned to find Stephen looking at her quizzically. It was obvious he hadn't the slightest idea what she was talking about.

She led him up to the bedroom, feeling his gaze brush across her legs and buttocks. She was trying desperately not to be distracted by his proximity, proximity she found undeniably erotic.

They both stood in front of the piece in silence. Stephen

appeared awed whereas Sara now felt like throwing miniature knickers over all the blossoms. Stephen's eyes slid down towards the heavy shoehorn now sitting next to the base of the porcelain sculpture. He picked it up, weighing it thoughtfully, then looked over at Sara, eyebrows raised. She shrugged apologetically.

'I wouldn't actually have ...'

'But you were thinking about it?'

'I might have got a little carried away, I suppose. I might be having some self-esteem issues and the piece is ... well ...'

'A little confrontational?' he asked.

'In the cold light of day, very confrontational.' She took the shoehorn out of his hand. As she did so she had the definite impression that one of the vaginas actually winked at her. Sighing, she dismissed the image from her mind. Stephen walked around the piece slowly.

'I guess the question is, does it belong in the bedroom?'

'I've tried everywhere else, the dining room, the hallway, the sitting room ...'

'It is a statement piece.'

'Sort of in the "yes, I am woman" school.'

'Well, you are female, Sara,' Stephen noted unnecessarily, at which point Sara wished she wasn't horribly aware of Stephen's beautiful tanned hands, the fingers of which appeared to be caressing the 'petals' of one of the flowers – a disconcerting sight for Sara who had now surrendered to the notion that she might indeed be on the point of wishful hallucination, perhaps some bizarre side effect of celibacy.

'A female currently suffering from major penis envy,' she announced, abandoning any semblance of etiquette. She collapsed on the ottoman placed at the foot of the bed. Stephen left off caressing the sculpture and walked over to the side table. He picked up the printout she'd abandoned by the phone and glanced down at it, then grinned. Mortified, Sara felt as if she were suddenly pinned to the ottoman by chagrin.

'Are you sure it's penis envy?' He held up the image of the porn star's vagina. 'Or am I missing something about your sexuality here?'

Sara leapt up and snatched the printout from him.

'Oh, I'm heterosexual. It's just that between that bloody thing over there …' here she gestured towards the sculpture, '… and all the images of perfectly neat young women, I'm feeling very inadequate.'

To her surprise he burst out laughing. 'And all of this because of one small sculpture,' he managed to say between guffaws.

Sara was speechless, then, to her own horror, all of the tension, the loneliness, the humiliating memory of the call to Hugh, her own aching sense of sexual futility, mounted up then collapsed on top of her as she threw herself on the bed. Covering her face, she burst into loud sobbing. Within seconds Stephen was sitting with his arms around her.

'Shh, shh … it can't be that bad,' he murmured, rocking her like she was a child. Sara buried her face into his shoulder; the cashmere of his Ralph Lauren blazer soft against her cheek, the scent of him enveloping her like some delicious blanket.

'It is, it is …' Her voice was ridiculously small between the sobs. 'All my life I've bought beauty, all because I've always known that's the only way I'll get close to it … Even my husband, Hugh Lander —'

'You were married to Hugh Lander? My God, now he *is* gorgeous!' Stephen exclaimed, unable to keep the admiration out of his voice, at which Sara burst into louder sobbing.

'Sara, stop ... stop, listen to me ...' He held her face up to his, holding his gaze steady until gradually she calmed down.

'Look over there, at the piece. If you look carefully, beyond what you think you're looking at, you'll see that those ... flowers are not perfect. Quite the opposite, they are all individual, all flawed. Some of the petals droop, some are longer than the others, some buds are bigger, almost bulbous, some are hardly there at all, but they are all uniquely different. And that's what beauty is – bespoke, if you like, individually crafted. And beauty doesn't wither with age. It changes but it doesn't get less.'

'Do you really believe that?'

'I don't believe it, I know it. Want to know what my last boyfriend looked like? He was sixty, overweight and balding, but he was the most captivating man I've ever known. And you know what? He left me.'

'Really?' She looked up at him, incredulous, but he averted his eyes. She could feel him retreating emotionally, and for the second time she had a glimpse into a vulnerable core he kept so well hidden under all the immaculate grooming and presentation.

'Really. The bastard broke my heart, but I'm still alive. Now, can I get you a drink or something? I could sure do with one.'

'In the bedside cabinet there's a bottle of cognac and some glasses ...'

He got up and poured them both a drink, then carried them over to Sara. He pressed one into her hand then held his glass up for a toast.

'To beautiful flaws, long may they reign.'

Their glasses touched. Sara leant back against a pillow, letting the warming cognac stream through her. It was still light outside but the sun had dipped below Piccadilly and filled the bedroom with a soft late afternoon glow, the reddish light catching at the gilt and bronze. It felt intensely intimate, as if they were old girlfriends or young girls at boarding school, and for once the habitual aloneness that had shadowed Sara all her life temporarily abated.

'Besides,' he added, smiling, 'we all have our challenges. I, for example, have only one testicle.'

At which the tension broke like a bubble and they both roared, their faces thrown close together as the laughter caught like fire from one then back to the other. In her hysteria, Sara's hand accidentally brushed across his naked arm, and suddenly he caught her wrist, pulled her towards him and kissed her. His tongue pushed passionately into her mouth, searching, probing, the taste of him so sweet that in a flash Sara found her body responding before she could think rationally, moistening for him, all the longing, the desire sweeping up through her centre. His hands slipped down into her blouse, searching for her breasts, her nipples. Gasping, she sat back.

'Aren't you gay?'

'Sometimes I falter ...'

'So you don't mind if you and I ...'

'I think in some circumstances it's best not to intellectualise. Besides, the trouble with living in the twenty-first century is how everything gets shoehorned into labels, genres, including sexuality ...'

He smiled up at her, one hand still caressing a breast, the planes of his face a beautiful patchwork of shadow and angles. Irresistible mystery.

'I always thought shoehorns were overrated myself,' she answered, desire thumping a tattoo across every inch of her. He drew her back towards him and kissed her for a second time. Sara had the sensation that she was sinking backward into a pool of warm water. She was losing control and she struggled against the sensation. She pulled away.

'Strip for me,' she said, shocking herself more than Stephen.

'That's pretty kinky,' he replied straight-faced, until Sara caught the glint in his eye.

'Strip for me. You're beautiful and I want to see it all – in the light.' Her voice became sultry, more controlling. She sat up straight. Now she wanted to be master, to choreograph when and if she touched him. She was determined not to subjugate herself to desire again, not after Hugh, not after the phone call the night before. Stephen stood slowly.

'In the middle of the room,' Sara ordered, pointing to the empty rug where a square of late sunlight pooled. He walked into it. Immediately the ray of sun illuminated his head and shoulders, creating an aura around him. Now Sara could see how the very shape of his skull had a sculptural elegance, his ears transformed into translucent seashells that stood away from the soaring planes of his cheekbones, his straight, neat nose drawing attention down to the full lips, sardonic in their pout. The timeless nature of his beauty made Sara think of a mediaeval Nordic knight, then something older. He spun slowly in the light, his arms outstretched as if he were underwater. It was a floating dance, a seduction so joyously abandoned, the power of it caught in her throat.

He stopped rotating and faced her, his gaze steady and deep, the blue catching her own black pupils. Defiant, wry and dead sexy. Without breaking this bridge between them he unbuttoned his shirt with excruciating slowness then let it fall away from his torso where it hung, like huge unfurled white petals, down from his leather belt.

His shoulders were broad – perhaps a little too broad for so slender a torso, but the width seemed to make him vulnerable, a flaw in his perfection. He obviously worked out, but Sara guessed he was a naturally slim man who exercised to plump out his physique. The curves of his chest swept down to large dark nipples feathered with fine blond hair and as he lifted an arm Sara caught for a moment his armpit, finely dusted with long straight blond hair, as delicate as an etching. And she knew that if she buried her face into him, into this junction of limb and soft skin, his scent would be delicious, would be the trigger, the pheromonal aftershock of which would vibrate from the back of her throat right down to her sex.

He slipped his thumbs into his belt loops, pausing for a moment in mock shyness, his head tilted as if to tease. 'Dare I?' Sara couldn't help dropping her eyes down to his crotch, caught in that fascination, that promise of discovery, of taste, touch and scent that sweeps both women and gay men away – the sweet moment of before. Even clothed she could see his penis, his erection now tenting out the front of his trousers. His cock looked beautiful and well formed, the clear outline of it visible through the linen. She lifted her gaze back to his face, and again caught a gleam of amusement in his eyes. Pulling the rest of his shirt out of his waistband he let it descend to the floor with a soft slither.

'Oh God,' Sara whispered to herself, unable to remember the last time she'd wanted someone so much. He took one tantalising step towards her. He ran his hands down the sides of his torso in a slow tease and stopped at his belt. Slowly he unbuckled it, allowing each notch to loosen one by one before pulling the leather belt out from his waistband. Suddenly he cracked it in the air like a whip. The sound resonated around the large high-ceilinged room, piercing the silence. Sara almost laughed but the intense expression on Stephen's face stopped her. She may be master now but he'd made it clear he too could take control whenever he wanted.

Without saying a word she knelt and shuffled towards him on her knees until her face, her mouth, was inches from his crotch. He stared down at her, his expression now changed again; he seemed almost tremulous, questioning and vulnerable. He lifted his arms above his head and struck the pose of a bound slave, the muscles rippling over his ribs. From Sara's perspective his body was a series of foreshortened curves, muscular sculptural arches, his erect nipples two apexes. She reached across and began unzipping his fly. Stephen stared down from above as his cock pushed out, hard and ready. The velvet head nudged her cheek, her lips. She looked up; Stephen's face was flushed. Under her palms she could feel his clenched buttocks. He groaned then reached out to steady himself against a chair.

With a sudden violent yank she pulled his trousers down to his ankles. Fully exposed, the perfect symmetry of him was wondrous. Wrapping her hands around him she ran her fingers down the shaft. Stephen, overcome with excitement, could barely stand. He roughly slipped his fingers through her hair and pulled her head towards him. But she resisted: this was to be her act, at her own pace and command.

Slowly, tantalisingly, she blew gently on the tip of his penis. It quivered, a drop of dew forming in a perfect tear. Moving closer she rubbed it across her lips, the pungent earthy scent of him filling her nostrils, making her wet. Again Stephen groaned, his legs trembling. A beam of sunlight momentarily illuminated her face buried in his crotch, crystallising the moment in golden warmth. She extended her tongue and slowly encircled the head. From the corner of her eye she saw Stephen's fingers, his hands now fallen by his sides, curled in pleasure. Now she took him fully into her mouth, greedily sucking, as deeper and deeper he drove, his groans and cries now filling the room. Her hands cupped each taut buttock guiding him until she felt the tremor of a climax starting at the base and then she pulled away. She wanted him to come inside of her. She wanted pleasuring.

Knowingly, Stephen pulled her to her feet then, with his naked body and erect wet cock pressed against her clothed torso, he kissed her deeply. The scent of him filling both their mouths, she could have come then, his obvious excitement and pleasure was almost enough for her. While their lips were locked he thrust his hand between her legs, the wetness of her sticky against his fingers.

'I want you,' he groaned against her cheek. He pulled her down and across the polished parquet floor. He then threw her skirt up over her head. Embarrassed by her own body, Sara struggled, murmuring protests, but he was beyond hearing. With a sharp tug he ripped her pants at the side and threw them across the floor. Sara was wearing stockings so now her vagina was completely exposed. Lacking confidence, she held her legs closed, but using his knee Stephen managed to part them and she finally surrendered, staring up into the tent of her own skirt, transformed into a planetarium of glowing patterns and flowers. She lay there spreadeagled, fully clothed except for her crotch, the sun warming this naked apex. She'd never felt so exposed and so aroused. There was no escape and her own fear stared back at her.

Kneeling over her Stephen buried his face into her, his full soft lips biting the inside of her thighs gently as he worked his way up. Slipping his large hands beneath her full buttocks he began nuzzling her, his tongue brushing across the tip of her erect clitoris in excruciating pleasure, before taking her completely into his mouth, sucking gently as his fingers probed both her arse and vagina, slowly plying her open, to the elements, to him, to a great unfettered rush of pleasure as Sara thrashed and moaned above him. Finally she came so intensely she thought she might die from pleasure. He waited then hauled himself over her. Staring down at her flushed face he suddenly grinned.

'Good to know I haven't lost my touch.'

She smiled back at him. 'I suppose it's like riding a bike – once you've learnt you never forget …' She could still feel his hard erection against her. 'But you haven't come yet?'

'That's because …' And here he slowly entered her, the size of him making her groan involuntarily. He grinned again. '… I haven't finished yet.' He filled her completely, lifting her legs over his shoulders, pulled back until the tip of him was nestled between her swollen lips and entered her all over again, this time as slowly as his excitement would allow. Over and over until he abandoned himself and they both galloped to a shuddering climax – his first, her second – while two flights below Rosa, the housekeeper, returning from church and hearing the cries, crossed herself at the homemade shrine she kept in her bedroom.

Afterwards they both lay entwined on the floor, watching the setting sun leave the grand old bedroom like the closing of life itself. And when the evening chill began to creep across the floor Sara took him to her bed where they lay like two slightly bewildered children, cradled against each other in faint amazement.

'Sara …' Stephen murmured against her neck. She turned but he left the sentence hanging like the question that had already fallen across them.

'You know …' he finally continued, catching the silence before it snapped in two, '… we can't have a relationship.'

Deciding to rescue him she replied, 'But we can have some fun occasionally?' She tried to sound casual and succeeded.

'I can't see why not.' Stephen laughed, his deep voice resonant. 'But there's one thing I want you to really understand …'

Sara found herself tensing in anticipation of rejection. Dreading the worst she interrupted: 'But you don't have to say it.'

'But I do, I really do … You're beautiful, no matter what you think. Don't change a thing, promise?'

She lay back and thought before answering. She couldn't remember the last time she felt so flushed with contentment, so elated to be in her own skin. At last she felt completely and utterly powerful.

'Promise.' She stared over at the shower of freckles that peppered his shoulders. She hadn't noticed them before. There was something else that had finally fallen into place, something that had been forming like a jigsaw at the back of her brain.

'You know this collection I want to put together? Well I want you to be the curator. And I think I've finally decided on the charity.'

There was silence from Stephen. Sara glanced across to find he'd fallen asleep.

The auction was in one of Christie's smaller, more exclusive rooms. It was already in mid-swing and the last two items had gone for three times their estimated price. Sara scanned the room. She and Stephen as well as a fantastic publicist had made sure that the rows of bidders read like a who's who of the wealthy, famous and infamous of London. The slow burn of satisfaction had already started spreading through her. This time Sara didn't mind being visible, in fact she rather liked the huge banner that hung on the auctioneer's stand reading 'The Sara Le Carin Collection'. She'd even enjoyed the radio and press interviews engendered by her unusual choice of charity and the unusually large amount of money the collection was expected to bring in, all of which was to be donated. For the first time in her life she found herself relishing who she was and what she was doing. She smiled up at Stephen, who was standing beside the auctioneer as the official curator of the collection. Stephen smiled briefly back down at her then helped one of the assistants bring out the next art work to be auctioned. They carried the huge photograph of her mother onto the stage.

'Lot six – a photograph of fashion model Daphne Le Carin, in spotted bikini, nineteen sixty-two. Originally taken for French *Vogue*, this is believed to be the only surviving print. Do we start at a thousand …? We have a thousand from the gentleman in blue …'

Sara swung around. She recognised the man, who was in his mid-seventies, as someone who was rumoured to have been a lover of her mother's. So he must have been, she concluded. As if in agreement there was a faint ripple amongst the older bidders, all as curious as Sara was to know the truth of the matter. Another bidder put up his hand; it was another old friend, this time of her father's, and a bidding war began. Delighted, Sara leant back in her chair. She was finally going to be rid of the photograph, and the idea of that particular sale going to her assigned charity – No Cut, a charity dedicated to the fight against female genital mutilation – thrilled her even more. And then there was Stephen.

She glanced back up at him. Here he was entirely in his element, and she'd never seen him more beautiful. An old familiar emotion swept through her, catching at her throat. As impossible as it seemed, she knew it was pointless fighting it.

THE
ALCHEMY
OF
COINCIDENCE

Jennifer sat staring out the window. The studio at the back of their large garden was a wooden bungalow with a tin roof and the heavy Australian rain beat across the metal as if triumphantly announcing the breaking of the drought. It was ironic, Jennifer thought, because it felt like the beginning of her own. Drought, dry, I am parched. She scrawled the sentence in the margin of her sketchpad with her thick 2B pencil; the rest of the crisp, creamy page was blank. She liked the writing – it was defiant, a declaration. Somewhere in the corner of the large studio rain had started to drip through the ceiling. A singular soft persistent plop she decided to ignore. She placed the drawing pad on the wooden foldout chair she'd been sitting on and walked over to her modelling table.

A couple of old sculptures from her last show sat on the simple worktable – two porcelain vaginas, one young, the other older, as delicate as orchids, the fragile lips as thin as petals. The one-woman show had been hugely successful and had landed her a London gallery as well as several wealthy English collectors. But that was last year, and her next one-woman show was only a month away and she hadn't even begun. Oh, she knew the theme. It was to be based around a theory she'd started to develop over the past few years, a theory based both on experience and whimsy. But that didn't worry Jennifer, who had learnt to regard inspiration as something as elusive as threads of gossamer that one had to gather in then make tangible. The artist had become an expert in such matters – she was good at making emotions and ideas manifest.

The theme of the show was to be the concept that an artist could induce coincidence through image-making. It wasn't a theory that her husband, Toby Gladwell, shared, but then Toby, although he too was an image-maker (a film director) was not a romantic. No, indeed, she smiled, bringing to mind his oft-repeated philosophy: Toby believed in *concrete realism*, the concrete being a reference to concrete playgrounds of the housing commission flats he often set his documentary-style movies in. Despite this championing of realism the film director was most renowned for launching the career of Australian film star Jerome Thomas, an actor most famous for his romantic leads.

As a practitioner of cinema verité, Toby regarded whimsy as the terrain of the middle classes – in other words, it was utter escapism and a complete waste of time. In this the couple differed greatly from each other – her art was all about whimsy, his art was about realism. And yet, despite this, the five-year marriage was passionate, a meeting of both the sexual and intellectual.

At least that was how Jennifer, the romantic, had viewed it. But lately Toby's long absences while shooting had begun to alienate them from each other. It felt to Jennifer that while Toby's life was filling up with actors, crew, media as well as characters from his scripts and general entourage, her own life was emptying out. It was the culmination of all her long isolated hours in the studio, and the way all her girlfriends seemed to be either getting married or pregnant, or leaving Australia to pursue their careers overseas. And finally there was the loss of her mother, who had been one of her best friends, which had suddenly pushed Jennifer over the edge. She felt as though her life and Toby's were like scales with a dish at either end – Toby's dish was weighed down while her own dish floated up empty. It wasn't how Jennifer had imagined her day-to-day existence would be.

Restless, the artist got up again and counted out the space between the stool and the empty easel stand in long strides like a child. Outside the rain had intensified and she had to fight off the urge to rush back inside the large terrace house and cocoon herself in the doona to spend the rest of the day listening to the rattle of the wind against the windows and the roof. She arrived at the empty easel, lifted up a whiteboard and clamped it between the wooden bars, then picked up a whiteboard marker, her hand poised over the board. What she required was an example, a working example of her theory which would be the subject of her one-woman show – half installation, half sculpture. But to begin she needed something or someone to be an inspiration, a muse. She wrote the word *Coincidence* then listed as many coincidences in her life as she could remember:

1. My first boyfriend had the same first name as my husband.
2. My mother was born in the same English town as Toby's grandfather.
3. My birthday is on the same day as the painter Van Gogh's.
4. We live in Verona Street, Hawthorn, and I first met Toby in Verona, Italy.

Written out like that none of it seemed very significant and yet Jennifer could clearly remember the absurdly large number of times she'd made a small sketch of a sculpture or a maquette and then seen an element of that sculpture or something pertaining to it the next day. Like the time she accidentally chipped the nose of a stone head she was working on and the next day Toby broke his nose; or the sketch she made of the reflection of a couple in a broken mirror, then six months later the very same couple suddenly separated. She was convinced that image-making was a kind of alchemy but the question was how to prove it.

The sound of the phone ringing inside the house jolted her rudely back into the prosaic. It was Toby from Rome, his voice sounding drained but hyper. There was pop music somewhere in the background, then a barrage of hooting car horns. He explained that he was standing in the Piazza Navona and it was about three am and the clubs were emptying out.

'How's the shoot?' Jennifer's voice emerged smaller than she wanted, and she wished she sounded stronger, happier, more self-reliant.

'It's okay but slow. How's the work going? You still working on that theory of coincidence?'

'Kind of ... I've just started now.'

'That's what I like to hear, you're like my own live-in sorceress.'

'Oh don't say that, you make it sound so trivial.'

'Come on, babe, you know I like your work. But listen, darl, I'm going to have to stay on for an extra week or so, and there's a producer they want me to meet ...'

'An extra week? But that will make it over two months.'

'I know, sweetheart. Do you want to come here?'

'You know I can't, I have my show ...' Her voice tensed as an old fear surfaced, the idea that her work was less important than his.

Picking up on it he snapped back, 'I just thought I'd ask. You can always change the date of your show.'

'You know I can't do that so why do you always say it!' She was shouting now as the car horns and the thumping disco music pulled him further and further away from her, the studio, the soft drumming of the rain on the roof. On the other end of the line she heard the sound of a woman's laugh.

'I have to go now, Jenny, we'll speak tomorrow. Love you,' his voice now pat, casual.

'Love you back,' she replied automatically as he vanished into the disconnected tone.

The next morning Jennifer had an appointment with her gynaecologist. It was the usual check-up – breasts, smear test and pelvic examination. She was only twenty-six but the thought of getting pregnant had already begun to hover somewhere in the recesses of their marriage. Sitting in the elegant waiting room with the pinewood furniture and gleaming steel-framed coffee tables, she glanced across at a very pregnant young girl sitting on a couch opposite. The girl smiled wanly. She was extremely pale and it looked like all her strength and energy had gone into her distended womb. Looking at her, Jennifer wondered whether she should discuss conception with the doctor, but the reality of ending up home alone with a screaming baby and no husband for months at a time was just too daunting. No, procreation would have to wait – and in any case her art was a kind of procreation.

She picked up a French edition of *Vogue* that was six months out of date. There was a photo shoot displaying a series of dramatic evening gowns in a Spanish bullring. The models – a statuesque African and an icy blonde with dead eyes – struck poses around the arena and a tethered straining bull. Behind them in the wooden stands were several rows of spectators. One of them, a tall dark-haired young man, appeared to be rising up in his seat. The serenity of his expression in a broad sculptural face was in stark contrast to the burning of his blue eyes. Fascinated by him, Jennifer stared down at the page, momentarily transported into the arena, the hot sun, the smell of the sand, the blood and the fear of the animal, the shouting in Spanish, the sharp inhalation of the mysterious young man, his fragrant sweat ... There was something about his proportions, the vulnerability of his expression and that rare combination of unusual good looks, that completely captivated her.

She looked around the waiting room. Now that the young girl had left, there was only one other person waiting – a thin, depressed-looking woman in her mid-forties. A name was called and, after getting up slowly, the woman disappeared behind the dark panelled door of the surgery. Jennifer glanced over at the receptionist. She had her back to the artist and was on the phone. Taking advantage of her distraction Jennifer tore the page out of the fashion magazine and slipped it into her handbag. Three minutes later her own name was called.

Jennifer smoothed the magazine page out on her workbench then carefully placed a sheet of glass over the top of it to flatten all the creases. Then she placed the thick orb of a magnifying glass onto the surface and ran it over the image to the man's face staring up from underneath. The details of the photo magnified curved up suddenly like a bubble of moving time.

Now she could clearly see the shape of his jaw, the balance between the fuller, slightly pouting lower lip and the thinner, more defined upper lip. The nose – strong, with a pronounced bridge and slightly asymmetrical at its tip – provided a pleasing counterbalance to the perfection of the shape of his whole face, a diamond broken only by the flare of his jaw. The eyes themselves were large but deep-set, the hooded eyelids giving him a Mediterranean look. The eyelashes were thick and black, almost too feminine in such a masculine countenance. His irises were a piercing cobalt shot through with golden yellow. They reminded Jennifer of a solar eclipse, with the sun's rays blazing up behind in a deep blue sky. They reminded her of that sense of eternity one has as a teenager, of time and age being infinite. It was a sense she, at twenty-six, had now completely lost.

His hair was thick, black and tousled. He did not have the grooming of the beautiful who are aware of their own beauty; instead he seemed to be at war with it – it was almost as though he wished to shake it off himself like a coat he'd inherited but wasn't comfortable wearing. The paradox made him more desirable, more complex and, within that, fallible. Pausing, she ran the magnifying glass down his torso. His white shirt was unbuttoned at the top and the olive skin of his neck and chest were visible. He looked as if he was quite hairless. He looked, she guessed, younger than her, around twenty years old.

Toby was fifteen years older than her and, at forty-one, had a chest covered in whorls of curly brown hair. This man would be like satin, she imagined, polished wood under the fingers. The man's shoulders were quite narrow, his torso long. Slim in both hip and shoulder, he had the leanness of the intense, tipping forward as if he were about to shout at the bull.

Jennifer sat back, feeling like a swimmer taken out by the tide and only realising it when it was too late. Was it a question of perceived loss of control? It would be risky to choose this image, this man, as her muse for the show. If she were to select a local photograph the chances of coincidence would be far higher, but Jennifer was renowned for her inability to compromise, a propensity she prided herself on. She had always set herself impossibly high standards. Besides, she now felt as if the mysterious man had chosen her and not the other way around, as if somehow he had sought her out. But the magazine was six months old and the photograph had obviously been taken in Spain. Who knows who the man actually was – a local, a tourist, perhaps even a hired model or actor? But that was exactly why she had to choose him. This photograph, the way she had come across it, was perfect. The process had been so completely random, and randomness, Jennifer felt, was exactly the right medium for her alchemy of coincidence to take place within. She would try to summon him to her and document her process. This would be her artwork. Toby might call it witchcraft, but she liked to think of it as an ancient science.

Jennifer reached for her sketchbook and studied the image under the glass. In an hour she had drawn his portrait, realistic enough for her to begin. She propped the sketch up on the easel and pulled her modelling stand out in front of her. A lump of cool white porcelain clay now stood passively on the metal turntable waiting to be spun into life. It was that moment before creation, the junction between detachment and commitment.

Jennifer dipped her hands into a bowl of water and began kneading so that the clay became a convex ball ready to be modelled into the man's face. For a minute she paused with her hands covering the curves of the soft blank clay, summoning up the feel of his face through her body, up from the ground where her feet touched the floor, down her arms to the ends of her fingers. Closing her eyes she imagined how the strong planes of his face – warm and yielding – would hollow and bloom. The two deep valleys that were his eye sockets, the T of bone that was his forehead and jutting nose, the pronounced arch of his mouth, the swooping curves of his cheekbones rushing back out to meet the jawbone.

Her fingers now flew over the clay, thumbs pressing in here, a wire tool subtracting mass there … the rough facsimile growing beneath her hands was like a primitive ancestor of the man himself, as yet unrefined and raw. The features blurred in a primordial struggle as Jennifer lost herself in the process, her conscious mind eclipsed by a far more direct and instinctive compulsion. This was what she loved about being a sculptor, this disappearance of self. It was as if she became one with the clay, the only conscious force being the creativity flowing through her hands. It was the purest emotion she knew and the only other time she ever felt something quite like it was during orgasm.

Toby had commented on this disappearance of self when he first watched her work. 'You vanish and something else enters you,' he'd said, and to Jennifer's surprise and dismay he'd sounded frightened. It had only been when she'd watched him at work directing on set that she'd realised why – when Toby worked he became more himself. He was the opposite; it was as if he was more present, more conscious, his mental energy ramped up to a rattling pace. It was another difference that widened the gap between them.

Jennifer's hands stopped modelling. She stared down and the primitive mask stared back up. It already had a presence; the alchemy had begun. Time for lunch, she thought.

At the end of the day the face was complete – a delicate white rendering that, unfired, looked uncannily like a death mask. It sat drying on a table just outside the sliding door of her studio, sheltered by the branches of an old eucalyptus tree that dominated the yard. Above her the leaves rustled in the breeze and a fly, attracted to the scent, buzzed in erratic zigzags around the clay face. The mask was so realistic that even resting flat it gave the illusion that the man himself might be lying on the table, his face tilted up towards the sun. All that was missing was the flushed skin tone and blood pulsing under that thin epidermis. Jennifer, creation still racing through her own flesh, oblivious to the cooling evening, glanced down then kissed it. Hot mouth on cold.

Inside the house the phone began to ring. She knew it was Toby with his daily check-in from Italy. With her lips still pressed to the mask she let the phone ring out into the garden, ignoring it as it bounced against the thin blue-green gum leaves to sweep around the corners of the studio like jealousy. His jealousy. She ignored it. The powder from the clay tasted chalky and when Jennifer lifted her face up from the mask her mouth was stained white. She didn't wipe the ghost kiss off. The tip of her tongue tasted the powder again. There was an under hint of salt, of some distant sea – perhaps even tainted with the metallic pungency of blood, but then again she could have been imagining it. The phone stopped ringing.

'Let him wait – I'm always waiting for him,' she told the clay face.

The next day she made two nipples and a penis, visualising an organ that would be proportional to a slender man of about six foot. As she squeezed the clay into a cylinder, running her hands backwards and forwards, the clay squeezing up between her cupped fingers, the penis grew in both length and circumference. It was as if she was actually pleasuring the man himself. For a moment she even thought she heard a faint sigh coming from the drying tray beside the kiln, from between the lips of the clay face. And as her fingers slipped across the viscous surface, she thought about herself, her own sex – she was making it to fit her, her ideal cock.

She came to the tip then paused, wondering whether to give him a foreskin or not. He only looked about twenty years old, which would mean, if he were European or Australian, he would most likely be uncircumcised, but from a sculptural point of view it was easier and more visually pleasing to make him circumcised, so she chose to model the tip without a foreskin. Toby's own rather short and stubby organ came into her mind, and she remembered her initial disappointment on their third date when she first slipped her hands down into his jeans as he fumbled with the buttons of her blouse.

But what he lacked in size he had made up for with his mouth, pleasuring her with a genuine and rare enthusiasm. And later, on that first night on the rickety single metal bed in the cheap Italian pensione she was staying in, his lovemaking had not disappointed her. But if she had the chance to redesign his body, to sculpt in changes to a physique she loved because of its fallibilities not its beauty, his penis would be one of the things she would change.

The erect clay penis was about seven inches long and she could just wrap her fingers around the girth with one hand, the tip was slightly larger than the shaft, curved so that she could imagine the way it would nudge against her, brushing across the tip of her clit. The testicles that sat at the base were large enough to be able to cup comfortably and were in perfect proportion to the rest of his organ. The whole sculpture lay supine, now drying next to the face, as if she had recently dismembered the living man and these parts were all that were left. But already Jennifer felt a growing god-like power, the adrenalin of complete control.

Two weeks later Jennifer had created and assembled all of the parts she had decided were important for the alchemy: the face, two ears, two nipples, two hands (with fingers), one penis and balls, two feet. She had cast multiples of all of these organs. They were all fired and solid. She left all of the pieces white and raw, without any kind of glaze, except for the penises. These she lovingly glazed so that the surface was polished like white glass, as if they had already been worn smooth by some fictional woman's body. She stared down at them, fixated by this idea. What kind of lover would her muse take? A beautiful creature like himself, someone who reflected his own physical perfection like a mirror? She glanced over at the magazine photo pinned up on her work board. She didn't think he was a narcissist like that; there was something in his expression, an intelligence, that made her believe he wasn't just some professional model they'd hired for the photograph – rather, he was some handsome passer-by the photographer had noticed and recruited. He would understand an artist like herself, he would understand what she was trying to achieve.

She lifted one of the penises. It was the perfect weight in her hand. Unfurled and erect there was a defiant poignancy to its arched form, as if it were a homage to fecundity itself – ancient, classical. She rubbed it against her cheek and closed her eyes. The glaze was so flawless it actually felt like skin, soft, soft skin, and a little hollow opened up inside of Jennifer. Sighing, she leaned against the wall. It had been a good two months since she'd last had sex and suddenly she realised she'd been so distracted she hadn't even masturbated the whole time Toby had been away.

Jennifer sank down onto the floor and lifted her skirt. She lay there with her legs apart, the coolness of the stone seeping up into her skin. The sounds outside – the noisy magpies squabbling in the ghost gum, the faint buzz of a plane flying overhead, the drone of the cicadas – faded away as she pulled down her underpants and ran the clay penis up her leg.

'Imagine if you were waiting for him,' she thought to herself. Imagine he was about to step into the studio, his skin still smelling of sun and sweat, of the dust of the bullring, of orange blossom and all the things you associate with Spain. Imagine he spoke no English but when he looked at you, you both knew you wanted each other, without talk, without hesitation, without any of the social constraints of culture and mores. Imagine …

She was wet already, and, as she played the tip over her clit, she imagined that the penis was real, was warm and hard, that he was pressing into her, his lips on hers, and that she was falling into those dark blue eyes. She slipped the penis into herself. The circumference pushed against her clit, then slowly at first, she began moving it backwards and forwards, her breath emerging in short stifled cries at the imagined pleasure of him as he took her faster and faster. His long lean legs pressed hard against her thighs, as deeper and deeper she thrust the clay penis until finally she came with a short scream. Outside one of the magpies perched on the lawn cocked its head up towards the studio.

Afterwards, filled with a sweet release, she stood up and straightened her skirt back over her legs. It was as if nothing had happened. She placed the penis back on the workbench next to its comrades then carefully arranged the pieces so that there was some spatial relationship between them all, like the jigsaw puzzle of outlandish prototypes of body parts waiting to be assembled into the perfect man.

Toby stayed in Italy. Jennifer spent her days in solitude, broken only by the clink of the garden gate when either the postman delivered the mail or the cleaner arrived to clean the house as she did twice a week. Her friends, knowing how insular and absent she was when preparing for a show, kept away. For once Jennifer hadn't minded. She worked with a frenetic energy, an inspiration she hadn't felt in over a year, and with each new piece the man's presence seemed to swell, pushing out the walls of the studio until he almost felt like a sound – a musical note. On the twelfth day she wrapped and packed all the pieces and placed them carefully into a box to take to her art dealer.

*

'Big secret, Jenny, eh? Big mysterious bloody secret yours truly is gonna have to flog to the public, God help me.' Max Reiner, a man who had an uneasy relationship with both his body and the large amounts of alcohol and food he consumed to maintain his Falstaff-like physique, was just back from lunch and, as was his custom, still tipsy from the two bottles he and a client, a banker from the Macquarie Group, had drunk. The art dealer's massive face, with its broken capillaries, unshaven chin and copious amounts of nose hair, was flushed. Jennifer was the only one of his many protégées he was secretly intimidated by, and her visit was unexpected. He sat heavily on the edge of his desk and stared suspiciously at the cardboard box Jennifer had just placed on the floor.

'It's the concept for my next show, the Alchemy of Coincidence,' the artist announced a little apprehensively.

Max, turning over the title in his mind, worried at a forgotten piece of his lunch from between his teeth.

'The Alchemy of Coincidence, too much of a mouthful, my dear, too intellectual for these times. What we want is snappy and flasher – something that will appeal to your average Australian nouveau riche, something that doesn't involve too much thought, too much intellectual analysis. Lifestyle, that's what the Australian cares about – lifestyle,' he finished, belching conclusively.

Jennifer did not reply, instead lifting out the first piece, she began to unwrap it. It was one of the man's hands, fingers raised. She put it on the desk where it sat reaching out towards the art dealer in a silent plea. Max was unimpressed.

'Okay, it's a hand, beautifully modelled, one could almost mistake it for being cast from life. As usual, Jenny, you have displayed your remarkable ability to create extraordinarily lifelike detail. I suspect that was what sold the vaginas – especially to the English. Now that was an easy, accessible concept – powerful, succinct and very sellable. Vagina as flower ... but hand? Of course we could put the two together, now that's a workable idea – "Hand and Vagina", or maybe we could go more street – "Hand and Cunt". Of course we'd have to make sure the gender of the hand is established.' He guffawed at his own wit.

Again, Jennifer ignored him and continued to unpack the pieces, the next one of which was a nipple, obviously male; imprinted into the clay were tiny pores from which hair would have sprouted. She placed the nipple next to the hand.

'This is far more ambitious, Max. The whole show will be more of an installation ...'

Max groaned audibly, but forced an indulgent smile. 'An installation – I guess there're always the state galleries and major collections – much harder sale though, especially in these economic times.'

In lieu of a response Jennifer reached into the box and unpacked the penis. She was sure it was the one she'd masturbated with and it gave her a secret thrill to see it now, disembodied, singular and proud. Max picked it up and weighed it thoughtfully in his hand.

'Now I might be able to do something with that.' Max smiled – he had a fatal love of the double entendre. Jennifer grabbed it back and placed it tenderly beside the other pieces.

'Max, I'm not selling them off individually – I am conjuring up an encounter with the man whose body parts I have recreated. A complete stranger I saw in a magazine photo, a magazine from the other side of the world.' She pulled the page out of her pocket and held it up for him. Pushing his bulk away from the edge of his desk he snatched it out of her hand and stared at it sceptically.

'You mean to say that all of these body parts belong to that bloke in the background? The one half out of his seat?'

'That's right.'

'Well, he's a looker. But he's not famous or anything, is he? I mean, why him? He's a totally arbitrary figure.'

'Exactly, and now he's not. I have begun to immortalise him by taking his image out of the temporal and into the permanent.'

Max pressed the side of his temple with a fat thumb ringed by gold. He usually made a point of having a quick nap in the back room after lunch and already the combination of the young artist's intensity and the esoteric concept she'd begun to describe was giving him a headache.

'I think I'm following – you are trying to direct events through making art?'

'An encounter with the man I am faithfully reproducing over and over.'

She unwrapped the face and held it up at about the height the man's face would have been had he been standing in front of them. Max shivered. He was a superstitious man despite a strong mercantile streak and, frankly, the mask's hyper-real appearance made him feel as if a ghost had just entered the gallery.

With a dramatic flourish Jennifer placed the face next to the other pieces and strolled over to the far wall of the gallery, the white walls broken only by the current exhibition of pastoral watercolours inspired by the artist's experience in the computer game Second Life.

'I'll blow up the original magazine photo to full length, then fill the space with as many duplicates of these body parts as I can make before September. They'll be placed in complete randomness on the floor – in other words there is to be no meaning or logic to the display.'

Max moved off the desk and stretched out his arms, they seemed to encircle the space he regarded as both sacred and entirely his own – no matter what his artists might assume. 'Linking the notion of randomness to coincidence – random events equal coincidence, whereas "meaning" is what we project to understand such things?'

'Exactly, Max, so you're not as drunk as I thought.'

'Cheeky minx. You know I met my first wife by complete chance. At Narita Airport during a stopover. Her flight had been cancelled and they put her on mine. Often I find myself wistfully wondering what would have happened if her flight hadn't been cancelled. I'd be a lot richer now for a start ...'

'You would have met her anyway, in another coincidence. It was destined.'

'Fuck, I hope not. Jenny, your theory is total cock, but the public will love it! We'll need some text and maybe some film footage ... I dunno – you prowling the streets, waiting for the encounter? Maybe Toby could shoot it, that would bring in the crowds – famous film director helps artist wife find mysterious man/love object?'

'Stop pushing the celebrity couple thing. You know Toby

would never agree and besides, I don't need Toby's name to push my own.'

'It wouldn't hurt. Are things okay with you guys?'

'I don't know. I haven't seen him for ten weeks, he's doing this movie in Italy.'

'But he rings you, right?'

Avoiding his query, Jennifer dropped her eyes. Through the glass front of the gallery a mother walked past clutching the hand of her child, who looked about eight years old. Catching her eye he stuck his tongue out at Jennifer before being pulled away. Jennifer did not smile. She'd forgotten about Toby's absence until then; did her work fulfil her so much?

'Every day,' she answered quietly, not wanting to confess she'd stopped answering Toby's calls days ago.

'We're fine,' she lied.

The art dealer sighed then, deciding not to probe her for the real answer, picked up the magazine page and examined it again. 'This magazine is over six months old. You really have no idea who the man is?'

'I told you, none whatsoever. But there is an affinity between us now, whether he's conscious of it or not.'

'This is messing with fate, Jenny. I hope you're ready for the consequences.'

'And I thought you were a non-believer,' Jennifer retorted, smiling for the first time since she'd entered the gallery.

Jennifer arrived back at the old terrace house in mid-afternoon. Although the sun was still high there had been a drop of ten degrees in temperature and the sky had clouded over. When

Jennifer had first arrived from Sydney, she'd loved the extreme weather changes that could happen in a day in Melbourne; the strange winds, sudden hail storms and extreme heat in the summer, then after a while she found herself resenting the unpredictability – somehow it destroyed the rhythm of the seasons. Balancing the box under her arm she let herself into the house. The darkened, high-ceilinged entry hall was eerily silent and an old raincoat of Toby's, along with a couple of battered leather jackets, hung off the coat rack.

'Hello!' she yelled out automatically, her voice echoing off the tiled floor. After putting the box beside the door she pulled her coat off and entered the lounge room. The curtains were still drawn and the air smelt stuffy. She realised she hadn't opened the curtains since she'd begun work, nor opened the windows. Marvelling at her own preoccupation, Jennifer walked across to the French doors that led out to the garden and the studio beyond. She pulled them open and the afternoon breeze pushed into the room with brisk impatience. Jennifer stared out, her eyes drawn to the studio. The temptation to walk out across the grass and lose herself again was overwhelming.

The house had always been Toby's domain; it had existed before she arrived, it had contained his first marriage, and this still lingered in objects she sometimes found hidden away in cupboards: abandoned photo albums, an empty jewellery box, an old fur hat, a pair of fairy wings left over from some forgotten fancy dress party. Jennifer had never felt entirely at home despite her efforts to claim territory.

It didn't help that the walls resounded with Toby's professional accolades: film posters, framed reviews, photographs of openings with him standing next to various famous actors, framed letters of congratulation from other directors. Even empty, the house shouted in Toby's loud blustering voice, whereas the studio was always silent, always her sanctuary. If only she could usurp his presence in the house somehow, reclaim some living space. Jennifer reached into the box.

In the bedroom she lay down on top of the coverlet of their double bed. She was still wearing her clothes and it was a deliciously naughty feeling to be lying on the bed in the middle of the afternoon – a sinful indulgence. She held the mask in one hand and, with her legs slightly apart and her head raised on a pillow, she carefully lowered it so that it fitted over her face. She closed her eyes, her eyelashes brushing against the inside clay surface, the scent slightly earthy, the surface cool against her skin. Now she was him, this man she had never met, and it was his long fine hands that travelled down her body and slipped between her legs.

Stroking her thighs, she imagined his lips, his white teeth biting into the back of her neck roughly, the olive-skinned hands gripping the flesh of her thighs, pushing between them, his long fingers reaching down under the elastic of her underpants, finding her wet and engorged, her clit between his fingers as he knew – through instinct, through connectedness – exactly how to touch her, the pulling and rubbing to and fro across the tip, broken only by the occasional finger entering her, testing her wetness, preparing her for his cock, faster and faster, playing out the moment so that he knew exactly when to enter her, to make her groan. Her breath quickened as she imagined his weight now shifting on her, his hands under her buttocks, lifting her up ready to take him, and then in he thrust, hard, with a passion that was both selfish, strange and thrilling. She wanted him to lose himself, to only think of himself, and within that her, because they were now one and she came, a great thunderous bolt, white, blue, red, rippling through her in a violence that eclipsed the separation of her and the rest of humanity, her fingers slippery with herself, and all that longing.

Somewhere in the house a door banged shut. It's the wind, she thought, just the wind. And she left the mask on.

The next morning Jennifer laid out ten more slabs of clay and modelled ten more faces – all of the man, all with a slight variation in expression from the first mask. It was important to her that each mask was an original and not a replica of the first. It was like she was attempting to encapsulate the full emotional range of the man's expressions, summoning him in his entirety into her world.

'What is important in a relationship?' she thought to herself. 'What is important in lovemaking? What is the essence of a lover – what parts?' These questions floated about her like dandelion seeds, tantalising, whimsical and very difficult to catch.

Every day she would go out to the studio, switch off her mobile, put Sibelius on the CD player and begin a new part of the man that would be complete by the evening – slick with water, the clay now shaped into flesh waiting by the kiln to be fired overnight. And every day she would let the phone ring inside the house, resounding out into the garden until it stopped, only to reverberate in her head afterwards. The mental echo sounded suspiciously like guilt.

By the fourth week she had made thirty faces, five penises, forty pairs of hands and twenty-six nipples. She was just finishing the modelling of the eyebrows on face thirty-one when she was interrupted by the sound of the studio door opening. She looked up. Toby, slim and tanned and dressed in a new Italian leather jacket, stood in the doorway. It took her a second to recognise him.

'Hello. Husband? Remember me?' He smiled wryly but remained in the doorway, both of them momentary strangers.

'Sweetheart!' Her voice sounded false in the sudden silence, but it broke the awkwardness between them. She put down her modelling tool and rushed over to him, pushing her face against his shoulder and armpit, nuzzling down, trying to find his scent, the anchor that would tug them back together. Tentatively he put his arms around her. They haven't kissed yet.

'You didn't answer my calls, my emails, my texts.' Now angry, he pushed her away. 'Jesus Christ, Jenny, what's been going on?'

She tried to pull him back into her arms. 'Nothing, sweetheart, I just got caught up with work, you know what I'm like.'

'For three whole weeks?'

'Has it been that long?'

'Since we last spoke, yes. Three fucking weeks, Jenny. I actually got worried, thought you might have been murdered, putrefying on the kitchen floor or something.'

'Oh baby, that's sweet. But I was just out here, working on my show.' She opened her arms to indicate the four work tables now covered in white body parts – luminous and macabre. Only now did he become aware of the work, of the crowded presence of it, his gaze sweeping dismissively across the studio before stopping at one table. In seconds he was marching towards it.

'What the fuck is this?' He picked up one of the penises, one of the more tumescent models, and waved it in the air as if it were a baby rattle, or perhaps even a weapon.

'It's a penis,' Jennifer answered calmly.

'I can see that, but whose? Because it sure as hell isn't mine. Jenny?'

'I'm not having an affair if that's what you're thinking.'

'No? Then why else would you not bother to answer my calls?'

'I told you, I've been working obsessively. I didn't even hear the phone.'

Now he looked at her for signs of change, for the mark of another man. She did look different, thinner, but more plumped up around the face, flushed even. She'd even taken some care with her hair. Now he was convinced.

'You're lying.'

Jennifer held her breath, terrified he might smash the clay penis against the table edge, but instead he put it back down, suddenly looking very tired. It was such a gesture of surrender that her heart went out to him as she wondered whether it was the age difference between them – those fifteen years that made him so distrustful of his own power, his own attractiveness. And she wanted to go over and hold him again, to let him fall against her, capitulated. But she didn't. Her feet were fastened to the floor and yet she knew that not to move would lead to disaster. The fact that they had yet to kiss began to grow into something more urgent, something more poisonous.

'I got caught up, that's all, caught up. It's the concept behind my September show, the idea that if you make an image of some event or someone, the chances of that event happening or the coincidence of bumping into that person increases to the point where it can no longer be counted as coincidence.'

'You told me before I went on the shoot, but I didn't think you'd choose some bloke as your subject. Who is he?'

'I don't know.'

'You're telling me you don't even know this bloke?' And again, he caught himself staring across at the thirty faces and found himself wishing whomever the face belonged to wasn't that young, handsome or, for that matter, so well hung.

'I found him in a magazine, a six-month-old issue of French *Vogue*, in a fashion spread shot in Spain, and he was one of ten men sitting in the background. I will *never* meet him.'

'And you expect me to believe that?'

'Toby, it's an art concept, a device I'm using to build a show on! It's not life, baby.'

'But why him?'

'That's exactly my point, why not him? I've picked a total stranger randomly and I have mythologised him and he will never know. That's another aspect of the work.' She started moving towards him now but it wasn't easy, every step was like wading in treacle. 'Sweetheart, I would never be unfaithful, you know I wouldn't.'

She was now by his side, one hand trying to curl into his, to soften those resisting fingers. But Toby couldn't meet her gaze and she thought she could smell something different on him, a shift in the prism of his sexuality. 'What about you?' It was practically a whisper and she did not expect an answer, both of them knowing the answer already.

'Did you miss me at all?' he asked gruffly, a foil to move away from the dangerous topic of infidelity. To his surprise his voice thickened in sudden desire.

'Yes,' she lied again, 'every night.'

Now he looked up and suddenly there was that old heat between them, the flaring from under the belly, a quickening of the heart, and Toby wanted to conquer her all over again, in the same way he'd wanted the first time he'd ever set eyes on her.

He pulled her towards him and they kissed, Toby's tongue probing her rudely, roughly, as if he had suddenly become a stranger, not caring whether she wanted him or not but out for his own pleasure. His gaze slid away from her face to take in the myriad of porcelain faces staring up at him from the work table – all the same man, the same image he was now determined to press out of his wife, to pound out of her body. And as they kissed he began to tear off Jennifer's clothes, the soft cotton of her work apron pushed down to the floor. Feeling the weight of her breasts under the light sweater, he grabbed one, pinching down hard on the nipple, dominant, he wanted to hurt and pleasure, he wanted her wholly present in her body, wholly his. His other hand now pushed down the front of her jeans as, fumbling, she unbuckled her own belt, his cock thick and hard against the linen of his trousers.

They fell back against the wall, a moan escaping from Jennifer that was so strange she didn't recognise it as her own. He tore down her jeans which caught at her ankles almost making her stumble, and she had to steady herself against the edge of a work table. It shook for a moment, one penis rolling towards another, a nipple rocking on its axis, and she was distracted by Toby's fingers now plunging violently between her legs, fingering her roughly, with brutal efficiency, no tenderness there, and this new expediency excited her. Distracted by fear for her work, she managed to step out of one trouser leg, but he roughly swung her around and bent her over a chair; forcing her legs and arse apart, trailing the head of his cock from her wet slot to her arsehole, teasing them both, penetrating them both slightly. His other hand curled around under her belly, playing her clit. Her wetness grew against the palm of his hand like a stain, like all the ringing tones he'd listened to pointlessly over the past three weeks – like the stain of others.

And he watched the faces, all of them staring back with their blank white-clay eyes, some smiling sardonically at him, mocking him, as if to say, 'We've been there before, she is not yours,' and the table of cocks, all longer and thicker than his own. He tried not to think, tried to be there, right there, but it was impossible, jealousy was flooding through him as bitter as bile.

'Who is he?' His voice was loud over their groaning, the creaking of the chair.

'No one,' she said to the floor, and the wood swayed up like the decking of some ship they had unexpectedly found themselves on. He rubbed his cock harder across her, now plunging the tip into her sex. Again she groaned.

'Who is he?' he repeated louder, more aggressively.

'I told you, no one!'

He thrust completely into her, violently, with a frenetic pace that was completely indifferent to her own rhythm, and yet she was close to coming.

'You're lying,' he almost screamed, then leant back while he was fucking her so that he could see the little pink button of her arsehole, her parts so much younger and neater than his own. Pushing his thumbs into it he pushed her buttocks apart, watching his own sex and fingers pumping her as she howled with pleasure.

'See! See what I can do!' he screamed as he came, and she thought he was talking to her.

That night while Jennifer was in the bathroom applying her face creams and brushing her teeth, Toby went through the laundry basket in one corner of their bedroom. He rifled through a pile of dirty linen looking for used underpants of Jennifer's. Finding a handful, he pulled them out and sniffed them methodically, one by one. He was looking for clues, for the scent of another man. He had convinced himself that he had sensed this man's shape inside his wife, the imprint of another body against her body, perhaps even in his bed. He smelt nothing but the familiar musky essence of her, and it made him hard despite his suspicions.

Meanwhile, in the bathroom Jennifer noticed a miniature soap still in its wrapper on Toby's soap dish. According to the wrapper it was from a hotel in Sicily, but Toby hadn't mentioned anything about going to Sicily. She opened his bathroom cabinet then paused, listening for movement in the adjacent bedroom; there was none so she rummaged around at the back of the shelves. Her fingers reached a small pile of condoms that hadn't been there before.

In bed they lay side by side. Toby, staring up at the ceiling, imagined for a moment the night car horns and chatter that would float up from the Roman streets through the open window of his pensione, while Jennifer, not thinking, was watching the shadows of the tree branches lit by the street lamp outside dance over the Victorian plaster fresco. Someone had to break the silence.

'It won't work, you know, your theory. Images don't make anything happen. You can't just conjure up events or coincidences. You understand that, don't you?' Toby finally muttered up into the space above the bed, but even as he said the words he was thinking of something else, of somebody else, and how, in fact, maybe some connections are destined – like the gathering of storm clouds, or the inevitability of having sex with someone, how you do just know, and to deny such knowledge would be as perilous as denying the rules of physics.

Now Jennifer turned towards him and curled up into his armpit, her hand trailing down to the comforting soft knot of his cock and balls, and an equilibrium was momentarily restored.

'I know that, but even if they did, we'd still be okay.' A lover's answer with a logic that might only have made sense to her, but it really didn't matter because Toby had fallen asleep already.

The next morning he woke to find a note from Jennifer pinned to the pillow, telling him she'd gone out for a run. He sat up and noticed she'd left the window open; the bedroom was fragrant with the smell of damp eucalyptus leaves and a night of forgotten rain. Yawning, he pulled himself up, remembering that he was back in Australia, back in his own house. Suddenly there was a beep from his iPhone sitting on the side table. A text had come in and he immediately knew who it was from. He decided to ignore it for the moment. His groin ached a little and the violence of the lovemaking the afternoon before came flooding back.

As he stared across the familiar terrain of his marriage he tried to remember why he'd fallen in love with Jennifer in the first place. It wasn't just the combination of youth, beauty and a lateral intelligence that seemed at the time to complement his own fixed, obsessive way of thinking, it was also that she always kept something back, like territory he couldn't quite have or conquer, and this had been a new experience for him. He had wanted to break her, to possess her entirely like he had other women. He hadn't succeeded. And now this, this new alienation between them …

Suddenly Toby became aware of a grainy texture beneath one of his bare buttocks. He stood up and examined the bed, finding grains of white clay – porcelain. Rubbing them between his fingertips the porcelain body parts seemed to float about him in the air, mocking him in their invisible omnipresence, and he knew then that he had started to hate this disembodied rival. He had to exist, he had to, and if Toby were to ever meet him he would kill him, destroy him for shattering the balance in his marriage. How dare he! How dare he even exist and be so handsome! Toby punched the pillow then tried to calm himself down.

Was it possible that the clay man really was only a construct Jennifer had created? Was it possible for an artist to be in love with their work? He certainly knew about the allure of the film shoot and how most actors and some directors always fell for the seduction of both the plot of the film they were working on and also the illusion of intimacy such intense atmospheres engender. How many leading actresses had he seduced, enthralled with their performance on set? Many. But Jennifer seemed to be dealing in something far more ethereal and esoteric, so why did he feel so uneasy? He examined his fear as if inspecting the sides of a prism. It was objective logic he always returned to when uneasy, but

Toby had also learnt to trust his instinct and the more he stopped thinking and just listened to the emotion reeling away under his rib cage, the more sure he was that his wife was having an affair. And then suddenly he thought he could see the man himself, a vision fabricated from jet lag, sunlight, fear and guilt, standing naked and silent by the bed, Toby's bed, his hand resting on the bedhead, that big dick of his defiant, erect and proud ...

'Fuck you,' he said, and the spectre vanished. Feeling violated, Toby reached for his cigarettes, pulled on a T-shirt and grabbed his phone.

The sensation of claustrophobia eased once he was in the garden. He lit up under the big ghost gum and exhaled, watching the smoke plume curl around the white-silver peeling bark. He was marking territory, because every time he came home lately, the house and the garden felt less and less familiar, as if the plane travel, the makeshift camps of the film sets, and the affairs had all started to claim his world.

Lifting his iPhone he checked the text. It was in Italian, profusely emotional and indiscreet. Luckily Jennifer did not read Italian but theatrics irritated Toby, and he was tempted to just delete it, but this new woman, as translucent as Jennifer was opaque, had burnt her mark on him and he couldn't let her go, not just yet.

Leaning against the cool bark he began texting back but as he struggled with the correct Italian spelling a growing sense of being observed distracted him. He looked up across the small lawn towards the studio window. The white oval of a face stared back at him. Startled, he almost dropped his phone then moved closer. It was one of the masks, propped up against a modelling stand, facing out towards the greenery. Something in his gut tightened and he turned back to his phone to finish his text. Three minutes later his lover's reply made him laugh then gave him an erection.

Later, wandering through the rooms with a sandwich in one hand, he noticed that Jennifer had left her laptop in the study. It seemed to tease him with its half-open top, like a beacon drawing him forward. He walked past it twice, then drifted back, trailing breadcrumbs across the carpet. He glanced at the clock – he knew Jennifer wouldn't be back for at least another half-hour. Opening the laptop he furtively typed in her password – he'd memorised it once watching her over her shoulder. He then trawled quickly through her emails looking for messages from him: this elusive muse.

She'd only had about twenty messages while he was away; most of them were work related and a couple of his own, but there were three whose subject line said, 'Hello darling …' Swiftly, trying not to dwell on the moral implications of his actions, Toby opened the first email, his stomach clenching in fearful expectation. It was from a close girlfriend who lived overseas, as were the other two suspicious emails. There was nothing, not even any flirtatious messages from ex-boyfriends or old lovers.

'There must be something, there has to be,' Toby muttered to himself. He pulled open the desk drawer to find a blow-up of the magazine illustration staring up at him. In colour the man's beauty was more disturbing. He seemed to look straight up at Toby, the heavy-lidded blue eyes defiant and challenging.

'Go away.' To Toby's surprise he had almost shouted and yet he found it impossible to shut the drawer. He had to look. He had to know. He pulled the image out to examine under the light. It was obviously taken from a magazine but Toby was still unconvinced. He walked over to the printer and made a photocopy of the image. Just then he heard the sound of Jennifer's footfalls outside as she ran up to the front door. He pocketed the photocopy and quickly replaced the original back in the drawer.

That afternoon, unbeknown to Jennifer, Toby went to see Max.

'So …' The filmmaker prowled around the gallery like a bored tiger edgy for lack of prey − or at least that's what Max thought, anchored firmly behind the reception desk.

'What do you think of Jennifer's concept for the new show? I mean, this alchemy of coincidence?' Toby swung back towards the gallery owner with a lunge that gave Max a sudden urge for a drink, something to slightly fog the filmmaker's intensity, a quality he shared with his young wife. Buying time, Max fiddled with a paperweight before answering.

'Ingenious, timely and very contemporary. It's all to do with the death of institutionalised religion, you know. This need to find meaning in the random. Like death, like quantum physics or string theory.' He threw in the last topics for the hell of it, because Max knew nothing about physics but quite a lot about death.

'Wanker,' Toby thought, while the gallery owner watched him warily from under his busy eyebrows (once immortalised in an unkind cartoon in *The Age*). Max smelt marital trouble and was overwhelmed by a poignant desire to rescue his little artist, who was so ingenuous in her fey philosophies, so different from her street-fighter husband. But Max suspected he was being old and sentimental, and he couldn't afford any upheaval before the show was safely installed.

Pushing his considerable weight away from the swivel chair, he waddled over to Toby. Up close he could sense an anger whistling around the filmmaker like wasps or static electricity. It was a wondrous sight to the older man, who pondered whether some of it might rub off and invigorate himself – it had been so long since Max had actually *cared* about anything. He put out a plump ringed hand that hovered uncertainly above Toby's shoulder.

'Is something wrong, Toby? Trouble at home?' The uncharacteristic gentleness of his tone thoroughly unnerved Toby and made him imagine the horns of the cuckold poking through the sentiment. Bristling, he turned.

'Who is he? Do you know him?'

'Him?' Max was confused, wondering if Toby was asking about the identity of the current painter whose abstract canvases were hanging on the walls. Toby strode back over to the reception desk.

'Him!' Toby jabbed a finger down onto the flyer on the desk advertising Jennifer's show, which was opening in two days. The blown-up face of the man stared out at them from under the exhibition's title.

'Oh, *him* ...' Now Max understood Toby's coiled fury. He even recognised it, the infidelity of his wife being the cause of his last divorce. Now he was able to place his hand firmly on Toby's shoulder.

'He, my dear boy, does not exist – at least, no doubt he does exist but not in our world, ergo Melbourne, therefore he is entirely irrelevant to you, Jenny, your marriage, even the show – unless, of course, he should mysteriously turn up and demand intellectual copyright to his own image.' Max laughed nervously, which only further infuriated Toby.

'Are you sure?' Determined not to be patronised, Toby shrugged off the hand on his shoulder.

'My dear boy, she adores you. You are her world.'

Toby crumpled the flyer without even realising it, then with a sweep of his hand indicated the whole gallery.

'No, Max, this, this is her world,' he countered with a vehemence that surprised both of them.

That night Toby made love to Jennifer with a pounding fury, but just before he was about to climax the image of the man's face slipped across Jennifer's flushed face, the hot tangle of moving limbs, the core of their rhythm, and as hard as he tried Toby couldn't come. He fell back against the mattress, his back slippery with sweat.

'What's wrong?' In the dark Jennifer's voice was reedy with anxiety.

'You tell me.'

'Toby, I'm not having an affair.'

Rolling away from her, he didn't answer.

'What can I do to prove it?' she asked.

'Jenny, he's everywhere, he's in your hair, in this house, outside in the fucking studio, in your body.'

'No he's not, I made him up!' She was cracking now, a great chasm tearing open between them, and he wanted to rescue her but somehow couldn't.

'It's just a question of time,' he muttered darkly.

'What do you want from me?' she screamed, but he had pulled the blankets over his head, huddling.

She went to sleep on the couch downstairs. As she wormed her way down into the lumpy cushions, an old doona pulled over her like a tent, she wondered how he could be so jealous and so doubting when both of them knew that she was the more faithful.

She tried to distract herself from her weeping by thinking about the sculptures sitting in her studio like silent captive performers waiting to be led to the theatre. She had made so many parts, the shape of her muse now resonated in her hands like the memory of a blind person. The familiarity was so real it was as if she knew him already. 'Is this infidelity?' she wondered, just as the shape of his penis, or at least her rendering of it, fluttered down the back of her head and tingled in her fingers and groin. Could you want someone you'd never met so much? Was this how some women felt about celebrities?

She tossed and turned, trying to fold her long legs into the crook of the couch. Finally she pulled a long pillow from another chair and wrapped herself around it as if it were a man – her man, her creation – and slept without dreaming.

The next day, Toby, his body clock still in a different time zone, got up early and, after slipping past the sleeping Jennifer, left the house to drive into the city. He wound his way around Studley Park at that time of morning when there is no one around except joggers and cyclists, but already the day had begun to heat up and a dryness lay over the morning air. He felt all jittery, as if something momentous lay just ahead but he couldn't quite see it. It was disorientating, this feeling of a premonition, and Toby, who liked to be in control of the events in his life, felt threatened.

On Lygon Street he had a cappuccino and a pastry at his favourite Italian café then walked around to the casting agency he'd always used for his films. Casey, a woman in her mid-fifties who'd worked with Toby for over fifteen years, was already in her office. A broad woman with a healthy disregard for the niceties of beauty, she was famous for her maternal earthiness and zero tolerance for the egotism of her more famous clientele.

Casey was leaning back in her chair, headset wrapped around her face as she talked furiously to someone in London. She was framed by the photographs of actors and actresses that covered her back wall; shiny in youth and hope. Smiling at Toby but not bothering to pause the rapid fire of her conversation, she indicated that he should sit. He threw himself down in a leather chair opposite her and, staring over her head, noticed a very early headshot of an impossibly young Jerome Thomas. For a minute Toby slipped back into memories of his own first film, the one that had launched the star's career. Casey finished her conversation and pulled off the headset.

'Sorry, trouble with a client in London. So Jesus, Toby, I thought you'd still be in Rome, or at best in an editing suite.'

'I will be in a couple of days, but I had a few days off and Jenny's got a show opening tomorrow.'

'That's right, I think I have an invite somewhere … How is the lovely Jenny?'

'She's okay. Listen, I have a question for you …' He pulled out the magazine image, unfolded it then lay it flat on the desk. 'Do you know who this is?'

She turned the photocopy around so that she could see it more clearly.

'I mean, I figure you know everyone, right? Actors, models, wannabes ... southern and northern hemisphere.' His voice tightening, he wondered whether he really did want to know.

'You know me, babe, I'm a total face slut. If he's anyone I'd know him.' She studied the young man thoughtfully. 'You thinking of casting him? He's definitely got presence, a little Keanu Reeves meets Hugh Jackman – but can he act?'

'Just tell me who the fuck he is, Casey,' he snapped.

Casey glanced up, surprised, then shrugged and pulled out a book filled with images of smiling actors – a casting reference book of A-list actors and models. She turned the pages, scanning the photos for a match. Finally she shut the book.

'Well, he's not a local actor or a model, that much I can tell you. And I don't recognise him from ICM America. Toby, what's this all about?'

'Nothing. Forget I asked.' He snatched back the photocopy.

Casey stood. 'So when does the film come out? People are saying good things about this one, Toby.'

'I reckon we'll be finished by Christmas. We're on track for the release date.'

'Well, if you need me for the Australian end on the next one you let me know, won't you?'

'Always, always. Thanks, Casey.' He was backing towards the door. 'And if you do think you see this guy anywhere, you ring me.'

'Who is he, your long-lost brother?'

'Something like that,' and he tried to laugh but failed.

When he got back to the house in the early afternoon, Jennifer had begun to pack the pieces up ready to be collected that afternoon to be installed in the gallery the next day. When she heard the car pull into the driveway, she hesitated; feeling furtive, she stood with one of the porcelain faces wrapped in tissue paper. This is not clandestine, this is merely art, she rationalised. Nevertheless she was nervous about seeing Toby. She hadn't spoken to him since their argument the night before and had spent the day checking her mobile every five minutes, expecting an apology or at least a text from him – instead there'd been nothing but silence.

Toby climbed out of the car and decided that he wouldn't go into the studio to say hello. As he left the concrete driveway he noticed the mail still poking out of the letterbox. He collected it on his way through to the house. He felt Jennifer, her presence stretching across the front lawn, catching at his back. He would not succumb. At the doorstep he shuffled through the mail: three junk flyers, one postcard from an actor friend for him and two letters addressed to Jennifer. One of them was elegantly handwritten in black ink. There was something disturbingly masculine about the handwriting, and he tore it open.

Hello, you don't know me but I got your address from
your London Gallery. Forgive my audacity but I just
wanted to write to tell you how much I enjoyed your
London show. Your work is a rare combination of both
the sublime and the sexual, and I have to say that the
beauty of the execution of your sculptures elevates it above
other artists of a similar ilk. I hope it won't be too long
before you will again show in London.

Yours, an admirer.

Toby's heart thumped uncomfortably against his rib cage and he felt nauseous. He slammed the front door shut and ran through the house out to the back garden then walked furiously towards the studio.

'This is from him, isn't it?' he found himself shouting. The pieces piled on one table seemed to push against his hot eyes, mockingly naked, mockingly realistic. All he wanted was a confession, something concrete he could fight against. Jennifer stood staring at him in her work smock, one cheek smudged with white dust.

'What is?' she replied, backing towards the wall, still holding a half-wrapped hand, the porcelain fingers strangely cold and tentative against her own. She was trying not to cry. He thrust the letter towards her.

'This!'

She still had the presence of mind to put the hand down carefully, the fingers upright. Trying to hide the tremor in her hands she unfolded the letter and read it. After a moment she looked up.

'I don't know who this is from. It's just some English fan – probably a buyer …'

'You're lying, Jennifer. You've been lying ever since I got back. I mean look at you! You even look different! And who are you dressed up for today? You're even wearing make-up – you never wear make-up unless it's a special occasion!'

'I told you before, I've never met him!'

'Then how could you know his body so well, eh? Tell me that much!'

She edged around to the front of the work table, so much

anger and so much fragility – both dangerously close to each other. She met his stare but she could not give him the answer he wanted.

'I don't know.'

Suddenly all of his fear, all of his frustration, burst through him and before he realised he had swept his arm through all the mocking faces, clawing hands, those loud penises, and they fell to the concrete floor, smashing in sharp clouds of dust and shards. Toby looked up to see that Jennifer's face was now as white as the broken masks, her mouth open. He ran out, out towards the car and away.

She was shaking from shock. She stared in total disbelief at the carnage he'd left behind. The floor and work table looked like a macabre operating table or butcher's slab, the broken body parts now tangled in with each other – the broken tip of a cock lying next to half a smashed face, snapped off. The whole show was ruined, unfixable.

Her shock was lacerated by the sound of a phone signalling an incoming text. She turned and realised Toby had left his mobile on the table. She was moving towards the phone when she heard the sound of a car pulling up outside the house. 'He's come back,' she thought, 'he's driven off then turned back around. He's realised what he's destroyed, how much he's broken.' The sentence pounded through her as she ran out through the garden, down the side of the house and into the front yard.

By the time she reached the pavement she was flushed and shaking. A man was standing by a white rental car, staring down at a piece of paper. Despite the fact that his face was turned away from her she recognised the profile immediately. He looked up at the house. She froze. He swung around and she saw instantly that he was exactly how she had imagined him to be – if not a little taller and a little more fully fleshed, his dark hair blacker and those deep-set eyes bluer.

'Sorry …'

He had a French accent, she thought, and now he smiled uncertainly, wondering at her flushed face and dishevelled state.

'Do you live here?'

But Jennifer could not speak. She could not assimilate his physical presence here in her own world, his very real existence. His smile wavered, uncertain.

'I'm looking for Toby Gladwell, the film director? I believe he lives in this house. I've never met him but I'm a journalist from *Le Monde* and I happen to be on holiday in Australia and I am a big fan. Would it be possible to interview him about his latest movie?' He stepped forward, a little tentative in his movement.

'You want to meet Toby?'

'If that's possible, I am happy to wait.'

Jennifer glanced up the street, there was no sign of Toby's car, it might be hours before he decided to return. She looked back at the Frenchman, his skin was exactly the shade she'd visualised and his lips curved out in a bow she herself had created. He was hers, not Toby's. Him standing there, outside her own house, was fate. A coincidence she made happen. 'And I am happy to wait with you,' she replied, then turned towards the house.

Acknowledgments

I would like to thank my partner Jeremy Asher, and all at HarperCollins Australia who have made this book possible, particularly Anna Valdinger and Katherine Hassett for their superb editing.

For an extra short story, go to www.tobshaeroticfiction.com,
hit on the link to a free download and subscribe to Tobsha
Learner's free quarterly newsletter . . .

Also available by Tobsha Learner

Quiver

Quiver's twelve interlinked short stories explore desire
and transport us into a world of love, power, pain,
pleasure and obsession. Experience the excitement
of lust at its most primal . . .

978-0-7499-5904-3

Tremble

In Wales, a young woman's sensuality is awakened
by an outrageous inheritance.

In Oklahoma, a rainmaker offers a drought-stricken
town salvation at a controversial price.

In Sydney, a record producer struggles to balance
wife and mistress – until one of them takes matters
into her own hands . . .

978-0-7499-5905-0